"Why?" Kate Tyler straightened, addressing the two mid-shipmen. "Why would Brian kill himself?"

A fleeting expression crossed Jordan's face. Wariness? Guilt? Pain? Kate could not be sure. Before she could speak, a voice in the hall cut through the charged silence.

"Did you hear the latest about Brian Tyler?"

"Do you mean the hanging? It gives me the creeps."

"No. Not that. The latest. Admiral Thatcher's having him court-martialed."

"You're kidding. Why?"

"For destroying government property—posthumously, of course."

Their laughter was obscene, spilling into the corridor, poisoning the air.

Webb began to speak, trying to interrupt, but Jordan cut him off with a look. As if hypnotized, Kate moved to the doorway and watched him confront two terrorized plebes. They stood in profile twenty yards away, their eyes locked on the rigid, furious first-classman facing them. . . .

EVERY
MOTHER'S
SON

ANNE D. LeCLAIRE

BANTAM BOOKS

TORONTO · NEW YORK · LONDON · SYDNEY · AUCKLAND

EVERY MOTHER'S SON
A Bantam Book / December 1987

ISBN 0-553-26952-6

Published simultaneously in the United States and Canada

Bantam Books are published by Bantam Books, Inc. Its trade-
mark, consisting of the words "Bantam Books" and the por-
trayal of a rooster, is Registered in U.S. Patent and Trademark
Office and in other countries. Marca Registrada. Bantam
Books, Inc., 666 Fifth Avenue, New York, New York 10103.

PRINTED IN THE UNITED STATES OF AMERICA

KR   0 9 8 7 6 5 4 3 2 1

FOR MY SON
CHRISTOPHER

Acknowledgments

This book is entirely a work of fiction and is in no way based on historical events. The characters are creations of imagination, and any resemblance to actual people, living or dead, is coincidental.

The U.S. Naval Academy at Annapolis, of course, exists. It served as both setting and inspiration for this story. Like Katherine Tyler, I came to the Yard as an outsider and am indebted to many people in the Navy and Marine Corps community for their assistance during the research and writing of this novel. I am particularly grateful to the following: Major Barry Bodine, Major Ed Kellogg, Captain and Mrs. Philip Ryan, Colonel and Mrs. Thomas Hucklebery, Major Andy Anderson, Professor Jack Sweetman, Colonel James McGinn, and Midshipman 1/c Richard McGrath.

I owe a special obligation to the dozens of midshipmen, past and present, who, with a rich blending of black humor and deep pride, talked about their life at that place called simply the Yard. Through their eyes and memories, I was able to walk the halls of Mother B. and Michelson, march across the grass of Worden and Farragut, attend tea dances at Dahlgren and football games at Philadelphia, survive plebe summer.

I would also like to thank Dr. Arthur Bickford, John Elliot, Edward Blute, Nancy Cole, and Susan Cockrell for their contributions, and Mike Ashford for volunteering to serve as generous host and tour guide during one of my visits to the town of Annapolis.

I am deeply grateful to Linda Grey, Jane Rotrosen, and Andrea Cirillo, and to Kate Miciak, who, in addition to gifted editing, graced the project with her wisdom, enthusiasm, and humor.

And lastly, I thank Hillary, Hope, and Christopher, who not only understood when I wept for citizens of an imaginary world, but willingly entered that world with me, sharing its joys and sorrows. Their love, patience, and support sustained me.

PROLOGUE

His death was not instantaneous. Nor was it peaceful.

This was not by design, for if the spinal cord is severed, a hanging will be instantly fatal. But the violent act was performed without skill, the noose improperly placed, and as a result the first three cervical vertebrae were not dislocated. Instead, three other factors contributed to his death. His windpipe was crushed, the blood flow to his brain was halted, and finally, the fragile nerve structures in his neck were ruptured. Death was lingering and painful.

His body did not surrender willingly. Oxygen-starved cells, bursting blood vessels, limbs dancing in convulsive spasms, all his bone, muscle, and fluid screamed in silent fury. Beyond conscious thought, his frenzied instinct to survive fought its doomed battle against the darkness.

Finally, death was demeaning. It occurred in a dark, forbidden place beneath the cold bars of a grill that had been used to anchor the rope. And when life had ended, the corpse's sphincters relaxed, soiling the body and its garments with the foul stench of death.

It was a lonely and honorless death and was not worthy of the man.

PROLOGUE

His death was not instantaneous. Nor was it peaceful.

This was not by design, for if the spinal cord is severed, a hanging will be instantly fatal. But the violent act was performed without skill, the noose improperly placed, and as a result the first three cervical vertebrae were not dislocated. Instead, three other factors contributed to his death. His windpipe was crushed, the blood flow to his brain was halted, and finally, the fragile nerve structures in his neck were ruptured. Death was lingering and painful.

His body did not surrender willingly. Oxygen-starved cells, bursting blood vessels, limbs dancing in convulsive spasms, all his bone, muscle, and fluid screamed in silent fury. Beyond conscious thought, his frenzied instinct to survive fought its doomed battle against the darkness.

Finally, death was demeaning. It occurred in a dark, forbidden place beneath the cold bars of a grill that had been used to anchor the rope. And when life had ended, the corpse's sphincters relaxed, soiling the body and its garments with the foul stench of death.

It was a lonely and honorless death and was not worthy of the man.

PART I
BLOOD

Sons are the anchors of a mother's life.

Sophocles

CHAPTER ONE

The locals still call it the Selby place.

The house, bathed this morning in the icy light of winter, is a Dutch colonial and stands proud and tall on a rise overlooking River Road. Its construction is sturdy. It has an admirable integrity of line, a geometric balance that pays homage to tradition. Yet there is about the house a satisfying hint of imperfection. Long ago the foundation had settled into the earth so that marbles dropped from a child's grasp roll across the dining room floor, coming to rest against the walnut-stained baseboards. Strips of felt encircle doors that no longer fit snugly within their frames, and near one end of the ridgepole there is a mismatched square of shingles. Ruts, carved by decades of New England winters and spring rains, scar the gravel drive; the side meadow has never been fully civilized into a lawn.

The owners of this home have accepted these shortcomings, seeing them as symbols of an inalienable truth: it takes a while for a house to develop a soul.

The house was built more than a century ago by Samuel Selby, a maker and engraver of watches. A sunny room on the second floor served as his workshop and study. From its window, he overlooked the rear half of the property, which stretches back into a wooded patch of hickory and beech trees, reaching its boundary at the shallow waters of a moss-banked river. There are fox in these woods, and ruffled grouse and chukar partridge, and glossy brown muskrats that play on the riverbank. The delicate engravings Selby etched in the hinged lids of pocket watches were inspired by this view.

When the watchmaker died, his only son inherited the estate, leaving it, upon his death, to *his* son. The last Selby to occupy the house, a great-grandson of the original owner,

moved out thirty years ago, selling the property to a director
from New York. The director lived there a year before
transferring the house at great profit to an insurance man from
Hartford, who subsequently sold it to a civil engineer and his
family of six, who turned it over to a Navy commander, a
lawyer attached to the Judge Advocate's staff at Groton on his
last tour of duty before retirement.

All who have lived here altered the house in some way.
The New York director painted the clapboards pink, which
the insurance man's wife immediately restored to the original
white. She also renovated the kitchen and replaced the
claw-footed tub in the upstairs bath, which the director had
lacquered red. The wife of the engineer installed olive green
wall-to-wall carpeting in the downstairs rooms, and her husband built a barbecue, constructing it by hand from boulders
wrested from the surrounding land. The commander's wife
ripped up the carpeting, painted the exterior trim Georgetown
blue, and sowed wildflowers in the vast expanse of the
meadow.

Every transmutation of paint, each aster and azalea planted,
was an attempt by these individuals to forge their own
identity on the house, to make the place uniquely their own.
Each family entered the front door with dreams woven from
the warp and woof of timber, glass, and brick. This home
represented a promise, a pledge of permanence, and roots,
security, and safety: *Nothing bad could happen here*. Owner-
ship was at once an act of hope and a compact of commitment.

Locals—men and women born in this tiny town with the
knowledge that they would be buried within its borders—are
suspicious of newcomers and their commitments. They witness change with jaundiced eyes. More than three decades
have passed since a descendant of the watchmaker has lived
in the house, but the natives still call it the Selby place.

A cardinal flew by the window, and catching sight of it,
Kate drew her breath in enchantment. She had seen the bird
almost every day this winter, but its beauty—the slash of
scarlet against the backdrop of snow—always caught her
unaware. She had felt the same way when Brian was newborn
and she would tiptoe to the side of his crib to watch him
sleeping; seeing as if for the first time the marvel of each

eyelash against his cheeks' poreless skin; the eyelids as thin as pale violet tissue paper with their delicate tracing of veins, the wonder of each intake of his milk-sweet breath.

From her bedroom window, she watched the cardinal, waiting for its mate to appear. The pair had arrived last spring, making their nest in a thicket of honeysuckle by the house. Each day throughout this interminable winter they had kept her company with their visits to the feeder she kept stocked with sunflower seeds and cracked corn. They were the shyest of all the birds she fed. And she liked them the most, especially the female. The dull brown bird had none of the showy plumage of her mate. Kate identified with her, knowing what it was like to be the less handsome half of a couple. When she was with Michael, he invariably drew the first glance. He carried himself with the confidence of a person who has been told since childhood that he was good-looking.

Not that Kate was ugly, only that hers were not conventional good looks. She was tall, with features too irregular to be called pretty. Her forehead was too high, her chin too pointed. She was not photogenic, for much of her appeal was born of animation and intelligence, qualities not easily captured by the shutter's eye.

At forty-two, she looked five years younger, although the first white strands had recently appeared in her wiry, red-brown hair. She had stared in horror at these signs of aging, then accepted them with resignation. As the mother of a twenty-one-year-old son, she reasoned, she had earned a few gray hairs.

Beneath her window, the two birds huddled on the wooden dowel of the feeder. While Kate watched, the male ducked his head beneath the plastic shelter that covered the seed and scooped up a kernel. Then he fed his mate, placing the seed inside her stout red beak with such gentleness that Kate felt witness to a moment of intimacy and devotion. The sweetness of it almost moved her to tears. She shook them off impatiently; her emotions were too close to the surface lately.

Aware she had dawdled too long, she turned from the window and quickly finished dressing. Catching sight of herself in the mirror—so sober—she forced a smile. The cardinals were a good omen. Brian would soon be home. The smile widened.

She reached the head of the stairs before she felt the silence. There was an eeriness to it, different from the claustrophobic stillness that marked the house when Brian was not there. She stood, listening. Even before her eyes encountered the mute proof, she knew what was wrong. The clock had died during the night.

Behind the hood door of the grandfather clock, the hands rested symmetrically, the hour hand frozen at two, the minute hand at ten. On the seconds dial, the silvered arrow touched thirteen.

The pale February sun, refracting off snow, lit the ivory-walled hall. She walked slowly through the pool of its light until her eyes were level with the face of the clock. The gleaming tubular weights hung high on their chains, but even before she checked them, she knew the clock had not simply run down, knew instead that some fatal illness had struck deep within its workings. Still, she unlatched the trunk door and nudged the cold bob with a finger. Obediently, it circumscribed its arc, but there was no life behind the movement, and the transversed curves became shorter and shorter until once again the brass orb stood perpendicular and still. Sighing, she shut the glass door. She looked up at the moon dial beneath the break arch. It was late in the month, and the face of the moon was partially obscured. Later in the dial's rotation, in two or three weeks, both eyes would be revealed, but now only one looked out. Kate studied the enameled face, and when she spoke, her voice reflected her affection.

"Don't you worry, Gramps Moon." The childhood name came easily to her lips. "I'll find a clock doctor and we'll have you ticking again before you know it."

The Seth Thomas was a grandfather clock in truth as well as in name, having belonged to her mother's father, and before him to his father. Decades ago Kate had measured her growth against its polished walnut housing. At some moment during each vacation visit to her grandparents' home, she would stand solemnly before her chosen yardstick and, never cheating by raising her eyes, gauge her progress by her line of vision. As each new field fell before her, she studied it, scrutinizing with serious brown eyes not only the workings of the clock, but the tiny nicks and scratches on plinth, trunk, and molding. In this way she came to know the Seth Thomas well, far better, in fact, than its owners had.

When both her grandparents died—first her grandfather from a stroke, months later her grandmother of a broken heart—Kate, the only grandchild, and then in college, was offered her choice of their furnishings. She did not hesitate, taking, of course, the clock. It had been an integral part of her life ever since, accompanying her through the succession of base housing that she and Michael had shared throughout their married years, traveling with her from Norfolk to Virginia Beach, Boston to Newport, no more successful than she had been at fitting into the drab, transient apartments and houses. Finally, four years ago, here in Connecticut, they had both found a home.

She spoke again, her eyes on the painted moon, her voice echoing in the hall. "We'll get you running again and—" She broke off. For one instant the lunar eye was seeing. More than seeing, it seemed malevolent. So real was this illusion that she took a half step back. Instantly shadows shifted and the face again became the benign moon of her childhood, flat, fat, and friendly. A trick of lighting, she thought, blotting out the memory of the evil glance.

Nina would know of a repairman. Blessed Nina. The day the Tylers had moved into the Connecticut house, Nina had arrived on the heels of the moving van, bringing with her a thermos of coffee and an invitation to dinner. Almost from the instant of meeting, the two women had become friends. Usually Kate held back. In the nomadic military life, too many friends and neighbors were left behind. Over the course of twenty years there had been too many partings.

But this time was different. This time Kate did not have to think of later pain. This time she was determined to plant roots, and for that reason her relationship with Nina was special. With each week that passed, she found herself growing more attached to the spunky, fun-loving mother of five. She came to rely on Nina's advice about who could repair a recalcitrant furnace, which doctor would respond to a Christmas Eve call, which plumber to phone when the septic system backed up, how to find a reputable accountant, car mechanic, and much later, a lawyer.

Thinking of Nina, Kate turned toward the stairs. Behind her, the clock's silenced pulse seemed to whisper a warning. She repressed a shiver. From the window on the landing she caught a glimpse of Nina's mud-spattered Chrysler as it made its way up the long twisting drive, and she smiled. Nina took the curves the same way she drove through life, with reckless merriment, ignoring bumps and curves. Five kids, two of them twins, must do that to you, she mused.

Eliot had it wrong, she thought. February is the cruelest month. She looked at the barren expanse of snow, broken occasionally by muddy smears of earth, and wondered if spring would ever come. Three taps of cheerful impatience on the horn prompted her to hurry.

In the kitchen, she pulled on her coat. The novel she had borrowed from Nina lay next to her purse. She scooped up the book and shoulder bag, and succumbing without hesitation, grabbed the last streusel-topped Danish from the box on the counter. Juggling book, bag, and pastry in one hand, she opened the door, then pulled it shut behind her. She gave no thought to locking it. This had been one of the things she and Michael had squabbled about. He was as security conscious as she was naively secure, and after he had installed an elaborate security system, they fought even harder because she constantly forgot the sequence of steps to deactivate it and was always accidentally setting it off. After he walked out, she turned off the alarm and hadn't used it since. A twenty-five-hundred-dollar security system couldn't really protect against loss. It certainly hadn't been able to safeguard their marriage.

Six weeks before, when Michael had stunned her with the news of his remarriage, one of the first things he mentioned to Kate about his second wife was that she never failed to lock the door. Nor did she ever lose her keys.

"She probably always wears her seat belt too," Kate had said to Nina.

"Sounds like they deserve each other," her friend had replied, with the unquestioning loyalty for which Kate loved her. Before the split the two couples had been a comfortable foursome, sharing Sunday suppers at the Tylers' and summer tennis on the Shaws' court, engaging in their social life between Hal's flights and Michael's hours of duty at the sub base. But later, after the divorce, Nina and Hal gave all their support to Kate.

Kate opened the car door and shoved aside a pile of library books, jackets, mittens, and a hockey stick, the handle of which was covered with jam-smudged, dirt-gray hockey tape.

Tennis balls, left over from the last warm days of fall, rolled around on the floor. She mumbled her hello through a mouthful of streusel and slid into the front seat. Nina eyed the Danish grimly.

"Of course, you know I hate you," Nina said.

"You'll just have to hope for divine retribution. In the hereafter you'll be a svelte celestial cherub with Saint Peter breathing down your halo, and I'll be an obese, thunder-thighed angel."

"Fat chance," Nina grumbled, and then groaned at the unintentional pun. "It isn't fair, you know. I exercise eighteen times a day and diet every second. It's been so long since I ate a piece of cake, I've forgotten what it tastes like. I'd kill for a hot fudge sundae."

"It'll all be worth it when you put on your bathing suit this summer."

"Are you kidding? In spite of everything, I'm gaining weight. Hal mentioned it when I got out of the shower last night. The man likes to live dangerously." She glanced over enviously as Kate finished up the Danish. "How do you do it?"

"Good genes. Actually, I'm probably rotten inside."

There was the briefest moment of awkward silence as both women thought about Kate's parents, and then Nina broke in with her common-sense tone, which allowed no sliding into grief. No thoughts of stricken parents, of cancer or strokes.

"God, I hope so. If there's any justice at all, your arteries had better be clogged with cholesterol. You know, some day a brilliant endocrinologist is going to walk away with the Nobel by discovering the secret of metabolism, and then we'll know why you gorge constantly and don't gain an ounce, while I merely *smell* lasagne and gain ten pounds. In the meantime, my patron saint is the inventor of the wraparound skirt. All set?"

Kate looked at her friend and smiled. She wanted to tell her how much she loved her and what their friendship meant to her, but her parents had believed emotional outbursts were excessive and in poor taste, and so Kate had learned to be uncomfortable about expressing her love. Perhaps if she could have said more to Michael . . . ? Now she said nothing as Nina spun the wheel deftly and headed the car away from the house.

As they approached the main road, the mail truck was pulling away. The flag on Kate's box was raised. After her first months in the house, and numerous futile trips down the long driveway to see if there had been a delivery, Kate and Wallace Simms had arrived at a system whereby he would raise the flag, which she could see from the second-floor landing window, when he left mail. It probably wasn't by the book, but that didn't seem to bother Simms.

"He never did that for me," Nina teased. "I've lived here for fifteen years and he still calls me Mrs. Shaw. I bet he's got a crush on you. I wonder if he's married." She laughed when she saw the color rise in Kate's cheeks. "Only kidding, Katie. Do you want to pick up your mail now or wait till later?"

"Might as well get it now. Not that I'm expecting anything more exciting than late Christmas bills and another exorbitant ransom note from the oil company." When Nina stopped the Chrysler, Kate reached into the box and pulled out a handful of advertising flyers, leafed through them half-heartedly, then saw the letter. "Well, I guess I got lucky after all." She couldn't suppress a grin.

Nina recognized the Naval Academy stationery. "Isn't Bri coming home next week? And he's writing you a *letter*? Good Lord, Robert hasn't written as much as a postcard to us during the entire two years he's been at Brown. What's your secret?"

"Damned if I know. Listen, don't get me started on Bri. He's such a great kid. Sometimes I wonder how Michael and I ever turned out such a perfect son. God, listen to me. I sound so smug." She held the letter tightly, and then, like a child who torments herself by saving the best treat until the last, decided to wait and open it later, when she was home alone and could savor it. She tucked it in with the other mail on the seat beside her.

"Well, Lord knows you have a right to be smug. Proud too. Bri *is* terrific. How is the romance going between him and Danielle?"

"I'm not sure, but I think it might be dying. He didn't see her when he was home over Christmas."

"Why do I have the feeling that doesn't upset you too much?"

"It isn't anything against Danielle. But after Bri leaves Annapolis he's committed for five years of service. I know I probably sound like the classic possessive mother, but he's only twenty-one. There's plenty of time for marriage later."

"How old were you and Michael when you got married?"

"Twenty and twenty-one, but that argument won't wash. Michael and I haven't exactly been an advertisement for early marriage." She fished for a tissue to wipe her fingers, sticky from the pastry. "I guess it's not just the thought of his marriage that bothers me. It's the fact that Brian's grown-up. It all happens so fast. One minute he's a boy, coming to me to zip up his snowsuit and tie his shoelaces, and now..."

She brushed a few streusel crumbs off her lap. "They're still there, you know, in his room. The science project is on the shelf in his closet, and that ridiculous stuffed tiger he called his teddy-cat is on his bed. They are still there, and he's a man. And now he's going off, and it's so damn hard, Nina, so damn hard to let go. Robert is two years younger than Bri, so you haven't had to face it yet. He hasn't really gone yet. I never guessed it would be so tough to face that moment when your child begins to make a life of his own. The whole thing is so damn ironic. You're supposed to raise him so that he's independent, but when it happens, it almost breaks your heart. When I look at Brian, one part of me wants to burst with pride, but the other part would give anything in the world to turn back time, to have just a few more years with him. You were smart to have more than one child, Nina. Maybe it's easier if you have several. When one goes, at least you still have others at home."

"Smart? I was just disgustingly fertile. The next time you get lonely for a child, Kate, my dear, I'm going to send the twins over for a prolonged visit. Just give me five seconds to pack their bags."

The thought of Sean and Seton, chattering, inquisitive bundles of seven-year-old hyperkinesia, made Kate laugh. "Not that," she begged. "Have you no mercy at all?"

"Mercy? Not when it comes to those monsters." It was common knowledge that anyone who so much as touched the Shaw children risked walking away with empty sleeves. "Now. Which shop shall we hit first?"

"The Company Store. Everything is thirty percent off."

"The Company Store, it is. Then let's have lunch at the Inn."

"The Essex? What's the occasion?"

"A celebration. Of children who grow up, and of the parents who raised them. And of friendship." Nina grinned her mischievous, infectious grin. "Besides, I have this unbelievable craving for a huge bowl of their borscht topped with a huge mound of sour cream."

"You're unconscionable," Kate protested, and the two friends laughed like children.

Although it was not quite noon, the dining room of the Essex Inn was crowded. Within a year of buying the property, Dale and Jane Conroy had converted the old building from a dark, second-rate country inn into the most fashionable restaurant within ninety miles of New York. White wicker tables and chairs stood out against the emerald green walls, and vibrant chintz curtains framed French doors that opened onto the length of a bluestone terrace. On each table, yellow and pink tulips bloomed in fat cranberry vases.

Jane Conroy could be as charming as her inn, and she greeted the two women warmly and then led them, chatting easily, to a table for two by a pair of French doors. Beyond the mullions, the desolate garden was blanketed with snow. Involuntarily, Kate shivered.

"Cold?" Nina asked. "We could move."

"No. This is fine." Kate quickly scanned the room. It had become a habit with her, this looking for Michael everywhere she went, although she knew there was little chance he'd be here. But even so, she looked. When she did not see him, some of the stiffness eased out of her shoulders.

"You sure you don't want to sit somewhere else?"

"No. Really. This is one of the best tables, and Jane gave it to us. She's been so nice since Michael and I split, I don't want to hurt her feelings."

Nina rolled her eyes. "Good God, will you listen to yourself? 'I don't want to hurt her feelings.' It's about time you started worrying about Katherine Tyler. And I'll tell you something about Jane Conroy—she's one sharp businesswoman, and I'll bet you the lunch check that she's just as sweet to the King of the Romper Room."

In spite of herself, Kate laughed. Six weeks before, just four months after the divorce, Michael had married a woman twenty years younger than he. In the painful days and weeks following his wedding, while Kate struggled to heal, Nina had compiled a roster of nicknames for him. King of the Romper Room was one of the more flattering.

"Is that what's troubling you, Kate? Michael?"

"Not really. I guess it's just a little bit of everything." She broke off when the waiter came to their table, grateful for the interruption. She was not ready to discuss Michael. Nina ordered an Old Fashioned, but Kate needed more time to consider.

"God," Kate said. "I didn't think anyone drank those anymore. I haven't had one since my sophomore year in college. My date took me to the Lord Jeff in Amherst, where I proceeded to disgrace myself by getting sick on Old Fashioneds. I think I'm allergic to the bitters or something. I haven't thought about that in years."

"You ought to try one," Nina urged. "Might do you good."

"I better not. My three o'clock class awaits. I think it's instant dismissal for any professor showing up with liquor on his or her breath. On the other hand, it's all right for half the class to show up reeling."

"They *don't*."

"Not really. Though I've had one or two who have."

"Oh, hell, Kate. At least have a glass of wine. I've got a roll of breath mints in my bag."

"I guess getting fired wouldn't be the worst thing that's ever happened to me. Just remind me to gargle when you drop me off at home." She ordered the wine and settled back in her chair, scanning the room again.

"Don't bother with menus," Nina ordered, when the waiter returned with her drink. "We're having the borscht." She looked at Kate, questioning, and when Kate nodded, she said, "Bowls, not cups. And a glass of wine for my friend."

"Very good," said the waiter. "Today's special is Cornish beef pasties. Excellent with the soup."

Nina groaned in mock despair. "Who am I to refuse Cornish pasties?" She leaned toward Kate and stage-whispered, "Another five pounds. Guaranteed. I must be out of my mind." When the waiter left, she studied Kate. "All right, let's have it. What's bothering you?"

"Take your pick. Mid-life crisis? The middle-aged, single-woman blues? Maybe it's just the 'Winter of My Discontent.'" Her delivery was deliberately husky and dramatic, but her friend didn't smile.

"Come on, Kate. It's *me*, Nina."

The wine came and Kate took a long swallow, then set the glass down and stared at it, running her index finger around the rim.

"It's pretty much the same old stuff, Nina. Boring conversation."

"If you can't bore your friends, who can you bore?"

Kate continued to fuss with her glass, her eyes averted. "I'll tell you something," she said finally. "I'm forty-two years old, and after the holidays I sat down and took stock. I'm starting over, Nina. The plan I thought I would be following until my old age has been scrapped, and I'm going to have to start all over. The thing is, I don't know if I have the strength to begin again. Or the courage." She took a sip of wine and looked up. "I warned you this would be a boring subject."

"You're not exactly back at square one, Kate. You're just continuing in a different direction." Nina's blue eyes studied Kate shrewdly. "Has something happened?"

"Not really. I'm just feeling vulnerable. A little lonely at night. Michael and I hadn't really talked for years, but I could always *pretend* to myself that there was someone there. I know things hadn't been great between us for ages, but I was used to it. I had hoped here, in the new house, we could straighten things out. We used to share things, but then it seemed like we grew apart, that his job and career came to mean more to him than me and even Brian. But the thing that stings like hell, if I'm honest, is that my husband left me for another woman."

"Ye gods, Kate! You're not going to allow that creature with a mentality half her age make you feel inferior, are you? You're twice the woman she is!"

"Apparently Michael doesn't think so." She winced. "Forget I said that. No, I was thinking last night about how different men and women are. If I had left Michael for another man, he would have been furious, but on a deeper level he could accept it. I would be an adulterous bitch, and he would get sympathy. But if I had just walked out, had said, 'I'd rather live alone than with you,' it would have destroyed him. His ego couldn't take that, and you can be damn sure he'd feel castrated. It's so much easier on a man if the rival is another man. A woman's different. The most devastating threat is always another woman."

"I hadn't thought about it, but you're right. If Hal wanted to leave me because he felt he had outgrown our marriage or something, I'd be sick, but it wouldn't be as bad as if he left me to marry one of those gorgeous bimbos he flies with." Nina's eyes narrowed. "Who am I kidding? I'd *kill* him if he left me at all."

"Not to worry. Hal will never leave you. Not for a stewardess or a mid-life crisis."

Nina motioned to the waiter for a refill. He quickly returned with the drink and two bowls of borscht. "To your three o'clock class," she toasted. "Speaking of work, have you sent out your résumé to other colleges yet?"

"I've thought about it. So far it's all thought and no action. A change in jobs at this point would probably mean moving, and right now I don't want to do that. Since the divorce, I feel the house has been pretty important to Brian. A source of security, you know, and I don't want to take that from him."

Even as she spoke, she knew she wasn't being truthful. The fact was that she—not Brian—needed the house. From the first moment she had seen the Selby place, she had loved it. It was the homestead she had always longed for, and she couldn't give it up now, even if it didn't make sense to keep it. Michael argued that she was crazy to stay there. "What do you need such a big place for? All by yourself?" She had not bothered to explain.

Financially, the huge house was a horrific drain, but she didn't mention this to Nina, knowing that her friend thought she should have insisted upon financial support in the divorce terms. That point of pride had cost her, but she was glad, in spite of what her lawyer and Nina said, that she was not taking money from Michael.

"It just seems that my whole life is on a downswing. First Michael. Then my job. Teaching at a third-rate school to a group of students who couldn't get accepted anywhere else. When I take a good look at my life, all I see is failure."

"You're being too harsh, Katie. Your divorce was Michael's fault, not yours. I don't know about your job, but I have a feeling you're a damn good teacher. One thing I do know for sure. You're a wonderful friend and a tremendous mother. Look at Brian. He's happy, and I can't name a better adjusted, brighter kid. My kids think the world of him, and the Shaw tribe has pretty high standards. Whether or not it fits the picture you want to paint of yourself, you have to take some of the credit for that. Bri didn't get to where he is by having a failure for a mother. Look, Kate, you took a bad blow to the ego and you're still reeling, but I know you, and you're going to be all right. You're a lot stronger than you think you are."

Before Kate could respond, the sound of laughter caught their attention. A woman entered the room clutching the arm of an attractive gray-haired man. She was dressed in a soft blue wool suit, and her streaked blond hair curled gently around her neck, but in spite of the softness she tried to achieve, the word she evoked was brittle.

"My God," breathed Nina. "The day just took a turn for the worse."

The blonde appeared oblivious to everyone in the room except her escort. Her head was thrown back and she looked up at him with adoring eyes.

"Who's he?" Kate asked. "This is a new one. I thought she was going with some carpenter. The young guy with the beard who was working on the Johnsons' restoration. I saw them at the Harringtons' brunch on New Year's Day, and she told me she was going to marry him."

"I guess she didn't tell him. He dumped her. Rather cruelly too. I guess he figured out that after the honeymoon was over, they'd have very little left to say to each other. Poor Liz. First her husband and then her lover. Maybe she terrorizes them with her desperation."

Kate studied the woman across the room, and it seemed to her that there was a sadness beneath the forced gaiety. "That's too harsh, Nina. I think Liz just erects barriers to protect herself, and then becomes imprisoned within them."

"There you go. Saint Katherine. That's transference for you. Liz Shannon has the hide of a rhino and is about as sensitive. Don't waste your compassion on her." Nina stopped abruptly as the object of their conversation detoured by their table en route to the ladies' room.

"Afternoon." Liz Shannon smiled coolly. Up close she looked older. Lines of age and lack of sleep creased her makeup. "I haven't seen you two for *ages*." She directed her attention to Kate. "I saw Michael a couple of days ago. I must say, I don't know what he sees in that new wife of his. She's a *child*." Too many cigarettes had made her voice raspy. "Did you see that lovely *hunk* of meat I'm with? He's Julie Weston's cousin. I just met him last night. He's from San Diego and is staying with Julie for a month. Just divorced. Julie arranged the date, and *don't* you just know I owe her my life. I almost *died* when I found out what he does for a living. You'll never *believe*."

The woman's habit of emphasizing every third or fourth word irritated Kate like an emery board run over her teeth. Beneath the table she felt the gentle nudge of Nina's foot.

"A *urologist*. Can you *stand* it? You know what I told Julie? Two men have pissed on me this year already. I sure don't need an *expert*." She laughed hoarsely. An elderly couple at the next table glanced their way, their faces stiff with disapproval. Kate shrank in her chair.

"Well, I must run. Can't let a piece of prime meat like that stay alone too long. Too many hungry women around." Liz brushed Kate's face with a cool look, and for an instant her smile faltered. Then she turned and walked away.

Kate spoke first. "If I ever, *ever* say another kind word about that creature, you have my permission to throttle me."

"The poor urologist. I doubt he knows what hit him. What an absolute bitch she is. That crack about hungry women made me itch to dump my borscht down her gaudy shirt."

Kate didn't laugh. "She's right, you know. There're half a dozen women in this room right now who'd jump at the chance to grab that man. He could be a closet alcoholic, a wife beater, or terminally boring, and it wouldn't matter. Fresh meat. Just like Liz said. Available men are at a premium, and middle-aged women are a glut on the market." When she looked up, tears glistened in her eyes.

"Kate, honey, don't. Why let that bitch get to you? I should have dumped my soup on her."

"God, she's just so awful." Kate's voice was low and frightened. "But it's not just Liz. It's me. I'm terrified I'm going to end up like that. Scared and bitchy and grateful for blind dates."

Nina leaned across the table and took Kate's hand in hers. "Not you, Katie. Never." She tightened her grasp. "You're vulnerable and you're hurt, Kate, but you're soft. You're soft and gentle, and never in a million years could you end up like Liz Shannon. Never. It's just not in you."

Kate clung to her fingers, wishing there was some way she could let her friend know how much these words meant. The moment passed. From across the room, the sound of Liz's giddy laugh floated to them. They turned and watched as her escort lit her cigarette. His arm stretched across the table to her, exposing his wrist. His gold-link bracelet glistened against the immaculate cuff of his tailored shirt.

"Oh, God," Kate whispered. "A urologist." Then they began to giggle.

The warm glow of lunch, born of wine and laughter and friendship, stayed with Kate while she returned home to pick up her car and gather her papers for school. Already late, she risked a ticket as she raced toward the college. But not even the prospect of this or of facing her three o'clock class could diminish her sense of well-being.

Composition II/Introduction to American Literature was a prerequisite for graduation at Lanchester Community College. The faculty had a humorless joke about that. It might be a requirement that the students take the course, they said, but not that they enjoy it. The general apathy of the class proved the truth in their words.

Early in her first year of teaching at the college, Kate—stung by their indifference—assigned her students a composition in which they were to give their reasons for enrolling at LCC. The essays had saddened her. Almost without exception the pupils were there, they wrote, because their parents had pushed them, and not because of goals or ambitions of their own. Education, the Holy Grail of one generation, had become the albatross of another. In spite of this, she had grown attached to a few of her students. Through their compositions, between the lines of crudely articulated thoughts, of poor grammar and poorer spelling, she came to know them as individuals. And perhaps because they realized that they had exposed themselves to her, they slowly came to trust her. Sometimes they hung around her office, usually for small talk. Now and then they sought advice.

Occasionally she had in her class the exception, a student who perceived college as the first step toward fulfilling a dream. Kate had come to regard such pupils as gifts. Usually they were reentry students: housewives recently divorced, or adults seeking career changes. Three years ago there had been a cop who had grown tired of his job and wanted to become a lawyer. Motivated, curious, challenging, such students often lit a spark that fired the entire class, and when that happened, Kate found that it was again a joy to teach.

This semester she had only one reentry, Wally Haines. If he contained a spark, he had so far effectively concealed it.

As usual, he was late, disrupting Kate's lecture on "Honor as a Theme in American Literature." She had grown accustomed to his tardiness. At the beginning of the first semester, she had learned that he held a job busing tables in the campus cafeteria. Without that job, and another one at night pumping gas, he could not have afforded the college tuition, low as it was. Like most of her students, Haines came from a modest background.

Today, as he noisily took his seat, provoking a bored chuckle or two, she continued with the lecture. Dutifully, her students took notes. A few, Wally among them, made no pretense of this.

"Mr. Haines, drawing on the assigned reading you have completed so far this term, would you give us an example of honor in our literature?"

He slouched in his chair, his long legs extended beneath the seat of the student in front of him, and using a blade on his penknife, began to scrape the line of motor oil from beneath his fingernails. The student to his left continued to draw hearts on her notebook.

"What about our most recent assignment?" Kate prompted. "How did Hemingway define honor?"

Wally watched the girl doodle. He didn't raise his eyes. "I didn't get around to reading that story yet." There was no apology in his tone. He continued to work on his nails. The room was still; all note taking stopped.

Kate stifled the impulse to ask him why he bothered to come to class, since he didn't feel the need to read the assignments. "Can you come up with *any* examples, Mr. Haines?"

He slouched deeper in his chair. At last he looked at her, lazily, as if debating whether or not to answer. He tossed his blond hair out of his eyes and carefully folded the blade back inside the knife casing before speaking. "I don't think there is any such thing as honor. If there ever was, it's dead now."

Kate felt a flash of irritation. She was keenly aware that every eye in the class was focused greedily on her. Even the doodler had shoved aside her artwork. "An interesting thesis, Wally. Can you back it up?"

"It's dead all right," he repeated smugly. "It died in Vietnam, and Watergate. Leaders cheat and people lie." The class was with him now. Malicious smiles appeared on several faces. "What about you, Mrs. Tyler? Can you back up your *thesis*"—the word was mocking—"that honor exists?" His eyes glinted malevolently.

A dozen rebuttals came quickly to mind, and just as swiftly Kate rejected them. "I disagree with you, Wally," she finally said, her voice soft. "I believe honor exists in fact as well as in fiction. I had hoped, through our reading this semester, that you would come to catch a glimpse of the magnificence of man and the glory of his potential. To see the fierceness of his courage and the power of his integrity; the pride, dignity, fortitude, and endurance he exhibits at his finest. I had also hoped that you would come to see that, as a member of this fellowship, you possess these qualities too. Whether or not you choose to allow them to flower is, of course, quite up to you. It had not occurred to me, quite frankly, that you would deny their existence altogether." She paused and then slipped her papers into her briefcase. While the class waited in uneasy silence, she erased the chalkboard and then pulled on her suit jacket. With unhurried movements, she gathered up her purse and briefcase.

"There will be no reading assignment for tonight." She was prepared for the astonished shuffle that greeted her announcement. "Instead you will each prepare a composition. You will have twice the length of time to write the paper, and it will be graded as two papers.

"I will also waive the rule, and for this one composition, concept and execution will count more heavily than punctuation, spelling, or grammar." She paused and watched as her students diligently raised pencils and grabbed notebooks to jot down every one of her words.

"The topic of the essay will be 'Honor.' You are to write a paper of any length on honor and courage as they exist in fact or fiction, using, if you can, illustrations from our reading thus far. I would hope you come to agree with me that honor does not exist only within the pages of a novel. If, on the other hand, you agree with Wally, I expect you to make your case convincingly." She opened the door to the hall. "And since I think it will lack purpose to return to Hemingway today, this class is dismissed."

On the way home, she stopped at the supermarket to pick up something for dinner. Standing in front of the dairy case, she reached for a quart of milk, and for the countless time that day, was reminded of Brian. When he was home, they went through a half gallon a day. When she was alone, she was amazed to see how long a quart could last. Sometimes the milk soured and she ended up pouring the last inch or two down the kitchen drain.

She put the carton in her cart and turned down the deserted meat aisle. Five o'clock. Too late for the housewives. Absently she scanned the cellophone-wrapped steaks and chicken pieces. After the lunch at the Essex, she wasn't really hungry, but she was haunted by the fear that if she skipped just one meal, she'd soon stop cooking entirely. She poked over the packages of chicken. Not tonight, she thought.

The frozen-food section was busier. Single people, she thought. Lone shoppers choosing single-portion meals. I guess it's better than a single's bar or a computer dating service. Then she giggled. A young woman standing next to her looked up and smiled.

"Thank God for Stouffer's," she said.

Kate got her giggles under control and smiled back, tossing a package of beef and green peppers with rice in next to the carton of milk. All in a boilable pouch. The marvels of modern technology.

On the way to the checkout counter she added a box of cherry Danish to her purchases. She was still smiling when she pulled out of the parking lot and headed home. An old Barbra Streisand song drifted out from the radio speaker, and Kate sang along with the melody. She was a Streisand and Sinatra fan. What would Wally Haines say about that? It would probably complete his image of her as a woman totally out of touch with the times.

By the time she approached her home, shadows of dusk were settling into night. The temperature had dropped, freezing the ruts in the drive into treacherous ridges. When they had first moved into the house four years ago, she and Michael had drawn up a list of projects: new gutters, blacktop the drive, buy a carpet for the upstairs hall, repaint the shutters. The driveway, like the carpeting, had been one of those projects they'd never gotten around to. Ahead, the house waited in the dark.

This was the time of day she felt the divorce most keenly. Returning to a cold and empty house in wintry twilight, she regretted there was no one waiting with warm coffee and a warmer smile. It isn't Michael I miss, she thought sourly. It's the pure protoplasm. Prime meat.

She swore softly. She had forgotten the light. Usually she lit the lamp on the table in the bay of the living room window to relieve the bleakness. In the days after Michael left, she used to leave the radio playing softly all night to assuage the raw silence. But today, after the lunch with Nina, and afraid of running late for her class, she had forgotten to switch on the light.

She pulled up the crest of the drive and drew in her breath. There was a car already there. She flicked on her high beams, capturing it in the glare. The silhouettes of the driver and passenger stood out in sharp relief. She immediately recognized the shape of the uniform hats. Caps, Bri called them.

Later it would strike her that never for an instant did she think one of the visitors might be Michael, although that would have made more sense. At the moment, she thought only of Brian. He had come home. Her heart leapt at the thought. In the final seconds as her car continued up the drive, a dozen thoughts scrambled through her mind. He must be frozen, sitting out here like this. How long has he been waiting? Why on earth didn't he go in? Bri knows the house is never locked. Who did he bring home with him? On the heels of these questions, others, fueled by a mother's anxiety, flooded in. Why has he come home early? I hope nothing's wrong. She pressed her foot against the accelerator and pulled abreast of the dark sedan. Then she saw it was not Brian at all.

She turned off her ignition, watching the two men get out of the car. She recognized the driver now. He was the deputy commandant of the Academy. The other man was, for the moment, eclipsed by shadows, and so she did not see his face. Then he skirted the car and approached. Again, recognition was instantaneous. Captain Richard Beck. The senior chaplain. He opened her door and held out a gloved hand to help her.

"No," she whispered. Even before she heard his voice, she knew it was bad. His eyes met hers, and she saw the effort this cost him. Ignoring his hand, she swung her legs out. Before either man could speak, she rushed toward her home, leaving them to stand in the shadows.

CHAPTER TWO

The men followed, the leather soles of their uniform shoes slipping on the icy walk. Uninvited, they entered Kate's home. The gold stripes and stars on their sleeves seemed luminescent in the dim hall.

They were both tall and wore their gray hair clipped short. In their black uniforms and from a distance, they could have been mistaken for brothers. Their faces were drawn with fatigue and strain.

Kate stood facing them in the darkened hall. The deputy commandant broke the awkward silence.

"Mrs. Tyler—" he began, but she cut him off before he could continue.

"Forgive me. You must be cold. Come in." She struggled to regain a small measure of the composure that had so hideously abandoned her outside. Avoiding their eyes, she turned on a light and hung up her coat in the hall closet. Her movements were jerky and overly precise.

"I hope you didn't have to wait long. I'm usually home earlier. I stopped on the way to shop. Oh, I forgot the groceries. They're still in the car. It doesn't matter. I'll get them later. Commander Kestler, isn't it? And Captain Beck? Would you like something to drink? Something hot? Coffee? Or perhaps something stronger. I have scotch. Or bourbon. Wine? I usually have a glass before dinner. Would you like to join me?" The words spilled out, allowing the men no pause for answers, giving them no chance to speak.

"Mrs. Tyler?"

Silenced at last, Kate turned to the chaplain in surrender, letting him cup her hands in his. Stripped of gloves, his fingers were icy, and she shivered but did not pull away. He led her into the living room. For an instant, her eyes darted about in terror—what had Michael always told her? They

26

only send the chaplain when the news is very bad. With visible effort, she pulled herself together, knowing nothing she could do would forestall their words.

"We've come about Brian."

She didn't ask if he was all right. She knew he wasn't. "How bad is it?" Then the silent bargaining began. Please, she prayed, don't let it be too bad. A broken leg. It must have been a car accident. A head injury. That was trickier. He always wore his seat belt. His father had drilled that into him. It probably wasn't a head injury. And all the while she prayed, she knew she would be able to accept any injury or illness, anything except the one black impossibility.

The chaplain did not prolong it.

"I'm sorry, Mrs. Tyler. Brian is dead."

"No." She intended to scream, to change everything with the power of her denial, and she was shocked when the word came out a broken whisper. From the moment she recognized them, she had known. *They only send the chaplain if the news is very bad.* "No," she repeated in the wounded murmur. She moved to flick on lights. "No, not Bri." Her ears were ringing. Beck leaned in to help her, but she shook him off. Before her knees gave out, she sank down onto the sofa.

"Brandy?" she heard him ask.

She nodded and numbly indicated the door that led to the dining room. When he returned, she took the glass from him, holding it tightly so that it would not slip through her frozen fingers. The liquor burned her throat. She stared down into the amber fluid. If she didn't look at them, maybe they would go away. But even as she tried to ignore them, she knew she had to ask. Had to know. "How?"

Kestler answered. Unlike the chaplain's, his voice was that of a man used to keeping his emotions under rigid control. "I'm sorry, Mrs. Tyler. It appears that the boy committed suicide."

"No." The denial was instinctive and complete. Finally this was something she could deal with. A mistake. Somehow, someone had made a dreadful mistake. In haste, a mistaken identity. Some other midshipman. Someone else's child. Brian would never commit suicide. She sat a little straighter, allowing the hope to flood in.

As if reading her mind, Beck took over. His voice was filled with sorrow. When Kate looked into his eyes, she saw he believed there had been no mistake. He believed that Brian was dead. She would let him talk and then she would explain, show him his error.

"His company officer reported him missing. His room-mates were questioned and admitted that he had been away all night. A search party was organized. One of the mainte-nance men found him."

"How did he die?" She must ask questions, because they were expected of her. She sat stiffly, careful not to move. If she did so, something inside her would surely break. They were mistaken, and soon something they would say, if she listened very carefully, would prove that.

"It appears that Brian . . . that he hung himself."

No. Oh, dear God, no. The brandy rose in her throat and she gagged. "Where?"

"In a tunnel. A tunnel for the heating ducts. It runs beneath the Yard."

Stop. Please, stop. Don't tell me anymore. "When?"

"We can't be certain until after the autopsy." Autopsy? Kate flinched, but the commander did not notice and continued remorselessly. "The medical examiner said he died sometime last night."

"Last night?" Fresh horror struck her. *Oh, God. All day— while I was shopping and drinking wine and laughing, while I was teaching class and walking down the aisles of the supermarket and joking with Nina—all this time Brian was dead. My only son was dead and I did not know.*

"Admiral Thatcher decided it would be better if we came to tell you, so that you wouldn't be alone."

"We've been waiting here most of the afternoon." Beck's hands were still cold, and this time Kate shrank from their touch. "Is there someone you'd like us to call? To be here with you?"

"Michael," she said. "Has anyone told Brian's father?" Suddenly it seemed strange that they hadn't gone straight to Michael. The military always closed ranks during times like this. Automatically she looked at her watch. Five-fifteen. Only fifteen minutes had passed. A quarter hour and a lifetime. "He should be home by now. I'll phone him."

They moved aside when she reached for the phone. Her fingers trembled so badly she had to punch out the number twice. When she heard his voice, for the first time she almost broke down completely.

"Michael? It's Kate."

His reply was impatient. He had been this way since the divorce, treating her as if everything had been her fault, barely suppressing his hostility.

"Michael. I have bad news. I can't tell you over the phone. Can you come over?"

"Kate—"

"Please. Please, Michael. It's important. It's about Brian." Her voice broke on his name, and that seemed to cut through the wall of anger that he had erected.

"Five minutes," he said. "I'll be there in five minutes. And Kate, this is damn inconvenient. It had better be important."

She set the receiver down carefully and walked away from the phone. Brian's picture stood on the piano. It had been taken the summer of his first cruise. He was dressed in his full uniform. He had been so proud. So proud and young and handsome. She sat on the piano bench and held the frame in her lap, staring down at the man to whom she had given birth. It became too painful to look at his face, and gently she replaced the picture on the piano top. The metal frame seemed to burn her hands.

Outside, the February night sheathed the house. In other houses on River Road, rooms were coming alive with the sounds and scents of early evening family life. People returning to their homes, bringing with them pieces of their days. Dinners were begun, television sets switched on, boots exchanged for slippers. In the Tyler house, Kate sat in silence, and with the two naval officers, waited for Brian's father. Death had already isolated her home.

The sound of the car coming up the drive broke the tableau. Kate reached the door and opened it before Michael had even knocked.

"All right, what the hell is so damned important that you dragged me out? Wendi was just starting to serve dinner. This had better be— Good God, Kate. What is it? What's wrong?"

"You'd better come in." Now that he was here, she lacked the courage to tell him. He looked so much like Brian. Tall, blond, blue eyes that crinkled when he laughed. A chin that jutted forward just a bit, daring the world. Kate turned away.

It hurt too much to look at him. The naval uniform he wore only highlighted their similarity.

He walked past her into the living room. When he saw Kestler and Beck he hesitated, and Kate saw the almost imperceptible hesitation when he braced his shoulders. *They only send the chaplain if the news is very bad.* She moved to the dining room sideboard and slowly refilled her glass, pouring out brandy for him as well. It was cowardly of her to leave, but she could not bear to be there with him, to see his face when they told him. She was grateful for his presence. Now her pain was shared. Only Michael could understand. He would tell them how impossible it was, how ludicrous even to think that Brian might have killed himself. If they were right, and Brian was really dead, it had to be some kind of terrible accident. That's all.

But Michael ignored the glass she held out to him. "Why?" Anger burned in his voice. "He was home at Christmas. Jesus Christ, Kate, didn't he say or do anything that gave you some idea that he had this in mind? He must have said something. Was he in some kind of trouble?"

Shaken, she sank back into the sofa. His anger did not surprise her. Anger was always Michael's answer for everything. She knew his grief was as keen as hers. What she couldn't believe was that he could so readily accept the idea that Brian had taken his own life. She withdrew into silence. She sensed that in spite of his outburst, Beck and Kestler were more comfortable with Michael. The three began to talk, settling the specifics of arrangements, ignoring her.

"Was there a note?"

"What?"

"Brian. Did you find a note?"

"I'm sorry, Mrs. Tyler. There was no note. Not with the body or anywhere with his belongings."

She withdrew again. It was wrong. Not just the suicide. Everything. She tried to think back to Christmas. He had spent the first days of his break visiting friends in D.C. When he had come home, he'd seemed fine. A little drawn, tired, but that was all. And he hadn't wanted to phone Danielle. She tried to concentrate, punishing her mind to recall more. Shrilly, the phone intruded on her thoughts, but she did not move. After the third ring, Michael strode to the study to answer it. She heard him speak to the caller, then lower his voice.

"No. No, she wasn't exaggerating. It's Brian, honey. There's been an accident."

Kate looked at Beck and Kestler but they would not face her. The three of them eavesdropped silently. *Don't tell her. She has no right to know. Brian isn't her child.*

"He's dead, honey. I'll tell you when I get home. Not long. Maybe half an hour. No, there's no need for you to come here. I know. I love you too."

Kate retreated to her cocoon of silence. He returned to the room, but she refused to listen as they continued to make their plans.

"Would that be agreeable to you, Kate?"

She pulled herself back. What were they talking about?

"Brian's funeral. Would you like the service at the Navy chapel?"

"No." The word was ripped from her.

"Where then?" Michael rubbed a hand over his eyes wearily.

"I don't know." She felt pressured. Talk of funerals, arrangements, the planning of death seemed so cold. She didn't want to have to think about it. If only they would leave.

The men exchanged glances, forming a conspiracy of maleness.

"We have to make some decisions now, Kate." Michael's tone was even, calm, as if he were appeasing an unreasonable child.

"I'll think about it later. Tomorrow. I just know I want him to come home, not be left down there."

With each word they were taking Bri further away from her. Dimly, she heard the sentences—interstate regulations regarding transportation of bodies, plane versus train, timetables, funeral homes. They dealt with death so professionally. They never mentioned his name anymore. *It's not "him." Or, dear God, "the body." He's Bri. Our son. He's our son, Michael. Our son.*

"What funeral home, Kate? We can't wait forever to pick one out."

"I don't know. Anyone. Pick one out of the phone book. Look in the Yellow Pages. Let your fingers do the walking." She started to giggle, and stifled the sound before it became a sob. Then she saw the shocked expression on Michael's face, and the giggle threatened to surface again. Beck brought her more brandy. He rested his hand on her shoulder for an instant, as if trying to give her strength, but she pulled away from him.

In the end, Michael did as she suggested and chose a funeral home from the phone directory. She heard him making arrangements, crisply telling someone on the other end of the wire that the body would be shipped home and that he would be in touch when they knew more details.

"No." She stood. "I'm going to bring Bri home."

"You don't have to do that, Mrs. Tyler. The airlines can handle it. We'll take care of it on our end. Why don't you just let us handle this for you?"

"Kate, that's madness. There's no need for that. You'll just exhaust yourself. Be sensible. There'll be enough for you to do here."

"I'm going, Michael. My son's not coming home alone, shoved in the baggage... in the baggage hold of some plane. At least I can be with him."

Shamed, he looked away. "Of course. I understand. I'd like..." His expression was a mixture of pain and guilt and pleading. "If you don't mind, I'd like to go with you. We'll go together and bring him home." It was uncharacteristic, this asking, and out of old habit she warmed to him.

"Commander Tyler," Kestler began, "it's totally unnecessary, you know." For the first time, the Navy man seemed uncomfortable with Michael.

"I know," he said. Kestler frowned, but did not pursue the subject.

Michael led the officers to the door. They came to Kate's chair first, reaching down to clasp her hand, bending to murmur condolences, to assure her that if there was anything at all they could do, she had just to call them. Kate did not answer, hardening herself against their sympathy. She did not want it.

She was glad they were gone. When Michael returned to the room, for the briefest moment, she thought he was going to come over to her and hold her. They had not touched since he had arrived. She leaned forward slightly and saw him stiffen.

"There are calls I suppose I should make," he said, and

turned toward the study. She heard him phoning the airlines for reservations, and listened while he again talked to Wendi, explaining he would be home shortly.

"Should we make a list of people to call?" He stood in the doorway, holding a pad of paper he must have taken from her desk.

"Tomorrow."

"What about your father? You'll have to call him."

"Not on the phone." Kate shut her eyes against the pain. "He's not well, you know. I'll see him when we get back. It won't help to tell him tonight. Not over the phone."

"Well..." He flicked the pad nervously against his leg. "Do you want me to call Nina? Have her come over and stay with you? You shouldn't be alone."

"I'm all right. I want to be alone."

"You're sure?"

She nodded, knowing it was a lie, knowing she wanted him to stay.

"I can stay if you want. I could call Wendi and have her come over."

"No, I'm all right. You go on home now, and I'll see you in the morning." The thought of Wendi here, in her home, witnessing her grief, was abhorrent.

He handed her a business card. "This is Beck's. He wrote the number where they'll be staying tonight. If you need him, you can call him there."

"I didn't even thank him for coming. They came all that way. I know they didn't have to, and I never even thanked them." Her voice was low, but it was steadier now, and she saw the flicker of relief cross his face.

She waited in the hall until he had gone, not moving or closing the door until the engine had turned over, headlights leapt to life, tires crunched on frozen earth. Then she shut the door and moved into the empty living room. Her footsteps echoed on the polished floor. The room was too big, too silent, too cold. She thought again of the people who would have to be told, and longed for the comfort of another voice to ward off the silence. She thought about her father and reconsidered calling him. She desperately needed his strength and love. But as she reached for the phone, she paused. Her first instinct had been correct. He was ill. The stroke had badly crippled him. Word of the death of his only grandson should not reach him over the telephone. She owed him more than that.

She wandered aimlessly, walking from the living room to the hall to the dining room, where she refilled her glass with brandy, willing alcohol to dim her pain. Brian smiled out at her from his photo, and her stomach rebelled; the bile of brandy rose in her throat. This time she could not stop it. She ran for the bathroom, reaching the toilet as the vomit gushed forth. The red beets from her luncheon soup splashed against the white porcelain like blood. Bent almost double, she clenched the edges of the bowl and threw up again and again until there was nothing left.

She dampened a facecloth with cool water and wiped her face. In the cabinet, there was a bottle of mouthwash, but nothing could rinse away the taste in her throat. The smell of sickness filled the room.

She took a sponge and a can of cleanser from the vanity cupboard and began to scrub the toilet. She flushed the water away and dumped disinfectant in the bowl. Still she smelled her vomit. There were spatters of it around the base of the toilet. She went to the kitchen, took a bucket from beneath the sink, and filled it with hot water and detergent. She moved like an invalid, her shoulders hunched as if she could not stand straight or something inside her would snap. Back in the bathroom, she got on her hands and knees and began to scrub the floor. Water spotted her wool skirt and a run started in the leg of her stocking, but she never thought of changing.

After she finished scouring the bathroom, she went to the hall closet and took out the Electrolux. She began to vacuum the living room, pushing the wand back and forth fastidiously over the same spot before moving on to the next. When she was done in that room, she moved on to the dining room and hall. The phone rang, but she ignored it. When the vacuuming was finished, she began to dust, spraying the wood surfaces with Pledge, polishing them until everything gleamed.

She attacked the windows next, washing them with Windex and polishing them with paper towels. Her blouse had pulled free of her skirt, and semicircles of sweat stained her underarms. Sometime during the cleaning, she had slipped out of her shoes. Now, barefoot and with her hair unkempt, her deranged image was reflected in the windows as she scrubbed the cold, dark panes. She polished frantically and gashed a knuckle on the wood sash. She stared at the spreading blood. She felt no pain. In the study the phone rang again.

By midnight she was ready to begin the kitchen. A hollow burning filled her stomach, but she could not think of eating. She swept the floor and scrubbed the countertops. Her feet were cold and her legs sore, but she could not stop. Her lower back ached with a deep menstrual pain.

She was in the bathroom when the door bell chimed, but she did not answer it. She was staring at the tile floor. It looked streaky. She had not done it right the first time. Immediately she knelt and began scrubbing again.

"My God, Katie. Are you all right?"

Nina stood in the doorway, her mouth open in shock.

"Go away. Please go away. I have to clean the house."

"Katie. Dear Katie. Stop. It's after one." Nina's voice was ragged; her face was red and puffy. She had been crying.

"Go away, Nina." Kate pushed the sponge violently against the blue-patterned tile.

Nina stooped and pried the sponge from her raw hands. "Michael called me. He's been trying to reach you. You didn't answer the phone. He's very worried." She sat on the wet floor next to Kate cradling her as she would one of her children. "He told me about Brian. I'm so sorry, honey."

"He didn't do it, Nina. Brian wouldn't do it."

"I know, I know."

"He didn't. I know—" At last the tears started. Embracing, the two women huddled on the wet bathroom floor and wept.

The first thing she saw when she opened her eyes was the teddy-cat. It lay next to her head on his pillow. The smell of it—the sweaty, sweet smell of Brian's childhood—filled her lungs. She reached out for it, hugged it to her breast. She was cold, her neck stiff. She sat up, swinging her legs over the edge of the bed. Everywhere she looked, there were reminders of him. But that was why she had come to his room in the night, wasn't it? How long had she been sleeping? She glanced toward the clock on his nightstand. A hard wad of chewed gum stuck on the wood. A nasty habit she could never break him of. Not even when he became a spit-and-polish mid.

She replaced the tiger on the pillow and walked to the corkboard next to his desk. In the dim light of dawn, she saw two pictures tucked in the corner of the frame. They had been taken when he was ten. Why had he kept them? In one he stood by her side, his face young and touchingly intent. He wore a blue blazer and striped tie and held a small violin, cradling it in one arm as he gazed straight at the camera. She had bought the instrument for him that year and enrolled him in the Suzuki program. Their mutual love of music had proved to be a special bond, or so it had seemed to her at the time.

She looked at the second picture and wondered why at the time it hadn't been clearer to her what she and Michael were doing to their only son. The photo was snapped during a Little League game. Brian stood in the batter's box, waiting for his turn at bat. He wore the same expression of intensity. Behind him, Michael stood cheering him on.

The same week Kate had enrolled him in the Suzuki Institute class, Michael had brought home a leather glove and a ball. "Can't have my boy turned into a sissy," he'd said, half joking. Throughout that spring, every night after supper, in the patch of green that bordered the officer's quarters on the base in Virginia, he hit pop-ups for Brian to field. Gracefully the boy had tried to please them both. Until, in junior high, he discovered track.

Kate brushed her finger along the row of plaques and trophies on the bureau top. The oldest, a tiny battered cup he always kept in the center, he had won at his very first race. After that victory, the violin and glove had disappeared into the closet.

She and Michael had had dreams for him; most were those they themselves had never fulfilled. But Brian had always been true to himself. A cross-country runner. A man for the long distance.

She had hoped to find some measure of comfort in his room, but there was only pain. The memories were too strong. The room weighed on her and, afraid of being crushed, she fled.

Aware Michael would soon arrive, she quickly showered. She stood at the closet, trying to decide what to wear. Each decision, each ordinary task, seemed insurmountable. At last she chose a gray wool suit and packed a small overnight tote bag. Downstairs in the hall, she picked up her handbag and set it on top of her overnight bag. She wanted to be ready when Michael came. Money. She didn't even know if she had enough to get her to Annapolis. She didn't get paid until next week. She went to the desk and took out her checkbook and charge card and stuck them in her pocketbook. She had thirty dollars in her billfold. Enough to get by. She would charge the plane fare and hotel. Even while she thought through her plans, she realized how ridiculous these matters were, and resented having to deal with pointless details instead of being allowed the luxury of giving in totally to her grief.

Michael arrived promptly at seven. He wore his uniform. His face was lined and hollow, and she knew at once that he had not slept. He held the door for her, and when he reminded her to lock it, there was no sarcasm in his voice. Then he carried her suitcase to the car. He was kinder to her than he had been in years. It was the kindness of an injured person toward another who was also wounded.

His car was new. A sports car of some kind. She was not good with the names of cars, had never had an interest in that kind of thing.

Someone stopped by to see you this afternoon, Bri. I told them you were at the track.

What kind of car, Mom?

Blue. A blue car.

What else? Old or new? Two-door or four?

I didn't notice. Just blue.

She closed her eyes, trying to shut out the memory; light-headed from lack of sleep, she stumbled.

"You all right, Katie?"

Michael had not called her that in years. Now, taking her arm, he guided her the rest of the way. The bucket seat on the passenger side was locked in the farthest forward position, and her knees jutted against the dash. He reached across her lap and pressed a lever, adjusting the seat. A much shorter person usually rode in this seat. Her presence stayed with them on the silent ride to the airport.

They were early for their flight. She let him take over, let him arrange their boarding passes, obtaining seats in the nonsmoking section. When he had finished, he led her to the

coffee shop and ordered coffee and corn muffins for them
both. He ate two of the muffins; she left hers untouched. She
sipped her coffee mechanically. At last their flight was
announced.

He waited until they were in the air until he began.

"Did he give any indication he was going to do it? Anything? At Christmas did he seem depressed or angry about
anything?"

"He didn't do it, Michael. I don't care what they say. He
didn't." Her voice was exhausted but firm.

Resentment flashed across his face, and she recognized the
closed, stubborn look he wore when he was being crossed.
He turned away from her.

In less than an hour they would be in Baltimore, and as
they drew closer the memories flooded in.

"Remember the first time we flew down for his interview?
Remember how nervous he was? And then, later, when he
had finished the tour and interview, what did he say? Some
silly thing? 'A piece of cake.' That's what he said. 'A piece of
cake.'" She bent her head, trying to stop the tears, but they
came anyway, sobs that caused other passengers to crane
their necks and then look away. Michael took out his handkerchief. He had brought two. Even in that he had thought
ahead. She used to love his precision when she was younger.

"Stop it, Kate. Don't talk about it. Try and get some rest."
He reached over and awkwardly took her hand, folding her
fingers in his.

They sat that way for the rest of the flight. When the pilot
informed the passengers that they were approaching Baltimore-
Washington International Airport, she turned to ask him if
he'd arranged for a rental car, and saw that he was asleep. She
knew it was irrational, but it angered her, and she slipped her
hand from his. As the FASTEN SEAT BELT sign flickered on, she
leaned forward and stared out the window, looking beyond
the gray span of wing.

Soon she would be with Brian. An hour's drive to Annapolis and she would be with him. And there—at the Academy—
she would find answers to her questions.

CHAPTER THREE

As they drove through Gate 1 and into the Yard itself, all her ambivalent feelings about the Naval Academy surfaced, vacillating between a pride so profound that her throat ached with the sweetness of it and a resentment equally intense.

Awe took hold first, generated by the overwhelming sense of tradition evidenced and celebrated by wood, steel, and stone: the foremast of the battleship *Maine;* the tomb and sarcophagus of John Paul Jones; the Tripolitan, Macedonian, Herndon, and Mexican monuments, masses of stone erected in the memory of honored dead; the stately buildings anchored amid the flawlessly groomed grounds.

There, too, was the aura of the place, the majestic pomp and circumstance epitomized by the dress parades on Worden Field, when nearly five thousand midshipmen become one, a splendid marching machine moving to the tattoo of drums so throbbing and relentless that one's own heart becomes synchronized with them and the earth itself seems to pulse with their beat. In the posture of the Brigade members, Kate saw a cockiness; these young men believed themselves an elite. Each had run the rugged course, a marathon won inch by inch, each measure grudgingly granted. And because Brian had belonged to this elite, Kate shared his pride.

But beneath her pride always ran a darker emotion, a chord of animosity and jealousy. Part of it related back to her ex-husband and her belief that the Navy had always been her rival. But with Bri the feeling was deeper. With him, she felt the Academy had assumed her place, taken her son from her. The mids even called their dorm Mother B., an open acknowledgment that Bancroft Hall, a sprawling eight-winged building, cradled the entire Brigade in her massive womb.

Nor could she overcome the belief that the Academy had consumed the unique soul of Brian Michael Sidney Tyler and molded it to fit its form, altering posture, gait, even language. (Stairs became ladders; floors, decks; a bed, a rack.) In each change, Kate felt the ache of loss.

Once, during his youngster year, Brian had laughingly told her that the Naval Academy was the only place in the world where a man's God-given rights were taken away at entry and then given back to him, one at a time, over the next four years as privileges. She had looked then at his animated face, but she couldn't laugh, for so, too, had she come to believe that the Navy had taken away her God-given son and then, piece by piece, returned him, inexorably transformed.

Now she looked across the seat at Michael. He stared stonily ahead, his face masked in anger, still smoldering despite the length of time that had elapsed since his argument with the car rental clerk in Baltimore. For him there was none of her ambivalence. From the moment four years before when Brian took his Oath—one of thirteen hundred brace-backed plebes to stand on the yellow bricks of Tecumseh Court in the baking July heat, immaculate and fresh in newly issued white works—pledging his loyalty (his life if need be), Michael had felt only pride that their son was following in his footsteps. New Navy paraphernalia bearing the Annapolis seal joined older mementos crowding the surface of Michael's desk: paperweights, a pewter letter opener, a coffee mug holding white pencils with U.S. NAVAL ACADEMY embossed in blue. Michael wore a Navy T-shirt while sailing his sloop in the Sound, and when he raked the first autumn leaves, he donned his blue-and-gold Academy sweatshirt. As many fall Saturdays as he could, he flew down for a football game, screaming himself hoarse for the Annapolis team. No, Michael felt no ambivalence. He had never been an interloper, here on sufferance. Well, Michael, she thought grimly, now we have both lost him.

Overhead the gray sky pressed down. The car's wiper blades swished and clicked against the windshield. The snow that had begun just as they landed in Baltimore now streaked the Academy grounds. The wind blew in from the Severn, cloaking the Yard with its icy breath. The car heater spewed warmth against her legs, but she shivered, dreading the answers she had come to seek.

Michael turned onto Porter, past the officers' quarters, then onto Buchanan and into the circular drive of the superintendent's home. As if by accord, they sat for a minute in silence. Michael turned to her, opened his mouth to speak, then shut it again and reached for the door handle.

He circled the car, opened her door, and she swung her legs out, swimming up through her grief and exhaustion to find the strength to move. As she took her ex-husband's arm and walked wtih him to meet the couple waiting at the door, she held her head high in the swirling snow.

Admiral Thatcher and his wife stepped forward to greet them. She was whip thin and all sympathy, her soft Southern accent blurring the edges of her words. He—erect, correct—spoke, too, of condolences, but it seemed to Kate that behind the wire-rimmed glasses his eyes, narrowed from years of fighting the glare of sun on sea, were as cold as dead love.

There was a flurry of welcome, the business of taking off coats and gloves and handing them over, nervous conversation about the unexpected storm, and then they were ushered into a stunningly appointed room. As Kate took in the Oriental rugs, the museum-quality paintings and furniture, she could not help but compare this gracious room with the Spartan ones of Bancroft Hall. RHIP, she thought wryly.

I'm a first classman now, Mom. Liberty. Every weekend. Rank Hath Its Privileges.

You sound like your father.

That's because we both know the rules. RHIP. The Navy's version of a carrot on a stick.

Marian Thatcher's musical voice broke into the memory. "May I get you something to drink? Coffee or tea, Commander? Mrs. Tyler?"

"Nothing, thank you." Kate turned to the admiral, cutting off anything Michael might have said. "They told us so little. How did it happen? How did he die?"

Thatcher took off his glasses and rubbed the bridge of his nose. Narrow indentations creased his gray hair where the frames had pressed against his head. He addressed his words to Michael.

"I don't know how much Commander Kestler told you, Commander, but I'm afraid there is not much I can add. Your son was reported missing by his Company Commander at 0700. We instigated a search by 0730. One of the maintenance crew found the body. He had hung himself from a grate in the steam tunnel." He turned stiffly to Kate. "I'm sorry, ma'am. I know this isn't pleasant for you."

Kate stared at the carpet until the muted blue pattern blurred. Scores of questions pounded at her brain, but she could give voice to none of them.

"Why?" Michael's face was ashen.

"I wish I knew, Commander. Marian will tell you I spent a sleepless night trying to make sense out of this. None of us know. I'm sorry. Your son was one of our finest midshipmen."

"Admiral, when did he die?" Kate asked.

A flash of irritation flamed for a moment, and then Thatcher again turned to her. His wife sat in a blue velvet side chair, and her hand stroked the arm nervously.

"We'll have to wait for the autopsy to be sure, but the local medical examiner believes it was sometime around 0200. Between 0200 and 0300."

A chill swept Kate, and she was back in the upstairs hall in Connecticut, surrounded by the encompassing sense of stillness. She felt the touch of the cold brass weight against her index finger as she nudged the bob, saw the trick of lighting on the enameled face of the clock and the frozen position of the dial hands. Remembering, she felt the pull of ancient Celtic blood, and a force stronger than reason told her that regardless of what the autopsy proved, the actual instant her son had died was 2:10:13.

"I want to see him."

Admiral Thatcher and Michael stared at her as if she'd gone mad. Marian Thatcher could not control a horrified flinch, as if Kate had spat on one of her costly rugs. Her fingers pressed against the nap of the dark velvet, smoothing out nonexistent wrinkles.

"Well, now, there's no need for you to put yourself through that, Mrs. Tyler. The necessary identification has been made. All of that has been taken care of. And it is my understanding that the body is already on its way to Baltimore."

"Why Baltimore?"

"For the postmortem. All autopsies for the state are done there at the chief medical examiner's office."

"Why do they have to have an autopsy?" The thought of her son's body being further brutalized was hideous.

"It's routine, Mrs. Tyler. In all cases of a sudden death, a postmortem is required."

"Please," she whispered. "Please, call and see if they have taken him yet."

Thatcher hesitated, then glanced at Michael. Receiving a nod in answer to his unspoken question, he left the room to make the call. Kate stared at her clenched hands, listening to the click of a distant clock, and wondered if she would ever wake from the nightmare.

"The storm has delayed things," Thatcher reported from the doorway. "The body is still at the funeral home. They will wait for you, but they asked that you hurry. They like to get the postmortem started as soon as possible after the death."

Marian Thatcher rose to get their coats. In the hall, her husband grasped Michael's hand. "My sympathy, Commander. In a way I feel as if I have lost a child too. It might surprise you, but in spite of the size of the Brigade, I feel I know each and every one of my men."

Marian fingered the pearls at her throat and shot him a subtly reproving glance.

"Yes, of course. Young women too. Forgive an old sailor. When I graduated in '51 there were no women, so I guess for me it will always be that way. You know the feeling, Tyler. Not like in your day either. Just one of the changes that Congress in its infinite—"

"What was the name of the funeral home, Admiral?"

"Hearst, Hall, and Smith." Thatcher's expression conveyed his displeasure. Clearly he was not used to being interrupted, especially by the ex-wives of officers.

Kate watched in silence while Michael said good-bye. His obsequious tone sickened her. She didn't fail to note Marian Thatcher's relief that they were leaving her elegant home.

"He didn't do it, you know." Her voice was shrill, but she couldn't control it. "Brian didn't commit suicide. He couldn't. I don't know how he died, but I know my son wouldn't kill himself." Without waiting for Michael, she stepped outside, anxious to escape the pity she saw in their eyes.

Admiral Horace Thatcher stared after the departing car, his face carefully devoid of expression. Flakes of snow twirled and danced through the open door, dusting his spit-shined shoes. He reached for the knob and closed the door. His grip was firm but not tight. His knuckles were not white; his hand

did not shake. He was not surprised by this. He was intensely certain of his self-restraint, supremely confident that no
one—neither family nor fellow officers nor the ranks he
commanded—could ever gauge his mental outlook on the
evidence of his physical appearance. He prided himself on
this. He was wrong.

Early in their marriage, Marian Thatcher had discovered a
chink in his diligently crafted armor. The correct and tightly
controlled officer had a vocal tic. He hummed. The sound
was as faint as the buzzing of a bee, a tiny, tuneless droning
that escaped from deep in his larynx and betrayed him.

She heard it now, and knowing from experience that this
Doppler signal signified either monstrous frustration or fury,
she wisely tiptoed her retreat.

Death had not been kind. The marks of the rope cut his
throat cruelly, and the surrounding flesh was swollen and
angry. His hands and feet, the last poking out from beneath
the sheet, were purple where the blood had pooled. When
she reached to touch her son, his skin was cool. Yet it still felt
the same to her fingers, muscles still strong and pliable. Once
she had touched him, she could not let go, and she had
enfolded him in her arms, stroking his face, crooning into his
hair, smoothing it. Behind her, Michael made a mewing noise
and fled the room, but she was aware of nothing but her son.

The tinkling sound of silverware and glasses brought her
back to the present. Kate shut her eyes, trying for the tenth
time to erase the vision that seemed burned into the very
tissue of her eyes. Michael had arranged for a table by the
window in the hotel dining room. Below, the harbor waters
reflected the lights of the city. The drinks he had ordered
were on the table, and not even knowing what she was
drinking, she swallowed half of hers. The waiter stood at her
side, mutely waiting for her order, but she could not speak.
After a minute, Michael ordered for them both, choosing the
onion soup Calvados and two entrées of spiced crab cakes.

When the waiter walked away, he turned on her, whispering
fiercely, "For God's sake, Kate, pull yourself together. You
can't go on acting this way. Christ, you were *rude* with
Thatcher this afternoon. He put himself out for us. Having us
to his home instead of to his office. A courtesy, for Christ's

sake, and you were rude. How the hell do you think that makes me look?"

"It doesn't matter now."

"What? What the hell do you mean, it doesn't matter?" Conscious of the stares from other diners, he lowered his voice. "How the hell do you think it makes me look? Brian kills himself, and then you come here and act like a lunatic."

Kate's voice was so soft he was forced to lean across the table to hear it. "It doesn't matter. I'm not your wife anymore. You won't be judged by my behavior." She paused when the waiter brought their soup and salad. Michael peppered the salad and slathered a roll with butter.

"Did you see his shoulder and arm? They were so bruised? Did you see them?"

Michael slammed his knife down. "Jesus, Kate. Please. Not now." The words were said half in anger, half in plea. She fell silent and watched him eat. He bent over the bowl and spooned up the soup. She finished her drink and signaled for another one.

He was finishing his third crab cake when he noticed that she had not touched her food. "You should eat," he said. He looked pointedly at her empty glass. She didn't respond. His mouth tightened and he resumed eating. The waiter returned, and Michael ordered coffee. She asked for a cognac. He narrowed his eyes, but she ignored the warning. The liquor was bringing shadows and dimness, and she welcomed them.

When they rose to leave, she realized the cognac had been a mistake. She reached out to support herself against a table. Furious, Michael grabbed her elbow, steering her toward the elevator. Once the door closed, shutting them off from view, he dropped his hand. She began to cry. He had pulled away, but she stepped closer and leaned against him. At that moment, in spite of everything, she needed him. She told herself the years of silence, the years in which they had grown apart, had never really happened. They had loved each other once.

"Please, Michael. Please, hold me."

Woodenly he put his arms around her, and she sank gratefully against his wide chest, into the warmth of his uniform. "I can't believe it. I just can't believe Bri's dead. I thought if I saw him, it would make it real, but I still can't believe it." She heard the noise of her sobs, great wracking sounds of despair.

"Shh, Kate. Don't do this."

"He needed me, and I wasn't there. Oh, God, Michael, Bri needed me. He was dying, and I was eating and laughing and sleeping, I was living and he was dying, and I didn't even know."

Her choking sobs filled the elevator, and when the doors slid open, the noise flowed out into the corridor.

"Come on, Kate. This is our floor."

She did not move. She buried her head against his chest, whispering the words into the fabric of his uniform.

"Please. Please stay with me tonight. I can't be alone."

Her need was overwhelming. The isolation of Brian's death had grown all day. Michael was the only one who could share her pain, understand her grief. She could forgive him everything—the divorce, his weakness at the funeral home, his appetite at dinner, everything—if he would just stay with her now and help her get through the night.

"I can't." He dropped his arms and stepped into the corridor. "Don't ask me, Katherine. I can't."

"Please. Don't turn away from me now. Not now."

"Oh, Kate," he said in a sad old voice. "Don't you see? I already have. Brian's death doesn't change that." He walked away, and she watched. When he opened the door to his room, she heard his telephone ringing. Fumbling through her tears, she opened the door to her own single, silent room.

The winter months at the U.S. Naval Academy at Annapolis are long and bleak. The river ices over, bone-chilling winds sweep in from the Chesapeake, and midshipmen walk from Bancroft Hall to Chauvenet to Macdonough with their heads down, taking it like an assault. The pressures—the all-pervasive, never-ceasing pressures designed to break a boy and turn him into a man by grinding away at mind and body and spirit—smother even the strongest among them. During these leaden months a collective case of cabin fever rages, and the promise of spring seems impossibly far away. The midshipmen call this period of doom the Dark Ages.

Crossing the Yard, Kate shivered. Her headache was excruciating. In the snow behind her, her feet left a solitary trail through the Visitor's Gate. She was the first outsider to enter this morning. In the distance, she heard the pealing of bells. She quickened her steps until the massive bronze doors of Bancroft loomed ahead. Inside the dorm, her footsteps echoed in the empty halls. It was nine o'clock, and nearly all of the midshipmen had already left for classes.

She turned the corridor which led to Brian's room. His nameplate had been taken down from its place on his door. As if they had known she was coming, his roommates waited inside.

She stood for a moment at the threshold and looked down at the snow melting from her boots onto the spotless green tile. Her eyes swept over the room, seeing the stripped bunk and emptied closet. The only sign that Brian had once inhabited this room was the sea bag, suitcase, and carton of books by the door. On his bed, a garment bag lay across the bare mattress. His grease cap—the ultimate symbol of Navy spit and polish, the stretched cloth immaculately white, whiter than the fresh snow that coated the Academy grounds outside—lay on top, never, she realized, to be thrown in the air in jubilation and victory, the gesture of triumphant release that marked the end of May's Commissioning Week.

Her grief was mirrored in the faces of the two boys—men—before her. They had both jumped up when she entered the room, and now stood in awkward silence. It hurt to look at them.

Jordan Scott, the smaller of the two, was a wiry, sloe-eyed boy. His face was lean, with finely chiseled chin and cheekbones; his nose led in a straight, strong line to a proud brow, which was broken by a comma of dark hair. Many mids, by the time they are first-classmen, slack off a bit, their shoes no longer as richly gleaming, the white of their hats smudged a bit on top. Jordan betrayed none of this. His belt buckle glowed as brightly as the day he bought it, and his black wool uniform was immaculate. He wore it with an easy elegance, as if he'd been born to it.

Webb Garrick, on the other hand, was forever doomed to draw the inspecting officer's critical eye. No matter how hard he tried, this gangling giant of a man from the Midwest looked unkempt, as if his uniform had been issued a size too small for his stilt-legged frame. With thin, receding hair, he

looked older than his age, and his expression in repose—
despite his reputation as the company prankster—was mel-
ancholic, as if he had already seen the sorrows of a lifetime.

"Mrs. Tyler—" Jordan began. Across the narrow room,
Webb Garrick twisted away and looked out the window. His
neck was rigid, but his back looked naked in its vulnerability.
Four years of intense indoctrination and rigorous training had
obviously not prepared him for this. The three roommates
had been a unit, and the unit had been destroyed.

"I can't believe Bri's gone." Jordan's voice was muffled. He
avoided facing Kate. "Nothing will ever be the same. I don't
think I'll ever laugh again."

The sentence struck a chord of memory in Kate. The same
words: another time, another death. Then she remembered.
After John Kennedy's funeral, Mary McGrory had said the
same sentence to Patrick Moynihan. Moynihan corrected her.
"Oh, we'll laugh again, Mary. We'll just never be young
again."

She turned away, unable to console Jordan. She walked to
the pile of Brian's belongings. On top of the box were two
heavy texts, and she drew her finger across the titles. *Modern
Italian*. His grandfather's influence. Her father had been the
only man in Congress to speak seven languages. A sense of
loss—waste—swept her as she reached for a small box that
rested on the textbooks. She opened it and saw Bri's watch.
It had been a high school graduation gift from his father.
Precisely engraved letters on the back spoke of a father's love
and pride in his son. Her hand shook as she set the box
down. Jordan and Webb watched silently as she picked up
Bri's wallet and flipped through it, glancing at his license,
Social Security card, and several pictures. In one photo, Bri,
Webb, and Jordan, dressed in civvies, were standing in front
of the Washington Monument, their arms around three girls.
She looked closely but did not recognize any of the women.
Did Danielle know Bri dated other women? All six in the
picture were laughing, and the frozen gaiety broke her heart.
Next to that picture was an old photo of her and Michael,
taken long before the divorce. It had been glued in the photo
album that she kept on the bottom shelf of the bookcase in
the study. When had Bri taken it? The edges were ragged
where he had pried it loose from the page.

He had never said much about the divorce. Twice Kate had

tried to talk to him about it, but he had jokingly avoided her attempts. How badly had they hurt him?

"Why?" She straightened, addressing the two men. "Why would he do this?"

A fleeting expression crossed Jordan's face. Wariness? Guilt? Pain? Kate could not be sure. Before she could speak, a voice in the hall cut through the charged silence.

"Did you hear the latest about Tyler?"

"Do you mean the hanging? Christ, it gives me the creeps."

"No. Not that. The latest. Thatcher's having him court-martialed."

"You're shitting me. Why?"

"For destroying government property—posthumously, of course."

Their laughter was obscene, spilling into the corridor, poisoning the air.

The words paralyzed her. Beside her a voice—steellike in its anger—knifed the silence.

"Boyce. Reed." Jordan's tone was low, but there was no mistaking the fury in it.

Webb began to speak, trying to interrupt, but Jordan cut him off with a look. As if hypnotized, Kate moved to the doorway and watched him confront two terrorized plebes. They stood in profile twenty yards away, their eyes locked on the rigid, furious first-classman facing them. The muscles of Jordan's cheek was bunched with rage.

"What were you saying?" His voice had grown deceptively soft, but the menace in it chilled Kate. The two uniformed plebes stared dead ahead, their chins tucked in a tight brace against their necks.

Behind her, she heard Webb whisper, "Christ."

"Give me fifty," Jordan commanded in a hushed, deadly voice.

The two dropped as if shot onto the polished tile of the hall. Fifty push-ups later their rasping breath was the only sound in the corridor. They moved to rise, but Jordan cut them short.

"Fifty more."

"Jordan," Webb said. "It's against regs—"

"Shut up, Spider." The first-classman did not take his eyes off the plebes. "Shut the hell up about regulations. What you're seeing is plebe indoctrination. That's not against anything. It's the duty of a first classman to provide proper indoctrination for plebes. Isn't that right, Boyce?"

"Yes, sir." The plebe's response was labored; his arms trembled as he pushed his body up, his full weight supported only by his fingertips.

"You, Reed. Against the wall. Fingertips. Understand?"

Reed, a red-haired, lantern-jawed youth whose closely cropped hair did nothing but emphasize his large, hooked nose, braced himself, his feet set more than a yard away from the wall until he was supporting himself only by his fingertips. Hatred spasmed his freckled face, but before he turned to obey Jordan, the careful blankness had returned.

Violence hung in the air like an odor. By now, Kate had forgotten why the plebes were being punished, forgotten that Jordan had come to Brian's defense. She was sickened by the scene and only wanted it to end. "Please," she whispered. "Please, stop this."

Abruptly, as if he, too, were tired of the game, Jordan stepped away.

"Get out of here, you sorry chickenshits. You're not fit to breathe the same air as the rest of us. I'll see you both at evening come-arounds. Now get the hell out of here."

The plebes scrambled away, squaring the corner and taking the stench of their fear and resentment with them. Jordan returned to the room. A sheen of sweat covered his forehead. For an instant, it seemed that he would say something to her, but before he could, Webb spoke.

"I'm really sorry about that. They didn't mean anything by it." His eyes held the haunted look of an ancient animal.

Kate sat on Brian's bed. Her head ached and she was so cold.

"Since I heard, I've been over and over it. It just can't believe Bri would do this. Was there anything he said or did that gave any . . . any hint?"

"That's the hell of it, Mrs. Tyler." Jordan's voice had returned to normal, as if the scene in the hall had never happened. "Webb and I have talked about it, and we can't think of why he'd do it. Everything's been going great for Bri. Right, Spider?"

Webb spoke slowly, reluctant to be drawn into the discussion. "That's right."

"When he wasn't in his rack all night, we thought he might

have gone into D.C. for the night." Jordan paused, aware he had made a slip. "He, ah, he did that once or twice before, and we covered for him. But this time he hadn't said anything about staying out." He again turned to his roommate for confirmation. "Right, Spider?"

Kate looked up at Webb, but he was staring out through the venetian blinds. She was seized by the belief that he knew more than he was saying. She rose from the bed. All the questions she had hoped to have answered were still there, but new confusion had been added. Brian had broken regulations to go to Washington. If caught, it would have been a serious breach of rules. Before this she would have bet her life that Brian would never violate the Academy's Concept of Honor. Heartbroken, she returned her attention to his meager pile of belongings. They had been packed neatly, efficiently. She was grateful that the task of emptying his desk, closet, and shelves had not been left for her.

"Do you have a car?" Webb's voice was husky.

"Yes. Brian's father rented one. I left a message for him to meet me here."

"We'll bring these things down to the front. Jordo and I will carry them to your car."

"That's not necessary, Webb. Don't you have a class or something you should be doing?" How often had she heard Brian grumble that there were very few free minutes at the Academy?

"It's okay, Mrs. Tyler. We have the time."

Kate looked again at Bri's belongings. "Are these all his things?"

"Yes, ma'am. Except for the stuff in the basement. We checked his locker there this morning, but it was empty. Someone else must have already shipped his things from there."

She picked up the garment bag and followed the others to the first floor. Michael was waiting there. Kate had not seen him since the scene outside her room the night before, and now she was glad the two midshipmen were there with her and she did not have to see him alone. She watched as he came toward them, shocked by his posture. He slouched, shoulders and head bent. No longer in uniform, he seemed to have shrunk. Throughout their marriage, and after, she had never seen him in defeat, and she suddenly realized how difficult this trip was for him. As he had once worn his pride, so now he wore his shame. His son was no longer the Annapolis Man, but the Suicide.

Webb and Jordan looked uncomfortable, uncertain whether to salute Michael or shake his hand. He was not in uniform, but he was a superior. He solved the problem by reaching for the box of Brian's books, accepting their awkward words of sympathy with an abrupt nod.

"I called Baltimore," he said. "They're releasing the body this morning. I've arranged for the casket to be on our flight this afternoon."

She knew that this was his gesture of conciliation, but it irritated her that he could not mention Brian's name. She nodded and busied herself with one of the boxes, then stepped around the car, slamming the trunk. A bloodred Corvette roared by, a midshipman at the wheel.

Webb followed her gaze. "Every plebe's dream," he said. "A 'Vette and a grease drag to share the front seat." Kate was surprised by his cynicism. "It's a mid's perk. For surrendering our identities, we are allowed our toys."

"Easy, Spider," Jordan said softly. He opened the door for Kate. Before he could close it, she took hold of his forearm, propelled by the sense that she was going with things left unfinished.

"Jordan, he wasn't in some kind of trouble? He hadn't done anything wrong, had he?"

"Bri wasn't in trouble. It doesn't make sense, what he did, Mrs. Tyler. No sense at all." His eyes met hers, clear and guileless, but Webb continued to stare at the frozen ground. His face crumpled, and for a moment Kate feared this giant of a mid was going to cry. Then a small knot of down-coated tourists approached, and she watched him stiffen and swiftly compose himself. There was a towheaded boy in the group, and as they passed by, he looked up at Webb and Jordan. A look of adoration shone on his pale winter face.

The two midshipmen stood and watched the car drive away. They stood stiffly, not waving, and when the car left their field of vision, Jordan turned to Webb.

"Spider? You all right?"

The other man walked away from his roommate without

answering. His gait was rigid and he did not bend into the wind, taking it instead full on, blinking back the tears its sting brought to his eyes.

Jordan let him go. He returned to their room alone. At the door he took in the emptiness. "Shit," he said. A helpless rage overwhelmed him. He needed to talk to someone, but there was no one. Briefly he considered seeking help from Captain Bellows, but he rejected the idea almost as soon as it occurred. The fact that it had even crossed his mind indicated his desperation. Buck. Buck was the only one he could talk to, the only one who would understand. Memories of the last few times he had seen his older brother swept over him, but he brushed them aside. Almost as if Buck were standing beside him, he heard his voice. Cool, sardonic.

"Tough it out, shithead."

The phantom voice gave him courage, and he picked up his books and headed briskly toward class. As he strode down the corridor, he unconsciously averted his eyes while passing the last door on the right. He wasn't home free yet. And he wondered, What had happened to the letter Bri had written? Why hadn't she mentioned it? No, he was a far cry from being home free. He'd have to call Buck after all.

They did not speak until the plane was airborne. "Brian broke regulations to go to Washington that night. Did you know that?"

Michael shook his head wearily. She wanted to tell him how she was beginning to be afraid she didn't know their son at all, but she said nothing. After a while, she tried again, reaching out tentatively. "He was so happy, Michael. So proud. It just doesn't make sense. Why would he kill himself?" Her voice dropped, low and scared. "Did you see his body? He looked so bruised. Why would there be bruises?"

Michael turned in the seat until he was facing her. When he spoke, his voice was cold. "What are you trying to say, Katherine?"

"I don't know. I just can't believe he would kill himself. Why would he? How can you believe it of him? You knew him, too, Michael—"

"Jesus, Kate, let it be. He's gone. For God's sake, just stop hounding me about it." The woman seated on his right looked up in alarm. Conscious of her scrutiny, he lowered his voice. "And Kate, let's get one thing straight. When we get home, I'm telling everyone his death was an accident."

Stunned, Kate did not reply. She pulled away from him. For the rest of the flight, she sat with her head averted from him, her eyes squeezed shut, wrestling with confusion, despair, and grief. As the plane descended to Bradley Field she suddenly realized more horror and grief lay ahead. She would have to tell her father that his beloved grandson was dead.

CHAPTER FOUR

Brian knew, of course, that the Academy had changed him, but only during his brief returns to life outside the Yard was he aware of the extent of this metamorphosis.

Take today, for instance. He had just finished a superior home-cooked Thanksgiving meal, and ahead lay the prospect of a free afternoon and evening, hours unpunctuated by the swarming sound of forty-six hundred other midshipmen or by the insistent pealing of bells. For weeks now he had been dreaming of this dinner away from the wardroom of Mother B., welcoming the idea of a meal during which no one bolted the contents of his plate, had food fights, or played games of Bug, and no plebe was forced to take part in his own degradation by eating pads of butter, then washing them down with Worcestershire sauce. Here at last he was in Jordan's home in Virginia, and by all that was right and true, he should have been reveling in this liberation. But he wasn't. Instead, he felt edgy, alien.

Even being out of uniform felt wrong. He was used to the fit of his blueworks stretched taut across his shoulders, and the sports shirt he was wearing now felt loose and untidy, like hair allowed to grow too long. Absently he ran a palm across his scalp, checking the length of his hair. He had worn it long throughout high school, but now when the slightest bit of whiskerlike stubble grew in on his neck, he felt irritable and disorganized until he could get to one of the barber shops in the basement of Mother B. Earlier, downstairs in the Scotts' living room, he had inhaled the scent of freesia and wondered if he would ever again feel at home in a room that smelled of flowers instead of Brasso and Pledge.

The problem, he acknowledged with a wry grin, was that for better or for worse, he'd been converted. He was now a genuine hundred-percent Navy man. The outside world had lost its appeal. It was undisciplined, and he had grown uncomfortable with its sloppy freedoms. No. There was no question but that Navy life fit him as neatly as his dress blues molded his body.

Even now he was surprised to acknowledge this. Initially he hadn't even wanted to apply to Annapolis. He had only sent off the application after the joint pressure of his father and grandfather had coerced him into it. Even then he had hoped that despite his grandfather's influence and his father's own exemplary record at Annapolis, he would be rejected.

When his acceptance arrived in the mail, it was too late to back out. He knew his mother would understand. Although she was careful not to talk about it, he sensed she shared his mixed feelings about Navy. But he knew, too, that his father could never accept a decision not to attend Navy. So with great misgiving and confusion he embarked on the terrifying experience known as Plebe Summer.

In the early days of that June three and a half years ago, Bri had not been sure he was going to be able to stick it out. Others had quit. Two left the very first day. One classmate, a husky boy from California, had been standing in line for the plebe haircut when he abruptly and loudly announced that this bullshit wasn't for him and walked away, leaving in his wake a stunned silence. The others in the queue avoided each others' eyes, but words hung in the air as clearly as if they had actually been spoken: *Christ, what a loser. Didn't he know what he was getting in for?* Their ranks closed, filling in the space the boy had occupied. He was gone. Forgotten. It was like he had never existed, and they never spoke of him again. He was but the first.

Each morning of that plebe year, their number diminished. The reasons varied. Some washed out for academic reasons, others for physical or emotional. When a man left, the survivors—for that's how they came to regard themselves— felt a surge of pride that they'd made it through another day. They had what it took to hack it.

At night, once, Brian heard muffled weeping in the corridor outside his room. Although he searched the faces in the mess the next morning, there was no sign of who in his ranks had spent a sleepless, troubled night. Twice, humiliated and exhausted beyond any fatigue he had ever experienced in his life, he decided to quit. *This bullshit is not for me.* Each time, he sat in the phone booth near his room in Mother B., shrinking down as if each upperclassman who strode by intuitively knew what was in his mind, and he dialed his father's number to tell him that he was coming home. (It would have been easier to talk with his mother, but he placed the call to his father, unwilling to let himself off the hook.) Twice he hung up. Even now he couldn't say for sure what kept him from completing those calls. Certainly a part of it was the thought of his father's absolute contempt. Part was his own stubbornness. He had never been able to back away from a challenge. But it was more than that, Brian knew. Somehow, over the endless hours and weeks and months of that year, he had come to consider the Academy his home and his family. Somehow, he had come to love it.

The immense irony of this was that he had spent most of his life hating the Navy. As a child he had resented it, jealous of the way it took his father away, usurping his loyalty and love, the things a man should reserve for his family. He was not the only service child to feel that way. He knew that Navy brats fell into two categories: those who loved the service and planned to follow in their fathers' footsteps, and those who wanted nothing to do with it. When his parents had divorced last summer, he'd blamed the Navy too. Their marriage was another casualty of the military. His profound and unequivocal sense of allegiance sometimes baffled him now.

Of course, this feeling was not something he could talk about—not even the most gung ho smack would profess to actually love the Boat School—but he sometimes wondered if others felt the same way. He looked across the room at Webb and Jordan. Webb stared balefully at the television. Jordan concentrated on his book. Each was unaware of his scrutiny.

Did they share this same ambivalent devotion? He realized, not for the first time, how seldom the three of them discussed personal things. He supposed he knew them better than anyone else at Navy. Through four years he had seen them grow, change, cope with pressure, and yet on the innermost level they remained a mystery to him. Even their bull sessions tended to center less on private matters and more on pragmatic issues, focusing on Academy policy, gripes about professors or company officers, and, of course, on women. Macho role-playing, his mother would call it. There

was a certain amount of truth to this, but there was also a
more practical reason.

There was no time. To confide—really confide—requires
the luxury of time, and one of the first rules each plebe learns
is that there is no time at Annapolis. The battle with the clock
begins the first year. Seconds have to be robbed from the
unrelenting call of classes, polishing shoes and brass, racing
to upperclassmen's rooms for come-arounds, memorizing Reef
Points. Precious energy or moments are seldom wasted even
to damn the stupidity of having to commit to memory the
titles of the movies playing, the menus for the next day's
meals, or, letter perfect, the prescribed answers for a series of
ridiculous questions.

*How long have you been in the Navy? All me bloomin' life,
sir! Me mother was a mermaid, me father was King Neptune.
I was born on the crest of a wave and rocked in the cradle of
the deep. Seaweed and barnacles are me clothes. Every tooth
in me head is a marlinspike; the hair on me head is hemp.
Every bone in me body is a spar, and when I spits, I spits tar!
I'se hard, I is, I am, I are!*

*How's the cow? Sir, she walks, she talks, she's full of chalk.
The lacteral fluid extracted from the female of bovine species
is highly prolific to the—*here a quick glance at the carton to
see approximately how many glasses remain—*eighth degree.*

*Why didn't you say sir? Sir, sir is a subservient word
surviving from the surly days in old Serbia when certain
serfs, too ignorant to remember their lord's names, yet too
servile to blaspheme them, circumvented the situation by
surrogating the subservient word, sir, by which I now belatedly
address a certain senior cirriped, who correctly surmised that
I was syrupy enough to say sir after every word I said, sir.*

The pressure was unrelenting. You quickly learned to get
by with shortcuts and tried not to fall asleep during class.
Some professors were kinder than others, choosing to over-
look exhausted plebes whose heads nodded over their texts.
As the four years passed, there was a slight letup, but there
was never enough time to open up and expose one's soul to
roommates. Or perhaps, he thought, by then the pattern had
been set.

Looking at them now, he remembered his first impressions
of his roommates, and he suppressed a grin. How he had
disliked them both during the early days of that long hot

summer. He had thought Webb was a slob and Jordan a priss. Like others who had judged them too quickly in those first hard days, he had almost missed their strengths.

Now Webb sprawled on the bed, valiantly fighting sleep while the football game blared on the television set. Just the sight of the prematurely balding mid made Brian smile. He had the burlesquelike look of a man who had been put together improperly, the creation of a drunken doll maker. His face, arms, legs, and ankles were match thin, his chest and torso broad as a football player's. In manner he was coarse and crude, a man who let off steam with practical jokes. The pranks and vulgarity were camouflage for intelligence and a soul of great gallantry. He was never alone. Brian seldom saw his roommate crossing the Yard but that he was ensphered by a group of classmates, their white caps bobbing about his shoulder or chin as they strode down Stribling. From a distance, he looked like an empyreal planetary figure orbited by moons.

His humor was legend. As a plebe he won the hearts of upperclassmen and his peers with his incessant practical jokes, many of which became famous. It was inevitable that within the first days of Plebe Summer, Webb would be dubbed Spider. Shortly thereafter he took to leaving his calling card between the sheets of other mids' racks. More than one man had recoiled in horror at the fuzzy black spider on his pillow before recognizing it as a fake, one from the boxful Garrick had bought in a D.C. novelty store. That first September he had managed to slip several of them into the rack of the company commander. Four years later the memory still made Brian chuckle. The captain had leapt from his infested sheets and backed against the wall, his mouth open in a shrill scream which brought men on the run. Later, red-faced with rage, Bellows had strode the corridors of Mother B., demanding that the perpetrator step forward. When he had threatened to discipline the entire company, Webb had promptly confessed, thus immediately earning the respect of both plebes and upperclassmen, several of whom spooned him after that night. (It was not until January that Brian had been spooned, the traditional term indicating that a plebe had received permission from a first-classman to call him by his given name.)

Spider was not the only one with a nickname after that

episode. Bellows, who would forever regret but never erase the memory of his scream cutting through the night, was henceforth known as B.B.—Babyass Bellows.

The whole phenomenon of nicknames at the Academy is curious. Almost every mid has one. Some are natural, bestowed because of a man's anatomical characteristics: Pumpkin Head Olsen, Some Strong Warner, Gorilla, Stork, Pencil Neck, Troll, Fox, Bear, Lardo. Others are given because of alliteration or a play on a name. As Webb had become Spider, so had Bill Haag become Hog and Jeff Potts, Piss Potts.

Other times, as in the case of Low Man Boyde, the names are the result of a particular experience. Brian himself had been dubbed Cow by his classmates because of the quantities of milk he consumed at each meal. Even now, faced with the choice of a quart of milk or a bottle of beer, he inevitably chose the former. But had he grown to hate the sight of milk, he would still be Cow and would remain so long after the reason for the name had been forgotten. Like Lardo, who had shed forty pounds during their plebe year and become trim and hard, but who would be forever, throughout his Navy career, always Lardo.

It seemed to Brian that these names were accorded out of affection or derision, but seldom out of indifference. A few never earned a nickname. Jordan had survived four years without having one attached to him. In some subtle way that Brian couldn't put his finger on, his roommate had discouraged this.

Jordan was as immaculate as Spider appeared disheveled. He looked like a recruiter's notion of the ideal naval officer. Elegant, with dark good looks, he wore his uniform as if he had been destined to wear it—which, in a sense, he had, since his father, grandfather, and great-grandfather had been naval officers. Like Brian, he had been weaned on Navy spit, polish, and protocol. He was intrinsically a fierce competitor and excelled at sharpshooting and fencing. Yet even before they had completed youngster year, Brian sensed that Jordan was not pitting himself against other Brigade members as much as he was against the specter of his older brother Buck, who had graduated from the Academy years before. James Buchanan Scott was a difficult act to follow, Brian acknowledged. Sup's list at Navy, All-American in rugby, hero in 'Nam. Sometimes Brian glimpsed in his refined Southern roommate an insecure man whose graceful manner concealed a bruising vulnerability, and he wondered how much of this came from living in the shadow of Buck.

For Brian, these two men, Jordan Thomas Scott and Webb Spider Garrick, were more than roommates. They were the brothers he had never had, and he loved them. He knew he would without hestitation entrust them with his life.

Spider broke into his thoughts with a shout. "Christ, did you see that? The friggin' ref called clipping!" He slammed the mattress in disgust. Across the room, Jordan turned from the textbook that had claimed his attention for the past hour.

"Keep it down, will you, Spider?"

Webb looked at his roommate in amazement. "You are un-American, you know that, Jordan? How can you possibly sweat the books when the Steelers are behind thirteen to zip?" He took a swallow of beer. "You know what would be absolutely perfect right now? A mushroom and pepperoni pizza, heavy on the cheese."

Brian groaned and loosened his belt another notch. "How can you even think about food now? You had four pieces of pecan pie."

"Three and a half. The last was just a sliver. But who's counting?" He drained the last of his beer and groped for another from the six-pack on the floor. "How you doing, Bri? You ready for another?"

Brian shook his head and set his nearly full, lukewarm can on the bedstand. A burp escaped his lips.

"You're a woop, Tyler. A disgrace to the Brigade. Here. Let me show you how it's done." Webb narrowed his eyes and let loose a rolling belch. He reached for his beer, satisfaction creasing his round face. "I think I got a lump up with that one. Save it for chowder."

"You are truly disgusting, Webb." Jordan didn't look up from his book.

In reply, Webb belched again.

"Gross, Spider. Truly and totally gross."

Sighing with pleasure, Webb stretched out on the bed, taking another long pull from his fresh beer. "Just think of all those poor bastards back in Mother B.—Christ, would you look at that? Another penalty against Pittsburgh. That friggin' ref must be blind. He's a goddamn imbecile, worse than Babyass."

Jordan was at last diverted from his book. "I don't think I will ever forget the look on his face this morning when he looked out into T-Court."

The previous night, a group of first-classmen, led by Webb, had transported the silver A-4 Skyhawk from its place by Worden Field across the Yard to Tecumseh Court. That morning the aircraft, festooned with toilet paper and a pair of Bellows's undershorts, stared straight at the statue of Tecumseh. "B.B. was so red, I thought he would explode. If he has a heart attack, Spider, you'll be listed as the cause of death. I bet he can't wait to see you graduate."

"That wasn't your best one." Brian sat up, grinning. "The best was the time you emptied out his office and put his desk in the third-deck head. Even the engineers in tenth couldn't outdo you on that one." A fresh wave of laughter flowed through the room. Webb threw back his head and roared noisily, thumping a pillow.

"What the hell are you three degenerates pissing your pants about?"

James Buchanan Scott stood in the doorway. He wore rubber flip-flops on his feet and a bath towel wrapped around his waist. His torso was well developed but with an overlying fleshiness, like a weightlifter gone soft. The glass of bourbon he held was still beaded with condensation from the steam of the bathroom. Like Jordan, Buck Scott was handsome, but there was a harshness in his face that his younger brother lacked. There were creases—pilot lines—in the flesh near his icy blue eyes, and the eyes themselves were as old as death. He had long ago isolated himself in a place that admitted no one. He glanced at the empty beer cans on the floor. "Getting in the spirit for the game Saturday? I hear Moskowitz sprained his hand and some friggin' second-string quarterback named Howley will probably play. You'll need more than beer to dim the pain if Moskowitz can't play."

"James Buchanan? Is that you?" The voice—soft, with a slightly flirtatious teasing modulation—floated up the stairs and through the open door. Brian thought back to all the Southern women he had ever known, and wondered why they always called their male offspring by their full names, as if they were one: James Buchanan, Jordan Thomas, John Davis.

"Yes, ma'am. It is I, fruit of your womb, flower of your maternal heart." Buck's voice dripped irony.

"Your father wants to see you, dear. He's waiting in the study."

An expression of pain flitted over Buck's face. "Yes, ma'am. On the double," he drawled with exaggerated courtesy. He leaned against the doorframe and twirled the slivers of ice remaining in his glass. "What have you three druids got on for tonight? Big night away from Mother B."

"Sleep." Spider gave the word a sensuous sound. Next to eating, sleeping was his favorite activity. "We're going to get some serious rack time."

"What a bunch of candy asses. Is this the product they're turning out now at the Boat School?" The words were slightly slurred.

"What about you? Who are you seeing tonight?" There was no mistaking the undertone of admiration in Jordan's voice.

"Judilynn."

"Again. This sounds serious." Since his divorce, Buck had dated the few holdouts in the airline he flew for, stewardesses who hadn't slept with him when he was married, and was now working his way through the roster of secretaries in northern Virginia.

"What can I tell you? The woman is wild for me. She does things that would make infants like you blush. My war stories really turn her on." The whiskey was gone now, and he set the empty glass on the top of the bureau and helped himself to a can of beer. "Women find war stories irresistible. Every one of them has seen *The Deer Hunter,* and they want to know if any of us really played Russian roulette. I'll let you three gentlemen in on a little secret. No matter how they deny it, women really cream their jeans when you hint at violence." He was slurring more now, and Brian suddenly realized he was drunk. "You want to know what is absolutely guaranteed to reduce a woman to jelly? My tattoo."

"Come on, Buck. You don't have a tattoo." Jordan threw a wad of crumpled paper at his brother. He had been the butt of too many jokes to fall for the latest.

"I sure as shit do." He knotted the towel tighter at his waist and swaggered into the room to the space at the foot of the twin beds, turning his forearm up to the light. "You see these?" The trio of upperclassmen leaned forward. Three shiny scars, each about the size of a dime, shone whitely on the underside of his arm. "These are my Vietnam tattoos."

Buck drew a finger slowly over the small circles. "Yes, sir, they love these. Can't keep their fingers off them. Got 'em one night in a bar in Saigon. Playing chicken with an Army puke."

Fascinated and repelled, Brian leaned forward. Even Spider ignored the Steelers game now.

"This Army turd was drunk as a skunk, and with great ignorance soiled the honor of the Corps. I, of course, had no choice but to defend the Corps." Buck gestured broadly. "I challenged the sorry prick to a game of chicken. Saigon style."

He looked from face to face, as if deciding which to challenge. "You mean not one of you ever played Saigon chicken? What about you, Tyler?" Without waiting for an answer, he thumped his beer can on the floor and picked up a pack of cigarettes from the top of the bureau. Then he sat down on the mattress next to Brian. He was so close that Brian could see the peppering of freckles beneath the mat of dark chest hair, could smell the scent of his deodorant and after-shave, could feel the heat from his body. A band of loose skin rolled over the top of the terry cloth, but at the bottom edge of the towel the muscle of his naked thigh was bunched and hard. Unbidden, Coach Lansky's voice echoed in Brian's mind. Christ, Buck was some kind of hero in Lansky's book, the awed way he sounded when he talked about the way Buck Scott used to train, straining at the weights.

"It's arm wrestling." Buck's voice called him back. He took hold of Brian's arm and grasped it with his hand until they lay palm cupping elbow, forearm pressed tightly against forearm. Brian's skin looked pale and young and vulnerable next to the dark arm of the older Marine. For an instant they sat without moving, then Buck, smiling, forced Brian's hand down until both clenched arms were flat on the surface of the bed. Casually Buck used his free hand to tap a cigarette out from the pack. He tossed the rest aside and put it in his mouth, pretending to pull on it, inhaling deeply until it almost seemed that the tip was red and glowing.

With the grin still on his face, he looked straight into Brian's eyes and dropped the unlit cigarette down in the crease formed by their arms. Involuntarily Brian flinched and pulled away, but Buck held his arm fast, crushing the butt between their forearms. Their eyes locked, Buck's cold and mocking, Brian's fighting fear. He could *feel* his flesh burning, could smell it. His arm ached. Far away, he heard the muted echo of the football game, the sound of Spider's breathing and Jordan's muttered, "Jesus!"

"The idea," Buck intoned, "is to put the butt out—'course, in 'Nam we used a cigar—and the first one to pull away is chickenshit." His breath brushed Brian's face. Brian could feel his palm sweating in the Marine's unyielding grip, and in spite of himself he responded to the challenge. The muscles in his arm and shoulder tensed as he put his weight and strength into the contest, trying to push the cigarette against Buck's arm. The Marine laughed harshly. His grasp tightened cruelly on Brian's arm—the cigarette was now flat, the paper damp from their sweat—and slowly he ground their arms together. Then, as if suddenly tired of the game, he abruptly relaxed his grip.

"I have to give that mother credit. He stuck with it. Three times we tried it. Neither of us ever did win. A fight broke out. I don't remember the trip back. Passed out. Forgot the whole thing. In the morning I woke up with a hell of a headache and my arm was festered and swollen. Even then I couldn't remember. My buddies had to tell me what had happened. I guess it was a draw. Neither one of us ever did pull away."

He lifted his arm and stared at the scars. Slowly, lovingly, he drew his forefinger over the pale circles of damaged flesh. "God damn, but women love that story."

Brian rubbed his forearm, as if smudging away dirt. He felt ill and humiliated. Violence had entered the room, and it seemed to him that he and his roommates were ill equipped to handle it, that they were too young and foolishly innocent. Their silence enraged James Buchanan Scott.

"What the hell's the matter with you pricks, anyway? You all gone soft? You might as well be in Colorado Springs wearing blue bus driver's caps, you're going to be such wimps."

"Bullshit." Jordan's voice was hollow, a child showing off for an admired adult. "Last night Spider masterminded putting the A-4 in T-Court."

Buck turned. "You disappoint me, Spider. No originality.

No originality at all. That poor plane has logged more hours on the bricks of old Tecumseh Court than it ever did in the air. Every class ever graduated had someone drag that son of a bitch across the Yard." He stooped for the last beer. "If you want to hear a really good story, wait till you hear what we did the night before the Army game." Brian wasn't sure why, but he was suddenly embarrassed for Jordan.

Buck was relishing his story. "Our West Point exchange officer that year was a stuffy fat prig whose only pride and joy was his car. A mint '57 Thunderbird. God, how he loved that car. Always driving it around the Yard. Only thing the smug prig would talk about. Well, the week before the game we sold chances to every man in the Brigade. Five bucks a chance. Every damn one of us bought one. We raised a fortune. Then, the night of the bonfire, we invited the woop to the rally. When he showed up, there was the Thunderbird on the field. We'd trashed it. Took five of us an hour using sledgehammers. He started to cry when he saw it. Funniest thing I ever saw. He ran across the field toward the car and tried to hold this mess of metal in his arms. The prig was crying. *Crying*. Tears running down his cheeks."

"What happened? Did he ever find out who did it?" Spider's voice sounded objective, almost disinterested, but Brian knew his roommate was affected by the story.

"You don't get it, Garrick." Buck was laughing so hard his handsome face flushed. He took a long pull of beer. "It wasn't his car. We'd bought another car from a dealer. It wasn't his car at all. We beat the shit out of Army that year too. Yes, sir, that was the last of the good classes. Every one since then has been nothing but chickenshit."

Spider's voice was deceptively soft. "Don't bet any big money on it. Our class is a damn good one."

"No, Garrick. You lost it. You want to know *when* you lost it? When Congress legislated that women could be admitted. On that day the last class of real midshipmen walked across the Yard." Buck drained the can and reached for a book of matches to light his cigarette. "What the hell do they call you guys now, midship-Ms.'s? Christ, look at you. Just last year a woman graduated first in the class. Let me tell you, that would never, ever have happened when I was there. Never."

"That was a fluke."

"A fluke? I'll tell you what I think, Tyler. I think you are all a bunch of pussies. Before long they'll be taking the urinals out of Bancroft, and you'll all have to sit down to take a piss."

"Bri's right." Jordan's voice was thin. "No way will any woman graduate first this year. I bet you there won't be a woman in the top ten."

"Ten out of twelve hundred? Not bad odds for you."

"The top twenty-five. How's that?"

"You mean it?"

"'Course I mean it. I'll bet you . . . I bet you a thousand there isn't a woman in the top twenty-five." His voice was stronger now, less reedy and scared.

"A thousand, little brother? Sure you can afford it?"

In answer Jordan stretched his hand toward his brother. After a moment Buck grinned and clasped it. In the November light from the window, the three circles of scar tissue gleamed as the two brothers shook hands.

The room was silent. Ignoring this, Buck turned to the others. "What about you two? Want to add to my bankroll?" Brian wanted to look away but couldn't. "'Course, maybe you agree with me. Maybe you deserve to have a woman calling the shots. Hell, you mommy's boys would probably love serving under a cunt's command."

"You're a real shit, you know that?" Webb struggled to his feet, towering over Buck. "But I hope you're a rich shit, 'cause I'm adding a thousand to Jordan's." He stuck his hand out, belligerently waiting for Buck to shake.

This is insane. Brian wanted to ignore them, to turn away from the look of triumph in Buck's eyes. He was *not* going to take part in this. Christ, the place a woman ranked in his class had nothing to do with his value, his masculinity. *Nothing to do with it.* And the women weren't so bad. It wasn't a bed of roses for them at the Academy, he knew that for sure. It was a dumb bet, anyway. As if honor had anything to do with having women in the ranks. The silence in the room weighed on him. He remembered how he had been the one to pull his arm away during the game of Saigon chicken. He felt Buck's derision. Fighting the voices in his head, he rose from the bed and thrust his hand toward Buck. "I'll match their bets," he said. Their handshake was firm.

Buck laughed. "You poor suckers. Thank you for the easiest three grand I ever earned." He stood in the doorway. "See you at the game Saturday. You don't want to bet on that, do you? Not a friggin' chance for Navy if Moskowitz doesn't play. Damn shame too. Best quarterback we've had since Staubach. No takers? Well, see you around." When the door slammed behind him, the smell of after-shave and cigarette smoke hung cloyingly in the room.

"Jesus Christ," Spider exploded, turning on Jordan. "What the hell made you get us into a dumbass thing like that?"

Jordan looked wounded. "No one *made* you bet, Spider. Don't blame it on me. Besides, I just couldn't let him call us pussies. I just couldn't."

Webb paced by the bureau, slamming one fist into his open palm. "You know damn well I don't even have five hundred bucks in the bank. And now I'm into your brother for a thousand."

Jordan snapped his book shut. "Not yet. I mean, it's only November, for Christ's sake. Relax. Maybe he'll forget. Maybe there won't be a woman in the top twenty-five of the class."

"And maybe you'd better piss in a bottle so I can see what you've been smoking." Webb continued angrily punching his palm. "There are already two women in the top fifteen right now. At least two. In our company. Greene and Cauley. Did you *forget* about them?"

"Lay off, will you, Spider? It's done." Even angry, Jordan looked cool. Ever the immaculate midshipman, Bri thought. "Besides, Buck's right. Do you think women belong?"

"That's not the point." As usual Spider didn't waste time disputing the acknowledged. "They *are* there. It doesn't matter if they belong or not. They're there." He sank down on the bed. "A thousand friggin' bucks. You must be crazy, getting us in a bet like that. It must run in the family."

For a moment Brian thought Jordan might swing at Webb. He spoke softly, deflecting the explosion. "Why do you let him treat you that way, Jordo?"

"What way?"

"Like shit."

The tension stretched out, electrifying the air like an exposed wire. Brian knew he had come perilously close to transgressing an invisible line.

"He's not always like that." Jordan's voice was measured, reasonable. Brian couldn't help but feel he was talking to himself more than to him and Spider.

"He's always been there for me. When Dad was away. You know what that's like, Bri. When I made Eagle Scout my father was in Europe, but Buck was there. It was always that way. When the other kids were getting screamed at or grounded, he'd encourage me. He taught me how to tie a necktie, bought me my first beer, and held my head the first time I got shit-faced. My father never talked to me about girls. Buck bought me my first pack of Trojans and told me how to use them. He prepared me more for manhood than my father ever did."

Brian could think of nothing to say, and when a roar went up from the television set, they were all relieved at the reprieve.

"Will you look at that?" Spider screamed. "That sucker is going all the way! Look at him! Look at him break that tackle. He's going ninety yards on the return. All the way for a touchdown. Will you look at that?"

At the Silverdome, the crowd went wild. In Virginia, the sound spilled out of the television console and into the sunny bedroom.

CHAPTER FIVE

Crunched together in their section of the stands, the midshipmen swore and sweated. The day was a record-breaker, the hottest November day in memory. Not the slightest breeze or hint of cloud relieved the intensity of the sun as it beat down on Veteran's Stadium. Even before the kickoff civilians, had shed their sweaters and the alumni had stripped off their blazers and sports coats and were now standing in shirt-sleeves. Down on the sidelines the television crews milled about in shorts and T-shirts, as if it were a summer day. For just an instant, Brian envied them. They were so normal. So free. Sweat rolled down his back. His collar chafed against his neck, and he knew the skin beneath the stiff fabric would be rubbed raw before the day was over. In the entire stadium, the only fully clothed people were the mids in their dress blues and—across the field—their opposite ranks in gray. The smell of steaming wool wafted across the bleachers. During the pregame show, when the midshipmen and cadets had marched on, five men had fainted.

But the heat could not dim the plebes' enthusiasm. Already they were screaming themselves hoarse, as if by the level of their voices alone they could determine the outcome of the contest. If Navy lost, they'd be in for weeks of hell, but if they won, it would be carry-on until Christmas. Few doubted that their team would be the victor. The alternative was unthinkable. Their enthusiasm was almost manic, a release for long pent-up emotions, not all of them having to do with the game. It was a rite of passage, this Army–Navy match, and this weekend would bring the plebes one step closer to becoming real midshipmen.

Around him Brian felt the tempo increase, and as it had every year since his first game—he'd been eleven, accompanying his father to the stadium—he felt his heartbeat quicken. The noise was now ear-shattering: the band was playing, but scarcely a note was audible over the frenzied screams. A classic, the newspapers and sportscasters would call it, akin to the Rose Bowl or World Series or Kentucky Derby, but Brian knew it was none of these things. This game was unique—a pageant that blended military pomp with historic rivalry second to none, hostility so ingrained it stretched back into the former century. What was the story his father had told him during that game ten years before? Something about a brigadier general and a rear admiral who had come close to fighting a duel over the outcome of a game in 1893, and how for the next seven years Congress had outlawed the event; his father, a living encyclopedia of naval lore.

In spite of the heat and his raw neck, Brian wanted the day to last forever. He wanted to remember every play, every cheer, even the feeling of the sweat soaking through his skivvies. This was the last Army–Navy game he would attend as a midshipman.

This sense of experiencing so many things for the final time had been with him since the day six months before when he had become a first-classman. It was a melancholy, sentimental bent that took him by surprise. Looking back, the four years had gone by so fast. Plebe year, a lowly fourth-classman, scared and proud as a virgin. Third-class year, the treasured diagonal stripe of gold displayed on his sleeve as proof of his advancement. Second-classman, Segundo, another diagonal stripe for the sleeve of his working blue "Alfa," almost there. And finally the top, a firstie, First Classman Brian Tyler. Even without the single gold stripe banding the edge of his sleeve, he knew he looked like a firstie. His walk, his eyes, everything about him betrayed the confidence of the first-class mid. *And it had all gone by so goddamn fast.*

The first time he had traveled to Philadelphia for the Army–Navy contest as a mid, a hyped-up plebe, Spider had thrown up in the bus all the way back to the Yard, one of the dozens of plebes who had welcomed the game as a vehicle for release from Mother B., come-arounds, and discipline, and then spent the next three days vowing never to drink again. In his second year Danielle had come down for the game, and Brian could still visualize the way she looked standing beside his parents, and even now he could feel the dim residual pang of hurt when he had glimpsed her, his first love, flirting with an older midshipman. Last year, for the first time, his parents had not come—the trouble apparent even then—and he had been the one who'd gotten drunk. This year—his last—was the most special.

He craned his neck, searching the stands to his left, scanning the rows of upperclass drags, looking for one face. At last he found it and smiled. She was tall, rawboned, not his usual type. He normally went for tiny women, creatures whose eyes were level with the stripes on his sleeve. Not this time, though.

As if sensing his eyes on her, Leah turned and looked at him. Then, laughing, she rose and formed a megaphone with her hands, shouting over the astounded drags who flanked her in the stands. "You owe me, Tyler! You know that? One night of ballet at the Kennedy Center. At least!"

Around him other midshipmen heard her words and the teasing began. "The ballet? Oh, Cow, you going to drink tea too?"

Once he would have been mortified by the attention she had attracted, but now he threw back his head and laughed. He was too much in love to care. Her total lack of pretense, now that he was no longer rankled by it, had become one of the things he found so attractive about her. For instance, she was at the game under protest. She loathed football, and when he'd asked her to come, she had refused. Stung, he'd argued, "Most women would give anything to go to an Army–Navy game with a mid."

"Ask one of them, then," she'd retorted, totally unimpressed. "And sitting half a city block away from the Brigade is hardly going to the game 'with' you, Tyler." He recognized the signs. She was just warming to the debate.

"Let me ask you something. How many of those women do you think really want to see the game? They probably hate football as much as I do. They just like the idea of being there. Now basketball, that's something else. . . ."

Finally they had hit upon a compromise: a ballet at the Kennedy Center for one Army–Navy game. And Brian knew she intended to make him uphold his end of the bargain. He grinned at her, loving her.

They were so different, in philosophy as well as political viewpoint. He was conservative, a Republican, and she was a liberal Democrat, as flamboyant in her dress and style as he was unimaginative. From their first meeting, a blind date arranged by one of Jordan's girlfriends, she had emphasized their differences, pointing out how little they had in common and refusing a second date. After four years at Annapolis Brian was accustomed to having women fall all over him. If not *for* him, he acknowledged, then at least for the uniform and the glamour women seemed to attach to it. This girl was a challenge. Physically, she was one of the most exciting women he had ever known, but her intellect and will stimulated him as much as the chemistry that flashed between them. "I love you for your mind," he'd say, trying to leer, but unsuccessful because of the truth of the statement.

Simply, he loved her because she was Leah. Because of her he was a better, more complete person than he would have been without her. She wasn't afraid to question, to challenge. Because of this, he found he could be himself around her, tell her things he had never told anyone before. She was the only one he had ever talked to about his parents' separation and divorce, to share his hurt and confusion. And anger.

She was straightforward about sex too. She didn't use lovemaking as an emotional pawn. For her it was clearly a commitment, and not easily given; but once made, it was given freely. She was completely without coyness. She was a woman, and until he met her, Brian now knew, he had dated only girls. In only a few months he had come to the point where he could not imagine living without her. He was so damn lucky, it sometimes frightened him.

He stood in the stands and waved to her, and ignoring his classmates' catcalls, motioned for her to meet him in the aisle by the concession stand.

As she wove through the crowd, she was greeted by appreciative whistles, and he could sense her discomfort. A wave of jealousy swept him. As always, he was affected by her beauty. She was tall, with athletic grace, rich brown hair—sun-streaked near her temples—a honey complexion, and brown eyes with flecks of green. Today she wore a loose lavender dress which was full across the shoulders but tightly belted at her waist. The buttons down the front were undone to expose an aqua T-shirt. There were small gold hoops in her ears and a simple gold chain around her neck. This was all the jewelry she ever wore, as if she instinctively understood that her beauty needed little to adorn it. Her hair fell in curls to her shoulders, and she lifted one hand to brush it back from her face. The gesture seemed infinitely sexual to Brian, and his throat closed with desire for her. With all his heart he wanted to touch her, but he was in uniform and it was not permitted, so he stood stiffly by her side, fervently wishing for the second time in the afternoon that he was allowed normalcy.

"What's with the livestock?" Leah asked, pointing to both sidelines.

"That's Army's mule over there," he replied, "and that goat on our side is Bill. Our mascot."

"Does the ASPCA know he's being abused like that?" Her eyes were alive with laughter.

"Okay, woman. What we have here, it seems, is a problem in attitude. It's time you had some indoctrination. Listen up, because tomorrow there will be a quiz."

"What if I don't pass?"

"Then I'll have to find me another woman. This is serious business. It's history. By virtue of your presence here today, you are part of history. Someday when you are old and gray—"

"Careful, Tyler. You're treading on fragile territory."

"I repeat, someday when you are old and gray, you can tell our grandchildren..." He paused. *Our grandchildren.* "You can tell them that you were part of the Army–Navy game. Do you realize this is a tradition almost a century old?" He knew he was retreating into a recitation of naval history, putting distance between them. "The first game was played at the Point in 1890 and Navy won 24–0. It was not a game without controversy. A Navy player dropped back to punt and then ran downfield for a touchdown. Army players—true to their wimpish tradition—protested the play and expected the officials to call it back. According to one player, Navy's play was clearly a false statement. It was dishonorable, he maintained, for an officer and a gentleman to announce he was going to kick and then do something else."

"You're making that up."

"On my oath, this is a true story. In that aforementioned game, Joseph Reeves, a naval player, wore the first football helmet."

Leah looked down at the Navy bench and giggled. "Don't

look now, but your mascot, unimpressed with tradition, is peeing on the sideline—"

"I swear, you are not paying proper attention. You'll unquestionably flunk the test at the end of the day."

"I don't think so." Her look was so openly sexy that Brian blushed, which seemed to amuse her more. Sudden shouts drowned out their banter. The Navy team took the field. Cries of "Tin Man! Tin Man!" filled the midshipmen's side of the stadium.

"Who's Tin Man?"

"I swear, you must be the dumbest drag in Philadelphia today." He leaned toward her, his attention already wandering toward the action which was about to begin on the field. "Tin Man is our quarterback. Bernie Moskowitz. A genius. He can throw better than Marino and scramble as well. The guy's incredible."

"Why do they call him Tin Man?"

"Because he's got a bad elbow, and knee problems too. It's a shame. If his arm holds up, he could name his place in the pros. After he's finished with his tour, of course. Staubach did it. I guess Bernie can too. He's the best we've had since Staubach. And his number's thirteen. Get it?"

"You mean unlucky?"

He shook his head hopelessly. "No, my poor uneducated dumbo. Number thirteen. You know, next after twelve. Staubach's number."

"Who is—"

"Don't ask."

Another roar went up from the crowd as Navy won the toss.

"Look," Brian said, "I've got to get back. Meet me here at halftime. Okay?"

Leah returned to her seat, this time unharassed by the mids, who were screaming through the silly yellow megaphones that hung from their necks on chains. The Brigade would stand throughout the entire game, Brian had told her. The West Point cadets had been commanded, in their pregame orders, not to sit down once during the contest, and not to be outdone, the mids had passed the word to remain standing too.

She felt Brian's loss as he walked away, regretting that she was unable to sit with him. It seemed a stupid rule, that midshipmen couldn't sit with their drags. Not as stupid, she decided, as calling dates "drags." She slid into her seat just as Army kicked off, and the roar from the Brigade almost deafened her. At her right, Jordan's date cheered wildly. She was a pretty girl, someone new, with long blond hair pulled back into a thick French braid. What was her name? Suzy? Sally? The girl watched the action on the field as if entranced, and behind her a man shrieked hysterically. Leah received a glancing blow from his arm and sighed. It was going to be a long afternoon.

"Where's the Tin Man? I can't find him," she said to Jordan's date, squinting into the sun.

"Army just got the ball. Bernie's on the bench." The girl was abrupt, and Leah settled back, determined not to ask any more. The heat was dreadful. She tried to pick Brian out from the mass of cheering blue uniforms. Although she had teased him about not wanting to go to the game, she would have gone to hell and back to be near him, even if it meant sitting yards apart. The thought of being separated from him made her almost physically ill. For that reason, among others, she knew she should draw back. Give them both more space. He was in the Navy. After Commissioning Week he would spend his next five years on active duty. He had told her about his childhood, how he hated having his father away at sea, the moving from place to place. She knew she blamed the Navy for his parents' divorce. Leah didn't know Brian's mother, but she did know herself, and she understood that she was not the kind of woman who would be happy as a Navy wife.

Another moan went up from the midshipmen, answered by a shout of jubilation from the cadets. She bent toward Jordan's date. The name finally came to her. Stacey.

"What happened?"

"Army scored." The poor girl actually looked close to tears.

Across the field, the black knight on his horse pranced along the sidelines, looking more like Darth Vader than a medieval adventurer. Behind him, an Army general, also on horseback, rode by the Army bench. The officer was rotund, and his round face was flushed beneath his snow-white hair. He yelled at the crowd and brandished a sword. The absurdity of the scene struck Leah. The general's horse was trotting now, and the crowd cheered frantically.

The Army player dropped back to kick for the extra point, and when the Navy men blocked the attempt, the stands to her right went berserk. In a orgy of release, the plebes were screaming now. On Army's side the plump general dismounted.

At last the offensive team ran on. She saw number thirteen and was at once disappointed. He looked so small and ordinary. Her attention wandered again, roving to the yelling and cheering men of the Brigade, falling at last on one woman, who fluctuated between watching the action on the field with great intensity and laughing at something the person at her side said. She was one of the prettiest females Leah had ever seen, willow thin with a milky complexion, pinked now by the sun. In profile she had the features of a cover girl, and the intelligence behind the face shone, even at a distance, with consuming vitality. Her most arresting feature was her hair, which was long and richly auburn. The woman wore the uniform of Annapolis.

The little remaining interest the game held for Leah disappeared. She was fascinated. Brian had talked with her for hours about life at the Academy, about how rigorous it was mentally, academically, and physically. The goal of Annapolis, he insisted, was to transform boys into men. And yet to Leah it seemed much of Academy life was designed to keep them boys. The enforced isolation, the rigid rules and regulations that demanded mindless obedience, seemed more likely to keep them immature, especially socially. Their allusions to women and sex, Leah found, were often more on the level of high school students than that of her classmates at G.W.

More than once she'd been puzzled and hurt as Brian regressed from a caring, intelligent, interesting adult to a crude and childish adolescent. One day he had appeared at her apartment with a badly bruised chin. "What happened?" she'd asked, alarmed. His grin was sheepish. "We had carrier quals last night." Still grinning, he'd explained, but she hadn't found it funny that drunken twenty-one-year-old men would race down a flight of stairs and onto a long table, landing on their stomachs like a jet setting down on the deck of a carrier. Boyishly, Brian had tried to win her over, but she couldn't rid herself of the feeling that he drank too much when he was with his friends, that their games were stupid.

Looking at the red-haired woman, Leah wondered what it was like to be a woman midshipman. She had overheard enough disparaging comments and jokes to know that many of the mids did not like having women in their ranks. At best they were tolerated; at worst, they were actively resented and the butt of cruel jokes. "What is the name for the women midshipmen?" she had once asked Jordan. "You mean the polite name?" he'd replied, grimacing. "Did you hear about the female who was rejected by Navy?" went another of his barbs. "She couldn't pass the physical. She was too pretty. Went to Air Force instead."

Leah believed that she was a liberated woman, the equal of her classmates, male or female, but she would not for the world have wanted to be a mid. She knew it was an opportunity to get a first-rate education at no cost, with a guaranteed future, but she knew as well that the military was not fair to women. Brian had told her that a female officer could be a flight instructor for fighter pilots but could not herself be a fighter pilot. There were no fleet assignments or combat duty for women, effectively barring them from reaching highest rank.

The frenzied screams of the midshipmen broke into her reverie, and she realized that it was at last halftime. In the midst of the jostling crowd, Brian was trying to get her attention. She nodded, understanding that he wanted her to meet him again at the stand.

He was so handsome. She used great willpower not to reach up and cup her palm against his jaw, letting her fingers brush against his close-cropped hair. She stared into his blue eyes, and her knees actually felt weak. She wanted to touch him so much it hurt. Did the fact that they had to hold back, were forbidden to kiss in public, increase the intensity of her feeling?

Out of the corner of her eye she saw the midshipman who had captured her attention during the game. "Who is she?" she asked Brian, but because of the noisy crowd, he could not hear her. He bent closer and she repeated the question. "And I was wondering who she was?"

He followed her gaze, trying to pick out which of the drags Leah was talking about.

"Who? What does she look like?"

Leah stood on tiptoe, craning to see above or around the jostling mass of uniformed men.

"There. That beautiful girl coming toward us."

"The brunette with Ted Powers?"

"No. There. The redhead." She pointed.

"Oh." Brian's voice was dismissive. "Ariel Greene. Engineering..." Uninterested, he turned his attention to trying to jockey into position at the mobbed concession stand.

"But don't you think she's gorgeous?"

"I guess. I don't know. I don't think about it much. She's just a mid. I think you're gorgeous, that's what I think." A chunky mid nudged his arm, spilling his Coke on him. "And I think I want to get out of this blasted uniform and be alone with you."

He stared into her eyes, and she forgot about the mid.

When the game resumed, Leah mused about Brian's tone when he had mentioned Ariel Greene's name. His indifference was real. She fanned herself in a vain attempt to relieve the dizzying heat. At that moment the Brigade went delirious. The men of Navy, led by Tin Man Moskowitz, had scored their first touchdown. The midshipmen, their voices already hoarse, screamed and shrieked, pounding each other on the back in jubilation. While all those around her cheered the players on the field, Leah found herself looking once more at Ariel. The midshipman stood with her head thrown back. Her hair flamed in the sun, and her arm was raised above her head in a victory salute. Like four thousand other members of the Brigade, she jumped up and down in exultation. Leah stared at her. How could Brian not think she was beautiful?

CHAPTER SIX

Winter covered the lushness of the Connecticut Valley, leaving the tobacco fields on either side of the highway looking deceptively benign beneath their veneer of snow. Kate drove down the familiar road toward her father's home, and unconsciously eased up on the gas pedal, delaying the moment of her arrival. She had not phoned ahead to say she was coming. She was afraid she would break down when she heard his voice. She dreaded the thought of telling him. Brian had been his only grandchild.

Within minutes she would be there. She tried to rehearse her role in the scene that lay ahead, but her mind was as dull and dormant as the fields she passed. Dread clenched her stomach. She cracked open her window, letting in sweet air. Yesterday's storm was over, as if it had never been, and the air was impossibly warm, an hour of spurious February spring.

She turned the wheel and pulled up the long driveway. On either side of the blacktop, barren trees cast stark shadows on the softening snow. Perhaps she should have accepted Nina's offer to accompany her. But she'd wanted to be alone with her father. She had an intense need to see and hold him, knowing that only he, her own flesh and blood, could share and understand her pain.

The nurse answered the door. Ida Roberts was a heavy, graceless woman with the muddy skin of a person who has eaten too many doughnuts, smoked too many cigarettes, and consumed too much coffee. She wore an olive green blouse that did nothing to relieve her sallow complexion, and dark blue, double-knit, bell-bottomed trousers that flapped around her sturdy shoes when she walked. A cloud of stale smoke permeated her clothes like sour perfume. The senator despised cigarettes. It had been a condition of the job that the woman not smoke, but Kate bit back words of reproach. It was so difficult to find a nurse who would take twenty-four-hour duty.

"Why, Mrs. Tyler. Come on in. Why didn't you let us know you were coming? Your father will be so surprised." She leaned in close to Kate, who instinctively stepped back. "He's in the den. He's watching his favorite soap."

The idea of her father watching afternoon soap operas was so incongruous—as alien as his office becoming a "den"—that she didn't know whether to laugh or cry. She turned and followed the sound of the television set, letting it lead her to her father. His profile was to the door, and he had not heard her approach.

She stood in the doorway and looked at him. She had seen him in December, but he seemed to have deteriorated in the last six weeks. She was not prepared for this. Dr. Carey had said stroke victims usually regained much of what they had lost, that the first days were the worst and that later, with therapy, things got better. Her father was not better. His gnarled hands rested on the arms of the chair. His left one was useless, but it seemed to her now that his right arm, too, lacked strength or life. His walker waited to one side.

Although the room was uncomfortably warm, there was a multicolored afghan tucked around his legs, and he wore a V-necked cardigan over his shirt. A large safety pin replaced one of the buttons in the sweater, and a thin elbow jutted through a hole in the sleeve. His hair had turned totally white. He seemed so frail, shrunken, and vulnerable.

He saw her then, and his mouth twisted with the effort of saying her name, the left side pulling cruelly. As she drew close to kiss him, she saw a speck of dried egg yolk on his sleeve. He smelled old, the sweet smell of damp wool. Anger stirred within her. A tray by her father's chair still held the dishes from breakfast and lunch, food hardened on the silverware. A similar tray, presumably that of Ida Roberts, topped another table by an armchair near the television. The room hadn't been dusted or vacuumed in weeks.

Looking at him, she felt sadness, frustration, and rage that her father, a man so meticulous about his grooming that he had worn a coat and tie to dinner every night of his life, should suffer the indignity of age and illness.

Their eyes met, miraculously his were unchanged—bright

blue and shining—and then her arms were around his thin frame, and for a moment everything was all right.

"What's up?" His voice was a surprise. It was strong, and she realized that she had expected it to be withered like the body that housed it. His words were slurred.

Ida appeared at the door, watching over them. Ignoring the nurse, Kate took off her coat and pulled a chair over to his side, gathering strength for what she had come to tell him. What words could she choose that would make it easier for him? Nothing could ever make the news painless. Her glance swept the room. In spite of the television, this was her father's room. There were books everywhere. They were stacked beneath the bay window, piled high in corners and on tables, and wedged in tightly in the floor-to-ceiling bookcases, filling every shelf with volumes; and when the shelves were filled, more books had been placed on top. There were biographies, histories, fiction, poetry, mysteries. Plato, Simone Weil, Shakespeare, and P. D. James, in seven different languages. During his seven terms in the Senate, Sidney Brian Baldridge had been the only congressman able to read both Latin and Greek as well as every language spoken by his constituents, including the Spanish of the migrant workers who arrived each year to work in the tobacco fields.

Before Kate could speak, Ida Roberts broke the silence. She pointed to a flickering image on the television set. "Why, would you look at that. He looks just like King Hassan. The spittin' image of the man." She turned to Kate. "I saw him, you know. I was visiting my son-in-law and daughter in Morocco. He was a Navy man, just like your ex." She spoke as if she were intimately familiar with Kate's history. "Well, I was doing some shopping for my grandchildren, and I saw him drive by." She lowered her voice with an insider's pride. "He was on his way to Madrid to have his hemorrhoids operated on. Gives you something to think about, doesn't it? Here he was King and all, and he still has piles."

"Mrs. Roberts." Kate's voice was sharp. "Perhaps we could have some tea. I'll help you in the kitchen."

She followed her out of the room without looking back at her father, afraid that if she did so, she would see knowledge on his face. He knew her so well. She never had been able to hide anything from him.

In the kitchen, she faced the nurse, determined to fire the

woman. Options flashed through her mind, and she quickly considered and discarded each. A nursing home was out of the question. It would kill him to enter one. Nor would he move in with her. Each time she'd asked, he had rejected the offer, refusing to be a burden. She had argued, saying truthfully that it would be company for her in the big empty house, but he would not be dissuaded. "No, Katie. Let me be in my own house. It's my home, you know, dear. It's where I want to be. Till the end, if it's possible."

"Mrs. Roberts," she began firmly, "this house is a mess. There's food on my father's clothes, and the place looks like it hasn't been cleaned in ages. Lord knows when you last dusted. My father pays you a good salary, the least we can expect is that you will take decent care of him."

Unperturbed, the woman unhurriedly filled the kettle with water from the faucet. "I'll tell you a secret about making tea. Always use cold water from the tap. Now, a lot of people will tell you to fill the kettle up with hot, the quicker to make it boil, but the truth is, the tea suffers if you do. Much, much better for the tea if you start with cold water. Tell you what my daughter says. She says when the water's still cold, the ions are still in it." She pronounced it "irons." It was as if she hadn't heard a word Kate said. "After the water's been heated once, it goes flat."

Kate struggled to remain in control. "I am not talking about tea. I am talking about my father's care. This place is filthy." She gestured to the sink, where piles of pans waited to be washed. The trash can was filled; another bag of garbage leaned against the wall. Coffee grounds soaked through the brown bag.

"I'm a practical nurse, Mrs. Tyler, not a housekeeper." The woman's voice held no trace of apology, and her attitude caused something to snap in Kate. She grabbed the nurse by the arm and whirled her around. Ida's moon-shaped face reflected her astonishment.

Stung by her placidity, Kate hissed, "My son is dead. They told me he killed himself."

Ida set the kettle down. "Mary, Mother of Jesus," she said softly. The words were a prayer. She sank into a chair by the table, and although she did not attempt to reach out to Kate, the pain in her eyes shamed Kate. All the fight seeped out of her. "That's why you came, isn't it? To tell him."

She nodded.

"Are you going to?"

Kate paused a minute before she answered. "I don't know," she finally said.

Ida reached into her pocket for a pack of Winstons. Kate said nothing. The woman's smoking no longer seemed important.

The nurse lit the cigarette and dropped the match into a cup of cold coffee that was on the table. Then she rose, and squinting against the smoke circling from the cigarette dangling from the corner of her mouth, busied herself putting tea bags in the pot and neatly setting out the teacups on a tray.

"He's pretty good today," she began. "It's good for him that you came to visit. Some days he's more confused. He forgets where he is. It frightens him when he forgets. And he can't always say the words he wants to say. That frightens him, too, and frustrates him. When I'm there, he's not so afraid. I think he'd rather have me sit with him than clean the house up, so I sit with him. We play gin or watch TV. He's better than a lot I've seen. Better by a long shot."

With mention of the television, Kate became apprehensive. So far they had kept the media at bay. Almost miraculously, no enterprising reporter had yet made the connection between a young midshipman's death and the retired senior senator from Connecticut. "Does he watch the news?"

"Doesn't like it. Just the soaps. And sometimes the Saturday morning cartoons."

Thinking of her father watching cartoons brought Kate perilously close to tears.

"Why don't you go on in with him? I'll bring in the tea shortly."

His eyes were closed, and for a minute she thought he had fallen asleep. "Dad?"

He opened his eyes and stared at her, waiting.

"Mrs. Roberts is making the tea." She paused. She had never had to make conversation with him before, not even in the terrible days after his stroke. "Does the smoke bother you? I suppose we could ask her to stop."

He shook his head, still waiting. For a split second his left eye turned slightly toward the right. Dr. Carey had explained about that, about how it might turn toward the lesion. The silence of the room weighed on them. Kate was used to her father being surrounded by people. All of her life he'd been the center of action. Visits from cronies, aides, and constituents had filled his days like the books that now crowded his library shelves. She wondered how often his phone rang these days.

"Have you heard from Ted lately? Has he been to visit?"

His eyes clouded in confusion, and she saw him reaching into the failing memory.

"Ted Calgery," she prompted.

The cloudiness ebbed. "Ted's a busy man." His voice was without self-pity, but because he slurred, Kate had difficulty understanding the words. "When you are busy you have no time for old goats put out to pasture."

"I think that's damn selfish of him," Kate said, then blushed as she realized that it had been six weeks since she'd last been here herself.

"Don't be too hard on him."

"Why not? He had plenty of time for you when you were the senior senator and his mentor." Why was she arguing? It seemed that she was fighting all the time. With Michael, her father, Mrs. Roberts. What was the sense of arguing about every little thing when none of it mattered anymore?

"Well, now, I'm just a senile old goat." He chuckled, and his face twisted into a grotesque semblance of a smile, but Kate could not laugh.

"Oh, Dad, you're no more senile than I am."

"Funny thing, the word senile." His s's slurred, but his eyes danced. "The Latin root is *senex*. The same as it is for senator." The effort of the conversation was beginning to tire him. He rested his head against the back of the chair. "Where's the foot?"

"The foot?"

He pointed to the door; frustration flamed in his eyes. "The foot."

Kate shook her head helplessly, and saw his frustration mount. She had seen the same expression in Brian's eyes when he was eighteen months old and could not make her understand his baby talk.

Ida appeared at the door with the tea tray. "What is it you want, dear?"

He pointed at the tray. "My foot!"

"Yes, dear. Your tea. You want your tea."

"Yes, tea." He was comforted.

Kate watched helplessly. Was it always like this. Alternating between lucidity and confusion? Memory died first, the doctor had warned her. The interior scrapbook of a person's life was erased. *Not now*, she thought. *I can't lose him too*.

Ida filled the cups, then settled with a soft sigh into her overstuffed chair and picked up her knitting. The yarn was the same multicolored thread as that in Sidney Baldridge's afghan. There was an intimate domesticity between the nurse and her patient, and Kate retreated, sipping her tea. She was so tired. On the television a handsome intern was telling a brash nurse that he would be unable to see her anymore, that his wife was getting suspicious. Ida Roberts nodded, speaking to the senator without taking her eyes from the black-and-white set. "And isn't that just what he told her last week, but he couldn't do it." The senator did not answer. The blue of his eyes had faded, becoming vague and watery, as if the soul behind them came and went at intervals.

She would never tell him about Brian's death. She would have to rely on Ida to protect him from the news. She would call the nurse later to talk about it. She drank her tea, and when she was finished, slipped on her coat and kissed him gently on top of his thinning, snow-white hair. He needed a shampoo. She patted his lifeless hand and promised to come back again soon.

"I'm glad you came," he said absently, his eyes still on the handsome, deceitful doctor.

She refused Ida's offer to walk her to the door, and in the front hall flicked on the outside light so that she would not slip on the way to her car. The melting slush had turned the driveway slippery. She walked gingerly, feeling intensely isolated. She had come here to her father's home in search of his strength and help. She had come, she now realized, to be comforted and consoled, but the father who had been the source of such things for her entire life was gone, and she resented the loss. *I don't want to be the strong one*, she thought, knowing her wish was futile.

CHAPTER SEVEN

The cemetery was swept of snow except for little mounds hugging the shadows of the stones. The mourners huddled around the grave like the shrunken survivors of a private, tragic battle. Kate's heels sank into the muddy earth and she stared at the coffin that contained the body of her son.

She stood with the Shaw family, but as the minister spoke the final words of the service, she barely heard them. She floated out of her body, retreating from the scene to a great distance. A chipmunk scurried across the hillock of a fresh grave and up the trunk of a pine tree, and with a glimmer of blue, a jay chased it. From her distant vantage point, she looked down on the pitiful group of grievers. They had nothing to do with her.

Each moment that she didn't break down was a triumph of tight control, but this exterior constraint contrasted acutely with her inner turmoil. Once, before the divorce, Michael had turned on her and accused her of being emotionally constipated. He had never understood. She kept her emotions under control because she was terrified that if she gave in to them, she would be lost. Only once, during this time following Bri's death, had she yielded. In the elevator of the hotel in Annapolis. She vowed she would not do that again.

At times during the past three days, she had felt crazed with grief. She began sentences and couldn't hold on to a thought long enough to complete them. Twice she went into the grocery store and twice left empty-handed, having forgotten what she needed to buy.

From the great distance of her retreat, she heard Wendi sniffle and saw Michael standing, Wendi's hand cupped in his. His wife was dressed in black and wore a small hat with a veil that hid her face. This dress of mourning made Kate's own red coat shout. She had worn it as a gesture of courage and life, of denial, a symbol of Brian's vitality, but now, here in the cemetery next to Wendi's somber black, it seemed inappropriate and frivolous, and she felt Michael's disapproval. Discreet yards away, behind a circle of bare trees, the crew from the funeral parlor waited in their pickup truck. Through the dimness she had put between herself and the others, she heard the minister issue the invitation to return to the home of Michael and Wendi.

Michael had told her that everyone should return to her house, but she had refused, saying she wouldn't turn her son's funeral into a party.

"People expect it," he'd argued. And still she had refused.

He kept his temper under control, but his sternness reminded her of the times throughout their marriage when she had felt that she failed him. "If you don't do it, Wendi and I will."

The funeral director moved to her side, handing her the book that contained the words of the service. "Is there anything I can do?" he asked. Kate shook her head. She crossed the dead winter grass and got into the Shaws' car, sitting in back next to seventeen-year-old Jennie.

"Do you want to go to Michael's?" Deep lines etched Hal Shaw's cheeks. Kate had never seen him look so old.

"I guess so."

"You don't have to, Kate."

"I know."

Nina turned around in the front seat. "You sure you want to go? We could go back to our house, kick off our shoes and have a drink."

"I'll go. Just for a few minutes." She didn't have the courage to stay away.

As soon as they arrived, she regretted her decision. Here, she was the intruder. Although the others had arrived only minutes before, everyone was already holding a drink. A waitress in black held a tray of appetizers toward her. A moment later a waiter proffered a hot artichoke and cheese dip with crackers. There was a bar set up in the dining room. Wendi's taste in decorating ran to blue velvet and distressed cherry furniture. Michael's recliner, a battered leather chair that had followed them twice in moves across the country—and the only piece of furniture he had asked for after the divorce—was nowhere in sight.

Hal and Nina stayed by her side, but they could not

protect her from the icy loneliness that seized her. Several officers from Michael's legal staff interrupted their conversation to speak with her. When she walked away they continued their discussion about a case, occasionally casting concerned looks in her direction. They seemed more at ease with Michael and Wendi. The couple stood in the living room, welcoming guests, gracefully accepting their condolences. Men as well as women bent to hug Wendi, whose eyes were red from weeping.

Kate listened to the murmured condolences with dry eyes and rigid shoulders, finding sympathy almost impossible to accept. Even as she ached with grief, she noticed how the others seemed to prefer consoling Wendi, and she resented the way her husband's new wife had usurped her role as chief mourner.

"I have to go home," she said. Without a word, Hal set his drink down and shepherded the children outside to the car, his arm tight around her. She sat in perfect stillness until they pulled into her driveway. The Shaw children peered at her out of the corners of their eyes, but did not speak. Jennie shyly reached over and held her hand. Of all the Shaw tribe, the teenager had most idolized Brian.

At the house, both Nina and Hal got out and she waved them off. "Don't bother coming in. I think I'd like to be alone."

Nina hugged her, holding on tight before letting her go.

"We're right next door if you need us," Hal said.

"I love you, Kate."

"I love you, too, Nina." There was a moment of clumsy silence. "We got through it, didn't we?"

Nina nodded, unable to speak.

"And I didn't break down. I was so afraid of that. So afraid I would cry."

"No, Katie. You were terrific. You didn't cry." Nina choked and turned away abruptly. Kate stood on the porch and watched them depart, inhaling the cold, still air of dusk. When she turned she saw the light in the window of her study. At a deep level of consciousness she realized that was wrong, like someone returning home to an unmade bed when she was certain of having made it before she left in the morning. Or a photograph reversed in printing. Something off, worrisome, but not the focus of conscious attention. Then she reached for the kitchen door. She turned the knob and was opening the door inward when she was flung to one side. Something hard—a knee? a fist?—slammed into her hip, bruising flesh and bone, and she stumbled, heavily striking the wall before she fell to her knees. She cried out instinctively, but her assailant did not pause. A minute later she heard the sound of a motor starting from down on River Road, followed by the squeal of tires on snow.

She stayed where she'd been flung, a crumpled heap on the kitchen floor; her bowels contracted in spasms of cold terror. She heard the pitiful mewing sounds of an injured animal, a rabbit from the woods perhaps, or a kitten. The kitchen door was still open, and the dark night yawned beyond. She was deathly afraid to leave it open, but as she made a tiny move toward it to close it, a hideous thought took hold. What if there were still another person in the house and she was shut in with him? Stunned by panic and fear, she huddled in a ball, her knees drawn into her chest, rocking back and forth. It was several seconds before she realized that the animallike sounds were coming from her mouth. She clenched her hand into a fist and pressed her knuckles painfully against her lips to cut off the noise.

For a long time she stayed like that, until, inch by inch, the disabling terror ebbed, replaced by a shaking so violent it was like a palsy. The first time she tried to stand, her leg gave out. Pain shot down through the entire leg from her hip. She wondered if the blow she received could have broken a bone. She tried again, clenching her teeth against the pain, and this time managed to limp to the door and close it. When she switched on the overhead light, she saw nothing out of place. The dining room, too, showed no sign of an intruder. Her mother's sterling tea service was still on the sideboard, flanked by matching candlesticks.

She swung open the door to the living room and gasped. Cushions had been pulled from every chair and the couch. Side tables were lying on the floor. Magazines were strewn everywhere, pages torn out and crumpled on the carpet.

The study was worse. Books, spines snapped on some, littered the rug. Every drawer of the oak desk had been emptied. In the chaos, it was impossible to determine if anything was missing. Kate stood in the middle of ruin, unable to move, barely breathing. Finally she crossed to the phone and called the police. While she waited for the patrol car she pulled the drapes across the windows. Now, if anyone watched from outside, they could not see her. But she could not get rid of the feeling of being watched. Through the crack between the drapes she saw the flashing light spill over the barren shrubbery as the police car pulled into the drive.

The officer who responded to the call was young. The beginning of a pot belly pressed against his uniform shirt. He looked pale, too, and she wondered if he was fit enough to chase someone if he was called upon to do so. Distracted, she realized he had a notebook open.

"Anything missing, Mrs. Tyler?"

"I don't know. I haven't looked yet."

He roamed from room to room, touching nothing. In the dining room he paused when he saw the silver service. "Looks like they didn't have time to take anything. You probably interrupted them."

"Him."

He looked at her sharply. "One? You saw him?"

"No. But he ran by me, pushed me down. I heard the car. I'm pretty sure there was only one."

"Some dumb kid. Probably getting money for drugs." Sighing, he tucked the notebook away. *Routine*, his expression said.

"I didn't see him. It could have been someone older." His readiness to blame a youngster annoyed her.

"Usually a kid, a case like this. Must have known you'd be out. Are you usually out at this time? At a job?"

"No. I teach at the college. I'm usually home now." She paused for a moment, reluctant to tell him where she'd been, and he picked up on her hesitation instantly. She had underestimated his shrewdness.

"I was at a funeral. My son's. His funeral was this afternoon."

He took the notebook out of his pocket and flipped it open to the brief page of notes. "Tyler. Of course." Kinder now, he offered her a seat, asking if he could get her a drink or call someone for her.

"Did you have someone here to watch the place during the funeral?" He finally resumed his investigation.

She shook her head.

"Damn them. They read the funeral notices, you know, watch and see when a house might be empty." Despite his words, he seemed inured to the horror of such parasitic behavior. "I'm surprised he broke in with the security system. Usually on a B and E they won't touch a place with a system. Too much of a risk."

"It wasn't on."

The warmth he had shown her chilled a degree. "You really should use it, Mrs. Tyler. It's like an engraved invitation to these kids if you don't. We do what we can with patrols, but we can't protect people who won't protect themselves."

"Yes, I know. I'll remember." She just wanted him gone. "Thank you for coming. Yes, I'll be sure to let you know if I find something missing. Yes, I'll be sure to use the alarm system. Thank you again." She closed the door after him and waited until she heard the sound of the car leaving.

She returned to the living room and began righting furniture, when the reaction hit. The tremors shook her entire body like a fever. She clamped her jaw shut to prevent it and sank into a chair. Someone had been in her home, touched her things. She felt violated and soiled, as if her spirit had been raped. Although the policeman had searched every room and found no one, she couldn't escape the feeling that a person was still there somewhere. In spite of locking the front and rear doors, she felt unsafe.

The lights they had switched on in every room during the search still blazed, but she did not turn them off. Light, she felt instinctively, was security. Her hip throbbed as she climbed the stairs to change from her dress. The funeral and burial had happened long ago, to someone else. As she stripped off her panty hose, she saw an ugly bruise was already forming. She thought longingly of taking a hot bath, but she wasn't ready to lie naked in the tub yet, in spite of the lights and locks and alarm system. She hung up the dress and slipped into her kimono, then went back downstairs, into the ruined living room. Before she began to work, she put a Vivaldi tape on the tape deck, as if unconsciously combating savagery with civilization.

Still needing security, she thought of calling Nina, was in fact surprised that Nina hadn't seen the flashing light of the patrol car and come over. She considered, too, phoning Michael, and rejected the idea immediately. Her stomach tightened. She would have to stop relying on either her friend or her ex-husband.

She stopped by the door to the hall and looked across at the table. Four days' accumulation of mail was stacked on the surface, some of it spilled onto the floor. A thrill of shock surged through her, like an exposed nerve prodded with a needle. How could she have forgotten? How *could* she have forgotten? Her hands trembled, scattering the envelopes. She gathered them together and sat on the side chair, sifting through the pile. She did that twice, faster the second time. After the third time she threw the envelopes on the table and fell to her knees, crouching to look beneath the table. Her hip ached when she knelt. Her hands trembled violently.

She tried to slow her movements, to control the shaking. Nausea filled her like morning sickness. *How could she have forgotten?*

Her movements were ragged now. Perhaps it was wedged behind the table. She roughly pulled the piece of furniture out from the wall, catching the lamp just before it fell. It had to be there. Had to. She could not bear to think it wasn't. It had to be. It wasn't.

She ran to the study, stepping over the wreckage left by the intruder. Furiously, she pawed through the piles of paper he had strewn around the room, methodical in spite of her shock and pain.

Nothing. Steady. She forced herself to close her eyes, thinking back to the afternoon when she had learned about Brian's death. She had come back from the lunch with Nina. She had been rushed and had dumped her mail on the hall table, where she always put it until it could be sorted. She remembered doing it, remembered thinking of his letter and deciding to save it until she returned home from class. Then, of course, when she had come home, the men from Annapolis had been waiting, and she had forgotten about it. It seemed incredible to her now that she had not once remembered the letter, the last one from her son, the one that might hold some explanation for this nightmare. But looking back, the past days had been a haze, a span of hours lived in a grief-dimmed limbo during which she had gone to Annapolis and returned, made funeral plans, picked out the coffin, chosen what clothes to put on the body of Brian, selected the words to be spoken at the service, talked to the minister, driven to see her father. There had been no reality to those days, no normal frame of reference.

Go back to the first day. The officers had arrived from the Academy. They had come in, spoken to her. She had phoned Michael and he had come over. Michael. She could still picture him standing in the hall, his back to her as he said good-bye to Beck and Kestler. He must have seen it then. Taken it. It was so obvious, she didn't know why she hadn't thought of it immediately. But why hadn't he told her? Had the letter been so painful that he had chosen not to reveal it to her? Bastard. He had no right.

Michael answered the phone on the third ring. Voices buzzed in the background, people from the funeral who lingered there, the warm, tinkling sounds of a cocktail party.

"What letter?" He sounded harassed.

"From Brian. The one you took, you bastard. The one that came the day he died."

"You had a letter from Brian and this is the first I heard of it?" The shock in his voice silenced her attack. "For Christ's sake, Kate. How could you forget a thing like that?" He paused, and Kate heard the muffled exchange of conversation. He had put his hand over the mouthpiece.

"Listen, Kate, I don't know a damn thing about any letter." The pause was strained. "Are you sure there *was* any letter?"

"I'm not crazy, Michael. There was a letter. And it's gone now." She paused, pursuing another idea. "What about Kestler? Do you think he might have taken it?"

"Kate, for God's sake get hold of yourself. Calm down."

She was afraid he would hang up. "There's something else. The police just left. Someone broke in here."

"The police? Jesus, Kate, what the hell is going on there?" He didn't wait for an answer. "What was taken?"

"Nothing was taken. Apparently I walked in during the robbery. Michael? The officer said burglars watch the obituaries for homes that might be left unguarded." Silence. "Did you hear me?"

His hand was again cupped over the receiver and she heard indistinct voices. "Wendi asked if you were all right."

"Yes. I'm fine. The house is all right. Nothing was taken—" The thought hit her with such force that she sank into the desk chair. "Nothing is missing except Bri's letter. Maybe that's what he wanted. Bri's letter."

More muffled sounds while he repeated her words to his wife. "Kate, listen. I don't think we need to talk about this now. We still have people here, and I have to go. I want you to turn on the security system. Do you understand? And I want you to stop thinking that there is any connection between any letter of Brian and the break-in. That's not very... very healthy thinking. Okay? I have to go. You take care of yourself, all right?"

She hung up the phone. He thought she had imagined the letter. His expression made that clear. Great weariness overtook her, and with it, doubt. Maybe she had. Maybe she *was* going crazy. Unbalanced. Insane with grief. Like the mother in a Greek tragedy. Next she would begin to beat her breasts, rend her clothing, tear her hair.

Exhausted, she shut her eyes. Behind the closed lids a form took shape: the outline of Brian's letter. She saw the envelope, his precise, sloping handwriting, the faint smudge of dirt on the corner near the Annapolis seal, saw it as clearly as the morning she had taken it out of the mailbox. Shrugging off fatigue, she opened her eyes, stood up, and began searching the study. She was going to look very slowly and carefully one more time for Bri's letter. And when she was finished in this room, she was going to look in the living room and hall and kitchen, and then upstairs in her bedroom. She wasn't going to stop until she had covered every inch of the house. And if she couldn't find it, she was going to call the Academy. She couldn't give up.

CHAPTER EIGHT

The warm spell ended during the night, broken by a cruel, encompassing cold that froze crocus buds lured out by the false spring, seeming twice as brutal in contrast to the days that had preceded it. The wind came up at midnight, licking the landscape with ice. Snow followed. It fell for seven hours, and the sound of snowplows and sanders scraped through the frigid air.

Kate lay in bed and listened to the noise of the plows as they passed in front of her home. She had slept fitfully, possessed by the thought of the missing letter. Her brain, her entire being was drained from going over and over the past few days, trying to latch on some elusive moment when the letter might have been misplaced. Her concentration was broken by the telephone's ring.

"Mrs. Tyler?" The words were gentle but direct. "I hope I haven't woken you up, but Reverend Davidson gave me your name. He told me about your son." The woman spoke more quickly now, as if realizing that Kate, having heard too many words of sympathy, wanted to cut her short. "My name is Ellen Kingsley, and I understand how you are feeling."

Understand? How could you possibly understand? The receiver was heavy in her hand. *Dear God, no one—no one could understand the pain. Not Nina or Reverend Davidson, and certainly not some stranger named Ellen Kingsley.* Kate started to speak, but the woman's next words froze her.

"My daughter died last year. Her name was Melissa and she was nineteen."

"I'm sorry." The sentence came automatically. *Why was she telling her this? It had nothing to do with Brian.*

"I don't need to tell you what it was like after she died—"

Wrapped in her own pain, Kate had no time for this woman. "I have to go—" she began.

"And then I met other parents who had lost children," she continued, as if Kate had not spoken. "A group of us meet each Monday night at the church. Compassionate Friends is what we call ourselves. We meet and talk—cry, if we want, shout, get angry, hug, support, whatever we need to do. The group is a lifeline, Mrs. Tyler. I know it saved my life."

"Thank you for calling, but I am not interested."

"Mrs. Tyler... Kate..." Ellen Kingsley's voice was very gentle. "When I said I understood, I meant it. I *want* to help. I *know* what you are feeling. You see, like your Brian, my Melissa also took her own life."

Shock hit Kate like a fist in the stomach. When she could speak, her voice was icy. "Well, you're wrong, Mrs. Kingsley. My Brian did not kill himself. Do you hear me? No matter what you think, Bri did not—could not commit suicide." She banged the receiver down. Her last words, so shrill she had almost screamed them, echoed in the bedroom.

There it was. So obvious. What her heart had been telling her from the moment she had first heard. *Brian could not commit suicide.* Everything she knew about her son, every bit of instinct and innate intelligence reinforced this belief. Scenes from his childhood sprang to mind. She remembered the time he was eight. They had been walking along the road and come upon the body of a pheasant killed by a passing car. Brian had been the one who insisted that they bury it. He had run home for a shovel and carried the corpse into the woods. She could still remember the heavy, damp smell of the forest floor, the soft mat of rotting oak leaves and pine needles. He had dug the hole—deep, so that animals wouldn't uncover it—and gently dumped dirt over the bird. When he was done, they saw a single, magnificent tail feather. She had picked it up and offered it to him, asking him if he would like to take it to school for science class. He stroked the feather longingly, and she had seen that he wanted it. After a moment he'd said, "I can't keep it, Mom. It belongs to the bird." Then, sweating from exertion, he had redug the grave and placed the tail feather with the pheasant before again recovering the bird.

And she remembered the time—he must have been thirteen—he had seen a news program about how calves were raised for veal. Tears of anger had filled his eyes when he saw the young animals confined in their tight cages. The reporter had explained that limiting the calves' motion ensured tender meat. "How can they do that, Mom?" he'd asked. She shared his helpless rage, understanding when he vowed never to eat veal again. And he never had.

Other pictures, other times came to mind. Just two years ago. Brian and Danielle talking about a touring exhibit of watercolor paintings. The artist, a paraplegic, had held his paintbrush between his teeth. "I couldn't do that," Danielle had said. "If I was stuck in a wheelchair like that, I would want to die." Brian had looked thoughtful. "I might at first," he'd finally replied. "But I think if it really happened, I'd still want to live. Look at that guy. He was a football player, lived entirely in a physical world, and now that's gone and he paints."

Her belief intensified. *Brian would not kill himself*. How could he have? She swung her feet to the floor and began getting dressed. Her stomach growled with hunger, but she did not waste time making coffee. She had to make them understand—Thatcher, Beck, someone down there—just had to make them understand that Brian couldn't have killed himself. There must be some other explanation for his death.

She began placing calls, and with each call her frustration mounted. She was told Thatcher and Kestler were not available, but they would get back to her. She did reach Beck. The chaplain had listened to her fervent, urgent words and then softly suggested she might want to speak to her own minister or to a doctor. She listened to his advice impatiently. He did not mean to be insensitive, he just didn't understand.

Unable to wait for him to return her call, she tried Thatcher two more times before noon, stammering out a message, incomplete sentences about how Brian wouldn't have committed suicide.

She spent the afternoon waiting, listening for the telephone, frustration and anger mounting with each hour that passed. At five o'clock she dialed again. "I'm sorry," an impersonal voice responded. "Everyone is out of the office until tomorrow."

Kate slammed the receiver down. Then, almost without thinking, she pivoted on her heel and left the house.

She drove recklessly, still simmering. Only when she climbed the steps to the police station did she realize with amazement how uncharacteristically impulsive and courageous her behavior was.

Phil Kadetsky, the Lanchester police chief, looked tired. He was in his mid-fifties, round, pink, and bald. He led her to his office and listened to her story in polite silence, occasionally scrawling brief notes. The building that housed the police department, and the fire department as well, was old, with thin walls. Kate was conscious that in spite of the closed door her voice could be heard outside his office, but she didn't care. She practically shouted her story: Brian's death, her belief that it must have been an accident, the missing letter, the break-in. She told him of her conviction that there was a connection between the burglary and Bri's letter. When she finished, she clasped her hands tightly in her lap. She couldn't breathe. She was afraid to look at him, afraid she would see in his face the disbelief she had heard in Michael's voice last night and again this morning in Beck's. Without remarking on her story, he excused himself, returning minutes later with a slender file envelope.

Quietly he asked questions about Brian, the Academy, Michael. He was good at this, thorough although appearing to ramble, and then allowing her answers to flow, each leading to another, revealing more. She found herself telling him about the divorce and Michael's remarriage, and even about her job. When he was done, he leaned back in the swivel chair and reread his notes. Finished, he placed them on the desk and stared at her for several minutes. She stared back hopefully.

"I want to, well, to help of course..." he began.

She knew at once he didn't believe her. "Then do something, damn it! Find out how he died."

His low-keyed manner contrasted sharply with hers. "Well now, let's begin with a cup of coffee. Okay? All we have—all we can offer—is black. No one ever remembers to buy milk. I'll be right back."

Alone in his office, Kate heard the banter of other men through the walls. Their voices rose above the clatter of the typewriters and teletype machine. Doors opened and closed, and she realized the shifts were changing. She sank back in the chair and fought to regain control. A plump young man poked his face in, looked around, and withdrew without speaking. Kate looked at her watch, amazed to find that it had been ten minutes since the chief had left her. She fussed with her gloves. The fury that had propelled her to this office began to ebb, replaced by hopelessness.

Just as she was debating whether to leave, Kadetsky returned. He set a Styrofoam cup down on the desk in front of her, sat in his chair, and sighed. He left his own coffee untouched.

"Is that right? Black? Black with one sugar?"

Dutifully, Kate sipped. The lukewarm coffee was heavy with sugar. Beneath the syrupy taste of the sweetener it was bitter, as if the coffee had been made early in the morning and now only these last sour dregs remained.

"It's fine."

Kadetsky's hands were short with fat, stubby fingers which Kate could not picture holding a gun. He stroked them absently across the top of his scalp, as if hoping to discover new growth of hair there. Opening a desk drawer, he took out a small container and plopped five saccharin tablets into his coffee. He stirred it with a ballpoint pen, the same one he had used to take notes with earlier. He had not looked at her since he'd returned with the coffee. "Weather cold enough for you? Seems twice as cold following that warm spell. Twice as cold." He addressed the words to the room.

With a sinking feeling, she began to acknowledge it had been a mistake to come. The chief was no different from the administration at Annapolis. She desperately wanted to leave. Kadetsky concentrated on the pen, drying it with a rumpled handkerchief, rolling it across the desktop, using the palms of his chubby hands. He talked more about the weather and road conditions, mentioning the number of minor accidents reported in the past eight hours. "Fender benders," he called them. Once, when he thought she wasn't looking, he glanced at his watch, checking its time against that of the large round clock on the wall by the window.

"I'm sorry. I'm keeping you." Kate said. *I shouldn't have come.*

"No. Not at all." He reddened.

She moved as if to rise, and he looked up in alarm, pulled his notepad toward him on the desk, and reread the notations he had made earlier. "Well, now, Mrs. Tyler, I guess you didn't come here to hear a briefing on our accident reports," he began, again running his hand over his bald head, his eyes focused on the pad, avoiding hers. "Mrs. Tyler, I'm real sorry about your son. Real sorry. The death of a child has to be . . . well, it has to be one of the hardest things a parent can ever face. And suicides, well suicides are twice as hard. The guilt, questioning, senselessness of it all—"

"My son did not commit suicide." The shaking began again, and the coffee slopped over the edge of the rim. She set the cup on his desk.

His voice, face, posture softened as he leaned toward her. "Mrs. Tyler, you're not alone, believe me. It happens. And every parent feels the same way. Confused. Hurt. Believe me." Frustration flared briefly in his eyes. "Since your son" —he checked his notes—"Brian died, have you talked to any professionals? Has anyone mentioned the statistics on teen-age suicide? Christ Almighty, it's unbelievable. *Unbelievable*. Over in Wilmington they've had five already this year. Five. It's like an epidemic. And every one of those five kids had parents who feel exactly like you do. Do you—"

The door behind Kate opened, and even as she turned, she saw relief flash on Kadetsky's face.

"Kate. What the hell is going on?" Michael's voice was harsh, but Kate ignored him. She flashed an accusatory look at the chief, and he had the grace to look embarrassed. He rubbed a hand over his hairless pate. The sound of voices from the outer room had quieted, and Kate knew the other officers were listening.

"I was hoping maybe you could help us straighten this out, Commander." Kadetsky nodded toward Kate. "Your wife— excuse me—ex-wife—seems inclined to doubt that your son took his life. She came to me because she thinks there is some connection between a break-in at her home, a missing letter, and his death. Naturally, under the circumstances, I can understand why she'd be a bit upset, but I think we can straighten this out, sort it out between us. This is a difficult thing to ask a man, but let me ask you, sir, is there any doubt in your mind, any doubt at all, that your son took his own life?"

The muscles in Michael's jaw jumped. He stood rigidly, ignoring the chair the police chief had offered with a sweep-ing gesture.

"It *is* painful for me to talk about my son's death, Chief, but there is no mystery about it. Brian committed suicide. Naturally, it is a shock, but there is no reason to twist his death. There was a brief investigation, of course. I'm satisfied with the results. The authorities at Annapolis are satisfied. I phoned them after I received your call, and I know they will confirm what I have said."

"I don't care." Kate's voice was shrill. "He didn't do it. I know he wouldn't—"

"I'm sorry if Kate has taken up your time," Michael continued smoothly, as if she hadn't spoken, as if she were not even in the room. "She's been under a lot of strain. I'm sure you can understand, given the circumstances."

"Of course, of course. Sorry to have bothered you, Commander. Just trying to do my job. Have to follow up when someone comes to me. Well, now, I know how busy you must be, and I surely appreciate your coming right over."

"Not at all." Michael's bearing was military, that of one officer reporting to another. "Again, I'm sorry for any inconvenience Mrs. Tyler has caused."

"No problem at all. That's what we're here for. To help." Kadetsky rose and smiled tentatively at Kate, but she froze him with a look.

Without speaking to her, Michael held her chair, and grasping her arm tightly, nodding at the chief, led her from the room. The tension of his fingers betrayed his fury. Fleetingly she considered pulling away, and as if reading her mind, he tightened his grip. Resentment at both men burned.

She tried to ignore the curious gazes of the dispatcher and officer at the desk as she walked through the main room of the station. Even outside, as they walked down the steps, Michael did not release her arm. He pulled her toward his car and opened the door. She felt the cold fury radiate from him.

"I have my own car." She tried to match his rage with cool dignity, aware her face flamed. Absurdly, humiliatingly, he made her feel like a disruptive child who had been reproved by adults. "Look, I'm sorry he dragged you here. This had nothing to do with you." She hated herself for the note of apology in her voice.

He ignored her. "We've got to talk. Do you know where the Copper Lantern is? Good. I'll meet you there. Can you drive?"

"Of course I can drive."

Again he did not respond. A muscle in his cheek jumped,

and his eyes were frigid. He slid into the seat of his sports car and closed the door. When he pulled away from the curb, tires screeched.

Kate shrank inside her coat. As always, his fury intimidated her, controlled her. *Damn it*, she thought. *I've done nothing wrong. He has no right to treat me like this.* Her hands trembled when she turned the key in the ignition. As she drove she concentrated on her anger, letting it build against Michael.

He was already seated at a table in the lounge when she arrived. There was a drink on the table in front of him, and as she approached he took a healthy swig.

"I'll have a Jack Daniels," she told the waitress.

"Do you think you should? You're driving."

Who the hell was he, talking as if she had a drinking problem or something. "So are you. Jack Daniels," she repeated firmly. "On the rocks." As the woman turned away, Kate intercepted her pitying glance toward Michael. Her anger intensified. All the suppressed emotions surged out.

"What right did you have to tell the chief Brian killed himself? What right do you have to interfere? I can call the police or the administration at Navy, or the President himself, and you have no right to interfere."

"I have every right. Like I told the chief, it's clear-cut. Brian committed suicide. What isn't so clear-cut is just what the hell you think you're doing. I am all too painfully aware, Kate, that you've been phoning the Academy. I've had dozens of calls about it already today. At the office. At home. The admiral even talked to the judge advocate about it. Asked what was going on with his staff. For God's sake, what the hell are you trying to do to me?"

His attack stunned her so thoroughly that she was unable to respond.

"You really don't understand, do you? You are wrecking my career."

"I thought that was all over, that this was your last tour."

He looked down into his drink. "I'm up for promotion, Kate. For captain. I just can't walk away from it."

"What about the law firm you and Jake were going to start? What about your promise to make this the end?"

"That promise was to you, not Wendi. She likes the life. She's proud of me. And I'll tell you one thing: she'd never,

ever mess it up for me." The words "like you" hung unspoken between them.

"I'm not your wife anymore, Michael. Nothing I do can affect your career."

"You know better than that. You know the way they think. It's bad enough about Brian, without you acting crazy too. That kind of thing doesn't look good. Thatcher called me and interrupted a JAG investigation today because of you. You think that doesn't reflect on me?"

He cupped his hands around the glass. His knuckles were white, and in the soft light of the cocktail lounge his gold Annapolis ring glowed dimly.

"I'm sorry he called you, Michael. I didn't intend to involve you."

"Well, I am involved. I'm so goddamned involved, it makes me sick." He drank deeply and signaled for another drink. "They think you're paranoid. Did you know that? They think you're having some kind of breakdown, all this talk of someone burglarizing the house just for a letter."

"I'm not having a breakdown, Michael. And I'm not crazy. I'm just trying to understand what happened to him. Someone did break into my house. And his letter—his last letter—is missing. I have to find out what happened. Can't you understand that?" They might have been speaking different languages. Even if he was able to accept the idea that their son had killed himself, wasn't he curious about what had happened to the letter? Why was it so difficult for him to understand her need to find out?

"Let's get this straight, Kate. What exactly are you trying to say? Are you saying that Brian didn't kill himself? Because, what then? How did he die? Are you saying someone else killed him? Are you saying that Thatcher and Kestler and Beck and half the damn Academy know he was murdered and are deliberately covering it up? Is that what you're driving at, Kate? Because if you are, then you are really sick. You better get some help. See a doctor."

He sucked in his breath. "Listen, Kate. You've *got* to stop this. We know what Bri did to himself. Let it go, Kate. Make your peace with it."

"I can't." Her voice dropped, and he had to lean across the table to hear her. "I can't because I just don't believe Bri could kill himself. Not like that. I can't help wondering. I can't sleep. I keep seeing the rope around his neck, the bruises on his arms."

"For God's sake, Kate." Michael's fist struck the table, knocking her drink over and sending the ice cubes arcing to the floor. The waitress approached hastily, as if in the dimness of the room she had been close by. She stooped, mopping up Kate's drink with a patterned napkin, making little clucking noises in her throat. At nearby tables, people turned. The bartender frowned at them, but when there was no further sign of trouble, he returned to wiping the long mahogany bar, dividing his attention between them and the TV.

Kate ordered another drink. Anything to make the waitress go away. Michael sat in silence, contorting the cocktail straw into rigid knots, until she had been served. "I loved him, too, Kate," he began. "You don't have a monopoly on grief. I was his father, for God's sake. I miss him, but I won't turn his death into something it wasn't." A spasm of grief distorted his handsome face. "It hurts so much." His voice broke, and for a moment Kate thought he was going to reach for her hand, to hold it with his. Then the moment was gone and he continued bitterly. "It hurts like hell, Kate. It hurts so damn much to know my son was a quitter. You said you felt like you didn't even know him. Remember saying that? Coming home on the plane? Well, I didn't know my son was a quitter, and it hurts."

She was too shocked to answer. She reached for her drink, withdrawing into the dark, private world where no one could reach her. It was icy there, as cold as the drink she held in her hands, but she did not care. She stayed there, far away from Michael, whom she'd once loved, in her own capsule of silence where his words could not reach her.

"Kate? Are you listening? Did you hear what I said?"

How long had he been talking without her hearing him? "I'm sorry, Michael. Could you repeat that?" Her words were without emotion.

"I said you've got to get hold of yourself. See a doctor. Maybe take a vacation. Listen, I'll be happy to help out. I'll even pay for it. Make the arrangements for a little trip somewhere and I'll pay for it."

She stared at him. During the divorce so much of his bitterness had been about money. Women always get the best of it, he'd complained. He listed friends who had gone down the tube paying outrageous alimony.

"I have money," she said impassively. "You don't have to worry about that."

"There's something else." He looked down at the table, bending the drink straw into a triangle. "It's about Wendi. You've got to stop calling the house about things. Like the letter. The robbery. Things like that. I can't . . . I can't be there for you, Kate." Even in her own pain she saw that he was having trouble with the words. "It upsets Wendi when you phone. I wasn't going to tell you this now. I was going to wait for a better time. It's Wendi. She's pregnant."

Even though he tried, Michael could not keep the edge of happiness from slipping through. It shone in his voice, knifing her.

The news of Wendi's pregnancy lodged in her throat like a piece of stone. She wandered around the house, picking up and putting down objects, switching the radio on to the Hartford Symphony, and then moments later turning it off. Finally she poured sherry into a crystal wineglass and climbed the stairs to the bathroom. She ran the tub full and hot, so hot she had to ease in inch by inch, drawing in her breath as the water bit each new patch of flesh. Even submerged, she felt weighed down, as if her weary leaden spirit transcended physics and was able to pull her body down.

She lay like that for a long time. When the bath grew cold, she flipped the lever with her toe and let the water drain out. Her untouched wineglass was on the edge of the tub. She wrapped a bath sheet around her and carried the sherry to the bedroom. She caught a glimpse of her reflection in the mirror and turned away. Like a shock victim, she walked slowly to the bureau and turned out the light. She did not need light to see the ravages of her body. She knew the flesh was no longer firm on her neck and upper arms and thighs. Her waist had thickened. She ran her fingers along the incision in her belly. The scar from Brian's birth.

She had not wanted a caesarean section, had argued for long hours with her doctor, willing her child to right itself. At last, exhausted, she'd surrendered to the surgeon. The operation had bisected her stomach, leaving a permanent reminder of Brian's birth. The scar of his death was invisible, but deeper.

At that moment, she came as close to hating Michael as she ever had. She pictured Wendi's swollen, blossoming belly, Michael's pride. By fatherhood he would manage to stay young. He'd found a way to replace Brian. She slipped on her nightgown and crawled into bed. She felt old, but more than that, she felt betrayed.

Her father had betrayed her by illness; Michael by his unborn child. She was alone and she was old and she could never be a mother again. She could feel this in the center of her womb. But as she lay there, one thought began to dominate her, and like a seed, determination grew in her. Brian had not betrayed her. Let Michael have his replacement child. She would find out why and how Brian died, and then she would be at peace again.

CHAPTER NINE

Leah walked beside him in stony silence. He didn't need a course in body language to know she was furious. They were in front on her apartment and he reached for her hand, but she pulled away.

"Okay," he said. "I'm sorry. I was just trying to be funny."

She didn't answer. She reached into her bag for her key, every motion precise and silent. She was so composed, it frightened him.

He wasn't controlled at all. In fact things were fuzzy from the wine he'd had to drink at dinner. More than he had expected at the table of a professor. He glanced sideways at her. Even angry she looked great. Even bundled up in that puffy lavender jacket. He loved her in lavender. He loved her even more in nothing. Desire flared, but her hostility shut him out. He tried again.

"I said I'm sorry. I was just trying to lighten up the moment. You have to admit the old girl looked pretty funny when the moth flew out of my mouth."

"How could you?" Each word was cutting. "You knew how much I wanted this evening to be special. If I get into grad school, Professor Mason will be the reason. You knew this, and you still acted like a child. God knows what she thinks of you."

So I popped a Ruley; big deal, he wanted to say, but bit back the words. He remembered the moment in front of the professor's door. While they waited to be admitted, he had watched a moth circle the porch light, and without thinking, he'd grabbed it and flipped it in his mouth. It fluttered its wings, tickling his tongue while he waited, and when he said hello to the woman who answered their knock, it flew out. "Popping a Ruley." It was the latest craze to storm the Yard. In class, dress parade, chapel, anywhere at all, it could happen: a mid would open his mouth and an insect would fly out. There was a plebe in the infirmary right now suffering from a bee sting. Who but a dumb plebe would pop a bee? The best goddamned popper of them all was Ted Ruley. He'd invented the trick and he had managed the show stopper. He popped a butterfly on Worden, and then while passing in review, opened his mouth and let it fly out. The funniest thing was the reaction of onlookers. After the initial moment of raw shock, they pretended nothing had happened.

He remembered the expression on Leah's professor's face, and laughter threatened again. He fought it. It would be deadly to laugh now, he knew.

Leah opened the door, her motions exaggerated and noisier than they had to be. He followed her up the stairs to her apartment. At least he wasn't being shut out. The need for her grew. All week he'd been waiting for her. He hadn't wanted to spend the evening with some old professor, had resented the idea, but she'd insisted. Now he'd blown it.

"I'm really sorry, Lee. If I could do it over, I would. I'd do the whole evening over and just change the beginning. It was dumb. Stupid. I was an ass. What more can I say?"

He tried hard to enunciate clearly, but it was difficult because he knew he was on the edge of a big drunk. He knew she didn't like it when he drank. But he wasn't really smashed. Just on the edge. Just fuzzy, and horny as hell. He reached for her as soon as they stepped inside her living room. She pushed him aside.

"Who are you, Brian?"

He pulled her close and nuzzled her neck. Although her body did not resist, unnervingly, it held no more life than her voice. "You know me. I'm the big bad wolf, and I'm going to eat you, Goldilocks."

She wouldn't play. Gently she disengaged herself and sat down in the rocker. "I mean it. I don't know you, Brian. Not really." She unzipped her coat and slipped it off; it fell in soft folds around her like a neon puddle. "The only thing I really know about you is that you drink too much."

Christ, he thought. *It was only a damned moth. We're fighting over a moth?* "You know who I am," he said, drunkenness making him obstinate. Her control frightened him, and that, in turn, angered him.

"The only thing I am sure of is that you drink too much."

"Ah. You have discovered the darkest secret of each midshipman."

"I'm serious."

"So I see." She had spoiled the mood now. He let his voice grow cold. There were plenty of other women who wouldn't mind a little joke with a moth. Actually, when you thought about it, it was pretty damn funny. "Maybe I better leave, and you can call me when you're in a better mood."

"It won't work." Her voice was calm. He looked at her face, and it hurt him. He had seen her laughing, concentrating when she was studying by his side, sleeping. He had seen her face when it was lit by the intensity of their lovemaking, and after, he had seen it grow soft. But he had never seen her look so sad. "If you want to leave now, I can't stop you, but I would rather talk with you. There are some things I need to say."

He wanted to walk away. He really wanted to turn and walk out the door, walk away from this room, from her, from them. He knew that if he left now, he would be walking away from something he would never be lucky enough to find again. Maybe he could come back. Maybe she would be there for him, but he didn't want to chance it. He sat down and waited for her to begin. All traces of alcoholic fuzziness were gone. He was stone sober.

"I love you, Brian. I love you a lot more than I was prepared to love anyone. Us—you and I—this whole thing is serious for me. You're not some casual affair for me. And I know I'm not for you. I know how much you've risked for me. But the thing is, I expect my lover to be a person, not a caricature. I need to know who you are.

"I've done a lot of thinking about it," she continued. "Most guys your age have begun to forge their identity. At Annapolis they tested you physically and intellectually, but I think you lack the space you need to stretch, to try out independence. Conformity is king there."

Anger surged defensively. "You don't understand."

"Explain, then. Tell me about it. Why did you go there anyway?"

"I've told you before. My father went there. I love it."

"Do you?"

"Yes."

"What is it that you love about it?"

"The discipline, for starters. The challenge to be the best you can be." He bent forward with his elbows resting on his knees and stared intently at his linked fingers. "Sometimes I see guys my age—guys I went to high school with, for Christ's sake—and they're already out of shape. Some have pot bellies. Twenty-one and they get out of breath running across the street. They're soft. Losers. They wouldn't know a command decision if it hit them in the face."

Her brown eyes concentrated fiercely on him, and for a moment he thought she wasn't going to say anything.

"You know what I think you love? Sometimes I think you like it at Annapolis because you can hide there. Just like you hide behind humor. Anytime anyone is in danger of getting too close to you, you make a joke. You use your humor as a shield. Everyone likes Brian Tyler, but who knows him?"

Her honesty, the sharpness of her perception, bruised him.

"You're dead wrong, Leah. And at least I don't analyze the world to death and bore everyone, Ms. Psychologist."

She ignored the hit. "And when I think about it, Brian, I'm not sure I could ever be part of a Navy life. You've told me how your mother grew to dislike it, how she felt trapped, unable to be herself. I think I'd feel the same way."

"You're going pretty fast, aren't you? Who even asked you to live a Navy life?" He could hurt too.

"Maybe I am going too fast." She met his eyes squarely, and he was the one who had to look away. "Aren't you ever lonely there, Brian?"

"Are you kidding? Lonely with forty-six hundred other guys surrounding me every waking and sleeping moment?"

"It's possible to be lonely in the midst of a million people."

"You know your problem, Leah? You think too much." He suddenly craved a drink, but didn't dare ask for one. He felt confused, and angry. But beneath the anger lurked fear. Could she be right? What had he heard his father say to his mother once? *Stop asking questions. You know the trouble with your questions? There are no answers.*

Maybe there were answers, and he didn't ask the questions because he was afraid of probing too deeply, afraid of the answers. Navy was his home, and he loved it. He'd invested four years there with an obligation for five more. He couldn't back out now. If he was wrong, where did he belong? His father would never get over his disappointment. That was part of the problem too. Sometimes he wished he had an older brother. As an only child he felt the weight of their expectations fully on his shoulders. They were understanding, but even the way they looked at him, the love and pride in their eyes, was their way of letting him know he couldn't fail. He, Brian Tyler, must excel. He was locked in their perception of the perfect son. Well, he wasn't perfect. He felt lost. His only anchor was Leah. She sat silently, a center of calm and peace and honesty. The need for her grew.

"I love it when you do that." Her voice was soft.

"When I do what?"

"That. When you're thinking you touch the tip of your tongue to your upper lip. It's the sexiest thing I've ever seen."

The air, which had been so tense with his resentment, now was galvanized with desire.

"I love you, Brian. I love the way you make people smile. I love the way your chin juts out when you're angry or obstinate. I love the way it feels when you hold me. I love your pride, your strength, the way you believe totally in things like Navy, this country. I guess I'm afraid."

"Of what?"

"Everything. Of getting in so deep I can't get out. Of being lost. I guess I'm afraid because I know if I'm not careful, I could be overwhelmed by this love, and you could walk all over me and I wouldn't have the strength to stop you."

"Oh, Lee, Lee." Her confession defeated him. "I wouldn't do that."

"That's not the point. You could, and I still couldn't walk away. Sometimes I feel like I'm fighting for my life."

"It's my life, too, Leah." He crossed the room to the fireplace and leaned against the mantel. A framed picture of the two of them stood inches from his elbow, and he looked at it with confused eyes. "I have fears, too, Leah. Look at my parents. Do you think I want us to end up like them? I mean, Christ, they were in love once. They were so in love, they couldn't even wait a year to get married. My mother left grad school to marry my father."

"We're not your parents, Bri," she said softly. "We're two different people."

"But they were just as in love as we are, just as much in love, and that's what frightens me. They were so in love, they couldn't wait to get married, then twenty years later, boom, divorce. No warning."

"Was it really such a shock, Bri?"

He shrugged, needing to be honest with her. "I don't know. They had little disagreements. No big shouting matches. My mother isn't a shouter. She just got quiet when my dad got upset. But they seemed happy. Normal. Happier than many couples I've seen. I can only remember one time in my life when they had a real fight. We were living in Virginia then, and my mom went to Washington to march in an antiwar rally. Dad was furious, madder than I'd ever seen him. He accused her of doing it on purpose to make him look bad. But mom didn't back down. She told him it had nothing to do with him. She opposed the war and for once she had to be true to herself."

"What happened?"

"We pulled out of 'Nam." He laughed without humor.

Leah sat without moving, her eyes never leaving Brian's face. "Do you think she was wrong?"

"It's confusing, Lee. I mean my mom's so honest about things, I can see how she felt she had to follow her conscience, but aren't people supposed to give in a marriage?"

"What about us, Bri? Suppose it were us. Would you ask me not to take part in a demonstration?"

"That's what I'm saying, Lee. Does marriage have to be a battleground with one person the winner? It was important for my mom to take a stand, but it hurt my dad. Maybe if she gave in that one time, Dad wouldn't have looked at another woman."

"You don't really believe that, do you?"

"Sometimes. I mean, Christ, it wouldn't have killed her." His voice rose in anger, then broke off abruptly. "God. I sounded just like my father then. Just like him." He looked thoughtful. "You just said you were afraid of being overwhelmed by our love, remember? You were scared I would walk all over you. I wonder if that's what happened to my mother? I wonder if she was afraid she was losing herself—overwhelmed—and that's why she stood up to him?"

Leah's eyes shone with tears, but she stayed silent.

"There are times when I find myself hating my father for what he did to her." His voice was low with guilt. "Her only fault was having integrity, and he walked away from her to marry a woman who is nearly my age. It's damn hard to see the moral principle in that. Damn it, Leah, I don't know who to blame."

"Is it important to assign fault? Your parents were married for more than twenty years. People change in twenty years. They grow. Maybe your mother and father grew apart, stopped sharing and trusting. Perhaps they simply grew tired of trying. There are probably just as many reasons for divorce as there are divorces."

Brian stared at Leah. In her cozy room—with her—he felt wise and mature and sure, far removed from his other half, the first-classman who drank too much and played too hard. "I love you. I'm sorry I had so much to drink tonight. I'm sorry if I embarrassed you in front of Professor Mason. I love you, Leah, and I promise you this: I won't ever stop trying. I'll never walk all over you, and I'll attempt to grow with you, not away from you. I love you more than I have ever loved anyone or anything."

She rose and the lavender coat fell to the floor. He crossed the room to her. He wanted to pick her up, to crush her against him, to carry her to the bed. He wanted to be strong and fierce and have his every move reflect the intensity he felt. With more patience than he had ever shown, he waited. He let her reach for his hand and lead him to her bed. He wanted then, more than anything, to have her truly trust him.

The ride back to the Yard went quickly. Confusion filled him. He flicked on the radio in the 'Vette Keegan had lent him and twisted the dial impatiently, tuning in one station after another, but the fragments of music and news could not rival the worries that flew through his mind. Finally, he turned off the radio and drove the rest of the way in silence.

The closer he came to Annapolis, the more he struggled with himself. He had meant what he told Leah, he did love her, and he wanted them to share everything, to understand each other, to be comfortable in each other's world. He remembered what she had said about Annapolis being a place where one learned to conform. The words rankled. She was wrong about that. She didn't understand. A man *was* tested at Navy, and he learned a lot about himself in the process. Couldn't she see that?

A new, troubling thought took hold, an idea so upsetting, he passed three cars before he realized that the speedometer pointed at eighty. What if she didn't like the Navy because she was jealous? His mother had sometimes been jealous of his father's work. His father had told him that once. Why did women feel so threatened and excluded by it? How the hell could you deal with that?

Annapolis's narrow streets were dark, nearly deserted, and he took the corners sharply, driving carelessly. He was going fast when he turned onto King George, and his right fender almost brushed the slight figure dressed in white. He stamped on the brakes, causing the rear end of the 'Vette to fishtail. He clung to the wheel with sweaty palms and forced himself to look through the windshield at the ghostly outline.

The man he had almost hit grinned foolishly at him. He wore a plebe's cap on top of his tiny, misshapen head, over which he wore a set of earphones so large they completely covered his ears. Brian rolled down the window. Even seated in the car he could hear the tinny sound seeping from the earphones.

"Crabtown," he said sternly. "You okay? Jesus, what the hell are you doing walking around here now?"

His grin widened, and the man the mids called Crabtown Earle drew himself to attention, and holding his elbow high and to the side like a child at a parade, saluted Brian.

Still shaken, Brian rolled the car around Earle. Christ, he'd almost hit him. That had been too close. He wiped his palms on his pant leg. That was all he needed. To kill the village idiot. He'd heard that Earle had a brother—Ray or Roy, something like that—a real tough townie who'd once beaten a mid senseless for ridiculing Earle. He hated to imagine what the man would do to someone who actually hurt his brother.

He passed through the gates onto the Yard, relieved to be home. When he opened the door to his room, he stepped back in surprise. The place was a zoo. Mids leaning against the lockers, sitting on desks, squatting on the floor. Christ, every first-classman in his company was crammed into the narrow room. At once, he saw they were not here to plan a prank. To a man, they were furious. He muffled a curse. He was tired. He wanted only to sink into the rack and pass out, not to fight a herd of indignant midshipmen. From the looks of them, he wouldn't be getting sack time for hours.

Jordan saw him first. "Did you hear?" He was rigid, his lean face dark with anger.

Harrison Keegan, a jock from Texas with a reputation for fast living and a short-fused temper, perched on the edge of his desk. Bri tossed him the keys to the 'Vette. "Thanks, I owe you. Hear what?"

"About Greene?"

"I've been in D.C. I don't know anything about Ariel. Christ, Hog," he shouted at a stocky mid who was leaning against his shelves, "look what you're doing to my shirts. What the hell is going on in here anyway?"

Spider's answer was clipped. "She won't make the tower jump."

The jump was required before a midshipman could graduate. Each of them had done it: felt the gut-wrenching fear as he climbed the spiral stairs to the platform high above the diving pool; inched out to the end of the board, wondering whether it was better or worse to look down, down at the still, deep water, at the large blue N at the bottom of the pool; trembled alone at the edge of the narrow board, enclosed in fear, surrounded by the echo and the faint chlorine smell of the natatorium, and overhead, the cool, unheavenly luminescence of the stark, angular skylight.

Each year there were several mids who were unable to take the final step, the step to nothingness beyond the board. It had to be taken independently, that step, with no allowance made for a helpful shove from a sympathetic classmate. Only the unremitting knowledge that you were washed up—*out*—if you didn't make the jump, proved ultimately stronger than the fear. Piece of cake.

"She'll have to make the jump, just like everyone else."

"No, she won't."

"What are you talking about?"

"Greene got a waiver." Spider's jaw was so tight, the words came out like extruded slots of steel.

"What the hell do you mean, she got a waiver?" No one *ever* got a waiver for anything at Annapolis.

"A waiver, asshole." The pitch of Jordan's voice rose. "She doesn't have to do it."

"That's impossible."

Keegan snorted. The room was hot, filled with the intensity of their anger. "In a pig's ass. Greene got some damn head shrink to come here and testify that because of some childhood trauma, little Greene has a mortal fear of high places. The doc had some pull in Washington and has been making all kinds of noises to a couple of senators." The Texan's drawl was shortened with anger.

Jordan took over the story. "The brass caved in and gave her the waiver. They covered their asses by saying the Water Entry is really only necessary to prepare for jumping off a battleship should the need arise, or some crap like that. Since Greene is a woman and women can't be assigned to duty with the fleet, she doesn't have to meet that standard."

"Jesus."

"I wonder what Stocker Wallace will do when he hears about it?" Two years before, Wallace, an extremely popular first-classman, had washed out because he hadn't made the jump. Just weeks before Commissioning they had given him the word. "I wouldn't want to be around when he fuckin' does."

"Buck was right." Jordan's mouth was tight. He turned his hard, intense stare on his roommates. "You remember, Spider? Bri? At Thanksgiving?" He faced the others. "Buck says his was the last real class of mids. He said since they let women in, we're all pussies."

"He's not the only one to say that," Keegan drawled. He pulled himself up to his full six-feet-three. "You know what the class of '79 had inscribed on the inside of their ring? LCWB." He paused dramatically. "Last Class With Balls."

"I wish to hell we could engrave LCWP on ours. Last Class With Pussy," Hog said.

Jordan's face was tense with resentment. "This isn't the only time the rules have been bent for them. Christ, look what they did last year: every damn mid in the place knows Mendosa didn't deserve to be first. It was all for public relations. A woman and a spick. Two minorities with one stroke. It sure looked good on the evening news."

"That's just talk," Ted Ruley objected faintly. "She earned the grade."

"Like hell," Keegan answered bitterly, slamming shut a book he had picked up from Spider's desk. "Nothing you can prove, but they adjusted her leadership grade. Why do you think they changed the rules and no longer allow peer votes on aptitude? 'Cause they know if we vote, there's no way any of the scum-fucking cunts will score higher than the bottom ten percent on leadership. That's why."

"Come on. They're not all so bad." Ruley's objection was weak.

A faint knock on the door froze the men, cutting reaction off. "Bellows is headed this way," a second-classman urgently whispered from his post in the hall. The room emptied like a sink drained of water.

"She shouldn't be allowed to get away with it." Jordan banged his fist against his desk.

"Easy, roomie."

"Easy, shit. Someone should take her for a swim right now."

"Hold on a minute." The mounting rage he heard in Jordan's voice made Brian uneasy.

"Hold on, hell, Tyler. Do you think it's fair? Christ, it wouldn't matter one bit what *you've* done here or who *your* father is. If you didn't make the Water Entry, you'd be out. Do you think it would make a damn bit of difference what any head doctor said? Damn right, it wouldn't. You'd get an Unsat and be out of here so fast you wouldn't have time to pack a seabag. Right, Spider?"

Webb Garrick was standing at the window, his back to them. He stared out into the night. He had been one of the men in their class who'd had a tough time with the jump. Time and again Brian had seen his tall roommate stand at the edge of the platform, his gangly body slick with sweat, working himself up to take the final step. And time and again, at unknown cost in humiliation and lost pride, Spider had turned and walked back down the metal steps of the tower. Only Spider knew at what cost he had finally made the jump. Brian certainly wouldn't know. The jump had been easy for him. He'd done it as a plebe, the first time he climbed up the tower.

Exhaustion suddenly overwhelmed him, and he began to unbutton his shirt. The whole evening—the drinks, the early argument with Leah, the near accident with Crabtown Earle, the scene in his room with his classmates—seemed distorted. He felt a band tighten around his temples, and walked to the sink for aspirin.

The thing with Greene had sure brought out a lot of unspoken hostilities about women. But by morning, he knew, tempers would cool down. In spite of what had been said in anger, most of the mids accepted females at Navy. It was the old grads who had the real problem with it. Jordan broke into his thoughts.

"Wait'll Buck hears about this. It just proves he was right. Women have turned this place into a pussy pit. You know what the real irony is? Not only did Greene get a waiver, she just cost us each a cool grand."

"What the hell are you talking about?"

"The bet, man. Did you forget about the bet we made with Buck? Well, Greene and her childhood trauma is going to lose it for us. The cunt is the only woman in the top ten percent of our company. The way it looks now, she'll stay there."

Spider kept his back to his roommates, his fists still clenched, his shoulders rigid. His voice, too, was unyielding.

"Maybe not."

"Keep dreaming, Spider."

"No dreaming, man. Maybe she'll make the dive after all."

CHAPTER TEN

Time at the Academy is not measured by the same gauge that governs the outside world. The civilian clock and calendar have no relevance here. Their metronomes beat off no seconds within these walls; their hours, days, weeks, and months flow by on a current that does not traverse this ground.

The parameter of existence here is demarcated by bells and classes, formations and studies, meals and sleep. Thus imprisoned in the timelessness of the Yard, it is possible to hide.

And in this state of timelessness did the days of the Dark Ages pass: December turned to January, and her bitter days gave way to February.

This was not the way Brian had envisioned spending his wedding night. He pushed the book across the surface of his desk and got up, restlessly prowling the narrow space between the beds. What was she doing now? He checked his watch. He had been married exactly five hours. Just five hours ago he had exchanged wedding vows. It was nearly impossible to believe. And here he was, alone in his room in Mother B. while his new bride sat alone in her apartment in D.C., cramming for a psychology exam. Not exactly the way he had thought it would be. He was alone. And he was horny as hell. Cold shower time. A bridegroom's nightmare.

But then the wedding ceremony itself had not exactly been the stuff of which maidens' dreams were spun. Not that Leah had seemed bothered. Remembering her radiant smile, his grim expression softened and he mutely vowed he would make it up to her if it took the rest of his life. She was the one right note in his existence. Everything else was such a mess. He sighed.

"Are you ever lonely at the Academy?"

Here and now, on his wedding night—a dismal and cold

night in late February without the saving warmth of a woman
or the sun—he thought about the intervening weeks since
that night in December when she had confronted him with
that question, and he thought about the events that dragged
on his soul. Yes, he longed to confess to her. Yes, I'm lonely
and afraid and confused. Confused, most of all. Not even
their marriage had provided absolution. He glanced at the
Academy calendar on his desktop. One more week in February. One week until break—and a trip home to Connecticut.
He flipped the calendar pages and counted. He really didn't
need to add them up. There were precisely three more
months until Commissioning Week. Three more months until
he could leave Annapolis behind. For four years he had put
up with and gutted out all the shit they could hand him,
looking forward to that one moment when he became a
graduate of USNA. Three more months and he had it made.

All he had to do was hang on. Hang in there for one week
until he could get home. Hang in there for twelve more
weeks until Commissioning. It sounded so simple—just hang
in, hang on—but he was increasingly aware that he couldn't
do it.

The silence continued to press down on him. Spider was
studying at Nimitz and Jordan had gone into town with
Keegan. Once inseparable, the three roommates were seldom together now. The room was icy with the piercing
bleakness of his isolation.

Yes, he whispered to his absent bride, *I am so alone.* He
had left her just two hours ago, but he needed her now.

"I'm behind you, whatever you decide," she had said when
they parted. He knew it was true, but not even Leah knew
the depth of his problem. She knew only about the part that
related to her. He was too ashamed to share the other with
her.

The Accident. That's how they had referred to it in the
days following the incident. *The Accident.* As if they could
deny their own part in it. God, how did he ever get in so
deep? Would he have married Leah, broken that basic rule at
the Academy, if he hadn't already paved the way by other
erosions of character and truth?

There were too many secrets, he saw that now. Secrets at
the Academy, secrets about Leah—even Leah herself was a
secret, for he had never told his parents about her.

He wondered now why he hadn't. Or at least told his mother. He supposed it was, in part, that he wanted to hold one section of his life private. Once, at home during the Christmas break, he had started to tell her about Leah, but the phone had rung, and by the time she had finished talking to Nina Shaw, the moment for sharing had passed. That one innocent secret had grown into another, more serious and important one: his marriage. Was that the way with deceptions? Did one lead to another until you were trapped in a hideous web of your own making?

Sick with guilt, he thought again about his mother. Fear of hurting her, of disappointing her, had ruled his youth and adolescence. On an inner level he had sensed that his father had made her unhappy, and so he had spent those years trying to live up to the image she had of a son. Or the image as he perceived it, which was one of the perfect son, an offspring who would always make her proud, always measure up. And he always did.

The intensity of her love, her belief in him, frightened him. His secret marriage would hurt her terribly—he dreaded having to see her face when he told her. Had it been a mistake? He and Leah had been over and over it, rejecting the idea one minute, deciding they had no choice the next. Well, it was too late now.

How would he manage to last until May? If he stayed at Annapolis, these remaining weeks would be hardest on Leah, but he knew she would never complain or emotionally black-mail him. After May, after he had walked away from the web, they could start afresh.

Even as he contemplated the idea, he knew he was fooling himself. Deceit and dishonor were not like clothes one wore for a bit and then tossed aside for a more desirable outfit. They were more like skin; one lived with them forever.

Was it possible to unravel the web? He yearned to—the idea struck him like a blow to his heart—he yearned to *like* himself again. Only one person could help him. He realized with surprise that this was not Leah. No, his instinctive turning at this moment was to someone else. He needed his mother. He needed to start with her. He realized suddenly that it was not the Academy alone that had nurtured his sense of honor. Long before he had spoken his Oath in the heavy July air four years ago, she had made it part of his character.

He dug in his desk for a blank sheet of paper. How would he explain the mess he had made of his life? As he began to write, the confusion he had lived with for weeks lessened its grasp, as did the soul-deep struggle for an answer. He knew with stunning insight that no matter how inept his words were, she would understand.

With equally keen intuition and great sadness, he knew his father never would. A memory swam unbidden from the past. He hadn't thought about the incident in years. They had been living in Norfolk, and a friend of his father's had stopped by for a drink. Captain McGreevy. Bud McGreevy. A classmate of his father's at Navy, the captain was a handsome man with a black crewcut, smiling green eyes, and the swagger of a Marine jet pilot. Except he wasn't smiling during this visit. He walked stiffly, legs bowed, and his hands were swathed in bandages.

When his father answered McGreevy's knock, their eyes had locked, and then they had disappeared into the living room, closing the door behind them. His mother, thin-lipped, withdrew to the kitchen. And what had *he* done. His face flamed with shame as he remembered how, knowing he was going to hear something he'd be happier not knowing, he had slipped across the room to the door, straining to hear the muffled voices.

I'm in a world of shit this time, Mike. There's a chance they'll take my wings.

For Christ's sake, stop pacing. Sit down and tell me what happened.

Stupid. It was just such a fucking stupid thing to go. I just can't let them take my wings.

Jesus, Bud. What the hell happened?

It happened at Willow Grove. I was taxiing out when the tower radioed there was an emergency, a bird was coming in with fire warning lights on. I knew there was going to be a hell of a wait, so I shut down and took off my helmet. Turned off the oxygen. Shut down. Ya know. It was hot, hotter than hell, and it looked like the wait was going to be longer than I thought. I don't know. I was just frustrated. I had a pack of smokes in the pocket of my flight suit and I just . . . I just took one out and lit up.

Jesus.

Stupid. I mean, I know it's against regs, but I thought,

what the hell. Then the next thing I know, the flame was shooting up, just shooting up, like a blowtorch. I tried to put it out, but no go. I mean the entire cockpit was ablaze. There must have been an oxygen leak in the mask or something. Some corporal on the ground crew saw what was happening and brought a ladder over and got me out.

Jesus. Are you all right?

Could be worse. Third-degree burns on my hands. Second-degree on my balls and legs.

I always knew you had hot balls.

For Christ's sake, this isn't funny, Mike. They're calling for an investigation.

Does anyone know you were smoking?

I think they might suspect. My CO called me in. Said he didn't know what happened and didn't want to know. Said he knew I was an honest man. Then he said, "There's a time in your life when you got to lie. You hear what I'm saying, Bud? There are times to lie." Other than that, no one's talked to me. What do you think, Mike. What should I do?

You want to keep flying?

Does a whore spread her legs?

I guess what I think is that your CO sounds like a pretty smart guy.

It had been years since that day, yet he could remember every word of the conversation. And remembering, he knew why he wasn't writing to his father. Even if he knew the reasons why he had to leave Navy, about the rules he had broken, his father would try to convince him to stay. *There are times to lie.*

He *was* going to resign. Brian knew that now. What had seemed an impossible thought only minutes before—leaving Navy, walking away from his life, his career, his *Commissioning*—had become not only right but inevitable. His letter reclaimed his attention. His fingers tightened on the pen as he reread the first sentence and then relaxed. Perhaps in writing those words his hand had been subconsciously guided by the true, deep part of himself that he wanted to be again. He prayed that he had the courage to hold on to that part of him while he tried to explain the events of the past months to his mother. Previewing the words, he caught a glimpse of the anguish he would cause her. Never in twenty-one years had he knowingly hurt her. He bent his head, fighting tears. Then he continued to write.

Jordan stood in the corridor and from the doorway watched his roommate. He shifted from foot to foot, suddenly hesitant to enter his own room. Whatever it was that Jordan and Spider and Bri had shared, they each knew it was now inexorably destroyed. He watched as Brian finished the letter and sealed it in an envelope, then, still silent, he walked through the doorway. Their greetings were subdued and they avoided each other's eyes.

"Where's the Spider?"

"Over at Nimitz."

"He's getting to be a geek. He shoulda come out with us." The smell of stale beer emanated from Jordan.

Brian fiddled with his pen. He had planned to wait until both of his roommates were there before he told them of his decision, but having written it to his mother, the telling became easier, and he didn't want to wait anymore.

"I just finished writing to my mother. I'm quitting."

Shock stained Jordan's face, then he laughed. "Very funny, Cow." He had not called him that for a very long time.

"I'm not joking. I'm going to hand in my resignation." He wanted to shock Jordan, realizing then that he still blamed him for the other thing. He pushed the thought away.

"What are you, buzzed?"

"I'm not the one who has been drinking." The tone was getting hot, and he worked to defuse it. "Leah and I got married today."

An expression of relief flashed across Jordan's handsome face. "So that's it. For Christ's sake, Bri. You're not quitting 'cause you got married, are you? Two dumbass moves do not make a smart one."

"It's not just that." His voice was very quiet.

Jordan ignored the warning. "Because you don't have to throw it all away for that. What is she, knocked up?"

Anger flared, then wearily he rubbed his hand across his eyes. "Midshipmen can't be married, you know that."

"Sure. Everyone knows that. Everyone also knows that there are at least two hot-pants segundoes who are married, and I can name you three firsties who have wives. One has a kid a year-and-a-half old. Hell, even their CO's know it. It happens all the time. They just close their eyes and pretend it doesn't exist. Christ, Bri, one of the guys was even counseled by his company officer. The guy as much as told him to get married if his girl held his feet to the fire."

Brian studied him. It was the first time in weeks that he had really looked at Jordan, and he was surprised to see that his shoes were scuffed and the top of his cap was dirty. "It's breaking the Honor Concept. Why have rules if they don't mean anything?"

"Oh God, Tyler, grow up. Does it really matter a gnat's fart if a mid is married? Will it make him a less effective officer?" Jordan crossed to put his cap on the shelf. Even in anger he displayed an officer's poise.

Brian tossed down the pen. "That's not all."

Something in his face must have alerted Jordan: he saw a flicker of fear set in. "It's the other thing. What we did in December. I can't live with that."

"You're leaving because of *that*? Are you insane?" He pivoted toward Brian. "And they'll ask why you're leaving. What are you going to say? Are you going to tell them that too?" Brian's silence enraged him. "Christ, don't be a fool. The stupid little bitch covered up, didn't she? We're home free. Why fuck it up? You wouldn't do that, would you?"

Brian didn't reply. He really didn't have an answer yet.

"Because that's a different story. I mean if you want to put your ass on the line, that's your business. I think you're crazy, but it's your tail. But if you go mouthing off, you'll bring Spider and me down too. Did you ever consider *that* while you were sitting around jerking off to glorious thoughts of *your* honor, Tyler?"

Brian accepted the anger. He understood it. That was part of his problem. His decision affected everyone he touched: His father. His mother. His grandfather. Spider. Jordo. Keegan. Leah. Eventually all his classmates. The list went on, a roster of innocent victims. There was no way to contain it. It was like crewing in Dorsey Creek. When an oar entered the water, the effect of the motion rippled out, spreading until it touched the distant shores on either side.

For an instant he faltered. Did he have a right to do this? The focus was too wide to consider, and he narrowed it. Leah. His parents. His grandfather. They were the most important ones, and he knew suddenly that each of them loved him, and he would have to trust the strength of their love. Even his father would have to understand.

He remembered a conversation with his grandfather before he left for the Academy four years before. "Sometimes you will have to make a decision that is difficult, and you'll be torn. But every man, Brian, has a moral detector inside, and it's situated right smack in the center of his gut. If you trust what that detector is telling you, no matter how much your mind will argue differently, you will make out all right. A man's mind can turn on him, seduce him with the smoothest passage, but his inner detector never will."

A sweeping sense of relief overtook him, and his fingers unclenched. His grandfather was right. It was that easy. Whatever the consequences, he now knew what he had to do.

"My mind's made up. I'm leaving."

Jordan stared at him with hatred. "You prick," he said. Then he pivoted and left the room.

Brian sat for a long time, staring at the envelope addressed to his mother. After a while he opened the desk drawer and searched until he found a stamp. He licked it and placed it precisely in the corner of the envelope, noticing the imprinted crest with an appreciation for the ironic. This was the last time he would ever use the stationery of Annapolis. He walked down to the mail drop and pushed it through the slot without a moment's hesitation. When he walked back to his room, his shoulders were held proud, straight even for a mid. He heard someone call his name but did not stop. He wanted to be alone. The crippling shame that he had lived with for ten weeks was gone at last. He had never felt more like a man.

The sounds of male laughter, spiced with mild curses and the high-pitched, laserlike noises of the games, spilled out of the video room at Dahlgren and filled the phone booth where Jordan sat.

His hands trembled as he dropped change into the slot. He fidgeted, counting the rings impatiently. "Answer, damn you," he whispered. "Answer." He did not dare to think of what he would do if no one was there. On the tenth ring the receiver was picked up.

"Buck? It's me, Jordan." He heard the panic in his words.

Buck's voice was sleepy. "Yo, little brother. What's up?"

"I have to see you, Buck. I need you. I don't know what to do." The words came faster, shot through with fear. It seemed as if all his life he had been repeating these words to his brother. "I'm in trouble, Buck. I'm in real bad trouble." Horrified, but incapable of controlling himself, Jordan began to cry.

CHAPTER ELEVEN

In early evening the living room grew chilly, but Kate did not rise to push up the thermostat. Five days had passed since the funeral, four since her visit to the police and hearing that Michael was an expectant father, but her pain had not lessened. She was exhausted, not only by the lack of sleep, but by the inner struggle that had waged during each night. *Accept.* That was the advice she had received from Nina. From Michael. From the administration at Annapolis. Accept Brian's death. Accept that he had taken his own life.

Accept? When every fiber of her heart and mind and soul rejected the very idea of his suicide? Couldn't they understand that it was impossible for her? Couldn't anyone understand? Brian would not kill himself. There had to be another explanation. There *had* to be.

"Accept the reality of this," John Stocker had advised, not unkindly. Stocker, a physics teacher at Lanchester, had lost a child three years ago, a lovely girl who had died when her car was hit head on by a pickup truck, the driver of which had been drunk. When Stocker had learned of the death, he'd driven over to visit Kate. He had listened to her, held her, wept with her, and when she'd repeated her belief that her son could not have killed himself, she had seen her pain and sorrow reflected on his face.

Accept reality. Whose reality? she wondered. For her, reality was the knowledge that Brian could not have committed suicide.

A sound of the door bell cut through her thoughts. It was a faint ring, as if the person on the porch, poised to run, had barely brushed the button with a fingertip. As she rose to answer, it rang again, stronger this time, with firmer purpose.

The young woman waiting on the steps was tall and pretty and faintly familiar. Kate had the nagging sense that she knew her. The girl was not one of her students, but probably someone from the college. She didn't conceal her irritation at the intrusion. What could she possibly want? Why was she bothering her? "Yes?"

"Mrs. Tyler?"

"Yes." Her impatience grew stronger.

The girl cut short the words she'd been about to speak. She was the same height as Kate. Their eyes were level, the girl's blazing with a nameless emotion while she stood silently, waiting. *Waiting*. Kate froze, fighting a desire to close the door, to shut out the wordless plea. They stood immobile for no more than five seconds, but in those silent, strangely charged moments, Kate studied the young woman's face with an intensity that surprised her, drinking in every detail—the tiny mole on the right earlobe, the subtle makeup expertly applied except for a tiny smudge of mascara on the left lid (had the hand that applied it been shaking?), the thick hair pulled back in a severe knot which should have made her look older but didn't, the faint pulse beat throbbing wildly in her temple, the bruising hurt that marked the lovely face as clearly as a birthmark. This vulnerability both touched and alarmed Kate.

Even while she studied the stranger, she knew that she was being scrutinized. She felt as much as saw the hunger in the girl's penetrating gaze. The words were out of her mouth even before she was aware her mind had formed the thought.

"You knew Brian."

The girl didn't answer—didn't have to, the answer was in her eyes—and Kate stepped back, drawing her into the house. Silently she stood to one side and watched as the girl looked around, her gaze darting about, drinking in everything. *So this is where he lived*.

"Yes," Kate murmured, aware even as she whispered the word that the girl had not spoken, that she had *heard* only the girl's thoughts. She reached behind her back and closed the door with trembling hands. She crossed the hall and entered the living room, pausing to push up the thermostat and turn on another lamp. The girl followed and sat down on the sofa.

Kate sank to the place beside her. All small talk had been circuited. "How did you know Brian?" she began.

"I met him last summer. In Washington."

Suddenly Kate remembered the photograph of Brian and his roommates in D.C. with three girls, and she understood why the girl had looked familiar. Unable to stop herself, she reached over to hold the girl's hand, cupping it between her own, as if by doing so she was able in some way to touch part of her son. This girl—this woman—had *known* Brian, dated him, laughed with him. Kate felt her hunger grow. It filled her with its craving, a great and greedy voracity that she had to batter down so as not to frighten the girl away. *She needed to talk about her son*. She knew her fingers were tightening around the girl's slender hand, and she willed them to relax. But she did not let go, would not let go of this link to Bri. Before she could begin to ask her questions, the girl spoke.

"Mrs. Tyler, my name is Leah." She paused, searching Kate's eyes, and what she saw there caused the flicker of hope to die in her own. "He never mentioned me, did he?"

In her own need to talk about her son, Kate didn't hear the pain in the girl's voice. "I'm sure—" she began.

"Mrs. Tyler," Leah broke in. "Brian and I—Oh God, I wish I knew a better way to tell you."

"Tell me what?" She should have known. Much later she wondered why she hadn't known. Wondered why the eerie telepathy she shared with the girl had failed her at that moment.

Now it was Leah's fingers that squeezed and held. "Brian and I are—" Her voice broke on the verb. "... were. Brian and I were married."

Kate pulled her hands back, as if they had been burned. Shocked. Yes. That was how she felt. She had received an electric shock; live juice had jumped from Leah's hand into her body, a current of such jolting, galvanic force that it flowed through every inch of her flesh and bone and blood. She felt it to the roots of her hair, to her toes, which had curled inside her shoes. She wanted to denounce the girl, deny her words, turn her from her home, but before she could move, Leah spoke again, and her words stunned Kate, causing her to sink back to the sofa, stilling her.

"They told me he killed himself, but I know he wouldn't do it. I know Brian and I just know he wouldn't do it." The girl looked at her, and Kate was moved to tears by the pain she saw in the other's eyes. "Jordan told me. He called me and told me that Brian was dead. He said it was my fault. And for a while I believed him. Nothing made sense, and he seemed so sure I was to blame. That's why I couldn't come for the funeral. Do you understand? But Jordan is wrong. Brian might have been guilty about lying and about dishonoring the Academy's code, but he felt good about us. He was so happy. We had so much to live for. I know he wouldn't leave me." Even while she spoke, Leah's hands fell to her stomach, pressing against the rough wool of her coat and the faint swelling it concealed. Her voice grew surer, stronger, and suddenly Kate caught a glimpse of her strength. It was the last time she would think of Leah as a girl. "He wouldn't leave me," Leah continued, "and I know he wouldn't leave our baby."

Long after Leah had finally gone, Kate sat in the silent room, reliving the scene, recalling every word, exhausted by the confusion that gripped her. Before Leah had gone, Kate had embraced her, consoled her, whispered words she could not even remember now. But only her shell had performed these functions. Kate—the real Kate—had withdrawn to an interior fortress, needing time.

She needed more than time. She needed her son. The need—to see him, touch him, hold him—was a hunger so severe, she was almost mad with it. It was worse, more consuming by far, than it had been the day she had stood by the steel gurney in the mortician's lab and taken his dead body into her arms.

Led by this desire, she crossed to the hall and climbed the stairs. She opened the door to his room and went in, bracing herself before the brutal knife blade of memories could sink in. The door had only been shut for days, but already it seemed to her that it smelled musty. She concentrated instead on the scent of her son. At the closet she reached for a shirt hanging there and balled up the fabric, dropping her face into it.

Cotton was no substitute for flesh and blood, memories no surrogate for physical contact. She wandered around his room, hungering, nearly crazed with the need to be close to him. She sat on the bed, running her hands over the smooth spread. The wad of his gum, embedded with the imprint of his teeth, was still on the bed stand. Without thinking, she picked it up put it in her own mouth, holding it there as it grew soft from her own saliva.

Leah is right, she thought. (Oh, how she resented admitting the other woman into her thoughts, into this room, but she pushed the resentment aside.) Brian did not kill himself. There is another explanation. The strength of this conviction surged through her blood. It propelled her down the stairs, to the phone in the study.

"Nina? It's me, Kate. No, I'm fine. I just wanted to call and tell you that I'm going away tomorrow. No, not to my father's. To Annapolis. Oh, Nina, I just had to talk to you. I'm positive that Bri didn't kill himself. I'll tell you about it in the morning before I leave. I'm going to find out why he died." Her voice was reedy with excitement.

Across the wire, Nina murmured caution, concern, but Kate shook it off joyously.

"What? No, I'm fine. Really. No. Absolutely not. I am absolutely not going to call Michael. No, don't come over. I'm tired and it's late. Listen, I'll call you in the morning before I go."

Hanging up before Nina could protest, she swiftly made a list of everything she had to do before she left. The college would just have to understand that she needed a leave of absence. She'd have Nina pick up the mail, check the house.

When the phone rang it was well after midnight.

"Kate? Are you all right?" Michael's tone was crisp, almost formal.

She masked her surprise. "I'm fine."

"Listen, could I see you tomorrow? We need to talk."

"Not tomorrow. I'm going away."

"So Nina was right. You have got some crazy idea of going to the Academy."

"She called you?"

"Kate? Kate, listen. You can't help Brian. He's dead. I know you're angry with me, and that you're hurt because of Wendi and our baby. Maybe I should have waited to tell you. I don't blame you if you're hurt. I don't know, maybe I can understand how you must feel. . . ."

Can you? Can you really, Michael?

"But the thing is, you can't go down there. You'll only hurt yourself. Can't you see that? I'm not talking about how all this affects me, Kate, because I know you don't care about that."

"I have to go. Bri didn't kill himself. Do you understand? I *know* it." She paused, trying to find the way to tell him about Leah, about Brian's secret marriage, his unborn child, but Michael cut her off.

"Kate, you have to stop this. People are beginning to worry about you. Do you know what I'm saying? You are beginning to sound irrational. For God's sake, get a grip on yourself."

Kate hung up, cutting off his words. Still hurting because of Nina's disloyalty, she dialed before she had time to think. "Nina, this is Kate." She heard Nina's sharp intake of breath at the chill in her voice. "You had no right to phone Michael. I trusted you, Nina. You had absolutely no right. No, I don't want to talk about it tomorrow. No, I haven't changed my mind. I'm still going to the Academy."

Tomorrow—no, it was after midnight—today, she would go to Annapolis. And this time she would not leave until she had the answers. This time she would not let her son down.

PART II
HONOR

Brothers all in honor,
as in one community,
Scholars and gentlemen.

Wordsworth

CHAPTER TWELVE

The seasons generate their own sounds at the Yard.

Each sound is so completely a measure of its own month and time that years later it will kinesthetically elicit for a graduate the memory of that season, cutting to the most central part of his being with such profound recollections of sights and sounds and feelings that for one terrifying, extraordinary moment he becomes again a mid.

In memory, the undercurrent of summer is soft. It is the harmonic buzz of lawn mowers as hypnotic as the droning of a P-51's engine. It is the soothing "kvik-kvik" of dusty-dark barn swallows as they bank on long slim wings, soaring gracefully from their nests beneath the copper roof of the Robert Crown Center to skim the riffled surface of the basin waters. And in Santee Basin it is the ringing carillon created by riggings as they chime against aluminum masts.

But against this symphony of summer is—always—another song: the harsh and screaming cadence of platoons of plebes as they march double-time around and across the Yard. They file out of Bancroft and across the courtyard of yellow bricks worn smooth by the soles of their shoes and traverse the Yard: behind Halsey; down Stribling and Porter, Buchanan and Decatur; beside Santee Basin; up and down the length of Farragut and Dewey. From dawn to dusk they march, and the air resounds with their cadenced echo, the shouted words a brazen disguise for the fear, anger, and despair that huddle within the heart and gut, but a vocalization as well for borning, spring-green buds of pride.

Eyes dead ahead, feet devouring miles of grass and concrete and macadam, with mindless precision the plebes trot double-time. They march to the tune of "Jesus Christ Superstar," and as each accented syllable escapes their lips, their left feet hit the ground as one.

Don't look down,
Tip your head,
Gotta be proud
Or you'll be dead.

Long after the platoon has passed, the hot, humid air holds
their words.

I want to be free,
But freedom isn't free.
It's gotta be bought
By you and me.

There is no escape from the heat of July and August; one
wears it like skin. It brings with it a lush decadence that
contrasts sharply with the austerity of Academy life. There is
no air-conditioning at the Academy, except in the mid store
and King Hall. And in the museum, where, amid desiccating
documents and ancient naval paraphernalia, sweating mids
stand and drink in the frigid air in stolen moments.

Summer is hell on the complexion. A glance in the mirror
confirms that sweat has brought on acne. The sign of a plebe:
zits, shorn head, desperate eyes. And a voice grown hoarse
from screaming. Yes, sir. Yessss, sir. YESSS, SIR.

That is summer at the Yard.

If the days of summer seem endless, autumn is too brief.
Its sounds are sharp and decisive, full of pride and power,
like the tattoo of drums on Worden Field. In autumn the
full Brigade returns, home to answer the call of the bells,
and the whistles shrieking at Farragut and Halsey, bells
and whistles that exhort them: to do more, try harder, run
faster.

From his post opposite Bancroft Hall, the scowling bronze
Tecumseh watches another fall begin, his noble face as fiercely unforgiving of weakness as any first-classman's could be.
But if a plebe, while rushing by on his constant treadmill of
classes and come-arounds, formations and inspections, dares
to raise his eyes, he perceives there a promise: he will
survive.

Of all the seasons on the Severn, fall is the most fitting to
house the midshipmen.

Winter? Winter is death. The wind screams as it tears in from the bay, bringing on its gray breath a hint of arctic ice. Around the Yard, naked trees stand like a coven of witches, and on either side of Turner Joy and Santee roads, the first-classmen's sleek and sporty cars are draped against the ice and snow and windborne salt, their fitted tarpaulins worn like shrouds.

Inside the granite and brick walls of Bancroft, the corridors echo with the pent-up voices of the mids as they yell their frustration. It is the Dark Ages.

In winter, even the drums lose their ability to lift the spirit, and the bells seem to knell, an ominous and mournful sound. The heat of summer is remembered with a false fondness, and the heart aches for April.

Spring begins with softness. Like wakening animals, the midshipmen stretch. Blood sings in their veins. Anything is possible. Victory is theirs. The vernal roundelay builds to a crescendo.

The drums are joyous now, the cadences triumphant. In the annual rite of recognition plebes scream in exultation as, torsos bare and glistening with Crisco and sweat, they scale the greased granite obelisk of Herndon to remove the cap placed there by first-classmen. By tradition, the first plebe to wrest the cap free will be the first in his class to make admiral.

For the first-classmen spring marks the end of the four-year tour. The parades, numbing spectacles of paralyzing boredom; the fears and deprivations; exams and summer cruises; the trials and successes end in the final moment at the stadium as they are commissioned. They shout their jubilation as, in their own ritual of passage, they send grease caps soaring into the air. One epoch is over in their lives. Another begins.

At that moment their class history begins to be written. In each mid's mind the four years become a mixture of fiction and reality, of what really happened and what he will later recall, recollections perceived through the imperfect scrim of a memory influenced by pride and tradition.

Spring is Sousa, and Wednesday, dress parades on Worden. In the chapel it is Wagner and Mendelssohn, as hour on the hour, each day for nearly two weeks, young couples exchange their wedding vows, then dash out from the chapel, ducking beneath an arch of benign and shining swords held aloft by the groom's smiling comrades. The brides wear virginal gowns; the grooms, in full dress, more resplendent than they. After months of denial, they are legally joined together. How many of them have married, coerced into wedlock by the magnet of tradition, the thrill of passing beneath that arch of swords, so that they can later say they had wed during Commissioning Week at Annapolis? But for now it does not matter. Their youthful faces glow with love and hope. The music and the marches and the glorious drums drown out everything else.

That is spring at the Academy.

But in the grip of winter it is hard to remember that spring will come, as difficult as it is in the middle of a black, interminable night to believe that dawn will surely break and that the insurmountable horrors that plague the heart and mind at two A.M. will by morning become insignificant.

CHAPTER THIRTEEN

It seemed to Webb Garrick that he would never escape the nightmare of this winter's deathly grip. Even as he descended from Bancroft and took the wind full in his face like a slap, he felt its imprisonment.

The tall, homely midshipman walked alone across T-Court, his gait the rapid, purposeful stride one learns as a plebe and never totally forgets, so that always—on liberty, with drags, everywhere, and long after he leaves the Academy—a mid seems engaged in a footrace. He passed classmates, nodding, but not attempting to join them. He was always alone now.

He proceeded down Stribling, heading toward Nimitz. The carrels in the library would be filled with midshipmen seeking refuge from the winter claustrophobia encountered in Mother B. He wondered if the engineers who had designed the library had factored into their computations the added poundage of the Dark Ages, when an uncommonly high number of mids studied there. Probably not. Probably the place sank more than the rumored inch per year. Typical Navy screwup, Nimitz Library.

The brass tried to hush it up, denying it, but the truth was that the architects and engineers who designed the building nearly two decades before had neglected to compute the weight of its 800,000 volumes when designing the library. The result was that the building settled into the earth at the rate of an inch a year. An inch a year!

Webb loved it. As a plebe he had been ordered by an upperclassman to stand on his chair before the entire Brigade in King Hall and quote from "Reef Points." He had amused them all with his brisk delivery. "The library has all the best features and services that one could expect to find in a contemporary college library," he announced. "It is located between Maury Hall and Rickover Hall," adding with the right touch of solemn dignity, "and should be observed before the year 2500, when it will disappear entirely." Word had come down from his company officer that he should cease his tour-guide act.

The brass did not like to talk about that inch per year. Of course, blame had been affixed to the civilians. "Cover your ass" was the maxim at Navy.

The March wind cut into his bare, bent neck. He turned up the collar of his reefer. Overhead the sky was steel gray, threatening another storm. Ahead of him, a group of midshipmen stood in a huddle, laughing and pointing up at the spire of the chapel. He knew what they were staring at. He had heard about it at breakfast. Dully he looked up to the top of the dome, one hundred ninety-two feet up. He'd had to learn that when he was a plebe, along with hundreds of other useless facts and words. Even now, four years later, if quizzed he could respond correctly: there are four hundred eighty-nine panes of glass in the skylight of Memorial Hall; the Japanese Monument at the north end of Luce Hall was presented to the Academy by the family of the late Japanese Ambassador Hirosi Saito, who died in Washington on February 26, 1939. Yes, Webb Garrick was a friggin' encyclopedia of USNA history.

Impaled on the tip of the spire a midshipman's cap, startlingly white, hung suspended against the winter sky, a lone celestial mote. He heard they were going to have to hire a steeplejack to get the thing down.

A friggin' steeplejack, for Christ's sake. He wondered who had put it there. The Dark Ages.

Last week a cadre of engineering students in Twenty-third Company had lowered the Neptune biplane that hung from the ceiling of Dahlgren, setting the yellow craft on the oval dance floor. They had painted the fat pontoons of the N3N with blue N's for Navy. Admin had screamed about that one. The Admiral himself appeared in the dining hall to deliver a lecture about respect for property and tradition.

Once, such pranks would have delighted Webb and acted as a stimulous, prodding him to even more outrageous deeds before his place as chief prankster was endangered. Now it no longer seemed to matter. The difference, he knew, was Brian Tyler.

Suddenly he detoured from his path to Nimitz and walked

swiftly toward Dorsey Creek, driven by the need to be alone. Really alone.

Each midshipman, early in his four years at the Yard, finds a place to which he can escape. Some find it outdoors. They walk along the seawall that flanks Farragut, or on the river-banks by Dewey Field. Others seek seclusion inside, in the hushed surroundings of the chapel or, perhaps, the space beneath the rotunda, where they stand by the crypt of John Paul Jones and soak in their surroundings, silent except for the hollow, measured footsteps of the lone Marine sentry as he circles the sarcophagus.

The most popular spot for the midshipman seeking solitude was Memorial Hall. The soul of Bancroft Hall, it is dedicated to those graduates who lost their lives while serving their country. Traditionally, it was supposed to be the most sacred spot on campus for midshipmen, but Webb avoided it. To him it felt haunted, the home of ghosts who asked him for more than he had to give.

Long ago, his search for solitude had led him to the Academy cemetery. There, passing among the graves of midshipmen who had died while at the Academy and those of admirals and other officers who had served their country, he read Navy's history, studying the simple stones as closely as he did the garishly ornate ones. Engraved in slabs of marble and granite and sandstone, were Celtic crosses and Roman ones, the etched wings of aviators and the dolphins of subma-riners. Beneath the giant elms Webb could stand and look back at the Yard, down on the playing fields and handsome copper-roofed buildings tinged green with age. Here he could try to gain perspective.

This afternoon he stepped off the paved drive and walked onto the grave sites. The ground was firm beneath his feet, holding the frost of winter. He knew by heart most of the grave sites. He knew where those who had been lost with the *Huron* in 1877 were buried: the grouping of slender shafts of sandstone standing in their memory were identical. There were names on some, but many more bore the legend: *Unknown*.

He could not shake off the feeling of desolation that had aged him a decade in the past few months. In front of him he saw the familiar tomb for the two midshipmen who had died in 1904 during target practice on the battleship *Missouri*.

Killed during training. He bet there had been hell to pay for that one. Now Midshipmen Ward and Neumann lay interred beneath one stone. Webb wondered if they had been friends. Perhaps, in life, they had not even liked each other. Now, in a cruel and cosmic joke, they would spend eternity together, closer than husband and wife.

His shoes were getting wet. The mud was making a mess of the leather, and he'd have to spend hours reclaiming his shine, but still Webb did not return to the pavement. He moved on, reading the epitaph of each stone he passed. Some were for mids who had died before their years at the Academy had ended, the stones erected in their memory by their classmates. It would have been nice to have done that for Bri, he thought. But Brian was not here. His mother had not wanted him buried at the Yard. Webb regretted that but understood why Kate Tyler refused to allow her son to lie here, knowing that she blamed Annapolis for his death.

He missed Brian terribly. He missed Bri's humor, his kindness, his courage and companionship. He grieved for him, but his grief was neither pure nor healing, for it was bound too closely with guilt.

He stopped in front of one modest stone. "Do not stand at my grave and cry," he read. "I am not here. I did not die."

Noble words, but lies. You *were* born, and you died before your twenty-first birthday. What loves and hates, disappointments and betrayals lay beneath the soil of this graveyard, secreted in the earth with decaying bones and flesh? As if drawn by magnetic ground, he pivoted and walked across the grass, heading toward a single stone. When he reached it, he stood silently, reading, perhaps for the hundredth time, the words carved in stone: THEODORE ELLYSON; COMMANDER; NAVAL AVIATOR #1; 1885–1928; DIED AT SEA.

He stared at the epitaph with a mixture of hurt and hunger and confusion. All Webb Garrick's life, for as long as he could remember, he had wanted to be a pilot. A jet jock. One of the chosen who climbed into a molded seat on top of engines capable of thousands of pounds of thrust and was shot off into the air, screaming through the clouds at 700, 800, 900 mph.

When other boys in his class in Hamilton, Ohio, had been reading box scores and memorizing the batting averages of Johnny Bench and Joe Morgan and Pete Rose, Webb immersed himself in the legend and lore and statistics of pilots and the planes they flew. While his best pal could quote Tony Perez's times at bat for the season, the number of bases on balls and extra bases he had accredited to his name, Webb knew the life stories of Claire Chennault, Joe Foss, Pappy Boyington, and Chuck Yeager.

At the first whisper of a telltale drone from the sky, he would crane his neck, and long before his friends could even catch sight of it, would shout, "F-18." He could recognize by their silhouettes the F-4's and A-4's and F-106's. The names of all military planes—Skyhawk, Tomcat, Harrier, Phantom, Starfighter—were like the powerful words of a wizard, part of a mysterious incantation that promised everything.

One day when he was nine, risking his father's wrath and a whipping, he had skipped school and taken a bus into Cincinnati to see an air show by the Blue Angels, the Navy's precision flying team. Entranced, he had stared into the heaven, watching their sleek, delta-winged A-4's maneuver, the midnight-blue jets almost black against the pale sky. His neck ached from bending back and a spasm grabbed hold of his muscles down into his shoulders, but he was never tempted to look down.

With a yearning in his heart so great that it bordered on pain, he witnessed the rolls, the low passes and sky bursts, the heart-stopping aerobatics flown in formations so tight the aircraft seemed in danger of brushing wing tips. And once when two jets flew over the field, one inverted over the other, just inches apart, so that each appeared to be a mirror image of the other, tears came into his eyes at the beauty, the sheer perfection of it.

After the show was over, he hung around, getting as close to the magnificent planes as he could, drinking in the presence of the pilots. The girdles of their g-suits revealed trim torsos, the fitted jumpsuits stretched over buttocks as taut as those of ballet dancers and disappeared into polished boots. He studied their rolling, cocky gait which was so much like a cowboy's, a swagger that bordered on arrogance except that it was backed up by the truth of their masterful performance in the sky. Theirs was the alpha chapter of a fraternity that celebrated maleness, power, and mystery, a fellowship that danced on the razor's edge. Even their ground crew walked with that characteristic swagger. When he got home, in his bedroom, he tried to mimic their stride, knowing with swift sadness that even if he perfected the walk, he would not belong to the fraternity.

That hour he knew his destiny. He would be a naval aviator. One proud day he would wear on his chest the gleaming wings of a pilot. He pursued that dream like a man possessed. He worked through high school to be the best, determined to win a nomination to Annapolis. Even there he did not stop. From the first day of Plebe Summer, unlike many of his classmates, he knew where he was headed, his choice for service selection preordained.

And now he was so close. He could almost reach out and touch the dream, touch it as if it were the wings etched in front of him on Ellyson's stone. In weeks he would be joining the fraternity of fighter pilots. He would be heading toward Pensacola to begin flight training, two months away from the dream born twelve years before on a dusty Cincinnati afternoon on the tarmac of an airfield. So close. So damn close to being able to wear those gold wings. He wanted it so much it was like an incarnate hunger.

He stared at Ellyson's grave. If he could have asked one thing of the man who lay silenced there, it would have been this: *Tell me what to do*.

With all his soul Webb Garrick wanted to believe that, if tested, he would do the right thing. He longed to be worthy of the heavy gold ring he wore on his hand. Corny, but true. He believed in the principles and philosophy of the Academy, believed in the Oath and the Concept of Honor.

But what if he chose now to operate on the Concept of Honor? If he talked, told what he knew, what then? Would it serve a purpose or would he simply be sacrificing himself, his dream? The questions that had plagued him for weeks demanded answers. His head ached with confusion.

What would be the sense? One tragedy had already provoked another. There was no sense in becoming yet another victim in a string. Let it stop here, reason said. If he kept quiet, he would graduate in two months. The price of honor was too great for him to pay.

This time the cemetery had brought him no peace. With an aching heart he headed back toward Fitch Bridge, walking straight into the wind, wishing with the intensity of a child that things would go back to the way they had been before.

It was way too late for that. Keenly, he felt regret. Dampness had seeped through the thin leather of his shoes, and he decided to return to Bancroft and change them. His teeth chattered from the cold and he quickened his steps, almost moving double-time down Stribling Walk. He was crossing in front of the chapel when he heard her call his name.

He froze for a second, unbelieving, and barely moving his head, chanced a swift glance toward the steps to his right. A quick look was all he needed. It was she. Again she called his name, but Webb pretended not to hear and jogged on, almost running. He inhaled the chilly air in ragged breaths. What was she doing here? Why would she come back?

As if pursued by death, the midshipman with the thinning blond hair ran from these questions and from Katherine Tyler, the woman who had called his name.

CHAPTER FOURTEEN

Again and again during the afternoon Jordan found himself watching his roommate. The big man seemed to be operating in a fog, going through the motions. In squash practice Spider endured without a sign of emotion the coach's dressing down for not giving the match his total effort. In King Hall he just sat at the table and picked at the food on his plate. The menu was steak and french fries, creamed corn, rolls and butter, cherry cheese pie, milk, and coffee—a portion of the midshipman's daily 4500 calories. Normally Spider would have eaten every bite. Jordan watched as he poked at the meat with his fork, and his disquiet grew.

After dinner they silently returned to their room to study. Across the expanse of two desktops he directed fleeting glances at Spider. Webb was hunched over his book, staring blindly at the page open in front of him.

As his uneasiness grew, so did Jordan's desire to talk to Webb, to break the icy silence that enveloped them. But the gap between them, born first of guilt and fear, had grown so large, so yawning, that it was now nearly impossible to ford. They had arrived at this silent state by a mutual, unspoken agreement. Too much had occurred to pretend everything was the same.

They avoided each other, seeing in the mirror of the other's face what each could not bear to confront in his own. They never talked about Brian. Suddenly, so abruptly that Jordan jumped, Webb spoke.

"I saw Bri's mother today. She's here."

"Are you sure it was her?" Jordan stared across at Webb. His eyes were guileless, his voice steady. Whatever emotion this news had provoked within, he kept it hidden.

"I looked right at her. It was her."

"Did she see you?"

"Why the hell would she come here? What does she want?"

Jordan pushed back the desk chair and stood. He swore softly and walked to the closet. He took out his uniform shoes, the can of Pledge, and the soft, lintless cloth he kept for this purpose, and began polishing. The attention was unwarranted. The patina was already flawless, a shine any plebe in the Brigade would surrender a weekend liberty to have. But he worked on them now as if he had just waded through a field of mud.

"Did she see you?"

"I don't know. I guess so. She called my name, but I . . . I ran." The confession was pulled from his soul.

"Christ." Jordan tossed the cloth down on the desk in disgust. He had almost shouted the word, and instinctively looked toward the open door, then back at his roommate, lowering his voice. "There could be a dozen good reasons why she came back, but now she's probably wondering why you ran away. Really smart. For Christ's sake, Spider."

Webb did not answer. He sat looking out toward the window, the dark shut out by the closed blinds. Involuntarily his gaze dropped to the stripped cot. The third empty bed.

He brought his hand to his mouth. The flesh around the thumbnail was ragged, and he chewed at it absently. All his nails had been bitten down to the quick.

"Look, Spider," Jordan said. "I didn't mean that." He crossed the room and pulled his desk chair closer to Webb. His voice lost its harshness, becoming softer, more Southern. "I guess I'm just upset to hear she's back. I try and forget, you know."

Spider continued to stare at the naked bed. "Sometimes there will be a bunch of guys laughing and, it's crazy, Jordo, but I'll swear that one of the voices is Bri's. I mean I hear him."

Jordan did not answer.

"Christ, Jordo, why'd he have to go and do it for? He didn't have to do that. We could have got through it somehow."

It was the first time they had mentioned Brian's death, and Jordan glanced again toward the open door. He got up again and paced.

"You want a Coke or something? I'm going down to steerage and get a drink. Want me to bring one back for you?"

He was almost out the door when Webb's low voice stopped him.

"Do you ever wonder, Jordo?"

"Wonder what?"

"About that night? About what Bri was doing in the tunnels? I mean, what the hell would he go there for?"

Jordan froze. He looked across the space and into Webb Garrick's haunted eyes. It's funny, he thought. I always thought Spider was the strongest one of us. For four years, I've envied his strength, his and Brian's. Now it looks like I'm the toughest after all. "I don't know, Spider," he said. "I can't figure it out."

He was glad to escape his roommate's questions and the almost accusing expression in his eyes. Shit, it isn't my fault Bri stretched his neck. Not my fault at all.

As he strode down the hall, his palms were damp. Webb's news about Kate had shaken him. It probably meant nothing, but he wished he had some reassurance. Not that it mattered. He was going to be all right. What had Buck called it? The quality that determined whether you were one of the ones that came back from 'Nam? S.Q. Survival quotient. Well, Jordan Thomas Scott had a very high survival quotient. He was going to be all right.

Funny, he hadn't thought about his brother in several weeks. Suddenly he felt the need to talk to him, to hear his voice. Maybe by the sound of Buck's voice Jordan would be able to elevate his S.Q. Instead of heading toward steerage, he went to find a phone.

The first booth was occupied. He swore and strode off to another, edging out the plebe who had just got his change ready to place a call. He ignored the boy's pained look. A pussy. Probably calling home to cry about how badly he was being treated. The candy ass was lucky he wasn't fried for standing in the hall with that hangdog look on his face.

The plebe shrank back, and Jordan pulled the booth door shut. He dialed Buck's number. The phone rang on and on. Suddenly he was aware of how anxious he was to confide the dormant fears that Kate Tyler's return had resurrected. He was about to give up when Buck spoke, his greeting slurred.

"Buck?" Now he felt foolish about the call. "Buck, this is Jordo. How's it going?"

"Fit and fine, little brother. Fine and fit. How about you? Made admiral yet?"

The slurring was thicker now. His brother had been drinking. He looked at his watch. It was early to be drunk. The thought seemed disloyal, and he laughed to hollowly cover this betrayal.

There was an odor in the booth, and he recognized it as the smell of midshipmen. Generations of mids—like the plebe now attempting to be invisible several yards away while Jordan finished his call, and like Jordan himself—thousands of mids had brought their scent to this enclosed space. No cleaning solvent would ever erase it. The booth smelled of fear, of a mixture of sweat and Brasso and after-shave, of hope and exhaustion, a scent that seeped from their pores while they sat and dropped coins into a slot, straining to reach the world beyond the Yard, reaching out to drags and parents, speaking lies and asking for truths.

From the corner of his eye he saw the plebe he'd displaced waiting, fidgeting with the change he held in his hand. Jordan pushed open the door. "Listen, douche bag, what's the problem? You hot for me? Get your ass out of here before I fry it blacker than overcooked bacon."

Terribly aware that he had pulled down the wrath of a first-classman, the plebe scuttled off. He had done nothing to draw this unjustified attack, his eyes seemed to say, but he knew the rules by which a plebe survived. "Yes, sir. Beat Army, sir."

Buck chuckled on the other end of the wire. Hearing this, Jordan was ashamed. The whole thing—the language, his treatment of the fourth-classman—had been intended to impress his brother. Christ, would he ever grow up? Maybe he should just hang up. Even as he considered the idea, he knew he wouldn't. It was just the way it had been his entire life. He needed Buck. There was no one else he could turn to.

"Buck? A funny thing happened today. Remember Bri? Remember what happened?"

"'Course I remember. What's going on? Something developing over that?" The edge returned to Buck's voice, all traces of booze erased. Maybe, Jordan thought in relief, it had been sleep after all.

"I don't know. Maybe it's just a coincidence."

"What? What happened, for Christ's sake?"

"It's Bri's mother. She's here. Spider saw her today. What the hell would she be doing here? Do you think she knows? You said you'd take care of the letter. You promised."

Jordan heard the soft intake of breath followed by a curse, then silence. Finally: "I told you. There wasn't any letter. I searched the whole goddamned house, and there wasn't any letter. You haven't been talking to anyone, have you? About what you guys did?"

"Of course not. You think I'm crazy?"

"What about Spider? You sure about him?"

"That's past. Why would we talk? Bri's the only one that wanted to talk. Before he decided to self-destruct. It's just funny that she's back again. You don't think she knows anything, do you?" He flinched involuntarily at Buck's curse.

"Listen, Jordo. Just hang loose. Don't worry. No one's going to connect you to anything. If the Tyler bitch wants to hang around asking stupid questions, let her. Just hang loose and keep telling her what you said before. You don't know nothing. What about Spider? Is he cool?"

"Yeah, Spider's fine." He pushed from his mind the image of his roommate hunched over his desk, his eyes red-rimmed, his nails bitten down until they bled.

"Listen, maybe I'll take a drive down there tonight, check out this Tyler, see what she's up to. You think she's staying there? In a hotel or motel? Never mind, I'll check around. Shit, maybe she does know something. Maybe she's likely to get her ass screwed, she keeps nosing around where she doesn't belong."

Jordan clenched his teeth. Buck's words grated. When his brother talked like that, he sounded like a stranger, and it chilled him. Only one thing frightened Jordan more, and that was the idea of not graduating from Navy. The thought of facing Buck's contempt was paralyzing, and he knew he'd do almost anything to keep from washing out now. Anything, except choose the route Bri had taken.

He replaced the receiver and walked away from the booth. Why the hell had Katherine Tyler come back?

CHAPTER FIFTEEN

A man—a civilian—was polishing the double bronze doors of the chapel as she approached. He held one open for her, touching his forefinger to his cap in the Southern manner she always found charming. She stepped into the vestibule and exchanged murmured greetings with a departing couple, all speaking in the reverent whispers reserved for churches and libraries. Hesitating at the rear of the chapel, she walked slowly toward the rotunda, awed by its magnificence, the glory of the vaulted ceiling, the stained-glass windows depicting biblical scenes related to the sea, the splendid pipe organ, and the rose and white marble that framed the jewellike Tiffany windows.

Although Bancroft Hall was, by virtue of its vastness, an impressive building, the chapel dominated the Yard. Its architect had designed it to be the crown of the naval complex, and the huge copper-sheathed dome towered above the granite, cross-shaped building. Wherever one stood at the Academy, the eye could always see it. It was a cathedral that celebrated not only God, but the Navy as well. Looking up at the intricate and beautiful windows, memorials to four heros of the sea—Mason, Porter, Farragut, and Sampson—Kate felt the power of the military, a reminder she did not need. She had just spent twenty minutes in Admiral Thatcher's office.

He had been polite, smiling, his offers of aid given with the silent, regretful understanding that there was really nothing anyone could do. But what really got to her was his damn patronizing manner.

He could not seem to comprehend why she had returned, what she wanted from him. This brisk, correct military man had suggested with chilly courtesy that perhaps she should talk to the chaplain.

In a subtle way, she sensed he was distancing the Academy
from her, as if the administration had already erased Brian
and his shameful death from its roll and thus had no further
business with her. Polite and patronizing. She recognized this
stance, having long ago become familiar with Michael's similar pose. As clearly as if Thatcher had said the words aloud,
she was the outsider, facing ranks immeasurably powerful
and closed. For years she had given in to that, bowing to
their superior strength.

But not this time.

She walked down the carpeted aisle and slipped into a pew.
She had not come to pray, but to spend a moment with her
son.

On the trip down to Annapolis that morning she had tried
to steel herself for the scalding memories that returning
would bring, but it hadn't been necessary. For Brian was with
her. She had felt it ever since she had passed through the
Visitor's Gate and onto the Yard. Although she could not
explain it, she felt intensely that he was beside her at every
moment. As she reached her hand out to rest on the pew
cushion, his strong, firm fingers seemed to cover hers. She
kept her hand there, afraid to break the fragile tie.

The pew immediately in front of her was roped off, reserved in the memory of all those who were MIA or POW in
Vietnam. She stared at the unlit memorial candle placed in a
stand by the pew and wondered how the mothers of these
men felt, how it must be to never know the fate of your child.
Their existence must become a limbo of horror. Does one
ever relinquish hope? Even if she did not know what had
brought Brian to his death, at least she knew where his body
lay.

Surrounded by the magnificence of the chapel, she knew
then, as she had subconsciously sensed for days, that she
could turn to neither her country nor her God for answers.
All that was left was her passionate belief and faith in her son.
That had brought her this far, and she was now certain that it
would sustain her until she uncovered the reason for his
death.

Standing, she turned to go, aware at that moment that the
flesh of her right hand was warmer than the rest of her body.
She held it close to her with the other hand, pressing it
against her sternum, making a fist of it to fit into the hollow

there. Maybe with the heat in this one hand she could warm her entire body.

Outside, the man who had been working on the metal doors had gone, leaving a can of polish and his cloth behind. Kate saw him sitting in the white bandstand, pouring coffee. from a thermos. The steam wafted between them like a veil, hanging in the air fleetingly before the wind dispelled it.

She was on the bottom step when she saw Webb Garrick. His name came unconsciously from her lips, and she stepped toward him, feeling her boot skid on the treacherous ice. She fell to one knee. Pain shot through her ankle. The workman in the bandstand rose hesitantly, holding his thermos awkwardly, as if uncertain whether or not to come help her. In the distance, Webb Garrick walked away. She stood unsteadily, gingerly putting weight on her foot. Her relief that it was not badly wrenched was swept aside by her fear that Webb would be gone before she could reach him. She called out again, shouting his name this time. He had seen her. She was certain of that. Later, she was absolutely certain that before he had fled—and it had been a flight—he'd turned and for an instant looked directly at her. She had unmistakably seen the surprise of recognition dawn on his face.

She ventured several steps in pursuit, ignoring her injured ankle, before giving up the chase as impossible. Even after she stopped she watched, following him with her eyes until he disappeared into a mass of black-coated mids striding toward Bancroft.

If Kate's feelings about the Academy were mixed, she knew she loved the city of Annapolis. There was a charming small-town air about it that was unusual for a state capital. The relationship it shared with the Academy was one of uneasy symbiosis. The midshipmen, she knew, spoke of the little town with derision, calling it Crabtown. And yet they walked its brick streets every time they got the chance, for it represented freedom.

For their part the townspeople were proud of the Academy and of the handsome uniformed men who lived there. Throughout the years a tradition developed whereby many families "adopted" individual mids, inviting them to their homes for dinners or just to relax, have a beer, let loose. But many other citizens resented the midshipmen, complaining that they strutted around as if they owned the place. They were rankled, too, by the influx of tourists the boys brought to their town, damning them even as they depended for their livelihood on the income they produced. The classic clash of Town and Gown, Civilian and Military.

She parked by the waterfront, emptied now of sailing crafts. The wind was colder and her feet and hands were beginning to feel numb. She turned toward Main Street; her stomach growled from hunger.

As she walked by Market Square, a jug-eared black man paused in his sweeping to grin at her. Across the narrow street McGarvey's Saloon seemed to welcome her with the same warmth. Its familiar mahogany bar and brass and dusky interior were wrapped in memories of the past. How many times had she and Bri grabbed a sandwich here?

While she waited for the glass of red wine she had ordered, she looked at the other diners. There were young professional people and blue-collar workers, congressmen and members of their staff, secretaries and shopkeepers. There were people from the Academy too. Even though it was midweek, she saw a table of midshipmen—first-classmen, looking strong and handsome in their winter works. The four were voraciously eating hamburgers, chuckling and bantering with one another. Watching them, Kate felt a yearning. The waiter brought her burgundy. When she took a sip, she had to steady her hand.

All the tables were full now, and she realized she was the only one sitting alone. No, there was one other man who was a single. He sat by the window, at a table set for two.

Sipping her wine, Kate watched him, envying him the ease with which he had settled into his solitary state. He was probably waiting for someone to join him. A business partner. Or wife. This thought brought a reflexive pang of regret, and she changed the imaginary tardy companion to a male.

The man simply sat and looked out the window, for all the world as if he were at home at his own kitchen table waiting for his meal. He was about her age, Kate guessed. Gray hair had begun to shoot through the black at his temples but had not yet touched his dark mustache. The skin at his jawline was just beginning to yield to the softness of middle age. He was good-looking, but in a kind, approachable way. It was his ears, she decided, amused by the absurdity of her logic. They were thick and curled and saved him from being handsome.

He turned and his eyes met hers. Embarrassed, as if he had the ability to read her mind, Kate reached for her wine and looked away. She returned her attention to the table of mids, cruelly probing a bruise. They were not familiar, and yet they were, as every midshipman is like every other in posture and bearing. Even without their uniforms she would have recognized them instantly as mids.

One, a blonde with close-set blue eyes, glanced toward her then and called out, his voice cheerful, beckoning.

"Brian. Hey, Brian, over here."

Kate froze. The blood stopped in her veins. Locked in that paralyzing moment of horror, she was numbly aware that outside her prison, action played on. The boy was beckoning to a mid who stood behind her. She saw the newcomer join the others, watched as they noisily made room for him at their table, saw them jab him playfully in the arm as men greet men for whom they have great affection. She knew they were talking and that the room was warm with laughter and the clatter of dishes, but all she heard was the sound of the mid calling "Brian," and all she felt was the instant that she believed her son was standing by her side. How treacherous the mind. How deceitful the heart in its need to believe.

But this time she did not cry. It was only after, after she had rushed from the place, her wine still on the table, that her eyes stung with tears. There, on a bench overlooking the harbor, she sat, finally allowing herself to weep. But the tears would not come. They were dried and dead.

Would it always be like this? It had been three weeks, and yet this grief had hit as swiftly and sharply as it had in the moment she had learned of Brian's death. Will it ever go away? Will things ever be normal again? She said the words aloud.

She heard a sound behind her, a soft, apologetic clearing of the throat. She turned. Standing behind her was the middle-aged man from McGarvey's.

"You left this behind," he said, holding out her pocketbook clumsily. "I paid for your wine."

Mumbling her thanks, embarrassed, Kate took her purse.

What must he think of her? He was staring at her, and she smoothed her hair back, knowing it was hopeless, she looked a mess. The days since Brian's death had taken their toll. She fumbled with the catch on her wallet and poked through her money. "How much do I owe you?" she asked. She sounded so ungrateful. Michael had always teased her that money embarrassed her.

Refusing, he shook his head, but she tried to press a five-dollar bill into his hands. Agonizingly, her nose had begun to drip, adding to her humiliation and frustration. Angrily, she searched through her pockets and then her purse, looking for a Kleenex. If only he would go away.

He proffered his handkerchief. It seemed too intimate to use his personal linen, but her nose was running, and vanity forced her to wipe it. Almost instantly she regretted taking it, for he seemed to regard this as an invitation, and settled down on the bench at her side. At least he looked away when she blew her nose.

The fabric of the handkerchief was thin, as if it had suffered through many washings. A blue M had been embroidered in one corner, machine-stitched, marking the hanky as inexpensive, the kind bought at the dime store as a Christmas gift for an uncle. Or a stocking stuffer for a husband. Can't stop, can you, Kate? she thought self-mockingly.

Unaware of her bitterness, he pointed to a long sailing vessel moored at the dock. "See that? It's a skipjack. One of the last in the country. They're a dying breed. Once scores of them fished these waters. Sail-powered vessels used to commercial fish for oysters. Now there's just a handful on the entire Maryland shore. A grace to it, though, isn't there?"

She liked his voice. It was calm and low and patient, as if he was used to explaining things to people. She guessed he worked at the capital. A lawyer or congressman, she thought. While he continued to talk about the boat—trying to make her comfortable, she knew—Kate studied him. He was wearing a porkpie hat. She had not seen a man wearing such a hat in years. His gloves reminded her of her father. Unconsciously she softened toward this stranger.

"What happened back there? At McGarvey's. Did someone say something to you? Bother you?"

The question was well intentioned, like the questioner. Kate shook her head. "No. Just . . . just memories." She looked directly at him then and saw a shadow of pain in his eyes. It wiped away her few remaining defenses. "I just had a bad moment when I remembered my son. He was a midshipman too."

"Was?" His eyes narrowed, but she did not notice.

"Yes. He's . . . he's dead. He died last month."

"I'm sorry." How many times had she heard the phrase in the past days? But his sincerity added weight to the simple words. And suddenly she found herself telling him about Brian.

At first, when she told him that Bri had been a first-classman, he had turned a sharp scrutinizing glance on her, but after that one look, he had stared at the construction of condominiums across the harbor. While she talked she picked unconsciously at the blue M on his handkerchief, her nail loosening the threads.

She told him everything. A pigeon strutted by their feet, pecking expectantly at the ground. The wind from the harbor ruffled its iridescent feathers. Kate pulled her coat tighter around her. Her hands were red, and she shoved them deep into her pockets. When she finished, they sat in silence.

"And there was never a note?"

Kate shook her head. She did not mention the missing letter, having learned it was a danger sign, evidence of paranoia, a signal she had clearly read in Michael's eyes, Thatcher's, even Nina's.

He stared out at the nearly empty harbor for a moment, and when at last he turned to her, his eyes were kind, with none of the wariness to which she had grown accustomed. She told him then about seeing Brian's roommate when she had left the chapel that morning, and how he had run from her. Yet even as she related the story, she wondered if she sounded crazy. Another symptom of psychosis. But he listened quietly, his gloved hands resting lightly on his knees, giving no indication of his thoughts.

The gloves, like his handkerchief, were old. They were slightly soiled, and the leather was soft with age, molding the outlines of his hands. Along the seam of his left thumb there were stitches of a brighter thread, where repairs had been inexpertly made. Kate knew when he took them off and dropped them on the table at night they would curl gently inward, as if remembering the fingers they fitted. Seeing his gloves this way—and his handkerchief earlier—Kate felt a sudden intimacy with the man, as though she had glimpsed the fabric of his life more closely than if they had shared casual sex. The thought made her face redden.

"What is it you hope to find here? Why did you come back?"

"I'm not sure. I just know that this is where he died, and it makes sense that the answer is here too." Honesty made her add more. "Brian's father thinks it is clearly suicide. Everyone else does. But . . . I just can't. Bri just couldn't do that. He isn't capable of it. I *know* that. It's not just . . ." She swallowed, finding it difficult to talk—to even think—about Brian's marriage, Leah, their baby. Even while welcoming the woman as proof that Brian would not have killed himself, she shrank from the knowledge of their marriage. But that, too, was something she would have to come to terms with soon. Then, as if reading his thoughts, "Perhaps every mother would feel that way, deny it, you know. I have wondered that. Am I just denying what is too painful to contemplate? But this morning, when Webb ran from me, I knew something was wrong. Something they haven't told me. I intend to find out what it is." Calm determination filled her, partly because of this gentle man who listened to her so nonjudgmentally. Knowing this, she felt a moment's regret that she had not met a man such as this years before. What would her life have been like had she chosen differently when she was a girl? But then, I would never have had Brian. She rose to go, holding out the rumpled, damp handkerchief.

"No, please," he said, rising too. "Keep it. It is not often I have the pleasure of assisting a lady in need."

They stood facing each other, and she saw he was no taller than she, almost exactly matching her height. As she murmured her thanks, she felt him stiffen. She glanced around but saw no reason for his sudden discomfort. They were alone, except for three midshipmen striding down the brick walk toward them. He drew in his breath as if to say something to her. But before he could speak, the midshipmen broke the silence.

"Hello, Dr. McNulty," they chorused.

Kate did not know if he responded. She stared at him in horror, her outstretched hand still offering the handkerchief.

"I'm sorry. I should have told you."

She heard his words, but in her shock ignored them.

"You're one of them. God damn it, you're one of *them*." At that moment a dim and sleeping belief that there *was* a "they" crystallized. She flung the balled handkerchief at him, a feeble gesture of rejection and anger. It hit his chest and fell at his feet. "Did they send you to find out if I've found out anything? Or did they just order you to follow me?"

If the words were unreasonable, she didn't care. She left him standing there, heard him calling to her, trying to explain while she walked swiftly away, a sob caught painfully in her throat as she tried to fight a growing sense of persecution.

CHAPTER SIXTEEN

In just a few weeks, Kate knew, Washington, D.C. would be one of the loveliest cities in the country. Tourists would pour in to view its rich pastel beauty, and the capital would greet them like a bride posing for her picture. She would be young and gay and full of promise, and delicately hued cherry-blossom petals would float down on her paths and basins and pools like confetti after a wedding.

But it was not appealing now. The tubs and plantings of tulips and jonquils and daffodils were not yet in bloom, and the mood, like the weather, was gray: raw and overcast and threatening rain. It perfectly matched Kate's spirit.

She walked along the sidewalks, bending into the wind and clutching the piece of paper in her chilled fingers. As she passed by buildings, she looked up and checked the numbers against the one written on the paper.

Since the evening Leah had appeared at her home with the news of her secret marriage to Brian, Kate had wrestled with a paroxysm of emotions: anger, resentment, guilt, shock. She felt that with Brian's death she had discovered she existed on the slopes of a long-dormant volcano, a powerful force that erupted with no warning, catching her with its seismic convulsions and leaving her unable to think clearly, to understand what was happening to her. Her son's marriage was another tremblor in the series. She had reacted by withdrawing into herself, letting Leah tell her story, listening quietly, asking questions, nodding, writing down the woman's address, promising to meet again, while inside her, turmoil raged.

Daughter-in-law. The words rang heavily in her mind. It sang of a son's secrets and betrayal.

And yet . . .

And yet in spite of the shock, the jealousy—for there was

that—she was being drawn to Leah. Because of Leah, Kate was no longer so terrifyingly alone in her belief that Brian could not have taken his own life. Someone else rejected totally the idea of his suicide. No matter how betrayed she felt, she and Leah were joined by a common bond. Because of this she was now walking along the Georgetown street, searching for the woman's apartment. And what of the baby?

She shut her mind to that, did not allow herself to think of it. In the series of quakes that had shaken her, that one was too overwhelming to deal with. Later, I'll think about that later, she told herself in the unguarded moments when thoughts of Leah's pregnancy slipped in. And then the barrier would settle firmly in place. She simply could not deal now with the thought of Brian's child.

But in those few unshielded moments when the idea of the child—her *grandchild*—edged its way into her tired mind, an unnamed emotion touched the space beneath her breastbone. But before she could identify it, she banished it—along with the image of Leah's pregnancy.

The street numbers were nearing the address written on the paper she held, not giving her much time to consider what she would say to Leah. Too soon, she found the building. She stood back and looked, checking the address again. It did not look like a place that housed students. A heavy door with double matching panels of etched glass waited atop the stoop. She drew a deep breath and mounted the steps, pleased to see her hand was steady when she pressed the brass bell. After a moment she heard a click and pushed the door open. Inside, the building looked even less like student housing. The tiles on the floor were polished, the hall walls freshly painted; the smell of paint still seemed to linger in the air. On the wall to her left was a line of brass mailboxes of the kind she had not seen in years. Above each box was a smaller square of brass which she recognized as a grill for speaking into. Kate checked the tiny white strips pasted to each mailbox, and when she found 3C, she caught her breath. *L. Tyler.* The smell of the fresh paint made her light-headed.

"Can I help you?" The man was close behind her. His face had the sharply chiseled features of a woodland animal. His nose did not indent at the bridge but went straight to his

forehead. Like a shark's. Yes, more a shark than a creature of
the forest. Kate's purse fell from her fingers. Before she
could move, he scooped it up. His fingernails were filthy.
He saw her looking at them and grinned as he returned her
purse.

"I heard you ring. I was in the basement. I'm the super."
He leaned in to peer shortsightedly at her face. "You all
right?"

"I'm fine." She recoiled from his breath and the menace
she sensed in his manner. Her fingers clenched. When she
spoke again, she was pleased to hear her voice was stronger.
"I'm looking for someone. Leah . . ." She forced herself to say
the words. "Leah Tyler."

"Oh, Tyler. She's in 3C. Should be in now." He glanced at
his watch, bending his sleek, narrow head. Kate was again
reminded of a shark. "She has fewer classes this term. What
with the baby coming." When he smiled, she saw his teeth
were yellow from tobacco and coffee and neglect.

She backed off. "Thank you. I'll go on up."

With the instincts of a predator, he stepped toward her, as
if not wanting to let her go until his curiosity was satisfied,
but she did not give him time to speak. Her heels clicked a
staccato tattoo on the wooden treads, and she did not stop
until she was on the third floor. Her pulse throbbed in her
ears.

Before she had a chance to knock twice, Leah answered
the door, as if she had been waiting behind the thick wooden
panel for this visit.

She was dressed in a oversized bulky sweater and fawn
stirrup pants. Her feet were bare. The yarn of the sweater
was a green-blue color like the ocean in the summer, precisely matching her eyes. There was about her a softness that
Kate remembered from before, a quality that even strain and
grief could not erase. With a pang, she suddenly understood
why Brian had fallen for her.

But there was a subtle difference about her, too, something
Kate could not quite put her finger on. Then it came to her.
Leah's wondrous, long, thick hair had been cut short. The
new coif fitted her skull like a cap, reminding Kate of the
tribal women who shaved their heads when mourning their
dead.

They stood facing each other. The world—the frantic laughter of a quiz show seeping from the apartment across the hall, the sharp odor of paint mixed with that of roasting chicken, a door opening and closing somewhere below—none of it intruded in the sphere that held Kate and Leah. Here was the last remaining link to her son. Then the younger woman smiled, a gentle smile of infinite sadness. She reached for Kate, impulsively hugging her in a quick, shy hug. "I'm so glad you're here," she said, and as simply and easily as that, Kate's barrier of hurt dissolved.

"Come in," Leah urged. "I just made myself a cup of tea. Would you like one?"

"That would be nice. I grew quite chilled this morning. I was at the Academy."

At the last word, pain briefly spasmed Leah's features, and Kate was surprised to feel an urge to protect the younger woman.

"Please sit down. I'll get the tea." She left without another word. While she waited for the girl's return, she wandered around the room, which was furnished with comfortable old furniture, the castoffs of another generation, but quite at home in this high-ceilinged room with the bay window and irregular shape. Beneath the window stood a long mahogany table strewn with textbooks and papers. Faded rugs covered the gleaming oak floor.

On the wall opposite the window there was a fireplace, its chimney exposed, the bricks painted white. A ceramic jug filled with dried grasses had been placed on the hearth. The mantel was old, the dark wood ornately scrolled. Most of its length had been put into use as a bookshelf. On one end Leah had grouped a dozen small, framed pictures. Kate crossed to have a closer look. She knew before she got there that she would find one of Brian, but she was still not prepared to see her son's face smiling out at her in these unfamiliar surroundings. The sight slashed her. Unable to resist, she picked up one of the frames.

The print was black and white, from one of those strips of cheap pictures people have taken in booths in bus stations or amusement parks. Kate could see at once why Leah had treasured it. Brian was sitting, Leah behind him, her chin resting on his head, her arms over his shoulders. Both young faces were hideously contorted. He was sticking out his tongue and she was crossing her eyes. In spite of the comic pose, there was a quality of tenderness in the picture, in the way her hand curled on his shoulder and the manner his face tilted toward hers, as if they were trying to be as close as possible. Kate replaced the photo and returned to the window.

"It's herb tea. I hope you don't mind. Doctor's orders. No caffeine." Leah set the tray down on the long table that served as a desk. "No caffeine, no alcohol, no tobacco."

Again the unfamiliar emotion knotted beneath Kate's ribs, and she stiffened slightly. "He sounds very thorough. Where did you hear of him? The University?"

"She. My obstetrician is a woman. And the University health services recommended her. She's wonderful." She sat down in the chair by the table, unconsciously cupping her palm around her belly. Beneath the sweater Kate could see the slightly rounded shape of her early pregnancy. She turned away and took a sip of the tea. It was weak, almost tasteless, and did nothing to warm her.

Leah carefully set her cup on the table by her chair without tasting the tea. She looked at Kate as if undecided what to say next. "Mrs. Tyler—Kate—what are we going to do?"

The basket by Kate's feet contained skeins of wool and a partially completed blanket. The wool was the color of old ivory, of thick, unhomogenized cream. Looking down at it, she had a sudden vision of Leah, alone in the evening, dishes and studies done, sitting in pool of lamplight and knitting an afghan for her unborn child. Twenty-one years ago she had done the same thing. She remembered the evenings spent dreaming about her baby's future, the weekend spent painting the tiny alcove that would hold the basinette when she returned from the hospital, the lists she and Michael had drawn up, numbering items they needed for the layette. The agony of deciding what to cross out. There was no room in Michael's paycheck for anything but essentials. Recalling, Kate felt a pang for the young couple she and Michael had been. What innocence they had been capable of as they moved with unswerving confidence toward a future they were certain would fulfill their dreams. A future that held no possibility of divorce. Or death.

"Mrs. Tyler? Are you all right?"

Kate looked across the room at the young woman with the

closely cropped hair. "Why didn't he tell me?" she whispered. "Didn't he know I would have understood?"

"He wanted to tell you. It bothered him terribly, but he said we couldn't tell anyone. He was afraid someone would find out and make him leave Navy. A question of honor, he said."

"'Honor is an island,'" Kate whispered.

"What?"

"'Honor is like an island, rugged and without a beach; once we have left it, we can never return.' Something my father taught me when I was a child. Funny. I haven't thought of that in years. Each week he used to give me a quotation to learn, and Saturday evening, if I had memorized it, there was a dime by my plate." She leaned forward, her eyes intently on Leah. "In my heart I just can't accept the idea that Brian killed himself. It doesn't make sense. Everything I feel and know and remember about him tells me it is impossible. He just wouldn't." She was silent for a minute, her gaze dropping to the skeins of ivory wool. She stared at the yarn, unseeing, and whispered. "But sometimes I think maybe I really didn't know him at all." There. The damned, tormenting thought was spoken at last.

Leah did not answer immediately. She picked up her cup. The tea was barely warm, but she sipped it, staring down into the china cup. Beneath the cap of hair Kate could see the bones of her skull, the vulnerable, exposed ear and temple.

At last she looked up at Kate. "I know," she said sadly.

Once when Kate was a child, her father's Irish setter had brought a bird to the back door. It was a harrier, one of the ones she used to hear scream as they soared above the back meadow. The dog had gently dropped the crippled bird on the floor, its feathers still matted from the setter's saliva. Her father had looked at the hawk with sad eyes and then begun the futile task of trying to save it. When he approached the bird, it had scuttled away, fluttering useless wings, to find shelter in a corner, where it turned to face its foes. Kate would never forget the look in the dying hawk's eyes. The fierce, savage look of a trapped warrior, which could not conceal the panic and pain beneath. That look was in Leah's eyes now.

She rose and moved to the window. It was twilight. The streetlights cast gentle shadows over Wisconsin Avenue, choked with homeward-bound drivers. A thin March rain fell meanly, and pedestrians hid beneath the stretched black roofs of their umbrellas like beetles, scuttling in and out of pools of sickly yellow light.

CHAPTER SEVENTEEN

The words were almost a whisper. "After he died, I wanted to die too. I couldn't bear to be alone."

Kate continued to look out the window. The scene below was blurred, surreal.

The girl drew a long shuddering breath. "Sometimes I thought I was going to go crazy. I keep thinking about him, trying to remember and memorize everything about him. I spent hours thinking about every minute we were together. I even made lists, of what he had worn, what he said, where we went, what we did. If I couldn't remember some detail—some tiny, inconsequential thing—it drove me insane. In class, anywhere, I would just stop until I had it. As long as I could remember everything, I still had him. Every time I lost a piece of the puzzle, a piece of him was lost. Finally I realized I had to choose. I had to choose between letting Bri go—letting all the questions and memories go—and living for myself and the baby, or holding on to Brian and—"

"That's not the only choice, Leah." Kate turned and walked to her. She knelt and took the girl's hands in her own. They were cold, as if blood had stopped flowing in her veins. "You could keep both."

"I know, but I have to keep the Brian I know and not some shadow figure, some person who wasn't who I thought. I guess that's why I have to know how he died."

Kate crossed to the chair and sat, staring into the distance. Finally she spoke. "I'm sure Bri told you, his father and I are divorced. That part of my life—the person I was for almost half my life—is gone. I'm a teacher, but my heart is not in it. Burnout is the term, I think. The only good, true thing I had in my life was my son. And everything I know about him tells me he couldn't commit suicide. But then, I never would have believed he would get married secretly either." There was no accusation in her voice. "I just have to learn what happened that night in February. I have to find the answers." The words were fiercely whispered. She was surprised to see Leah smile.

"Bri told me you were a fighter."

"Me? No. His father. He probably said Michael. He was the fighter in the family, not me."

"No. It was you. Bri said that when you really wanted something, you got this funny tight look around your mouth, and then watch out."

"Brian said that?"

"Ummm."

This idea was new, and Kate tasted it, surprised. Michael had always been the one who took on the family's battles. Yelling if someone slighted Bri. Banging the kitchen table if he felt a teacher or coach had been unjust, ranting if he believed a repairman was taking advantage of them.

And yet... Kate remembered the times she had gone to school to meet with teachers. The time Bri had been accused of cheating. She had been sick with anxiety, but she had believed in Bri and stood up for him. Later, when the truth had surfaced, she had been so glad she had.

Funny, she had forgotten that. Still, she was amazed that her son would describe her as a fighter. She wondered if parents ever fully understood their child's perception of them.

"Thank you," she said. "Thank you for telling me that." She would remember the words later, hoard them like nuggets of gold. Now, more than ever, she knew she could not let him down.

"But what if..." Leah shrank back into her chair. "What if we found out that..."

"Found out what? That he did kill himself?" Kate held herself motionless. "I have to know. With all my heart I don't believe he did, but if so, then I want to know why. Don't you?"

Again Leah cupped her hands around her belly. "Yes," she finally whispered. When she looked at Kate, her eyes were fierce with unshed tears.

"Tell me about the wedding," Kate said after a moment.

"Are you hungry? I mean, I was thinking maybe we could go to this place down the street—only two blocks actually—

and have dinner. We could talk, and I'd tell you about the wedding and everything."

"I'd love to," she said, and to her great surprise found that it was true. For the first time since Brian's death she was really hungry.

"It's Italian food. Good and cheap and tons of it." They walked along the street quickly, sharing an umbrella. Kate bent slightly to avoid the wind, but Leah stood straight, her belly—three months pregnant—going before her like the prow of a ship. There was pride in her carriage. "Junior has a terrific appetite," she teased. In the familiar protective gesture, she again cradled her arms about her stomach. "Did I tell you? It's going to be a boy." She said the words softly, as if giving Kate a gift.

"How can you know so soon?"

"I just do. It's definitely a boy." This absolute and absurd logic struck both of them at once. A student hurrying past turned and smiled at the sound of their laughter.

Once again Kate felt that odd emotion knife her sternum, and suddenly with both pain and wonder she recognized it for what it was—the pinprick of joy. Joy and hope and love. For an instant every fiber of her body tightened and froze, and then with a sharp intake of breath and enormous daring, she allowed it life. "Oh," she said softly.

"What is it?"

"I'm going to be a grandmother."

Leah looked at her sharply. "Does it bother you?"

Kate didn't even have to think before responding. "Not at all. You know, I loved it when Bri was a baby. I loved every stage. I liked the smell of him sleeping, the powdery, sweet smell of him, the perfection and innocence. I had friends who hated that age, but I loved it. The baths, feeding, all of it. And everything that followed. Even the terrible twos weren't terrible. He was so curious and bright. So funny. And his energy..." She looked over at the woman by her side. "But that time for me has passed. I hadn't really thought about it until this minute, but that time for me is past. I don't have the energy for it. Just thinking of it makes me tired." She laughed. "But, yes, I think I'll love being a grandmother. You know, it's the wisdom of the ages: to

everything there is a season. The season to be a mother is
when you are young."

"I'll bet you were a wonderful mother."

"I made my share of mistakes." She fell silent. She would
have Brian's son. For the first time since she'd learned that
Michael and Wendi were expecting a child, her sense of
betrayal, of isolation was gone. "Thank you," she said.

"For what?"

"Just because." She pointed ahead to a red-and-green neon
sign. "Is that the place?"

The restaurant was tiny, its clientele mostly students from
the University. The booths were worn, the wood polished to
a high sheen from decades of use. Red-checkered paper
placemats added vibrant color. Huge jars of grated cheese
and napkin dispensers flanked the Chianti bottles which
served as candle holders. They ordered lasagne. Wine for
Kate. A glass of milk for Leah. Over salads, Leah talked.

"Our wedding was wonderful and awful. We went to a
justice of the peace in Virginia. We didn't have anyone with
us. Like out of a short story, really. We laughed about that
later. I thought Bri might want Webb Garrick there, as best
man, you know, but he said he didn't want anyone else there.
Just the two of us. I couldn't get over the feeling that it was
my fault and he really didn't want to do it, so I kept asking him
if he was sure. He kept saying how happy he was, and I guess
he just said it too much. But in spite of all that, it was
wonderful."

"I wish I could have been there. What about your parents?
Do they know?"

"Not yet. I know I have to tell them, but I'm just not
strong enough to face them yet. I mean, my mother will
come in and take over. She'll cry and then lecture and then
make arrangements for me to come home and have the baby.
And she'll be so strong that I'll give in. I don't want to do
that."

"How will you manage?"

"By taking it one day at a time, I guess. Finish the year, get
my degree, have the baby. Get a job, day care for the baby. If
I look too far down the road, I get overwhelmed. One day at
a time." She laughed at the look of astonishment on the other
woman's face. "I know, amazing. I just eat everything. I listen
to the women in my Lamaze classes talking about how sick

they are and how they can't touch a bite, and I don't dare mention what a pig I am."

Leah laughed again, and Kate joined in. For a brief, miraculous moment, their grief was forgotten.

And then, remembering, Kate turned away.

"What's the matter?"

"I was just thinking how much Bri would have enjoyed sharing this."

Leah put down her fork. "Mrs. Tyler—"

"Kate. Please call me Kate."

Leah leaned forward. "How did he die?"

There it was, Kate thought. "I think," she began slowly, "that it must have been an accident." She ignored the tiny noise Leah made and continued, her words spaced precisely, as if she were thinking out loud. "I've gone over it and over it, and I think what happened is that some prank, some silly prank went wrong, and whoever was with Bri became frightened."

"A prank?"

"Oh, I don't know. A joke or something. You've heard them. They're always doing crazy things. Bri's brought home stories of their pranks for four years. Really crazy, juvenile things. I think it was something as simple and awful as that. Maybe he was alone, or maybe there was someone with him and that person got scared and ran for help."

"It doesn't make sense." But even as she said the words, Kate knew by her expression that Leah saw the terrible sense it made. She, too, remembered the stories and jokes, the games they relished.

"Or," Kate added tentatively, "maybe it involved hazing. I know there isn't supposed to be any of that going on anymore, but when Bri was a plebe I overheard him once talking to his father about several cases when indoctrination was carried too far." She remembered the look in the two plebes' eyes when Jordan had forced them to do push-ups, remembered the sense of violence that had flowed in the air.

"Oh God, how terrible," Leah murmured. "If someone knows . . . and he's just let us go on thinking that—"

She paled and ran from the table, stumbling awkwardly between tables and booths. When she returned, Kate knew she'd been ill. The waitress cleared the table, and they sat

without speaking. "Anything else?" Kate ordered Sambuca;
Leah followed suit. "Do you think you should?" Kate started
to say, but catching sight of the expression in Leah's eyes, cut
the words off.

They stayed silent, sipping the biting licorice liqueur. It
felt sticky on Kate's lips.

"How will we find out?" Leah finally asked softly.

"I don't know. I guess I'll just go there and keep asking
questions, talking to everyone who knew Bri. I've written a
list of everyone who might help. I thought I would just start
at the top and ask questions."

"Have you started yet?"

"With the questions? Yes. Early this morning I flew to
Annapolis. I went to the administration, but got nowhere
there. But sooner or later I'll hear something that doesn't fit.
Or maybe someone will want to talk."

The thought that someone might have hurt Bri deliberately
made her stomach churn. She had never shared these thoughts
with anyone, and now, saying them, she realized how insane
they sounded. Maybe it was easier to believe the suicide.
Maybe Michael was right.

"How can I help?" Leah's voice was steel-edged. "What
can I do?"

"I'm not sure. When I was there this morning I got a
definite 'closed-case' sense about Brian's death. As far as
they're concerned, they're satisfied with the suicide verdict.
I'll have to start with his friends, members of his company.
Maybe you could look at my list, see if there is anyone I'm
missing. The only boys I really know are Webb and Jordan,
Bri's roommates."

"I don't know many of the Brigade members. Bri and I
only met in late August. Most of the time we were alone. If
we did spend time with anyone else, it was usually Webb or
Jordan. What about his professors? Have you talked to any of
them?"

"Not yet. But that's a good idea." She remembered the
man on the pier. "There was one... I'm not sure. Now it
seems like I was overreacting, but I thought maybe someone
at the Academy suggested he follow me, meet me.... I know.
It sounds paranoid, but the meeting was such a coincidence.
I told him all about Bri, and he never once mentioned that he
was a teacher there. If he wasn't hiding something, wouldn't

he have told me he knew Bri or worked there or something?
It seemed so odd."

"Why would they have him follow you?"

"I don't know. Maybe they're afraid I will uncover something. Maybe they're not as positive as they want me to think
that they're convinced his death was a suicide."

"Do you think they would cover up an accident?"

"I honestly don't know. I used to believe in the integrity of
the military. I'm not naive. Not everything we hear from the
Pentagon is the gospel. But I believed, I guess, in honor at
lower levels. But you know the kind of bad press within the
last few years. Midshipmen convicted of cheating, of stealing,
those rumors of hazing. Maybe there is a cover-up. Maybe
they prefer not to look too deeply at why he died. Over the
years with Michael, I've seen staffs cover up for commanding
officers who were alcoholics, who were having affairs with
enlisted personnel under their command. Their staffs laughed
at them behind their backs but always closed ranks to protect
them. Once I remember hearing about a Marine staff sergeant who sent a damaging report off to Washington, detailing
his superior's alcoholic behavior. The officer wasn't punished,
but that sergeant will never get another stripe."

"Were you sorry Bri went to Navy?" Leah reached for
her coat and wrapped it around her, not meeting Kate's
eyes.

Oh, Lord, Kate thought. You've hurt her, tainted her
memory with your bitterness. Aware of the need growing
within her to protect this girl that Brian loved, she answered,
"No. I was very proud of Bri, and nothing he ever did could
change that. Now, let's say we head back. I've got to drive
back to Annapolis, and by the looks of that stack of papers on
your table, you've got assignments to work on."

The rain had stopped and the street glistened with an oily
sheen. The muted sounds of the city accompanied them as
they walked: tires on wet pavements, horns, a distant siren.
They did not talk on the way back to Leah's apartment, and
Kate said good-bye outside the door, on the sidewalk.

She opened her pocketbook and wrote the address and
phone number of her motel in Annapolis on a sheet of her
notebook. "Call me if you think of anything."

"I will. And thank you for dinner," Leah said. She seemed
reluctant to part. They stood for a moment, two lonely,

bereaved women, and then tentatively Leah leaned over and embraced Kate. In the distance she heard the wailing of another siren, and in the shadows of the apartment vestibule, she saw the shark-faced super. "Take care," she said to Leah. "Of both of you."

As she walked away she held the image of her daughter-in-law's shy grin.

CHAPTER EIGHTEEN

Roy Banks had not slept.

He lay on the couch, curled in the fetal position, like a garden slug at dawn. Like the gastropod, he was soft and white. Doughy flesh lay in folds at his neck, and his pectorals sagged beneath his T-shirt, flaccid like an old woman's breasts.

The winter sun filtered through the window, brushing his face with its sour rays. Moving only his head, he checked the alarm clock on the end table: four P.M. Two more hours until the evening shift began, an hour before he had to get up. He didn't close his eyes. Even if he managed to fall asleep, the nightmare would return. It had been that way for the past two months.

His face was gray with fatigue. The room stank of stale sweat and smoke. It was the stench of his nightmare, of death. Resolutely he pushed the thought with its haunting, damning picture out of his mind. His ham-sized hand moved beneath the stained blanket. He scratched his crotch and listened to the sound of the empty house.

"Earle?" He bellowed the name, repeating it a second time, knowing even as he did his younger brother would not answer. "Jesus H. Christ." He threw the blanket off and reached for his shoes, buttoned his green work shirt, and pulled a heavy wool sweater on over that. His knit ski hat and coat were flung on a chair, and he grabbed them on his way out the door.

The blue pickup waited in the drive like a loyal but mistreated dog. The body was battered, and a plastic sheet had been taped over the broken back window, but the engine caught the first time Roy pumped the gas. He switched the heater on full.

Cold, it was so friggin' cold. He hated the cold. He couldn't wait for summer. Half the people he knew complained about the humid Annapolis summer months, but he loved them. It would be all right with him if it was summer for twelve months. One of these winters he was moving to Florida. Miami Beach. That's the life. Humping the free and easy women. Never be cold again.

"So help me God," he muttered, "next year for sure I'm moving, and Earle can look after his own friggin' self." Anger at his brother welled up as he pulled out of the drive and headed east toward King George. Fifty-two years old. You're fifty-two years old and still baby-sitting. Taking care of the dimwit. Your brother's keeper. The promise he'd made his mother tightened around his chest like iron bands.

That damn Earle was going to be late for work again. If he showed up late many more times, he was going to get shit-canned. This was the third job he'd had since last summer. Christ, Earle'd fuck up a free lunch. Couldn't even keep a job as a dishwasher, as a pearl diver at O'Brian's Harbour Inn.

He turned the corner and drove toward the gates to the Academy. He knew, even before he saw his brother, that he would be there, standing on the sidewalk near the gates. His face darkened with anger. Jesus, he wished his brother would stay the hell away from there. His hands tightened on the wheel. With a squeal of brakes he pulled to the curb, reached across the bench seat and unlatched the passenger's door. "Get in," he growled.

"Hi, Roy." Earle beamed up at him. He was dressed in his white dishwasher's uniform. Unlike Roy, Earle didn't mind the cold. His coat wasn't even zipped up. A white sailor hat topped his small head. Over that he wore huge earphones for his Walkman.

"Get in, okay, Earle. I'll drive you to work."

Earle Banks's attention wandered from his brother. He caught sight of a black Porsche approaching. Moving quickly, he stepped off the curb, crossed in front of the pickup, and stood at attention. When the car was several feet away, he raised his hand in salute.

Even inside the cab of the truck Roy could hear the mids' laughter floating from the Porsche, and he beat one meaty hand against the steering wheel.

"Get in the fuckin' truck, Earle," he roared. He looked through the windshield, watching the sleek auto pass through the gates, past the guard, who was laughing too. "Friggin' queers."

"They wike me." Earle hopped eagerly into the truck. "Did ya see them sawute?"

"Like you?" Disgust twisted Roy's features. "For Christ's sake." Angrily he twisted the wheel, and the tires squealed again as he U-turned and headed toward O'Brian's.

"G-g-guess where I w-w-went today?" Earle smiled coyly.

"I don't know." Roy's face was flat with resignation.

"Come on. G-g-guess." He showed a child's sly joy at the game.

Roy sighed, knowing the question and answers had just begun. "To the harbor."

"A wittle crowser."

"The State House."

The cunning grin spread. "A wittle fahver."

Roy hated his brother's games. He hated the way he talked, the way he looked. That was just the beginning of his hatred, a powerful, deadly loathing that coursed through his veins and poisoned his heart's blood. He hated his parents for dying and leaving him with his brother, his older brother who at fifty-six had the brains of a five-year-old. He hated Annapolis, and he hated the Naval Academy. And most of all, with every fiber of his being, he hated the mids. The high and mighty midshipmen. He hated their fancy cars and their fancy clothes, and he hated the way they walked, their cocky, I've-got-the-world-by-the-balls way of walking. And he hated the fact that all his life he had worked for them, worked under their spit-polished, holier-than-thou shoes. It ate at his guts. Piss on you, he wanted to say each week as he was paid. Take your fucking job and shove it. He never did. And he hated himself for that.

Only twice had his terrible hatred boiled up and spilled over. The first time was thirty years ago during June Week. He had watched with a spreading sickness when one of the mids picked up a girl. Not just any girl, but Maggie Snowdon. Christ, but he'd had the hots for her. Miss Maggie, Queen of Annapolis women. He got the nerve up once to ask her out, but she had given him the cold shoulder. Thought she was too good for him, but she wasn't too good to go driving around town with a mid, sitting real close to the driver's side, practically in the fucker's lap. A red-and-white convertible it had been. A Chevy. With spoked hubs. Real fancy. Roy had followed them, waited until the mid dropped Maggie off. Then he jumped him. Right on the sidewalk. The guy was a good six feet. Had at least five inches on Roy, but he beat him up before the stupid fucker could get in one blow. Broke his arm. It had felt so goddamned good. After, he'd gone home, gotten drunk, and waited for the cops to come. Wondered if they would send the city cops or military ones. No one came. It took him ten years to find out why. Ten years later he finally took Maggie out. She was divorced for the second time. Washed up. Didn't think she was too good for him then. He asked her about the mid. She didn't know what he was talking about. Finally she remembered. The guy had said he'd fallen when running on the seawall. Roy laughed then and told her sourly how he had sandbagged the guy. For a minute she didn't believe him. Then she looked in his eyes and knew it was the truth. She never would go out with him again.

That was the first time he couldn't contain the hatred. The second time was just two months ago. He broke out in a fear-drenched sweat. He wouldn't think about that. No one knew. If he didn't panic, everything would be all right. Next winter he'd be in Florida. For sure.

"A wittle fahver." Earle's voice brought him back.

"I don't care where you went, okay. Just stay the hell away from the fuckin' Yard."

"They wike me, Woy." Hurt flooded Earle's pale eyes.

"For Christ's sake, Earle. They don't like you, understand? They *laugh* at you. Do you know what they call you? They call you Elmer Fudd. Elmer fuckin' Fudd. Or Crabtown Earle. And you think they like you, you stupid son of a bitch." He looked over at his brother, saw his tiny microcephalic head, the angry sebaceous cyst on his cheek, almost as big as his nose, the nose itself red, hooked. The sailor's cap, and the two huge earphones. Earle looked like a freak. He was a freak. And every day of his life Roy Banks looked in his mirror and searched his features for the imprint of his brother's face.

Earle giggled and smiled at him, and his anger drained as quickly as it had flared. He pulled up to the kitchen door of the inn. "You go on to work. I'll see you in the morning."

Roy drove off before Earle walked into the inn. It was

steamy in the cab now, and he turned down the heater fan. Driving with one hand, he reached over to the glove box and twisted the knob. Inside was his stash of Milky Ways. He took one out and tore the paper off with his teeth, eating the candy in two bites. The chocolate, soft from the heat, smeared his fingers. He was still swallowing the last mouthful when he leaned over and reached for another. He just finished it as he drove through the gates of the U.S. Naval Academy. Once in the Yard he drove slowly, inching down the length of the streets, eyes searching patiently. At last he found what he was looking for. He edged the Ford into a parking slot and hopped out. The wind hit him, and he pulled the ski cap down until it touched his eyebrows. Reaching into his pocket, he fished out his key chain, which held a dozen heavy keys. Staring into the horizon, he strode down the sidewalk. As he approached the black Porsche, he slowed down, edged closer to the curb.

Casually, he curled his hand into a fist, holding the keys so that the heavy shank of one extended out between two knuckles. He looked around once, quickly, and then passed by the car. The noise of metal against metal was like silk tearing. Up ahead two mids jogged along. The sound of their breathing, of their soles hitting the pavement, floated back to him. From the distance he heard bells pealing. He smiled as he imagined the scar along the length of the polished black paint. Still smiling, he returned to his truck, gunned the motor, and drove off, wondering what the bastard would say when he came back to his precious set of wheels and saw the damage. Envisioning the expression on the bastard's face, Roy's grin broadened. He would think about it all night, all night long when he worked in the tunnels beneath the Yard.

CHAPTER NINETEEN

Dr. Maxwell Taylor McNulty, Associate Professor of History at the U.S. Naval Academy, Annapolis, felt guilty. It was a new emotion for him, and one he decidedly did not like. And because he felt guilty, he was furious.

He closed the door of his office in Sampson Hall, hoping this would discourage fellow faculty members from dropping in for a chat.

"Damn it," he muttered. "She had no right to attack me." But the argument wouldn't wash. The auburn-haired woman with the sad eyes had trusted him, and he had betrayed that trust.

It was late, long after he usually went home, but he made no move to pack his briefcase and leave.

Max McNulty was forty-six years old and had been teaching at Navy for twelve years. If he could have chosen two words to describe his existence, they would have been these: comfortable and safe. He taught at a good school, his students were motivated and bright. He was as fond of them as they were of him, for he was a good professor and brought humor and life to his classroom.

Outside the Yard, his home was his refuge. It had not always been so, but he had now manufactured this isle of safety, this haven, and he cherished it and let nothing endanger it. Less charitable colleagues might have characterized his life as dull, but that did not bother him. He remembered when his life had been defined by havoc, remembered too well the pain of that.

His present peace had been costly.

He had been married to a beautiful woman, a charming woman who loved to dance and laugh. In some deliberately silenced part of his soul he knew even before he married her that he would not be able to give her all that she required, but he wanted to try. He tried long after his pride pleaded with him to stop, and sometimes wondered if he would still be trying if she had not walked away.

She fell in love with a captain in the Navy. She had not cried when she told him. He remembered quite clearly that her face had been alive with defiance and with love for this other man. After she had gone, Max did not speak about her, and gradually the pain eased. The life he rebuilt was calm, careful, and safe.

He did not share his home with anyone. He did not have a pet. There was a striped cat in the neighborhood that seemed to have adopted him. Every night the animal scratched on his back door, and in response Max let it in and fed it half a can of food from the supply he had purchased after the cat's third visit, a store he kept replenished. But he was not responsible for the cat. It was not his. Even in his choice of a pet he was safe.

In the intervening years since his divorce there had been other women. He had occasional dinner dates with divorced friends of his married associates, and now and then a casual date with one of the professional women who were beginning to flood the city. He seldom went out with one woman more than twice. His life was, for him, extremely satisfying. His classroom hours were limited, and in his off-hours he worked on a history of the Civil War which he hoped to publish soon.

But today this comfortable equilibrium had been upset. In the hours since he had left Kate Tyler, he'd been unable to get her out of his mind. The ferocity of her belief in her son had been impressive. Yet he knew it was not unusual. He had talked many times during the past twenty years with parents who believed in their sons' innocence in the face of irrefutable evidence to the contrary. Just two years ago a mid had been caught cheating, and even when presented with proof, the boy's parents had refused to accept his guilt, threatening to call their congressman, sue the Academy.

Very few cheated at Navy. A good advertisement for the honor concept, he mused. The amazing thing, he reflected, was that the code did work. If forced to put a statistic to it, he would guess that ninety percent of the midshipmen believed in and were bound to the concept.

While midshipmen occasionally died in car or motorcycle

accidents, suicides were extremely rare. Max had several theories for this. For starters, it was out of character. As a group, Brigade members were bright, highly motivated, goal directed, and hardworking. Hard chargers, the lot. And they had precious little time to brood. More than that, they were not what he identified as the suicidal type. They were not highly introspective. Of course there were some who were, but the majority fell in the bell curve. Highly disciplined but not inward directed.

He leaned back in his chair and clasped his hands behind his head. Closing his eyes, he tried to pull from memory young Tyler's face from the thousands he had taught. Was there something about this one midshipman that would place him outside the bell curve?

But he could not recall the face. Another kept getting in the way. Damn her. He sighed, acknowledging that she had gotten under his skin. But it was more than just her attractiveness or sorrowful determination that stuck with him. It was her accusation that the Academy was in some way at fault, and that he had been sent to spy on her.

That charge rankled. As much to prove her wrong as anything, McNulty toyed with the idea of walking over to Bancroft Hall and having a talk with the dead boy's roommates. The prospect irritated him. The last thing he wanted was to get involved. There was no doubt in his mind that Tyler had killed himself. The administration would have been under heavy pressure to investigate the death. If it had been anything but suicide, it would have surfaced, McNulty was certain.

Still, he could not forget Kate Tyler's face. Sighing, he pulled on his coat, set the battered felt hat on his head, turned out the lamp, and left his office. He would do this one thing and then he would forget about it.

As he pulled the door shut, he saw the sheet of paper tacked there. Taped to it was a news photo of four Navy F-14's escorting an Egyptian liner back to Egypt so that four PLO kidnappers on board could stand trial. In scrawling penmanship he recognized as that of a mid, was written: *Beat Terrorism, Sir.*

In those three words McNulty read humor, bravado, and a deep sense of pride.

It was rainy and raw, and he walked swiftly down Stribling

toward the huge dormitory. By the time he dashed up the steps and through the double doors, he was chilled and his nose was running. He dug in his pocket for a handkerchief and remembered too late that he had lent his to Kate Tyler. He poked a knuckle against his nostril and sniffed. It was the first time in years he had been in Mother B. He looked for a mid to ask for Webb Garrick's and Jordan Scott's room number. With his luck today, they'd probably be on the rear wing, fourth floor. He was not up to the climb.

The upperclassman who gave him the information stared after him when he walked away, unused to seeing professors in his home.

Max was lucky. Garrick and Scott roomed on the first floor, second wing. Turning down the polished corridor, he tried to remember the mids' schedule outside of classes, hoping they would be in, aware of the curiosity his visit engendered. Outside their room he stopped to check the names on the nameplate before knocking. Tyler's name, he observed, had already been removed. The lamp in the room was on. Inside, Webb Garrick was alone. Seeing his history professor, he jumped to attention.

"Good evening, sir!"

God, they were so damn polite, so downright eager. McNulty knew it was extremely unfashionable within the ranks of his colleagues at civilian colleges to actually like students, but looking across the spotless room at the clean-featured, handsome young man, he felt a rush of affection. Apprehension shone on the young man's homely face. It was unusual to have a professor knocking at his door, and anything unusual at Navy invariably meant bad news.

"May I come in?" The room was so immaculate, McNulty felt unkempt. He was aware of his dripping nose. "I don't suppose you have a tissue, do you?"

"Yes, sir. Right here, sir."

"Thanks. Listen. Forget that sir, okay? We're not in class here." The tall mid shifted from his rigid stance only long enough to reach for the box of tissues. "I wondered if you could help me." He took the offered Kleenex. "Thanks. I lost my handkerchief. Actually, I didn't lose it. I lent it to someone. In a roundabout way that's why I'm here. I lent it to someone you know. A woman named Tyler. The mother of your roommate Brian."

"Mrs. Tyler sent you here, sir?" The boy's forehead furrowed. He had quickly covered up his panic, McNulty granted him that. If he had not been watching him closely, he would have missed the brief flash of fear in the midshipman's eyes.

"No, she didn't send me. She just asked some questions. She can't seem to accept that her son killed himself. What do you think?"

The tension eased from the first-classman's shoulders.

"No, sir." His eyes held only sorrow. "It's hard to understand, but Bri did kill himself." Webb was still standing at attention beside his desk, and now he grasped the back of his desk chair so tightly his knuckles went white. "The thing is, I just wished he felt he could talk to me."

"No sign he meant to do it?"

"No, sir."

"What about your other roommate? Scott? Was Tyler closer to him? Could he have given him any hint about what he had in mind?"

Something flickered again behind the blue eyes. "No, sir. Nothing."

Max looked around the cubicle. He found it stark, and the M16 leaning against the rifle rack seemed incongruous in a college room. The room was one of the few in Bancroft designed for three occupants. Three desks, three beds, three closets with shelves for skivvies and immaculately folded shirts. Oddly enough, although the shelves holding Scott's and Garrick's belongings were full, they had not usurped any of the space formerly used by Tyler.

His bed, desk, closet space were empty, as if they were saved for him. The mattress of his bed was bare, the surface of his desk clear. Something struck Max as not quite right about that.

"Excuse me, sir? Why the questions? I mean, we've been over this before. We told them everything we knew right after Bri did . . . it. There's nothing more."

"Yes. Well, thank you, Garrick. Sorry to bother you. I guess I just wanted to satisfy myself. Mrs. Tyler is an oddly convincing woman. I'll be going along."

Webb could not hide his relief. As he walked away, McNulty turned back to the tall firsty. "Good luck," he said.

He walked slowly away from Mother B. Satisfied now? he

quizzed his conscience. You've done all you can. More than you needed to. His last words to Garrick echoed in his ears. Why did I wish him good luck? But he knew why. He knew that the third mid still lived in that Spartan room. Brian's ghost had not been exorcized. And his roommates knew that too.

CHAPTER TWENTY

Webb stood for a long while after McNulty left, not moving, barely conscious of breathing. In the distance he heard the sound of running feet, followed by other feet, a slamming door, laughter and splashing, like a pail of water thrown on the deck, followed instantly by more laughter and a torrent of profanity. The noise came from another corridor. Not in his company. There was something eerie about his company now. Even the plebes felt it. There was no horseplay at night, a slackening in come-arounds.

Webb's hands were very cold.

The shock of having McNulty come to his room asking about Bri began to wear off. But he felt no relief. He closed his eyes with great weariness. It was not over. He knew that instinctively. Maybe he had known that since the moment that morning he had seen Kate Tyler walking out of the chapel. It was all beginning to disintegrate.

His hands were trembling, and he clinched them, folding one inside the other like a boxer, tensing all his muscles: forearms, upper arms, shoulders, then his chest and back, holding them in taut control until the shaking stopped.

I'm beginning to fall apart. The thought brought with it a flood of panic. He laughed harshly. Nothing new. The disintegration had begun weeks before. The little signs betrayed each of them: the way they couldn't meet each other's eyes, their nervous laughter, the inclination to talk too much or too little. Little evasions. Maybe Brian had taken the easy way out, Webb thought.

Like a cancer, everything looked the same on the surface. Oh, there were times, hours, days even, when it was forgotten. But never totally gone. Like a disease in remission. Never totally cut away, always working its poisonous way.

He pulled on his reefer. His subconscious knew where he

was going before his mind acknowledged it. He was heading to the place he had been avoiding for days.

The Yard was deserted. The vitality that marked it by day was gone. There was a peacefulness about the place, and it soothed Webb.

He walked down Stribling. He had the sense that he was being followed, and looked over his shoulder, but no one was there.

When he reached Sampson he almost turned back, but it was far too late for that now. Unable to shrug off the feeling of being watched, he glanced around again. He walked to the edge of the grate and knelt. The grill was wet and frigidly cold. He gritted his teeth and lifted. The sound of metal scraping against concrete harshly ripped the silence, echoing across the deserted Yard. He froze, half expecting a security guard's flashlight to flood his face. After a split second he continued, pulled the grate free. He wiped his perspiring hands on his uniform.

Squeezing by the valves and pipes, he descended. It was a tight fit. When his shoulders were even with the surface of the sidewalk, he reached over and pulled the grate back over the opening, imprisoning himself. The sound of his shoes on the ladder echoed eerily. The cold went deeper than his flesh, chilling the core of his body and soul. It was the first time he had been in the tunnels since Bri's death. He was confronting the childish superstitions and fear by going to this graveyard, going to this place where death had dwelt.

Then, as they always did, the tunnels began to work their magic on him. The Ho Chi Minh Trail. Who had named them that? Who had actually discovered them? Jordan, he thought. Their plebe year.

There had always been rumors of a maze of tunnels that bisected the earth below the Yard. Steam tunnels, really. Whispers that they were kept secret because of the Admin's fear that they would be used by thieves. They were rumored to come up inside the houses on Porter Road, and the concern was that they lay open the senior officers' housing to threat of theft. It was whispered that the tunnels could be followed until they led to the giant generating plant outside the gates. Freedom.

It was the promise of freedom that had first enticed the roommates. Yes. He remembered now. Jordan was the first to learn about the trail. It had been in the middle of their plebe year, and Jordan had learned about them from Buck, who had discovered them when he was a mid.

In January of that year, the roommates had finally decided the time had come to investigate. It had begun as a joke, each daring the others to go down into the tunnels, challenges that began in jest but grew more and more barbed as the days went by. If they were caught, they would chalk up so many demos it would be a record. Perhaps that was part of their appeal. Typically, Brian had been the first to accept the challenge.

Beneath the ground of the Yard, they entered another world, a secret territory that held such appeal that the three found themselves risking more and more to escape there, sneaking through the buried labyrinth, discovering which turn lead to which of the various grates.

Jordan even made a map. The narrowest of the branches— so narrow that they had to half crouch and walk single file—led directly to the basement of Mother B. Eventually, to their disappointment, they discovered that none of them led beyond the Yard.

The biggest threat of discovery came from the maintenance man who sat in a room to one side of the main tunnel branch. He had chased them once, nearly catching them. This added greatly to the game, and the next time they descended into the lair, they had carried, at Webb's suggestion, smoke bombs to toss near the guard room.

In their third-class year, the tunnels lost some of their appeal. Once, during the beginning of that year, Webb had put on too much weight and had used the tunnels to train in, piling on sweat gear and running through the steam heat until, exhausted and sweat-soaked, he would return to Mother B. But during the last two years they had used the tunnels less frequently.

They were not the only ones to discover them. Occasionally other mids left evidence of their visits. But generally it was a well-kept secret in a place where there were few secrets. That, Webb knew, was part of its seduction.

During the past year, he had not gone to the tunnels at all. Why had Bri chosen this godawful place for his death?

Now he crouched six feet below the surface of the Yard,

feeling lonely and slightly foolish. The impulse that had
brought him here evaporated.

"Why, Bri? Why?" He was unaware that he had spoken
aloud until the whispered words echoed back, tormenting
him with a question he could not answer. Anxious suddenly
to be above ground, he headed back to the grate.

Then he froze. There was the sound of someone breathing.
Rasping, ragged breaths. He tensed, holding his breath. It
was silent again.

What had frightened him was the sound of his own breathing.

At the grate opening, the metal bars bisected the evening
sky. Was that the last sight Bri had? At that moment Webb
felt—piercingly felt—what those final instants of his friend's
life must have been like. In an unconscious movement he
brought one hand to his throat, half expecting to feel the
rough bite of rope encircling his flesh. He opened his mouth,
as if it were suddenly not possible to get enough air in his
lungs.

Had there been one last moment of conscious thought? Of
what? Fear? A fleeting moment of regret as the feet slipped,
too late? Or was it just relief? Relief at his escape. Relief to be
freed finally of the paralyzing guilt.

There was to be no escape for him, Webb knew. Oh God,
he sobbed silently. It isn't fair. Are we going to have to pay
our entire lives for one night? Is that what finally drove Brian
to this friggin' place? He bit his lip to keep from crying out.
Hands fumbling at the task, he lifted the grate and pushed it
aside, scrambling from the ladder to the ground, ignoring the
noise he made, not even stopping to check to see if anyone
was in the area. At that moment he didn't care if he was seen.
His single thought was to escape the tunnel and the hideous
knowledge of his best friend's last moments. They had fit his
skin too closely.

Back on the brick walk, he headed back to Bancroft. The
Yard was a graveyard. The monuments—Heradon, the granite cross at Soley and Chapel, Macedonian, Tripoli, the
cannons so thickly placed throughout that it was almost
impossible to be out of eyesight of one, the crypt of John Paul
Jones—the entire Academy ground seemed haunted by watching
spirits.

Webb knew that he had gone to the tunnels to exorcize

Brian's ghost. And he knew, just as certainly as he crossed the hallowed grounds of the Yard, that he had failed.

Despair swept over him. The shock and disbelief had dissolved, but not the guilt. He could not forget his part or absolve himself in the roll of events that had culminated in Brian's death.

"Oh, Bri," he silently cried. "Why didn't you come to me? I would have talked you out of it."

CHAPTER TWENTY-ONE

The motel where Kate had rented a room was one of the inexpensive ones on Riva Road. Like thousands of similar rooms across the country, it was furnished with a cheap dresser and a desk with a laminated top designed to look like maple. The advertised "kitchenette" was comprised of a small sink, under-the-counter refrigerator, and a two-burner gas range top, all set in the corner of the bedroom. As she opened the door Kate regretted the impulse of thrift that had caused her to choose this place instead of one of the lovely and convenient motels in town. She had left the bedside lamp switched on, but even the soft glow of its light did not diminish the feeling of impermanence that was part of the room. Its lack of personality was felt even more keenly after the warm evening she had just spent with Leah. She pushed the thermostat up a degree.

As she set her purse down on the desk, she noticed the red message light blinking on the telephone. Who could be phoning her here? Leah, she thought, with pleasure.

The desk clerk did not answer her call for several minutes, and she wondered if he had been sleeping.

"This is Mrs. Tyler in room 24."

"Yeah. You had a call from Commander Tyler. He left a number where you could reach him." She immediately recognized the number. Michael's office number. He wouldn't be there any longer.

Kate thanked the clerk, unable to keep the disappointment out of her voice. There was no reason for Leah to have phoned, she told herself. She slipped off her damp raincoat and hung it over the tub, smoothing out the wrinkles, then flicked on the television. She twisted the dial impatiently before snapping it off. Nothing but sitcoms. The room seemed claustrophobic. She opened the door of the small refrigerator, hoping against hope that the previous guest had left something.

It was, of course, empty. Even the ice cube trays were empty. She filled them at the sink and returned them to the freezer compartment.

She slipped out of her shoes, sighing with relief, and massaged her cold toes. A shower would warm her. She moved the raincoat to a hanger, which she placed on the doorframe, and then stripped. She let the water run hot, letting it beat down on her shoulders. She stayed there a long time, shampooing her hair, standing motionless under the water until her face was free of makeup. When she finally turned off the tap, the bathroom was steamy and fragrant. She slipped into her robe. She was still toweling her hair dry when the phone rang.

"Kate? Didn't you get my message? I called hours ago."

"Hello, Michael." She tried to think of something more to add, but there was so little to say to him. It was as if she had finally left him behind.

"Kate, we need to talk about your going to Annapolis." His voice was calm and controlled. Kate met it with an equal measure of moderation.

"There's really nothing to talk about."

"Just what the hell are you doing down there? The admiral called me today. He wanted to know if I was dissatisfied with the investigation. Jesus, Kate. I didn't know what to say. You made me look like an idiot. I mean, what the hell does it look like when a man can't even control his wife?"

"I'm sorry, Michael. I thought the admiral knew we were divorced."

"Don't be obtuse. Our divorce has nothing to do with it."

"I told you I was coming down here."

"And I told you—strongly told you, in fact—that you should forget the whole thing. Let it go, for God's sake."

"We disagree about Bri's death, Michael. I don't expect your blessing, but you can't stop me." Her determination in the face of his anger was new for both of them, and he met it with a brief silence.

"Listen, I'm sorry I jumped at you. I guess I'm under a lot of pressure here."

Kate stared at herself in the mirror above the desk. Her hair was drying in ringlets around her face, and it looked softer. She pulled a few strands over her forehead, experimenting. How long has it been since I changed my hairdo? she wondered. She thought about Leah and the girl's reaction to Bri's death. The long hair shorn. Evidence of grief, but also a sign of change. Maybe it was time to cut her hair.

"Kate? Kate, are you listening?"

She heard the strain in his voice, the gritted-teeth attempt to be reasonable.

"Yes, I'm here, Michael."

"As I was saying, I'm up for a judgeship. It would mean everything, Kate. Frankly, I'm surprised I'm still being considered. Brian's suicide was a black mark on my record."

The words hit her like sleet against bare skin, and she fought the temptation to bang the phone down. "Michael, what is it that you called for?"

"I'm ordering you to go home, Kate. Leave it alone. If you persist in this abnormal behavior, running around annoying people, you're going to ruin it for me. You have no right to destroy my career."

In the face of her silence, his flinty control broke. "God damn it, Kate, I thought you could see reason. I swore I wouldn't let you make me lose my temper, but you've done it again. I mean, this is just so damn typical of you. You run around doing what you want, like you always have, not considering how your actions affect others. Half the people I talk to think you're nuts. Straighten yourself out, Kate. Think about others. For God's sake, think things through. A perfect example of the irresponsible actions I'm talking about is the way you've handled this with your father."

"What?" The woman facing her in the mirror went white.

"I called the senator." His voice was righteous.

"Oh God, Michael— You didn't tell Dad about Brian?"

"Of course I told him. And that is just another example of your lack of responsibility. You don't think things through—"

"God damn you, you had no right to tell him—"

"No? How the hell did I know you hadn't told him? I called him to find out if he could make you see this thing clearly. I mean, Jesus, Kate, what if he had read it in the papers? What if some reporter called him up? He's not exactly an unknown. Think, Kate. That's a perfect example of how irrational you've become about this thing."

Kate squeezed her eyes shut, willing herself not to give

him the satisfaction of knowing he had gotten to her. "I've got to go, Michael." The inside of her mouth, her tongue, her cheeks and throat, tasted of salt.

She hung up. "I just didn't want to hurt him," she whispered to the hollow-eyed face in the mirror. "That's why I didn't tell him." She felt like a carrier of an infectious disease, spreading it, contaminating everyone.

Selfish. Headstrong. Thoughtless. The accusations burned. Then she remembered Leah's voice. *He said you were a fighter.*

Should she fight for Bri or give up? Even as she asked herself, she knew the decision had been made long ago. She had to know the truth. But in following that path, she would try not to hurt others. She glanced at her watch. It was not too late to try and talk to her father.

Mrs. Roberts answered the phone. Kate heard the surprise in her voice, and then affection. "Why, Mrs. Tyler. He was expecting your call. Let me get him. Yes, he's still awake."

"Wait a minute, Mrs. Roberts. I just had a call from Mr. Tyler. He said he had phoned Dad, told him about Bri."

"He did. I'm sorry, Mrs. Tyler. It's my fault."

"It's not your fault. I just need to know. Is he all right? I mean, did the news . . . hurt him?"

The wire hummed; there was the thin, constant drone of a television in the distance. "Your father is an amazing man, Mrs. Tyler. I suspect you are a lot like him. I'll be going now, to tell him you are on the line. He's anxious to speak with you."

"Katherine?"

His voice was terribly faint. It hurt her to hear it. When had he last called her Katherine?

"Dad? Dad, I just talked to Michael. He told me he talked to you. I'm at Annapolis, Dad. Can you hear me all right?"

"I was watching the Celtics. Got a bet with Mrs. R."

Kate gripped the phone tighter. The plastic housing of the receiver was damp in her hand. "Dad, I'm sorry I didn't tell you about Brian before. I wanted to protect you, and that was wrong." She spoke slowly, almost shouting the words into the phone, as if her father were deaf. "I don't know how much Michael told you, Dad, but I don't believe Brian killed himself. I'm here to find out what happened, but I don't want to hurt anyone anymore. I'm tired, Dad." She talked faster now, aware that her father probably could not understand what she was saying, sensing he was protected from reality by his illness, grateful for that, but needing him too. Her voice softened, and she turned to her father, as she had turned to no one else in the past few days. She did not care that her effort was doomed to be futile. She just needed to ask.

"Am I wrong, Dad? God forgive me, am I wrong?"

There was only silence from the other end of the connection. Hadn't he heard her? A wave of helplessness washed over her.

Her father's words came from a place in him he had long ago left behind. The voice was frail, but the words were strong with belief. For a moment she did not understand them, and her heart sank at the gibberish. Then she grasped the miracle. He was speaking Latin. She did not even need to translate the words. She had learned them long ago at his knee, and she repeated the last words in concert with him: "*Veritas vos liberabit.*" He had understood. *And the truth shall set you free.*

"Godspeed, Katherine."

Suddenly Kate had a dozen things she needed to say to this person she believed she had long ago lost. With all her being she wanted to hang on to him for one more minute, but he was already gone, returned to that gray place beyond her reach. "Good night, Dad. I love you."

After she hung up, she sat for a while. Tomorrow she would return to the Yard, to talk to Webb and Jordan. If she had to, she would talk to every one of the midshipmen at the Academy, but this time she would get answers. A knock on the door interrupted her thoughts. She jumped, heart thumping. There's nothing to be frightened of, she whispered.

"Yes, who is it?"

"Mrs. Tyler? Can I talk to you? I need to talk to you."

She cracked open the door, peering out into the drenched darkness of the motel parking lot.

The first thing she saw was his porkpie hat.

"What do you want?" Lord, I must look terrible, she thought, bringing her hand up to smooth her unruly damp hair back, uncomfortably aware that she had washed off her makeup. Then, because her first thoughts had been about what she must look like, she grew angry. "How did you find me anyway, Dr. McNulty?" Her tone was biting.

He grinned sheepishly. "I just began calling every motel, boardinghouse, and bed-and-breakfast in Annapolis. Found you on the seventeenth call." Having said that, he appeared at a loss, and they stared at each other for a moment.

"I'm not dressed, I'm tired, and I have nothing left to say to you." She started to close the door.

"Please . . ." He put out an arm, holding her with the gesture. "I wanted to talk with you. To explain. I've been thinking of you all day. You made me feel guilty, and it wasn't a feeling I liked. Could I please come in for several moments? I won't stay, I promise."

"I don't think there's any point," she began. *Why not?* an inner voice whispered. Because you don't have any makeup on and you look terrible. This thought so annoyed her that she wordlessly swept the door open, letting him in.

She pointed to a chair, ungraciously inviting him to sit, but he remained standing. The bedside lamp and light from the bathroom cast a soft light on the room, creating an uncomfortable, false intimacy. Kate thought about turning on the overhead light, but hesitated, knowing it would be unflattering. Again her reaction exasperated her, and she snapped on the light. Conceit be damned. Let him see me at my worst.

Now that he was in the room, he seemed as uncomfortable as she. He stopped just inside the door, looking as if he already was regretting the impulse that led him to her. "You look different."

"I don't have any makeup on." The words were defiant.

"No," he said. "It's your hair. It looks nice." As soon as the words were out of his mouth, he flushed.

The compliment further infuriated and flustered her. "What was so important that you had to come here?"

"I wanted to talk with you."

"So urgently that you had to run through the Annapolis lodging directory and then come here in the middle of the night?"

"I am sorry about today. I should have told you who I was, that I taught at the Academy, when you first began to tell me about your son, but I couldn't. You seemed to need to talk, and I was afraid you would stop if you found out who I was. I didn't think it would hurt. Haven't you ever held off, so as not to hurt someone?"

Kate thought of her father.

"I guess I'm trying to apologize and tell you that if you want to talk—about your son or the Academy—I will give you my home number and address. You can find me during the day at my office in Sampson Hall."

His discomfort was acute. Kate began to guess what it had cost him to come to the motel. "Thank you," she said reluctantly. "I suppose I owe you an apology for my outburst. It just seemed such a coincidence that you should turn up when you did. I appreciate your offer to talk. Perhaps I could come to your office in the morning." Another door opening. Any door, any lead, was welcome. There were so damn few.

"My first class is at ten. My last class is over by two. Any time before or after." He glanced at his watch.

"Well, I won't keep you," she said. "Your wife will be getting worried."

"I'm not married."

Kate felt her cheeks redden. Damn.

"What about your husband? Did he come here with you?"

"I'm divorced. Michael—Brian's father—has remarried. He's in the Navy. Are you a Navy man, Dr. McNulty?"

"Max. Please, call me Max." He removed his hat and fingered the brim nervously. His fingers were long and square, the nails clean and trimmed short. He set the hat down on the desktop, as if deliberately to rid himself of it so his fingers could not fidget. "No. I'm a civilian. To the eternal disappointment of my father."

"I take it he was in the Navy."

"Army. West Point. That's what he wanted for me too. From the moment I was born he had it all mapped out. Even chose my name with an Army career in mind. Maxwell Taylor McNulty. Quite a mouthful for an infant. He had served with Taylor and hoped the General would be a mentor for me. It doesn't hurt to be named after a man if you're hoping to attract his notice."

He perched on the edge of the motel desk, and after a moment she sat down in an armchair, self-consciously tightening her robe around her waist.

"But you didn't go to West Point?"

"The decision was taken out of my hands. During my first physical they learned I was color blind and hearing impaired, 4-F. Not West Point material. My father's most bitter disappointment. No, the closest I ever got to the military is teaching here at Navy. I guess I was meant to teach military history instead of make it."

"Do you mind?"

"For myself, no. Just that I couldn't fulfill my father's dream. But perhaps that is the destiny of each generation: never to meet the expectations of our parents. Just as it is their destiny to be doomed with disappointment."

Kate fell quiet, reflecting on the sad words. Had Brian chosen Navy for his father's sake? Knowing she could never have the answer to that now, she prayed that her son had chosen for himself.

"I went to see your son's roommate tonight. Webb Garrick. Nice young man. They all are, you know." He responded to the question in Kate's eyes. "I told him you felt he had run away from you."

"What did he say?"

"Claimed he never saw you. But I had the interesting feeling that my presence made him uncomfortable." He paused for a moment as if deciding whether or not to continue. "You know, if I had a son and he died, I think I wouldn't want to accept the fact that he had died. I think I'd run from the sense of guilt and failure."

"Is that what you think I'm doing? Trying to place blame because I can't accept the truth?"

"I'm just wondering what you will do if you find in the end that Brian did commit suicide. Are you prepared for that?"

"It's funny. You're the second person today to ask me that." She looked at him unflinchingly. "The answer is yes. I believe in Brian. I don't think he killed himself. But whatever happened, I have to know the truth."

For a long moment, he studied her. She could not tell what he was thinking. Then he rose. "I hope you find what you are looking for, Mrs. Tyler."

He moved to the door, and she rose, following him. He took a small notebook from his pocket and rapidly jotted his address on a page, then tugged it loose. "Don't forget. If I can help, give me a call."

She took the address. "Good night," she said. Their eyes met, and both glanced away swiftly.

Impulsively, he leaned forward, and for a moment, panicked, she thought he was going to kiss her. Then he abruptly pulled his hat on and walked away. She stood at the door and watched him as he crossed the darkened parking lot to a battered blue compact. Not a tall man, good posture—not military, but good—feet pointed the slightest bit outward when he walked. Hands relaxed at his sides, curling in slightly. She smiled at the hat. It was absurd.

When she closed the door, the room felt warmed by his presence. She was comforted by it. Her exhaustion had disappeared. McNulty would probably never know what it had meant to her that he had bothered to speak to Webb Garrick.

Her reflection in the mirror smiled wearily back at her, and she leaned closer to it, tentatively pushing the hair up with her fingers, feathering it. She tilted her head to one side, her eyes narrowed critically. It does look nicer, she decided. I wonder? Was he actually going to kiss me or was I imagining that?

Then, impatient with herself, she shook the daydreams off. All business now, she pulled the notebook from her purse and opened it. The list of names she had written under the title "Annapolis" was unchanged. She put a note next to Admiral Thatcher: *Nothing there*. Next to Webb's name she put a question mark. She would talk with him tomorrow.

She turned to the next page. At the top of the blank page she printed *Allies*. Beneath the heading she wrote: *Leah*. She hesitated for a moment before writing the next name. Strictly speaking, Max McNulty was not an ally. She guessed, correctly, that he had come to her motel simply to put his conscience at ease. And he did belong at the Academy, technically enemy territory. She hesitated a fraction of a second more and then added Maxwell Taylor McNulty to her list, copying his address and phone number there as well.

Before she was finished she added one more name, for good luck as much as anything. The last addition to her brief list of allies read: *Dad*.

She closed the book and headed toward the bathroom to brush her teeth. The tap was running, and at first she did not hear the phone. She answered it on the third ring. It was Leah.

"Mrs. Tyler?"

"Yes."

"I hope I didn't wake you."

"Not at all. Are you all right?"

"I'm fine." Leah laughed softly. "No indigestion yet. I'm calling because I just remembered something. Or someone, actually. As I said, I don't know many of Bri's friends there, but I did think of another midshipman you might want to talk to."

"A friend of Brian's?"

"Not exactly. One of the mids in his company. I don't know. I just remembered and . . . It's just a feeling I have."

"Woman's intuition." Kate's heart sank. She had hoped Leah had remembered something important.

"Her name," Leah corrected softly. "Ariel Greene. She's in Brian's company. I saw her at the Army–Navy game in November. Bri pointed her out. I just thought, you know, being a woman and all, maybe she would talk to you."

"Thank you, Leah." Holding the phone between her shoulder and ear, Kate reached for her notebook and jotted the name beneath those of Brian's roommates. "I'll try and reach her tomorrow. I'll call you tomorrow night and let you know how I make out. Thanks. Good night, dear."

Good night, sleep tight, don't let the bedbugs bite.

Brian's baby voice giggled in her ear. God, would the memories never end? Some day in the distant future memories might be comforting, but not now.

She stared at the name Leah had given her. Ariel Greene. Bri had never mentioned the name. It was probably nothing.

Afterward, lying in the dark, Kate tried to ward off discouragement. After the past twenty-four hours she was no closer to learning why Brian had died than she had been on the day of his death. Exhausted, she slept.

CHAPTER TWENTY-TWO

He drove in from Virginia, crossing the Potomac by way of the 14th Street Bridge. It was after eleven, and there was little traffic. He turned left onto Constitution Avenue and then left again into the parking lot by the Washington Monument. Only one other vehicle stood in the lot, a camper with Oregon plates. He left the car unlocked and headed west. His destination was six blocks away, but he chose to walk the distance.

He did not stay on the sidewalk, although the grass beneath his feet was still wet from the earlier rain. A few papers floated in the water of the reflecting pool. They would be gone by morning, removed by the park maintenance men. As he drew closer to his goal, he slowed, staying in the shadows.

At midnight the floodlights switched off. Darkness fell on the park like a soft cover. The man crossed the remaining yards with swift, stealthy steps. He was unaccompanied but did not feel alone. He never felt alone when he came to this long black wall of death. He reached out and touched the names engraved in the onyx stone, as if he were reading braille. He did not need his eyes to visualize the names. He knew their looks by heart: the clean, boldface print, all capitals, with each of the thousands and thousands of names— nearly sixty thousand of them—separated by precisely chiseled dots. The names on the wall were unalphabetized; their placement determined not by age or letter but by date of death, a listing punched out on a computer in Atlanta, Georgia. There were no indications of rank on that wall. No evidence of a man's race or religion. A democracy of death.

From yards away the man was almost invisible. His jeans, British commando sweater, and Reebok jogging shoes were black. Except for the skin of his hands and face, he knew that he could melt into the wall. Yet because of his pale flesh, he felt exposed. He wished he had dared to smear camouflage grease on his skin, but that would have been dangerous. Get him shot as a burglar. He had survived too much to be shot now by some nervous D.C. cop.

Before him and behind him and above his head, the wall reached into the night. It was actually three walls, each nearly two hundred fifty feet long. At each of its three vertexes, it stood ten feet tall. The individual walls were comprised of seventy inscribed panels. The largest of the panels held one hundred thirty lines of names, five names on each line. He stared at the point where it vanished from his vision. It was as if it had no end, but stretched on into infinity.

He came to the wall at least once a week, and always after midnight. The first few times he had come during the day and quickly realized that night, when the others were not there, was more appropriate. The majority of those who came were tourists. The wall was the most visited monument in the capital. He despised the tourists: they had no right to be there. The first time he'd stood back and watched them, he wanted to shout, "It's too late! Where were you when we came home?"

But many who came had known the men whose names emblazoned the wall. He did not want to be witness to these, family and friends who came and wept and took pictures to bring back to their houses where little flags were pasted in front windows or larger ones hung from poles in suburban lawns. He did not want to know about the color snapshots of the wall they snapped to tuck in the corner of frames, superimposed over formal pictures of smiling men in dress blues. Some of those who came, he knew, were related to a name on the wall, and others who made the pilgrimage, maimed men on crutches or in wheelchairs, he recognized immediately as his peers. He could not bear to watch them as they shuffled along the wall, their eyes seeking one name. Or to witness when they found it and wept, or knelt, or pulled from a bag some token. They left behind flags, and teddy bears, and bibles. Often they left photographs, propping them up against the base of the immense parapet. He'd seen the pictures. They were snapshots of families, or of girlfriends, or of the family pets. Usually dogs. The sentimentality of it sickened him. He wondered if they knew that the park service took their treasures away each night and stored them in a huge dark room.

They left flowers too—roses and carnations—pushing the stems into the narrow strip of grass that lay between the wall and the adjacent granite walk.

There was a flower by his feet—a white carnation—and he deliberately stepped on it. It was already almost dead from lack of water. What a waste, he thought, grinding it beneath his foot.

He felt nothing but contempt for the people who left flowers. They knew nothing of death. They had no conception of what death in 'Nam looked like. He knew.

Once he had been the identifying officer after an A-4 went down. The pilot came back in a body bag. A crispy critter. It was the first time he'd been assigned the duty, and he wanted to do it properly. The corpsman had said it wasn't necessary, but he had insisted on opening the bag, on making an identification by the books. Months passed before he'd eat red meat after that.

He continued along the wall. He had been running his fingertips along the wet stone for so long that they shriveled. Some of those who were memorialized here he knew, but he never sought a specific name. He felt as if he knew them all. This wall was his: he belonged here.

A sharp noise echoed somewhere behind him, and he spun, fists clenched, ready to swing. Motionless in the shadow, his back to the wall, he waited, straining to hear another sound. He hated loud noises. The doctors they sent him to after 'Nam had told him that would go away. It will take time, they had assured him. They never said how much time.

The sound was not repeated. He tensed, waiting for it, afraid that it was the precursor to one of his occasional flashbacks. They promised the flashbacks would cease too. When he could forget, they said. But he would never forget. It was always there. It never left him. Maybe for one day. Two at the most, but underneath it was always there.

After a minute, when the silence continued, the man in black continued his walk, but his concentration was now less intense. He should be leaving. It was an hour's drive to Annapolis, and he would be lucky to get a motel room. Still, he was reluctant to leave the wall. It was his talisman, a symbol of his ability to survive.

Finally he walked away. He did not look back at the shiny black granite, and before he was ten yards away he broke into a jog, running along the nearly deserted, darkened streets of the capital. He felt good. God damn, but he felt good. Strong and invincible. Alive. Like the best days in 'Nam.

CHAPTER TWENTY-THREE

The enlisted man on guard duty at the Visitors' Gate nodded to Kate as she drove through. She had never been stopped at the gate, and she wondered if his presence were strictly ceremonial. Under what circumstances might he actually stop a car, deny admission?

She pulled into the visitor's parking lot by Halsey and parked. A small group of mids filed out of the fieldhouse, and she watched as they jogged down toward the athletic fields. It was a lovely day, prematurely warm, more like late April than March. Although it was only shortly after nine, the sun felt good on her face after the rain and cold of past days. Impulsively she turned away from Bancroft and the complex of classroom buildings and walked past Halsey and toward Annapolis harbor and Chesapeake Bay, where several white sails glided through the lightly rippled waters, the sloops piloted by winter-weary sailors coaxed out by the first spring-like day.

She inhaled the salty air, breathing in the sharp tang of winter and the promise of spring. Behind her she heard someone shout her name. She turned and saw Max McNulty, his arm raised in greeting. She stood and waited for him to come to her.

"I was afraid I'd missed you. I called the motel to see if you wanted to join me for breakfast, but you had already left. I don't have a class until ten. What about it? Can I buy you a cup of coffee? We could grab a cup at the snack bar in Rickett's."

"I've already eaten," she said.

"So have I." His smile was sheepish. She studied him, wondering why he had been waiting for her. The smile was a little crooked, the left side curved slightly higher than the right. She had not noticed that before. She liked it.

209

"How about a walk instead?"

For twenty-five years Michael had been the only man in Kate's life. After the divorce she had been totally uninterested in all males. Now, confused by McNulty's presence, and a little shaken by the way her heart had jumped when she had seen him, her voice was sharper than she intended. "Why were you waiting for me?"

He shook his head slightly and shrugged. "Damned if I know." he said, his face a blend of sincerity and confusion. Kate laughed out loud. His rich chuckle joined hers.

More comfortable now, they headed toward Lejeune Hall, passing within feet of the bronze statue of Bill, the Navy's mascot. Max pointed toward the charging goat, pointing out that his gonads were brighter than the rest of the body because generations of midshipmen rubbed them for luck. As they walked by the statue of Tecumseh, he told her about the mids' other superstitious gesture said to guarantee good fortune. "They call him the God of 2.0," he said, pointing up at the statue. "During exams the mids throw pennies at the quiver. According to legend, if the coin falls into the quiver, the mid will receive a passing grade on the exam."

Kate listened quietly, enjoying the sound of his voice. She did not tell him how well she already knew these legends. A squirrel cut across their path. Another followed in close pursuit, both darting up the trunk of a giant elm. McNulty chuckled. "Now there's a sign spring is here. Damn squirrels. I think there are more of them here than mids."

They walked by Tecumseh, by the benches reserved for first- and second-class mids, and by the cannons flanking them. As they neared Michelson and Chauvenet, handsome and stately halls that blended with the older architecture even though they were boldly contemporary, Kate heard a muffled thud. It was a haunting sound, a series of dull noises coming in a rhythmic pattern. Whomp, pause, whomp, pause, whomp. The sounds hung in the air like smoke.

"What is that?"

"Cannons. Must be a service at the chapel today. A lot of naval officers chose to have their celebration of interment here at the Academy. The chapel here is the Naval Cathedral, you know."

"I know." She did not mention her belief, reinforced during

her visit the day before, that the church celebrated the Navy and the country as much as it did God.

"They fire the cannons after the service. When I finally leave this place, I think that is the one sound I will take with me."

In spite of the sun on her face, Kate shivered. "Appropriate, isn't it? There is so much death here."

He looked at her, uncomprehending. She pointed around the Yard. "Look. Everywhere. Symbols of death." Her rigidly extended hand swept in an arc, stopping momentarily at each shaft of granite, each gun. "There." She pointed to the twin cannons mounted on pedestals on either side of the entrance to T-Court; "and there," the ornate ones by the green benches at the head of Stribling; "and there," the four bronze guns flanking the Mexican War Monument; "and there," the four dark carronades at the base of the Macedonian. "It's not possible to go anywhere here and not be in sight of a gun or cannon. In some ways this place is as much a national cemetery as Arlington."

"I never felt that way," he answered. "In the twelve years that I have taught here, I always had the feeling that the Yard was very much alive, that it celebrates life and youth and the future. I find it very beautiful." He checked his watch. "Look, I hate to do this, but I've got to run. I have a class in ten minutes." Again he seemed uncomfortable. "I guess I just wanted to say good morning and see that you were all right."

"I'm fine."

"What are you going to do today?"

"I'm going to talk to Bri's roommates, and there was one other mid in his company I wanted to see. Ariel Greene. Do you know her?"

McNulty paused, squinting up at the spire on the chapel as if trying to remember something. The mid's cap that had decorated the spire yesterday was gone. "Ariel Greene," he mused. "Why the hell does that sound so damn familiar?" He turned back to Kate. "You're out of luck. She's gone."

"Gone?"

"She left. She was a first-classman, and just before Christmas break she left."

"What do you mean, she left?"

"She resigned. Quit."

"She *quit*? She was a first-classman and she quit just like that?"

"Not exactly. The whole story escapes me. I haven't had her in a class for two years. But I do remember her leaving caused quite a stir. Wait a minute. It's coming back. She quit because of some mandatory physical test she couldn't pass." He chewed on his lip, nudging his memory. "It was a swimming or diving requirement, I think."

"I want to talk to her. How can I find out where she lives?"
"Why?"

"I don't know." Little things that didn't fit. Ariel's story was one of those things. It seemed odd that a midshipman only months from Commissioning would quit. The woman was in Brian's company and had known him. "How can I find out her address?"

"I guess Administration would be your best bet. Listen, I have to run." He took off his hat and eased the battered fabric of the brim between his fingers in what Kate was beginning to recognize as a nervous gesture. "If you don't have any plans, how about joining me for dinner?"

The idea was tempting. She had grown to like this gentle, kind-eyed professor. But her feelings were ambivalent: he was still connected to the Academy. His loyalty lay there.

She refused softly. "Maybe another night." She read disappointment in his eyes and a flicker of something else. Relief?

He nodded and murmured good-bye, moving off toward Sampson Hall. He did not look back at her. She stood for a moment, wondering if she should have accepted his invitation. Then she remembered the glimpse of his relief. She straightened her shoulders the tiniest bit and headed toward the Administration Building.

In the gleaming marble lobby she stood at the foot of the curving staircase, her hand clutching the brass rail. A young officer descended the steps, nodding to her as he passed. At the door he turned back and looked at her. "Can I help you, ma'am?"

"No, thank you," she replied. "I'm fine."

He hesitated, then strode away. Still Kate could not take the first step up the wide, gracefully winding staircase that led to the administration offices.

What the hell are you doing down there? The Admiral

called me today. You made me look like an idiot ... selfish ... irresponsible. ...

It was damned hard to break old patterns. Her entire adult life had been defined in terms of Michael's needs. When and where they would move, picking up and setting down the family and belongings whenever and wherever he asked her to. Entertaining people he asked her to. But that had been her own choice. His reproach echoed in her head as clearly as if he stood on the marble stairs above and flung the words down at her over the balustrade. *You're ruining my chances for promotion. What are you trying to do to me?*

Her hand tightened on the polished brass. Other memories flooded in, unwanted. She remembered how pleased they both were when Michael earned a promotion: the champagne, the hugs, the dinner out to celebrate, the toast across the table. Always, from the first days, he would say the same words, deliberately delivered obeisance to her rarely acknowledged support.

"We did it, Kate," he'd say. "This promotion is as much yours as it is mine. I couldn't have done it without you."

But he never asked, not once, the price she'd paid, the needs of her own she had put aside so that he could advance. But then, she acknowledged, neither had she.

The door behind her opened again as another officer came in. She felt the spring air pulling her back. Finally she moved. She was almost jogging, but when she reached the top of the stairs she was not even out of breath.

I'm not doing this because I'm selfish, or because I want to hurt your chance for a judgeship, Michael, she said in silent words he would never hear or understand. *I'm doing this because I have to, and because what you are asking of me is too much.*

From the window by his desk Admiral Thatcher followed Kate Tyler's progress as she walked away from the Administration Building. He watched her thoughtfully, humming tunelessly. The steel bows of his glasses pressed against the veins that swelled out across his temples. He dropped his gaze to a point between her shoulder blades as one would zero in on an enemy through a gun sight, and was consumed with loathing, an emotion he usually reserved for reporters and liberal senators. Still humming, he crossed to his desk and sat down. The outer door, leading to his assistant's office, was still closed. Kate Tyler had shut it on her way out.

He reached across the expanse of desk and picked up a yellow brick. The top of it was smooth to the touch, more like polished marble than brick, and he absently stroked it with his thumb. An engraved brass plate had been glued to the top surface. He stared at the words: TECUMSEH COURT, 1908–1983, U.S. NAVAL ACADEMY. Years ago Plebe Horace Thatcher had marched on this brick. Put in his hours. Paid his dues. When they resurfaced T-Court, he had taken a token brick. It represented more than four years at Navy. It was a symbol of his career, a carefully molded set of steps that had led him to this office, which in turn was a station on his journey's destination. He said the words silently, reverently. Joint Chief of Staffs.

His thoughts returned to Kate Tyler. He was not going to let her ruin his career, as his predecessor's had been destroyed. Admiral Whitaker's road had ended when he left Navy, the victim of two scandals. Cheating and stealing. Two crimes not tolerated. Those and any whiff of a sex scandal could cut short a man's career faster than a sword through a ceremonial cake. Well, Horace Thatcher vowed, it won't happen on my watch. *Not on my watch.* Still humming, he returned the brick to its place on his desk.

He had had to give her the name she wanted, but someone would have to shut her up. He shouted for his assistant.

The door opened immediately. "Sir?" The young officer looked drawn.

"Do you still have Mike Tyler's number?"

"Yes, sir."

Thatcher removed his glasses and rubbed his temples. "A good officer, Commander Tyler. You'd think he'd be able to control his own wife."

"She's his ex-wife, sir," the officer said, immediately regretting it.

"Get him on the horn for me. And I want to see First Classman Decker ASAP." He paused. There was someone else. The professor he'd seen talking to Kate Tyler. "And Maxwell McNulty, Professor McNulty. He's over at Sampson. I want to see him as soon as his class is over." McNulty wasn't Navy. Could be a problem, but not if he knew what was good for him. He was a civilian, but he still worked at the Academy.

The assistant nodded, waited a moment to see if there would be further instructions, then bowed out. Thatcher straightened his shoulders. Already he felt better. Taking charge always improved his outlook. He reassessed his opinion of Michael Tyler while waiting for the call to go through. Ex–wife or not, Tyler should have been able to straighten her out. Thatcher allowed himself the smug certainty of knowing that whether or not Marian was legally married to him, she would always obey him. She knew what it meant to be loyal. He drew a sheet of paper out of a drawer and began making notes. *Loyalty*, he penned, as he thought of how he would impress upon Tyler ways to gain his ex-wife's cooperation.

By eleven the motel was little more than half full. The two chambermaids finished cleaning the occupied rooms. They had only had three checkouts, and none of those had left yet. Check-out was at one.

When they had vacuumed the last of the occupied rooms, they took the laundry cart to the basement and put a load of sheets into the machine. Then they turned on the small portable television set to their favorite game show and settled down to have lunch. They would finish the checkouts after lunch. As they munched on sandwiches, they called out the answers before the contestants could. It was a musical quiz show, and the older of the two—Mary Louise—held the edge. She knew all the old standards. Belle, the other chambermaid, was better at the show where a correct answer resulted in a letter being flashed on the screen. She could guess the secret phrase or name long before Mary Louise had a clue. She could just see the phrase up there, as if all the letters were right in front of her.

They laughed a lot while playing, and their laughter usually brought the desk clerk down to join them. If it wasn't busy, he'd stay for the entire show. Then they'd turn the set down so they could hear the front desk bell if someone came in wanting a room.

The desk clerk was a bit younger than the two maids, and they competed for his attention as avidly as they did over the television games.

Across the street from the motel the man in the dark
Porsche watched. He had been there most of the night,
moving once, near dawn, so that he would not call attention
to himself, and a second time, at sunrise, to get coffee and
doughnuts. He had not eaten since late afternoon the day
before.

He had not slept much. Just a few minutes on and off. Still,
he felt sharp. He had gone much longer without sleep in
'Nam. As he watched, he toyed with the idea of getting a
room in the motel, but decided to wait and rent one in
another place. Safer.

Earlier, on the coffee run, he had bought three cups at a
McDonald's and had been opening the third when it spilled.
Because he'd been mopping the liquid from his jeans with a
napkin, he had almost missed the woman when she came out.

He had straightened up and rolled down the window to
get a better look. He had never seen her clearly, only a
picture of her in her home. Not bad looking, he decided.
Looking for a resemblance to her son, he found none.

After she drove away, he pulled his car into the space she
had vacated. Her room was on the far end of the building,
away from the office, but he had still been cautious. Perhaps
she was just going out for a quick breakfast. While he waited
he checked the rooms on either side. He watched the chambermaids cleaning one after the occupants had driven off. The
room on the other side was filled, the curtains drawn across
the picture window that fronted the parking lot. There was
no sign that the occupants were awake. Finally satisfied, he
moved in.

He turned and walked to the office, careful to open the
door slowly so the bell attached to the inside frame did not
ring. High-pitched laughter floated up from the room below
the office, cresting over the sound of a TV game show. He
crossed to the desk swiftly. The keys hung from a board on
the wall, and he slipped behind the partition and scooped up
the key for room 24. It was now the only empty hook on the
board; the others all held at least one key. He eased one key
from a hook to the left that held two and put it on the hook
for room 24. At first glance the board looked as it had before
he took the key. All of this, from the time he'd entered the
office, had taken less than ten seconds.

There was a copy of the *Washington Post* on a battered side table by a wooden armchair, and he tucked it under his arm and strode, whistling, back to Kate Tyler's room.

Although he did not really expect to find anything of significance, he felt it was essential to get inside her room. It was as if by searching the room he would get to know the enemy, and that was reason enough to take the risk. He looked in the bathroom first. It was cluttered, and looked like a woman used it, having the cosmetic, warm scent he had come to associate with a female's room. Several crumpled tissues lay in the wastebasket, but nothing else.

He moved everything on the counter, opening the jars and smelling the contents, touching every article. He liked the perfume she used. He pictured her, nude and damp from the shower. He had never had an older woman. He felt the stirring of desire. Anything was possible.

When he reentered the bedroom, the bathroom looked precisely as it had before he'd searched it. He prided himself on this. The same with her bureau. He opened every drawer, lifting out each piece of clothing. By fixing a mental image of the things as they were when he first saw them and matching that image when he was done, he was able to replace everything exactly as it had been before he'd touched it. It was a trick he had learned as a child. It wasn't hard, once you got the hang of it. Using it, he had claimed access to every drawer and closet in his parents' home. Their bedroom and his father's desk had been as familiar to him as his own. Long before his mother had, he'd known that his father had other women.

Days before, when he had searched Kate's home, he'd torn it apart intentionally, partly because he hadn't had time to do a careful, thorough search of his invisible kind, and partly because he thought she could be frightened off. This had been a mistake because apparently it had just made her suspicious. It had been a failure too. He had not found the letter Jordan said that Brian wrote before he died.

There was nothing beyond the ordinary in the dresser, but he struck unexpected pay dirt on the table by the bed. The small pad by the phone had a name scrawled on it. The penmanship was poor, as if the name had been written while a receiver was held in the crook of the neck at the same time the person was trying to jot it down.

Even so, he understood it. *Ariel Greene*. He stared at the

scrawl for a long time, letting his breath out slowly. His reflection in the mirror on the opposite wall revealed his smile. Still smiling, he sat on the bed. Then he stretched out. There was a chance the chambermaid might appear to do the room, but he figured his car outside would deflect that. It would appear that the room was still occupied. The chambermaids would never notice it was a different car from the one that had filled the slot earlier. There was a chance, too, that Kate could return and find him there. He acknowledged that that might even be the reason he stayed. The sharp thrill of danger made him feel more alive, sharper, when treading its perimeter.

He buried his head in the pillow, which smelled of Kate's shampoo. Setting his mental alarm for ten minutes, he closed his eyes. The smile still played on his lips. Within seconds he was asleep.

Exactly ten minutes later, refreshed, he woke. He rose and smoothed out the bedspread and pillow, erasing the imprint of his body. He moved quicker now, with purpose. Crossing to the window on the rear wall, he pulled aside the cheap curtains, revealing a narrow strip of grass and a stockade fence. The thin smile reappeared on his face, and he took a folding knife out of his pocket. Using a small blade, he unscrewed the swivel lock on the window. He lifted the bottom section of the window. The storm glass was still in place, and he pinched the clasps and raised it, locking it in position at the top half of the window. That done, he closed the window and drew the thin net drapes closed.

There was no particular reason to remove the lock and provide for an easy entrance. It had been instinct. But he knew being prepared was essential, even if he wasn't certain why the preparations were necessary. That knowledge would come.

He stared again at the name on the pad of paper, then picked up the copy of the *Post*, and whistling under his breath, left. He turned back at the door for one last look, then satisfied, locked the door. There was no sign anyone had been in the room.

Noises came from room 23 now. The people there had awakened and would probably be leaving soon. It was after twelve, and he knew they must be hungry. He tossed the room key into the air. Every moment he stayed was risky, but it was more dangerous to leave something unfinished. Walking as fast as possible without drawing attention, he crossed again to the motel office. Within eight seconds the key to room 24 hung on its hook. He tossed the newspaper back on the table and was closing the door when the clerk and chambermaids began climbing the stairs. Then he drove off. He would need a motel for a night or two after all. He was amazed at how totally alive he felt. He didn't even need a drink.

CHAPTER TWENTY-FOUR

They sat on the carved marble bench opposite Bancroft. Midshipman Cynthia Decker's body was rigid and distanced from Kate's. The meeting was not going well. Kate wanted to like the woman, to reach her, but the mid was as stiff and formal as her uniform—working blues: dark wool shirt and trousers, black shoes. The dress was similar to that worn by her male counterparts, and it neuterized the young woman.

"You must be pretty excited. In two months you get your commission. I guess it must have been a difficult four years."

"Yes, ma'am." The courtesy was faultless, but it was a wall.

"Has the time gone by quickly?"

"With all respect, ma'am, may I ask what was it you wanted to talk about? I don't believe you got my name and called me to meet you just to chat about my commission or my years here."

"You know my son died last month—"

"Yes, ma'am. He was in my company. I was sorry to hear about your son's suicide." She gave her condolences with correct politeness, but there was cruelness in the way she mentioned the manner of Brian's death. Aware of a growing dislike for First Classman Decker, Kate forced herself to go on, unconsciously making her own sentences as brief as the mid's.

"I want to know why he died."

"I wish I could help you, but I don't see how I can. It's true, I was in the same company, but I didn't know your son well. We weren't friends or anything."

"I see. I was hoping you could tell me something about a first-classman named Ariel Greene—"

"She left." Decker's expression was closed.

"I know that. I was hoping you might be able to give me her address."

Decker looked at two long-legged mids dashing down the stairs from Bancroft, taking the steps two at a time, then turned back to Kate. Her face was unreadable, but for a moment something—a flash of fear—surfaced in her eyes. "What does Ariel have to do with your son?"

The break in Decker's composure had been fleeting, but it betrayed her. Kate did not answer, but kept her gaze on the other's face in a silent, strained battle of wills. Decker broke first.

"She was attractive," she finally said. She was not quite successful in suppressing a note of bitterness.

For the first time Kate looked at her, seeing beyond the uniform. Decker's brown hair was worn short, clipped straight across at the collar. Her eyebrows, too, were straight and unplucked. Decker was plain. Kate found herself wondering what she would look like in civilian clothes, if she would be more feminine. Then she knew what bothered her most about Midshipman Decker. She sounded just like Michael at his worst: hard, directed, male.

"If that's all, ma'am, I have a class I can't be late for."

Kate was as anxious to leave Decker as the mid was to leave her. "Certainly. Just one more thing. Could you give me Ariel's address?"

Decker looked directly at her. "I'm sorry, ma'am. I don't know it."

With absolute certainty, Kate knew that the mid was lying, and the lie was more chilling because the woman's gaze was clear and unwavering. It was not the first time that Decker had been untruthful with her. Kate knew all classes for the day were over. "Surely you have her name written down somewhere."

Decker did not answer, and provoked, Kate's voice grew loud, "I will get it, you know. If you don't give it to me, someone else will." The coldness in the mid's eyes made the hair on her arms lift, as if an icy breeze had touched her.

They did not say good-bye to each other. Kate left the woman sitting on the bench on Stribling and headed toward her car. A late afternoon wind had come up, and the sailboats she'd seen earlier on the Bay were now gone.

CHAPTER TWENTY-FIVE

From one of the tall windows lining the face of Chauvenet Hall, Midshipman Jordan Scott watched Kate walk away from Ariel Greene's former roommate.

"Shit," he muttered. Other midshipmen bumped into him as they rushed by, but he did not move. "Shitttt." A plebe pivoted and gaped, but Jordan ignored him. *Buck said he was going to frighten her off. That's what he said last night. He said he'd let the bitch know she wasn't wanted nosing around here. But she's still here.* Worse, she was talking with Decker. Could it be a coincidence? Jordan wanted desperately to believe it. What the hell was she doing hanging around? Spider said she had talked to McNulty. Now here she was talking with Decker. Although he would never admit it to Spider, Jordan was scared.

Why won't she just leave things alone? He looked at his watch: 1600. Two hours until meal formation. He had to get away from the Yard. He headed into town.

The Middleton Tavern was nearly empty. It was too late for the lunch crowd and too early for dinner. It suited his mood perfectly. He ordered coffee, wanting a beer. Giggles, high pitched, designed to catch his attention, broke into his thoughts. A quartet of teenage girls sipped soft drinks at a nearby table. Their laughter irritated him, and he hunched over his cup.

The girl's voices grew more animated. Without wanting to, he took in their signals, knowing how aware they were of him. He called the waiter over for a refill and allowed himself a casual glimpse of the four girls. One looked familiar. He remembered. She was a regular at Dahlgren tea dances. He tried to guess her age. High school. She couldn't be older than that.

There was a fresh outburst of half-suppressed giggles, and one of the others nudged the girl he watched. He could tell she knew he was looking at her by the way she bent to conceal her flushed face. She wasn't attractive. Ten or fifteen pounds overweight. She wore a blue denim skirt that fit tightly over her round hips and thighs, and a pastel oversized flannel shirt. Suddenly he wanted her.

As if she could read his mind, she lifted her head, looked at him, and smiled. He returned the smile. An unseen signal was given, and the three other girls scooped up their things and left. Their giggles crescendoed as they went out into the street. She rose and walked to his table.

"I know you, don't I?" Her hands were plump, dimpled.

"Join me for a cup of coffee?" He avoided her question. He wanted her so badly, it shook him. She wasn't pretty at all. A dog. He looked to see if there were any other mids around. He'd never live this one down.

She took the seat on the other side of the table. Her knees bumped his, pressing slightly against his before she shifted them. "I mean it," she persisted. "I've met you before, haven't I?" He sipped his coffee. Her uncertainty made her look younger. "I mean, sometimes I go to the dances, you know. Maybe we've danced."

"Sure. Maybe."

She nodded happily. "I knew it. When you smiled at me, I knew we'd met before." She looked down and long lashes swept against her cheek. She had nice eyes. He'd give her that. His uniform felt tight against his crotch. "It's funny, us meeting like this. I mean, there's so many of you, and here we meet again. A coincidence, you know what I mean? Having danced together before and now having coffee." She did not have a cup of coffee, and he made no attempt to get her some. He sighed soundlessly. He recognized the signs. She wanted soft talk, to be seduced. For a moment he considered dropping the whole thing, but his groin ached with his need. He sighed again, softly, and began.

"It happens that way. Sometimes in life, people meet. They're in cars going in different directions, but for one moment on the individual trips, they come together for one special time. Do you know what I mean?"

"Yes," she said softly. She let him seduce her, wanted him to make it easy for her to go with him. So he did.

They used her car. Her father's actually. A Toyota two-door that had a plastic litter bag hanging from the knob of the radio. She was allowed to use it after school if she would pick him up after work. She drove. "My name is Jane. Isn't that a terrible name? Boring. But my friends all call me Janey."

He was silent, staring out the window as she deftly drove out of the city. He saw a pile of textbooks on the back seat. High school books. Christ. He prayed she was at least a senior.

She flashed a nervous look at him. "Aren't you going to tell me your name?"

"Buck." Now why the hell had he said that?

"Buck. I like that. It sounds masculine. Hard. You know what I mean." She giggled nervously, brushing her hair back from her face with a gesture he guessed was meant to be sexy.

He didn't ask where they were going. She drove confidently, as if she'd made this trip before. Aware she had given something away, she said, "There's this place my friend Beth told me about. She sometimes goes there with her boyfriend. It's private, you know. A road not too far from here. Beth was the one with the blond hair and pink sweater. Do you remember her? She was sitting next to me back at the Middleton. She was the prom queen." Her voice was proud. "She's real pretty, don't you think?"

Jordan didn't want to talk. Not about Janey or Beth or Beth's boyfriend or some friggin' high school prom, but he recognized the prompt. "Not as pretty as you," he said.

"Thank you." She looked at his uniform sleeve. "I've never had a date with a first-classman before. Mostly just plebes. They're so young, you know."

"They're young all right." A date. Christ.

She looked again at him, staring at his hands.

"Better watch where we're going," he said. "Don't want to land your father's car in a ditch."

The color in her cheeks deepened. "You don't have a girl, do you?"

He was surprised. "Why did you say that?"

"You're still wearing your ring. I mean, you haven't given it to anyone."

He twisted the heavy gold ring around his finger, pressing his thumb against the stone, then the shank, rubbing the embossed seals, as if for luck. There were two intricate engravings on each side of the stone: the Academy's crest and that of his class. Spider had helped design the class crest. Impatiently he cupped his one hand over the ring, cutting it off from her view. "How much farther?"

"We're nearly there." She turned into a narrow dirt road. About one hundred yards down the road there was an open grassy patch on the left side where the early spring grass had already been worn thin in two bare strips from car tires. She pulled in. Before she turned the ignition off, she took time to turn the car around so that they were headed out.

He undressed her completely. At first she resisted, feebly protesting she was cold, but he didn't pay attention. He stayed fully clothed. When he unbuttoned her oversized shirt, her breasts surprised him. They were enormous. Almost bigger than he liked.

"You on the pill?" he asked, his voice crude. It was the only time he spoke to her after she was undressed. Her cheeks reddened and she nodded. He did not say another word to her.

She didn't come. He didn't care. After, she tried to cuddle against him and he clenched his teeth to keep from shoving her away. The sweaty smell of her, of them, disgusted him. The late afternoon sun stained her shoulders, and it was growing colder. "I guess you'd better get the car to your father," he said. "You better get dressed."

"That's okay. We've got time." She pressed against him again. "How come you don't have a special girl, you know? One to give your ring to?"

He pulled his arm out from under her and looked at his watch. "Christ," he said suddenly. "Look, I'm sorry to hurry, but I've got to get back. I didn't know it was so late." He flashed her a smile. "Rules, you know."

She took the rejection silently. While she dressed, he looked pointedly at his watch, and this made her nervous. She fumbled with the buttons and zipper until he wanted to scream.

She sniffed slightly as they drove away, but he pretended not to notice. There were stains on the front of his crotch, and he swore again and scrubbed at the material with a flowered Kleenex she gave him from her bag. Finally she asked in a small voice, "Do you think I'm a whore?"

"It doesn't matter what I think, does it?" he asked cruelly. They didn't speak again until she turned onto King George.

"Buck?"

He had almost forgotten he'd told her that was his name.
"What?"

Her voice was tiny. "Those cars you were talking about
before—"

"What cars?" What the hell was she talking about?

"The ones going in different directions? Do the passengers
that meet . . . do they ever start going in the same direction
together?"

He remembered then. Christ, she was taking it seriously.
It's just a line, he wanted to shout. For Christ's sake, it's just
a line. "Look, I'll just hop out here. Thanks for the ride. It's
been terrific."

He jogged toward the Yard. There was no sound of the car
pulling away, and he knew she would keep watching him
until he was gone from her sight. He couldn't wait to get
away. Only when he was climbing the steps to Mother B. did
he feel relief and realize that he'd been afraid he would not be
able to perform. He had needed to know that, but it hadn't
helped at all. Not even being with a woman could make him
forget his fears about Brian.

CHAPTER TWENTY-SIX

Kate returned to her motel, stopping on the way at a convenience store to pick up juice, tea bags, crackers, and cheese, and at a liquor store for a jug of wine. The wine, she hoped, would help dim the raging frustration and confusion. She asked herself the question a dozen times between the Yard and the motel. Why would Decker lie?

Juggling her purchases, she clumsily inserted the key and entered her room. For a fleeting moment she was certain that someone had been there in her absence. Then she remembered that the maid would have been in to clean, and scolded herself for being paranoid.

She set the few groceries on the tiny counter near the sink and put the wine, juice, and cheese in the refrigerator. Although it was only late afternoon, she was exhausted. She thought about opening the wine, but decided to make tea instead. The kitchenette was outfitted with the bare essentials: a small teakettle, saucepan, and skillet. While waiting for the kettle to boil, she put in a call to Leah, who did not answer her phone.

Disappointed, Kate looked at her watch. Four-thirty. She wondered if Leah had classes that late. She longed to talk with her, to talk to anyone outside of the Academy. She felt she was losing perspective. The growing sense of paranoia that had taken seed that morning while she was talking to Admiral Thatcher threatened to overwhelm her. Sighing, she poured water over the tea bag and set the cup on the bedside table. She dialed Leah's number again.

The tea was too hot to drink, and while it was cooling she took a shower, hoping it would ease the restlessness that had been building all day. It didn't.

She sipped the tea and again flicked the television on and then off. Again she tried Leah's number. When it went unanswered, she sat by the phone, undecided. Sighing, she pulled her pad from her purse and flipped to the page where she had noted McNulty's address. She stared at the words, wondering whether or not to call him. He had offered to help her. After all, he'd been the one to give her his address, and he'd been waiting for her at the Yard. And he had invited her to dinner. Her stomach was as nervous as it had been when she was a teenager waiting for a special call. Exasperated, she reached for her coat. I won't call first. That way, she reasoned, I can always change my mind.

She found McNulty's home easily. Although the street was only ten minutes from the hectic traffic rush of Church Circle, it felt like a distant suburb. The house was Victorian, with dormers, a steeply pitched roof, and a deep front porch—the kind of house that from the outside looks large but surprises one because the interior is so much smaller than one expects. There was a sloping lawn with towering shade trees, the tips swollen with buds. Someone had given attention to the plantings around the front door. Carefully shaped forsythia bushes stood on either side of the steps. The earth at their roots had been weeded, and shiny green shoots of early jonquils poked up through the soil. As she pushed the recessed doorbell, an attack of the jitters hit her.

He had changed out of his suit and was wearing a soft, faded flannel shirt over blue jeans, most of which was covered by a large white chef's apron. When he saw her, he made a feeble motion to remove the apron but left it on. She saw at once he was surprised. Then she glimpsed again the flash of withdrawal that she had seen earlier, and something else. Something like apprehension. The easy companionship they had shared that morning was gone. After a moment's hesitation, he invited her in. She immediately felt tongue-tied. She shouldn't have come.

"I'm sorry to intrude." The formal words rang in her ears. She would have given anything to be back in her motel room.

"I'm having a drink. Could I get you one?"

When he disappeared down the hall to the kitchen, she waited in a room to the left of the entrance. In the light from the hall she caught a glimpse of the living room to the right. The room in which she now stood had originally been a dining room, converted to a study. The furnishings were haphazard. There was an old morris chair and an equally worn stuffed chair opposite it. The room was cluttered but clean. There were brass rubbings framed on the wall. A stack of student's papers rested on the step table near the morris chair, and it was this, she decided, that gave the feeling of such familiarity to the room.

A partially completed model of a three-masted schooner stood on a card table set up by the front window. Vials of glue and paint and a glass jar of slender brushes were scattered around the work space. She was admiring the meticulously crafted boat when he returned with her drink.

"Will you join me for dinner?" It was the invitation of a man being scrupulously polite

"Oh, I don't want to intrude," she repeated.

"I have plenty. It's no bother."

She followed him to the kitchen in the back of the house. It was small but efficiently laid out and cheery, with a wall of exposed brick, old wood cabinets, and by a large window that overlooked the backyard, a drop-leaf table which bore a woven placemat and setting for one. She liked that he had set the table. So many people who lived alone ended up eating over the kitchen counter. She knew.

Efficiently and carefully, he sliced vegetables for the salad. Into a large wooden bowl he tossed spinach leaves, walnuts, chive blossoms that had been shredded into dozens of tiny lavender flowerettes, pieces of raw carrots and cauliflower and broccoli. Then he crumbled blue cheese over the top. While he worked he gave her directions for making a dressing. He did not ask her how she made out at the Academy, and she was grateful. She did not want to talk about it now. When the salad and dressing were finished, she sat and sipped wine. He put two potatoes into the microwave.

"Do you like teaching at the Academy?" She felt the need to make conversation, as if she were on a bad blind date, even though he seemed more at ease now that they were in the kitchen.

"Very much." He seemed relieved at her question. "It's a dream. Sound like the company line? It's true. Where else could I teach where kids rise when I enter the classroom, do their assignments conscientiously, are bright, highly motivated and pleasant? There's no worry about drugs or skipped classes."

Kate felt pang of envy. "I don't know. To me, your students seem regimented, programmed, if you will." She knew she was being perverse. Her son had been one of those students.

"Programmed is not the right word. They are disciplined, taught to respond without hesitation. That is part of their training. It's what plebe year is all about. Indoctrination. The ability to make decisions without wasting time which could be precious. That doesn't mean they haven't trained their minds to question. Don't do them an injustice." The criticism was soft-spoken. "Beneath the uniforms my students are individuals. What about Brian? Was he less of an individual because he was a mid?"

She wanted to answer honestly. She couldn't get over that cheated sense that the Academy had taken her son from her and transformed him into someone else, foreign, one of many, but that impression was countered by another one: her son's face, the lines and flesh molded into a new maturity and set with determination. "No," she answered.

When the potatoes were baked, he split them and spooned a mound of sour cream on each. Then he sprinkled a table-spoon of caviar over the snowy cream.

"I hope you like caviar," he said, although he hadn't asked her before he put the roe on the potato.

"I love it," she said, with more enthusiasm than she felt.

She was glad he hadn't decided to eat in the formal dining room. Their growing sense of ease seemed too fragile to survive the move. She brought the salad to the table while he poured more wine. Seated opposite her, he lifted his glass in a silent toast.

Kate took a bite of potato and the tiny bubbles of caviar exploded in her mouth like a salty fusillade. "It's wonderful," she said, surprised.

He was pleased. "I'm glad you like it. It's a standard here. I'm a vegetarian."

She took another mouthful, savoring the taste.

"You're frowning," he commented.

"Was I? I don't know. I guess I'm surprised. You don't fit my idea of a vegetarian. I think of you as part of the military complex."

"And you don't look like the kind of person to categorize people," he reproached gently.

Before she could respond, there was a scratching at the back door. "Ari's late," he said, setting down his glass.

"Ari?"

"Aramis," he grinned. He opened the door wide enough for a black striped cat to slip in. While Max opened a can of food and spooned it into a plastic bowl, the cat waited by the brick wall, its sober face watching every movement, its tail flicking rhythmically against the tile. It ignored Kate totally.

"How old is your cat?"

"He's not mine." He set the bowl on the floor. "I just feed him. I'm not even sure who owns him."

"Does he come every night?"

"Just about. Sometimes he's off fighting or doing whatever street cats do. When he turns up again, he has a fresh scar."

"Duel marks?"

Max looked at her, delighted. "No one else ever made the connection," he said. Having emptied the bowl, Aramis strolled to the door and waited. Laughing, Max let him out.

After the cat was gone, Kate was more keenly aware of being alone with him. She fiddled with her fork. When she swallowed her wine, the noise seemed very loud. Finally, her appetite lost out to her nerves, and she gave up any pretense of eating. "I talked to Ariel's roommate..." she began.

"And?" His voice was wary and he avoided her eyes.

"I don't know. I found myself disliking her. She seemed so tough." She fell silent for a minute. "It was like she had grown tough to survive. What do you think about women at the Academy? Do you think they belong there?"

"A moot question," he replied. "They are there." He continued eating with gusto, either ignoring or oblivious to her nervousness.

Annoyed at his composure, she pressed, "You're avoiding the issue. *Should* they be there?"

He put his fork down. Her glass was empty, and he refilled it. "I guess a lot of the old grads would string me up for this, but yes, I do." He studied her before continuing. "I'm surprised at you, though. If I read you correctly, you're not too sure."

"If the cost of admission for a woman is to become a male, maybe the price is too high."

"They aren't all like Decker," he objected, leaning back in his chair.

"What about the mids? Do they accept the women?"

"For the most part. It's not like it was back in '76. The mids at the Academy now have never known anything different. The most difficult years were during the transition. The all-male upperclassmen who watched women enter as mids fought it, but it isn't really an issue anymore." He paused and took a sip of wine, and when he continued, he spoke more thoughtfully. "But to be honest, it isn't that simple. After we spoke this morning, I went back and looked up Greene's class picture in the yearbook. She was very pretty, almost frail, and I was reminded of my first impression of her. I was amazed that she had survived Plebe Summer.

"Being a mid is twice as hard for a woman. The average woman mid scores higher on her SAT's, achieved a higher high school comprehensive grade. As plebes they have to have their shines brighter, their rooms cleaner, their 'table salts' faster. If one fails, her failure reflects on the rest. It's a chorus of 'I told you so. Women don't belong.' If one succeeds, she is often resented. Her achievements are looked on with suspicion, the results of a public relations ploy. No one talks about this. In fact there is denial, but last year a woman ranked at the top of the first class. When she was commissioned —the first mid of her class—members of the Brigade did not cheer. They saved that acknowledgment for the mid—a man— who ranked second. Afterward no one mentioned it. It was like it didn't happen.

"Their future, too, is not assured. The chances that they will make flag rank are almost nonexistent. They can't make admiral because they can't serve with the fleet. To make admiral, a sailor has to serve with the fleet."

"Why would a woman want to go here?"

"For the same reasons men do. For the challenge. To test themselves. Because they think they are the best there is."

"It sounds terrible."

"I gave you the worst scenario. It isn't all like that. In fact, as I said earlier, it's a lot better than it was in '76 and the beginning years."

They sipped their wine in silence. "I want to see Ariel Greene," Kate said.

"Why? What does she have to do with your son?" Again he betrayed that cool wariness.

"I don't know. Maybe I'm just reaching for anything. Women's intuition."

"I am too old and too smart to argue with that," he said.

He wouldn't let her do the dishes. They went back to the study and drank their coffee. He put on a George Winston tape. Full and now totally at ease, she teased, "Don't make it too comfortable here or I won't want to leave." She meant nothing by the words except to compliment his warmth and hospitality, but he recoiled—there was no other word for it—and she wished she had cut out her tongue. Then she got angry. *Don't worry*, she longed to say, *I'm not going to throw myself at you*. She finished her coffee and waited a moment or two, then stretched. "I didn't realize how tired I am. I hate to eat and run, but I've had a long day."

He made no attempt to persuade her to stay. He walked her to the door, performing the duties of a correct host, his words containing just the right portion of warmth. Careful to match his tone, underneath, Kate was seething. She felt like a teenager who had made an unwelcome advance. She was also honest enough to admit that the wine and music and warmth of the shared mood after so many months of solitude had made her acutely aware that she was a vulnerable woman alone with a man. Uncomfortably, she keenly recalled the moment in the restaurant days ago when she and Nina had been witness to Liz Shannon's desperation.

She waited at the door while he brought her coat. "Thank you for the meal. It was delicious." She extended her hand for him to shake. After a moment he took it. Their eyes met while he held her hand. A brief but unmistakable sexual charge passed between them, giving her the courage to ask her question. "I wonder," she said, "could you get me Ariel's address? Cynthia Decker didn't remember it."

"I wouldn't know how to go about getting it for you. Maybe someone in Administration could." Like Midshipman Decker, Max McNulty lied badly.

He stood in the pool of light by the front door, watching as she got in the car. She pulled the keys from her purse, and after fumbling a moment with the unfamiliar key, slid it into the ignition. The motor caught immediately. She put her purse on the seat beside her and gasped. Her hand had brushed something soft. Instinctively, before she even knew what she'd touched, she drew back in horror. From the doorway, Max still looked on. She felt panic building, knew she didn't want to see what lay on the seat at her side. She was aware now of a sweet, terrible smell. Trembling she flicked on the dome light and let out a whimper. A striped cat lay curled on the seat by her side. Aramis. It was dead. There was little blood, but by the angle of the cat's head, she knew its neck had been broken.

Its death was an obscenity on this quiet suburban street with its carefully maintained homes. The image of the animal sitting in Max's kitchen, waiting patiently for him to open the can of cat food, flashed through her mind. She reacted with fury, swearing, the words filthy and angry, words she never used. She picked the body up and cradled it in her arms. Max was still in the doorway. She knew that he saw something was wrong, and she felt a knifing of regret that she would be the one to bring the cat to him. Getting out of the car, she crossed the lawn to him, blinded by tears of rage.

"Oh God." He reached out to take the limp body from her. "Aramis." For the first time Kate saw his vulnerability. Anger had not hit him yet, but she was angry enough for both of them. They took the cat to the kitchen. The room still smelled of coffee and baked potatoes. They did not speak.

Later they were astounded that they hadn't wondered immediately why the cat had been killed and placed in Kate's car. She held the corpse while he opened a drawer and took out a large plastic bag. Then he lifted the cat and placed it inside. He was so gentle that watching him made her throat ache.

He set the bag by the back door. The inky fur shone through the plastic. Kate stood by helplessly. There were no words to say that would not be wrong. His face was grim and he said nothing. She felt guilty, as if the cat's death were somehow her fault.

He washed his hands at the kitchen sink; the suds flowed over their dinner dishes. When he finished with the towel, he turned and his eyes fell on the plastic bowl on the floor by the brick wall. He walked over and picked it up. When he dropped it in the garbage pail, she saw a glitter of tears in his eyes. "Don't," she said, aware that she was crying now.

He turned to her and then they were face to face, clinging to one another. It was impossible to say who had moved first, as it was impossible to guess whose was the greater need. They kissed each other with a hunger spurred by loneliness and fear as much as chemistry, and the hunger was heightened because it had been touched by a glimpse of death.

Finally, he stepped back. He grasped her arms and intently studied her face. "You think there's a connection, don't you? Between Brian and Ariel?" He read the answer in her eyes. Whatever confusion he felt earlier was gone. "I'll call you in the morning. I'll give you the address then. I'd get it now, but it's too late." He did this willingly, not telling her he'd been advised not to help her. Nor did he tell her the picture the admiral had painted of her—a neurotic, driven woman trying to destroy the Academy's reputation with lies in an effort to whitewash her son's suicide. It was a picture he'd had difficulty accepting all along. It did not match the one he had of a gentle, honest woman who believed in her son. Not for the first time he wondered why the admiral had bothered to warn him about her. "I promise. I'll call you in the morning."

Kate didn't notice the smear of dried blood on her hands until she had returned to the motel. She was washing it off when she heard someone at the door. The knock was loud, imperative, and she jumped. "Yes?" Her voice shook.

"Open the door." Michael's voice surprised her, but when she saw his face, she was paralyzed. His features were rigid with hate. It was directed at her, and she felt physically ill from its force.

"Michael, I—"

"Sit down." The hate burned in his voice. He had never hit her—she would have sworn once that he was incapable of hitting a woman—but now she shrank from him in fear. She had seen him in the courtroom, knew he possessed the acting skills every lawyer needed, but knew as well that the emotion directed toward her was not feigned. There was a streak of the cat's blood on her skirt, and she creased the material between her fingers, instinctively hiding it.

"You had to keep at it, didn't you? *Had* to know. I told you to let it go. But no, you had to keep pushing. Had to keep pushing until you ruined me. Well, okay, Katherine, I'll tell you. I'll tell you why your precious son killed himself, and I hope to hell you're satisfied. I'll tell you, and I hope it's worth knowing. Worth ruining me, hurting your father."

Kate wanted to prevent him from saying any more, wanted to cover her ears like a child. She raised her hand as if to ward off a blow. The death of Max's cat now seemed only a preview of a new, more terrible nightmare. Michael ignored the feeble motion.

"You want to know why he died? I'll tell you. He killed himself. Oh, yes, Kate, he killed himself all right. Your perfect, precious son hung himself because he was a cheat. That's right. He was a goddamned cheat and he got caught."

"No." The denial was no more than a whisper.

"Oh, yes, Kate. He was a cheat. You thought they were covering something up? Well, you were right. Admiral Thatcher *knew*, his roommates knew, for all I know half the bloody Academy knew. Is that what you wanted to hear? The truth." She tried to get up, to escape his voice, the knowing black gaze, but he pinned her arms to the chair. "Don't like what you're hearing? Well, it's too damn bad. You forced this. I didn't want to tell you but you wanted to hear the truth, so you're going to hear it, and I hope you hear it in your dreams for the rest of your life.

"Three months before your precious son was going to graduate, he panicked and cheated on an exam. He got caught. They didn't tell you that he was a cheat because they didn't want to destroy your memory of him. They knew how hard it would be to learn your son was a suicide, a coward" —he spat the word—"without also having to know he was a cheat. They tried to spare us that." She heard in his voice no horror, no shame or sorrow. Only hate. It was the only emotion she could read in his voice, face, and posture.

She bent her head. She felt as if the spots of blood on her skirt had leaked from her body, dripped from her heart. She fought for her breath. "It can't be true."

"Oh, it's true, all right. How do you like this precious truth you were so damned determined to find?"

"It just can't be true." She raised her eyes, pleading. "I

mean, why would he cheat? Why would he kill himself? He was married. His wife is pregnant."

"You're shitting me." At last she had shocked him. Michael rarely swore.

"Her name is Leah. She is a student at George Washington."

"Well, that's just fine. Just dandy. Any other grand news you've been keeping from me? Any other admirable traits come to light? A cheat, a coward, and a liar as well, this son of yours. Secretly married, huh? He broke just about every rule in the book, didn't he? Do you know how that makes me feel? It makes me wish to Christ I'd never even had a son." She was still sitting in the chair when he left.

CHAPTER TWENTY-SEVEN

Webb didn't want a drink. He hated the bar. He hated the smoke that filled the room with a thick blue haze that would cling to his skin and hair and pores until he showered it off. He hated the good ol' boys who lined the bar, drinking, boasting, eyeing the uniformed midshipmen, hoping one of the mids would provoke a fight. "Let's get out of here," he said.

Jordan fidgeted, making circles with his beer glass. "Not yet," he muttered.

"What did you want to tell me? What was so important that it couldn't wait?"

"I'll tell you. Wait until he gets here."

"Who?"

"Buck. He's meeting us."

Spider shoved back his chair. He didn't like the bar and he didn't like Buck. "Look. I don't want to wait. If you don't want to tell me now, forget it."

Jordan looked toward the doorway, relief spreading across his face. "Here he is."

Buck pushed his way across the crowded room. The only empty chair was across from Webb, its back to the men at the bar. "Hey there, brother. Let me sit there. You sit here." He jabbed Jordan brutally on the shoulder, a tight, hard jab that Webb could see hurt, but Jordan mutely relinquished his chair to Buck and took the empty one. Leaning back in the chair so that it was balanced on two back legs, Buck lit a cigarette and took a drink of Jordan's beer, flipping the match to the floor. Webb's regret that he had agreed to come deepened.

"What kept you?" Jordan asked. "We've been waiting for almost an hour."

"A little chore I had to do." Webb tried not to flinch at the nastiness in Buck's expression. "What was it you had to tell me, little brother?"

"It's about Bri's mother. She's still hanging around. You said you'd keep an eye on her, scare her away, but I saw her."

Webb looked from brother to brother. "You said you would scare her?"

Jordan ignored the interruption. "And I saw her talking to Decker. Damn it, Buck. She was talking with *Decker.*"

He had known all along that it would all come out. Well, it was coming down now, and there was no way anyone could stop it. Webb felt an eerie sense of relief. Later it would hit him that it meant his dream was ended. He would never be a Navy pilot.

When neither of them answered him, Jordan raised his voice petulantly. "Didn't you hear what I said? I saw them talking. On the bench by Stribling. And I'm telling you, she *knows.* Why else would she be talking to Decker? She's found out something."

Webb stood up, took a bill out of his wallet and tossed it on the table.

"Damn it, Spider, where are you going?"

"Outside. I'm finished here. When you're ready to go back, I'll be in the car."

He walked away. Jordan made a move to follow him, but something Buck said stopped him. Spider didn't hear what it was and he didn't care. He walked outside, greedily inhaling the fresh night air.

At the car he leaned back against the doorframe, his face toward the heavens. The spring stars were out, jewellike, forming a brilliant canopy in the sky overhead. He looked up at them for a long time, staring with such intensity that they blurred and then, like the sighting through a telescope that has been brought back into focus, became clear and distinct again. The ridge above the doorjamb dug into his back but he did not move. The Copernican universe strained down on him. He'd had to memorize the constellations for a class in navigation. The stars could never help him regain the course he had lost. Nothing would fill the emptiness he felt. Not a drink. Or a woman. Or a prayer.

He straightened and slid inside the car, keeping the door open, his right foot on the pavement. The dome light was on, and he reached up and flicked it off. He waited a long time. Finally he saw Jordan come out of the bar.

Buck was with him. The brothers walked so close, their shoulders touched.

Across the lot, Buck's drunken voice came to him. Webb watched as he did a little dance, shadow boxing, a parody of a boxer, jabbing the darkness. They were still talking. He watched, as disinterested as if they were strangers.

Suddenly Buck jabbed at Jordan, his clenched fist brutally striking his arm, as he had earlier inside the bar. Jordan stepped away defensively, putting distance between them. His arms hung limply by his sides.

As if enraged by this refusal to play, Buck circled the slender, elegant figure of his brother; the punches became stinging jabs. Crouching low, he danced and darted. His voice rose. "Go on. Try and land one. One good punch."

"Come on, Buck. I don't feel like foolin'."

"What's the matter? You a wuss? Is my baby brother a wuss?" Buck reached over and slapped him, a cruel, open-palmed blow to the cheek. The sound ricocheted across the deserted lot.

"Come on, Buck, cut it out." Jordan backed away.

Buck edged forward, slapping him again, first one cheek then the other. "Come on, wuss, aren't you going to stand and fight?"

Halfheartedly protecting himself from the blows, Jordan hunched his elbows.

"Hit me," Buck hissed. "Hit me and I'll stop." Slap. "Come on. One punch." Slap. "Come on, cunt." Slap.

Watching, Webb felt his fists curl. He leaned forward, setting his right foot flat on the pavement. Then he forced himself to unclench his fists. He looked away. Disgust washed over him. He wanted to get away. There was a cry. And the sound of footsteps moving away. Webb finally turned and looked. Jordan lay on the ground. He saw Buck disappearing back into the bar.

Webb did not move. When his roommate got into the car, he did not look at him.

Jordan wiped his nose on his sleeve, checking it for blood. He glanced at Webb. "He was just foolin' around. He didn't mean anything by that." His voice was apologetic. Webb did not answer.

"I couldn't hit him, you know. I never could. Even when we were kids. He was always trying to make me fight. He'd give me an Indian burn that would stay red for hours, just to make me fight. I never would." He sounded proud.

When Webb still did not speak, Jordan glanced at him nervously, then started the car. "Everything's going to be all right, though. He's going to take care of it. You know what I mean. About Ariel and everything. There's no need to worry about that."

"Sure." Webb didn't bother to disguise his bitterness.

"You don't like Buck, do you?"

"Let it alone."

"I can tell. He's not like you think he is. The last years have been hard on him. You know. 'Nam. All that. It wasn't easy on him there."

"A lot of guys were in Vietnam. He isn't the only one."

"It was different for Buck. All the time he was gone my father kept telling him he was a hero. Feeding him stuff about the Navy and pride and doing your duty to your country. But when Buck came back, he couldn't even get a job. Dad was telling him he was a hero, and people were throwing rotten eggs at our house. Calling my mother on the phone and swearing at her. We had to get an unlisted number. Kids would spit at Buck. Little kids. No more than ten years old. They spit at him and called him a baby killer."

"It's over, Jordan." Webb felt bathed in exhaustion.

"What are you talking about?"

"Can't you see that? It's *over*."

"What the hell's the matter with you, Spider? Haven't you been listening? That's what I'm telling you. What are you, soft? You afraid of Tyler's mom?" Not "Brian" anymore, Webb noticed.

"Listen—the last four years have been hell, and I'm not just going to walk away, give it all up because of some cunt. No way. No way in hell."

"It's over."

The words, the repetition, infuriated Jordan. He turned to Webb, screaming.

"That's what I'm telling you. Buck's going to fix it. Everything's going to be all right."

Webb didn't answer. He stared out at the dingy parking

lot. No way, he said to himself. No way, buddy. This is one
thing your big brother can't fix for you. Grow up.

Normally Roy Banks's blanched complexion was that of a
man who shunned the sun. Like a miner. Or a prisoner. Now,
as lack of sleep began to tell, it had bleached to the ashen
shade of a man under sentence of death.

In the past day or two he had begun to develop a tremble.
His foreman had noticed it. Earlier Roy had seen him staring
at his hands, and shoved them into his pockets, but not
before the man had stepped closer to get a whiff of his breath.
He'd recoiled immediately, stepping away from the sour smell
of decay. Roy could read the disappointment on his face. The
jerk would have loved to smell whiskey. Just once. He was
just looking for an excuse to fire him. Well, ol' Roy Banks
wasn't about to give him the satisfaction. Not that he hadn't
thought of crawling into the bottle lately.

It was a tempting idea, but the thought that kept him from
it was that it might make the nightmares more terrifying. As
bad as they were now, he didn't think he could stand it if they
got worse.

Maybe he would ask for a transfer. He'd done his stint on
the night shift. More than his stint. Once he had liked
working nights, when everything and everyone was asleep.
He'd relished the feeling of power that came to him when he
was one of the very few working and eating in the hours
while the world above him slept. And he had loved the
tunnels. Hot. Private. His own private world. But no more.
Now he was beginning to dread the midnight hours. And
working in the tunnels. He wanted out.

From the distance he heard a hollow ringing. The noise of
metal striking metal echoed, rolling through the tunnels to
him. He knew he should investigate, but he sat tight, trying
to ignore the sound. No way was he going to go looking for
trouble. He had enough trouble to last him a lifetime.

The ringing echo trembled and then disappeared, the last
silver sliver of sound hanging eerily before melting entirely.
Roy began to breath normally again. Florida. That's what he
needed. A move to Florida. He'd leave this freakin' job.
Leave the half-wit. For once in his life he'd be free.

He swung his lunch pail down from the ladder rung. The

greasy smell of doughnuts, of ham and cheese, filled his work space, and he fought back nausea. It went with lack of sleep. That was the source of his problems, he told himself. If he could sleep, everything would be all right.

At first the dreams had been mercifully dim. They were anxiety dreams in which he was running away while something black pursued. He'd wake from these with a pounding heart, sick with the knowledge of what the black thing was. Too soon, it invaded his sleeping hours. A midshipman, limbs convulsed, maggots drooling from the darkened, swollen face, crawling out of nostrils, mouth, and eyes. But in spite of the maggots, the eyes—accusing—could still see. And the mouth moved, begging. Sometimes the face of the dead midshipman was transformed, and it was his idiot brother who stared at him with damning eyes and worm-eaten mouth. In these dreams the dying man wore Sony earphones.

Roy thought that was as bad as the nightmares could get, but he was wrong. Lately the man had reached for him with dying hands, and Roy felt them touch the flesh of his neck, tightening, like a rope. After these nights, after the dead man had touched him, Roy knew there would be no escape. Not unless he confessed.

He closed his lunch box. From the tunnels around him he heard faint, shadowy noises; he tried to shut them out but was no more successful than he had been at turning off the dreams that damned him.

CHAPTER TWENTY-EIGHT

"Kate? Kate, please, open the door. It's me, Max."

He had been knocking for some time, but the noise did not register with Kate. She continued to sit, frozen in the same position Michael had left her in the night before.

"Kate? Please, can you hear me? Are you all right?"

When she finally opened the door, he was shocked. "My God, what's happened?"

She did not answer, having no words, but let him lead her back to the chair. He didn't ask her anything else then, but busied himself preparing tea. He filled the kettle and set it on the motel stove top. While he worked he stole glances at her, but she did not notice. When the tea was ready, he sat on the edge of the bed. Their knees were almost touching. She looked at him and her eyes cleared.

"Michael was here. Brian's father."

Max's jaws tightened but he did not speak.

"It just keeps getting worse," she said. Her eyes filled, but she did not cry. "He said they told him why Brian did it. They said he cheated."

He listened while she repeated the details of Michael's visit, his forehead creased in a worried frown. "What class? Did he say what exam Brian was supposed to have cheated on?" It troubled him that he had not heard about this. Rumor—especially about mids cheating—spread rapidly in the Yard.

She lifted her shoulders and let them drop. "I don't know. Does it matter?"

He chose his words carefully, aware of how fragile, how terribly vulnerable she was. "It might. Do you want me to ask around? I could start there. Or you might ask. They'd have to tell you."

She dropped her face to her hands. "Please. I just want to

be alone. I don't want to think about it anymore. I—I don't want to do anything about it. Could you just go? Please."

"What will you do?"

"Stop picking at me, will you? Just leave me alone."

He saw how very close to the edge she was. He bent and kissed her on the cheek. "I'll call you later. When I get home this afternoon. Try and get some sleep." At the door he turned back. "I almost forgot. Here. This is why I came. I thought you might like this." He put a sheet of paper on the desk, slipping it beneath an ashtray. "There's two things you might think about while I'm gone, Kate. First, for some reason people don't want you to have this address." He could not tell by her face if what he said was registering. "Second, for what it's worth, I don't think your son was a cheat or a coward."

Like many of the roads in Boxton, Vermont, Ellis Hill Road was unpaved. Deep ruts carved during the past winter cut down into the surface. Kate gripped the wheel and concentrated on keeping the car's tires straddled between the ruts. Her shoulders ached from the strain. She stared straight ahead, not even looking at the landscape. So far she had passed only one house, a farmhouse at the base of the hill. She was not missing much. Of all seasons in Vermont, March is the ugliest. It has neither the lush fertile green of summer, nor the brilliant foliage of autumn, nor the pristine snow of winter, which can transform the country into a miracle of sparkling snow and ice. In contrast, March is brown. Even the patches of snow that still cling to survival in the woods are mottled with brown. The oppression of a long winter soils the spirit, both human and natural. The rocky landscape is mean, reluctant to release winter and welcome spring.

Kate was reminded of a description by Willa Cather, something about winter in villages or country towns. That was it. The entire phrase leapt to mind: "Winter lies too long in country towns; hangs on until it's stale and shabby, old and sullen." The truth of this cut like a blade.

"It could be worse," the man at the Burlington Airport rental-car booth had said. "Just be glad you didn't arrive in mud season."

The road narrowed; the ruts grew deeper and more frequent. One wheel was entirely off the road. Kate's hands felt clammy inside her gloves. She had no idea what she would do if the car got stuck. On the verge of trying to find a place to turn around, she saw the house.

It was like hundreds of others in the back country of this state: a two-story farmhouse with several outbuildings in various stages of disrepair. Behind one, a crumbling shed, rested the hulks of old cars. They had been driven until they died, and then abandoned to rot, pieces stripped from them as they were needed. A dog, its pedigree and color as indeterminate as the landscape, barked shrilly, racing toward the car and pressing muddy paws against the top of Kate's door. From the driver's seat Kate stared out at the house. From this home to the U.S. Naval Academy was a quantum leap.

A woman came to the door. Sharply calling the dog off, she stood on the porch staring at Kate, her eyes and posture radiating suspicion. She wore faded denim overalls, a hand-knitted navy-blue sweater, and a red turtleneck shirt. The neck of the shirt hung around her neck in limp folds. Tendons ran up from her collarbones to her ears like cords. She watched motionlessly as Kate crossed the muddy driveway.

"Mrs. Greene?"

The woman nodded, giving nothing up. Her skin was taut, lined. She wore no makeup.

"Mrs. Greene, my name is Katherine Tyler. I'm looking for a woman named Ariel Greene."

The thin woman snorted derisively.

"Does she live here?"

"Oh, sure. 'Ariel' "—the word was sarcastic—"lives here. What would you be wanting with her?"

"I was wondering if I could talk to her." The dog nosed against Kate's body, spattering her coat with mud and saliva. The woman saw this but did not call the dog away, seeming to get a mean satisfaction out of the dirt the dog left.

It was raw standing on the porch. In spite of her coat, Kate shivered. "Look, if Ms. Greene lives here, I would like to talk with her."

"Why?"

"My son went to the Academy with her." A flicker of something akin to loathing crossed the woman's face, but was quickly gone. "I wonder if she would talk to me about him?"

"Why?"

"He's dead. I'm trying to learn why and how he died."

Mrs. Greene looked Kate up and down, taking in the leather boots, the stylish tweed coat that swept to the top of her boots. Then she backed through the door. Inside, the house smelled of wood smoke and dog. The living room was dark. Stained red wallpaper hung on the walls, some of it peeling down from the ceiling. The couch was covered with a crocheted throw made of brilliant, jarring colors. Two cartons of Christmas tree ornaments stood in a corner. A shapeless knitted stocking drooped from one corner of the mantel. Kate wondered who it had been meant for.

The woman sat, brusquely indicating the couch to Kate. "Her name is Shirley, you know. Shirley Jean. Named for my sister. Her aunt. Not fancy enough for her. Her and her highfalutin ways. Just like her father." The sense of spiritual poverty inside the house was more pervasive than that caused by lack of money. Kate sat, knowing her coat would be covered with dog and cat hairs, but not wanting to brush the cushion off before sitting.

"Ariel?"

"Who else. Started calling herself Ariel when she was around twelve. Wouldn't answer to nothing else. I should have taken the strap to her, but it wouldn't have mattered. I could have beat her senseless and she wouldn't give in. Not that one. A mind of her own, that one. 'Course, that's her father's fault. Called her his little princess all the time. *His little princess*." The words were said with a mixture of anger and resentment. "He's the one who gave her the idea she was better than the rest of us. Too good to stay here, that one was. Got herself picked to go off to that school. Lot of good it did her. Imagine going to a man's school that way."

Kate tried to fight her growing dislike of the woman. She remembered Leah's description of Ariel. Beautiful, she had said. How could something beautiful come out of this arid environment? Kate suddenly understood what it must have been like for the mother as she watched each painful step her daughter took toward a better life. To her mother, Ariel's attempts to escape must have stung like rejection.

There was a table in front of an east-facing window. It held several tall plants, spindly leaves trailing from the stems toward the light. The plants were more yellow than green, as if even plants could not flourish in this environment.

"She thinks she's better than the rest of us, you know. Always has. For all the good it did her." A spotted cat jumped onto the woman's lap and curled into a circle. Mrs. Greene made no move to stroke it. The tail flicked up and down while the cat eyed Kate. There was suspicion in both pair of eyes. "Your son went to the Academy?"

"Yes."

The woman stared. The cat's tail continued its slow flicking. It stretched once, its nails extending and contracting, then closed its gleaming eyes but did not purr.

"None of them come up here, you know. Never called or visited to see how she was doing, or to see if we needed anything. Not one damn one of them bothered to call or send a letter. Bodda says I should talk to a lawyer, says we could get some money out of this. I want nothin' to do with them."

"Who's Bodda?"

Mrs. Greene flushed. "My boyfriend. Shirley's father left five years ago."

It took Kate a minute to realize that by Shirley she meant Ariel.

"It was her own fault. I told her before she went there, it wasn't her place. The place is for men, not women. She wouldn't listen. Same as when she changed her name. Well, she can call herself anything she wants, but her name is Shirley Jean."

Kate desperately wanted to get away from this woman. There was something contagious in her hate.

"Could I see her?"

"I guess so." The sentence was grudgingly given. She stood, knocking the cat to the floor, and led Kate to a room on the other side of the hall. A new door, wider than normal, had replaced the one that used to be there. It had not been painted, and already the wood around the frame was stained from the oil and dirt of human hands.

Without looking back at Kate, the woman opened the door. "Shirley? Shirley. Someone here that wants to talk to you." It was dark inside, and she crossed to open the shades, letting them up with a snap.

Kate's knees went weak and she reached out to the bureau

for support. The slight figure in the wheelchair stared at her with dull eyes. "Speak up, girl. You have a guest."

She wanted to turn and run. She did not want to look at this ruined shell of a girl, did not want to talk to her; above all, she did not want to hear what the girl was going to tell her.

"She's been like that since they brought her home." Now Kate could hear the pain in the woman's voice. She recognized the sorrow.

"What happened?"

"She fell. Had an accident in the pool. She told them she couldn't dive, you know. Was afraid of it. Since she was a child. I guess she tried, though." A note of pride entered the brittle voice. "She won't walk. The doctors said she could. There's no reason for her sitting in that chair, they said. They said she has something called hysterical paralysis."

She pronounced it "high-sterical." "Shirley, this woman's come to talk with you. Says her son went to the Academy too. What's his name?" She twisted back to Kate, the mid-afternoon sun aging her face cruelly.

"Brian. His name was Brian Tyler." From the moment she'd stepped inside the room, Kate had known that whatever this crippled woman had to tell her would alter her life irrevocably. She knew too, that what she would learn here would be far more painful than anything Michael had told her the previous night. She wished she had never come to Vermont—that she had never returned to Annapolis to learn why Brian had died. Ariel began to speak, but Kate did not want to listen. It was too late for that. The mother left them alone.

"I didn't jump and I didn't fall," she said. "That's not the way it happened."

CHAPTER TWENTY-NINE

Brian knew the natatorium better than almost any other place in the Yard. As soon as Jordan unlocked the door, he breathed in the damp warm air scented faintly with chlorine. They crept into the huge, dim room. It was so different at night. The two pools were still, their waters dark.

"How did you get the key?" He spoke in a whisper, but the echo was macabre, bouncing off the walls like sonar. He was not sure whether or not Jordan heard him, but he received no answer to his question. He began to regret that he had come.

It was too dark to see the cavernous room clearly, to see the triangular skylight in the roof above the diving pool, or the blue and gold pennants that hung from lines above the length of the swimming pool. He walked carefully; the tiles beneath his feet were damp. Jordan disappeared somewhere, and they waited in silence for his return.

Where in hell has he gone? Brian wondered. Did Spider want to back out now too? A moment later a pool light flicked on, casting flickering shadows. Brian saw that the water polo nets were still in place from a late game. Behind him the diving tower loomed. He didn't need light to see that. He could visualize it in his sleep: the round gray concrete tower enclosing the flight of circular stairs, stairs that led to the three levels and the diving platforms.

He craned his neck and peered upward. The first platform was only five meters from the surface of the water. Up another level, to the left, was the seven-and-a-half-meter board. At the top, the height of the tower, was the ten-meter platform. Beside him he heard a tiny sound, a mouse noise. little more than a breath of a whimper. The sound sent a cold finger of apprehension through him.

He turned his attention back to the highest board, the

feared ten meters. He could never understand the terror this platform held for his peers. The very first time, the first try, he had jumped off, stepping off without a moment's hesitation, thrilling to the exultation. His only regret was that it was over too soon. In 1.3 seconds he hit the water, his feet shooting toward the large N painted on the floor of the pool seventeen feet below water level.

Sometimes, although he usually abhorred any form of exhibitionism, he made the leap two or three times. But at least he never yelled. The Marines did that, shrieking battle cries as they leapt. He didn't like that. No style in showing off. He liked to cross his arms across his chest, cross his legs, and then step forward into midair. Then, too fast to think about it, there was the swift downward flight. Once he forgot to cross his legs. The water hit him like a two-by-four between the legs. He never forgot again.

To receive his commission, every midshipman at the Academy was required to make the ten-meter jump. Not just make it, but make it unassisted, without a push from a sympathetic shipmate if he stood paralyzed at the foot of the board. It was easier now, with this new natatorium and the concrete tower to the platforms. In the old natatorium, over at Macdonough, the platform was suspended from the ceiling and the mids had to climb a Jacob's ladder to it before making the jump. That must have been something. This new tower made it a piece of cake.

The rationale behind the jump was to prepare mids for the eventuality, that remote possibility, that someday they might actually have to abandon ship. For that reason, they were told, the tower was the same height as the deck of a ship at sea. There had been a lot of flack about that theory lately. It began when a mid had been kicked out two years before for refusing to jump. The mid's congressman was still making quite a fuss. The word was that the whole thing was ridiculous anyway, since one probably couldn't survive a jump off a battleship deck, thus there was no need to prepare for it. But it was tradition.

What Bri couldn't understand was how someone would rather wash out than make the jump. To go through three or four years and wash out because you couldn't find the courage to make a simple jump. It wasn't like you had to dive or anything.

Of course, from the ground it looked easy. It was another thing entirely to be up there on the sucker. Ten meters. A little more than thirty feet. Just walking out to the end of the board took nerve, especially if heights bothered you. Spider had had a terrible problem with it. He had even thrown up before making the jump. If it hadn't been for the inescapable knowledge that no jump meant no commission, Bri knew Spider never could have done it. And there were always those who couldn't swim. Why the hell would anyone come to the Academy when they couldn't swim? It was a mystery. They were dubbed the sub squad, these mids who couldn't swim: aqua rocks. Throw them in the pool and they sank to the bottom.

Some mids got hurt when they jumped, he knew. They surfaced struggling to conceal their tears of pain or with a bloody nose.

Jordan emerged from the shadows and motioned them to follow him to the tower. The silence was beginning to wear on Brian. There was no hint of the angry words they had exchanged in their room, the building of rage that led to this moment. Only silence.

Spider was in the shadows behind him. The rear of the tower was dark, untouched by the single light Jordan had switched on. The beam of Jordan's flashlight fleetingly lit the sign, a standard Navy regulation sign with white letters. "This tower is locked for your safety when the pool is unsupervised. If you are found on the tower while the pool is unsupervised, disciplinary action will be taken."

Jordan fumbled with a key and then unlocked the tower door. The seriousness of what they were doing suddenly hit Brian. Behind him he heard Spider's whisper. "Where the hell did you get the key, Jordo?"

"Marine Corps ingenuity. Something you Navy puke selectees wouldn't know about."

In the shadows Brian saw their faces. Beside Spider's bulk the third figure looked startlingly fragile. He could see her coldly furious, beautiful face, even in the dim light. Even when she had realized where they were taking her, she had not been afraid. Anger and disdain shone on her face, and Brian flinched before it, suddenly ashamed.

He turned to Jordan. "Hey. Let's call it quits now. Let's just throw her in, get her wet, then go back."

"No way." His whisper was fierce. "No way. She's not getting away with this. She goes off." They began their ascent up the stairs, and the metal was cold beneath their bare feet. Jordan reached out and pulled Ariel into the tower.

Someone—who?—had tied her hands behind her back with the cord of a bathrobe. Even then she hadn't screamed. Except for the first inhaled breath of surprise when they woke her and dragged her from her room, she hadn't made a sound. In a queer way it was as if she had entered the conspiracy with them. Later Brian was to wonder what would have happened if she'd yelled, fought them when they tried to take her. And he was to regret bitterly that she hadn't.

He didn't even want to think about all the rules they were breaking. Decker might be awake and contacting administration right at this minute. If they got caught, he'd be spending every liberty from now until Commissioning Week on restrictions. If he was lucky.

They climbed in the blackness, single file, spiraling up, Jordan first, then Bri, followed by Ariel and Spider. The bobbing circle from Jordan's flashlight was the only light in the tower.

Once the girl stumbled, falling against him, and he reached out instinctively to help her. It was the first time he had touched her, and he was surprised at how frail her arm seemed. Her hair was soap scented. He was reminded of Leah, and again he was ashamed.

"Okay, Jordo," he said quietly, "we've had enough fooling around. Let's cut the crap and get back to our racks before we get caught."

"Shut up, asshole. It's too late to wimp out now."

They filed past the door that opened onto the five-meter board and relentlessly continued upward. For the first time the circular stairs made Brian dizzy. They passed the seven-meter board, up and around to the top. When all four were there, crowded at the base of the platform, Jordan turned and pushed Ariel out to the board.

"You bastards are going to pay for this." Her voice was shaky, but Brian saw by the expression in her eyes that she thought they were faking. Bile rose in his throat.

"Shall we leave her hands tied? Bri, you want to jump in and pull her out? That way we can leave her hands tied." Jordan's voice was vindictively purposeful. Webb hung back,

near the tower, refusing to step out on the narrow board
which stretched out over the silent water. The shallow rasp of
his breathing echoed in Bri's ears, and he remembered how
much his roommate hated and feared the ten-meter board.

Jordan pulled the girl forward to the end of the stainless
steel railing that edged each side of the board. The last four
feet jutted out into the darkness, no railing, no safety net.
She was dressed only in her white pajamas. Her feet were
bare, and in the dim light she looked terribly vulnerable.

At last, standing in this dizzying darkness, surrounded by
space, Brian saw that Ariel began to believe they were not
fooling. A whimper escaped her throat. It was the most
horrible sound he had ever heard. He moved up to stand
next to her. Jordan flashed his light on her face. The sheen of
sweat polished her cheek and slender neck. A pulse beat in
her throat. There was no name for the expression in her eyes.
Involuntarily Brian stepped away, contaminated. Shame was
too mild a word for what he was experiencing. The regret and
disgrace were marrow deep. It would be an eternity before
he could cleanse himself of this sense of degradation. He was
sick to his soul for the part he had played in this stupid prank.
All for a stupid bet.

Her whimpering grew louder now as she began to plead
with Jordan to let her go. Bri couldn't bear to listen to the
inhuman sound of her voice. He retreated to where Spider
stood. Jordan alone was with Ariel at the end of the board.

"Let her go." He sounded weary, old.

"No way, Bri. Not now. She tricked the brass, but she's not
going to get away with it."

Jordan prodded the shadow near him, but she tried to
crouch, hands clenching and unclenching, working at the ties
on her wrist as her fingers reached abortively for support.
Jordan flicked the beam of the flashlight on his roommates,
and in its light they saw Webb's pallor. He turned and ran
down the stairs, not even trying to be quiet. His footsteps
rang sharply on the metal steps.

"For Christ's sake, Jordo, that's enough!" Brian cried. A
horrible sound, moaning, inhuman, was coming from Ariel.
He took a step toward the end of the diving board and raised
his voice. "Enough. The joke's gone far enough."

Jordan stepped in front of Ariel, putting himself between
Brian and the woman. She fell to a crouch, suddenly silent.

"She's going down, Bri."

"What's the matter with you? Have you gone crazy? Let her go."

"No way." He reached down and yanked her up, shoving her forward. The low keening began again. She was just inches from the end of the board.

Brian took another step toward them. "It's okay, Ariel. It's okay. It's over. We'll get you down."

"Back off, Tyler. I'm telling you. Another step and I'll dump her over."

Brian stopped, desperately trying to gauge the distance. Scott was in front of him, still as a statue. He knew that Spider was below, by the edge of the pool. The sound of his breathing floated up, ragged and noisy.

"Bri's right." Spider's voice was disembodied in the empty natatorium. "Let her go, Jordan."

"What the hell's the matter with you? You want to fork over one thousand bucks to my brother? We agreed on this." Jordan's voice shook with rage.

While he was distracted by Webb, Brian saw his chance. He covered the last feet, grabbing for Jordan's arm, trying to reach past him to Ariel.

"God damn you, Tyler." Jordan yanked his arm away. The board jounced beneath their feet. "Cut it out or we'll all go over!"

Stepping to the left, Brian's foot lost contact with the board, encountering only emptiness. He countered by leaning to the right, frantically fighting to keep his balance.

"Jesus," Webb whispered.

Jordan was forgotten. All of Brian's concentration was now fiercely focused on the struggle to keep from going over. Freed, Jordan twisted and grabbed for Ariel. The movement made the board spring.

"For Christ's sake, back off, Jordan! You don't have to prove anything to us. We're not your brother. You don't have to show off for us."

Jordan's face was contorted. "Fuck you, Tyler," he shrilled. He reached toward Ariel, and instinctively she twisted away and fell, striking her head sickeningly against the board. Then she went over.

She screamed, a brief high-pitched shriek that ended when she hit the surface of the pool. Brian's blood ran cold with the sound of it. He knew it would haunt him until his dying day. Then he realized that her hands were still tied. He stood, his body drenched with sweat, and peered down into the black water. "Spider? You got a light? We need more light! Quick, on the pool!"

The flashlight Webb held had been transfixed on the end of the board, but now the beam swept the water. There was no sign of Ariel. Cursing, Brian pushed forward, and ignoring Jordan, jumped out into the blackness.

His feet knifed through the water; the impact knocked his breath away. Gasping air into his lungs, cursing the feeble light, he dove to the bottom, but the water beneath the surface was black. For the first time in his life he felt the weight of claustrophobia. He came up for air, gasping painfully, spitting water. His eyes burned.

"To your left, Bri!" Webb swung the beam. Following the circle of light, Brian saw her. Her red hair fanned out like seaweed. She lay facedown.

In seconds, using the lifesaving grasp, Brian had pulled her to the edge of the pool. She was unconscious. He knew by her limp body that she was unconscious. "Shit. Shit. Shit." He said the words aloud, caught in an interminable nightmare.

Webb knelt at the edge of the pool. He leaned in and grasped the body, pulling it up effortlessly with one huge hand. The knot was still firm at her wrist, and he tore at the wet material, swearing. Bri pulled himself up. He was not worried about water in her lungs, she hadn't been in the pool long enough. It was the dark stain of blood spreading through her hair that frightened him.

Jordan stood to one side, chest heaving. Brian didn't know when he had come down from the tower. They avoided each other's eyes. At that moment Brian hated his roommate.

"We've got to get the fuck out of here. Leave her."

Bri flashed a look of contempt at him. "I'm telling you, you bastard, just shut the hell up or I'll kill you."

Ariel was moaning now, softly, motionless, her vacant eyes fixed on the black triangle of the skylight. Even though it was almost oppressively humid in the natatorium, they saw that she was shivering. Sickened and scared, Brian felt the growing rage within himself. How had he let himself be talked into such an idiotic scheme? The worst part of the anger and shame was the inescapable knowledge that he had joined the plan willingly. True, it had been Jordan's idea, but he'd been quick enough to go along. In their room in Mother B. it had not only made sense but seemed innately appropriate and fair. Now he wondered at their madness and the terrible result of their plan.

"Lock the tower," Webb snapped, self-preservation taking over. Brian heard it in his voice, but knew it was too late for any attempt at self-protection. When she reported them, they would all be out. The knowledge made an acid ball of fear and regret in his stomach. He recognized the same emotions in the shadows of Jordan's face. Four years of terror and work, gone. And they would be gone. The brass wouldn't whitewash this one, couldn't whitewash it. The newspapers and politicians would swoop down, demanding an investigation and retribution. The Secretary of the Navy himself would probably be in on it. There was no question but that they would be out. He was glad then that Jordan had moved to lock the tower. If he'd been closer, Brian knew he would have killed him.

"Ariel, are you all right? Ariel?"

The midshipman did not answer. They heard Jordan's footsteps and saw the beam of light from his flashlight. It was pitch-black by the edge of the pool, and Brian felt a moment of vertigo. He needed desperately to see. He was soaked and trembling. He heard Spider by his side, felt his roommate's gentle hand on his arm. "Jordan's right. Leave her. Let's get the hell out of here. We've got to get back to Mother B."

Numbed, Brian allowed himself to be led away.

Bri lay in bed. In the dark he could hear the breathing of both of his roommates. He knew by the sound that neither of them was sleeping. He felt terribly alone, but he did not call out to them. He did not want to talk with them. He wanted to cry but there were no tears. He had wrenched his shoulder landing in the water, but he welcomed the throbbing pain. He wondered who would come in the morning to ask them to leave. He finally fell into a sleep, dreamless, as if no nightmare could be worse than the night that preceded it.

The bells woke him in the morning. His last day. He woke, remembering immediately. No reprieve. The three showered and dressed in silence. Once Jordan tried to say something, but Webb and Bri both turned on him, snarling. The air of the room seemed unfit to breathe: it was full of fear and anger, poisonous.

Still no one came. They went to the dining hall, but Bri could not eat. He craned his neck, trying to pick out in the sea of black uniforms the face of one midshipman. She was not there.

The waiting was dreadful. He sat through his classes, waiting for an officer to appear at the door, waited to hear his name, a hand fall on his shoulder. His shoulders were braced, as if for gunfire from an ambush. Somehow he got through the day. Noon formation. Afternoon classes. Waiting for the blade to fall.

There was a swim meet. An important meet. Eastern Conference. He pleaded an earache and got out of it, unable to look his coach in the face. He hated to let him down; Coach Nelson was the best there was, but there was no way he could face the natatorium.

By evening he was ready to confess. Anything to end the waiting. He kept looking for her, searching every face. Nothing.

He couldn't hold down the burgeoning hope, hope he saw reflected on the strained faces of Webb and Jordan. Somehow a miracle had occurred; for some inexplicable reason she wasn't going to tell on them. He did not trust this hope, but as the hours passed and nothing happened, it could not be held down. Relief was so powerful, it weakened him. Somehow he'd got off.

Jordan found out first. Ariel Greene was gone. She had been given a medical discharge. Rumors raged through Mother B. like fire through dried hay. She had been injured. The word spread. Apparently she had foolishly tried to make the dive alone. At night. The roommates were giddy with relief. At first.

Bri avoided glancing into Ariel's room when he passed the door, but once he passed Ariel's roommate. Cynthia Decker's look was scathing. Did she know? Her eyes told him she knew. He no longer walked to class with Garrick or Scott. By unspoken agreement they avoided each other.

With each day that passed, Ariel Greene seemed more removed. If she was remembered by members of the Brigade, it was as the firstie who had been given a psychological excuse from having to make the tower dive. The general, unspoken agreement was that it was just as well she was gone. She really didn't fit, didn't have what it took to be at the Academy. Rumor whispered that the doctors who examined Greene agreed her paralysis was psychological. That raised a few eyebrows, and privately many argued that it was further proof that women didn't really belong at Navy.

For Brian these days were the loneliest. He ached for someone to talk to. He couldn't tell the only ones he loved what he was going through. He could picture the horror in his mother's eyes. And Leah's. To talk to his father was out of the question.

For two weeks he didn't go into D.C. Leah phoned, offering to drive to Annapolis if he was too strung out with work to come to see her. But he refused, afraid of what she might read in his face. He missed her terribly. He made a tremendous effort to keep the strain from his voice.

With each day that went by, amazingly, the memory of that night dimmed. He began to breathe more normally. The tension in his shoulders eased. The blade would not slip in. There would be no ambush. The enemy had been recalled. It would be all right.

He had gotten off. *He had gotten off!*

It was going to be all right. He was going to graduate. Spider would go to flight school, fly the jets he loved. Jordan would be commissioned a lieutenant in the U.S. Marine Corps, following in the footsteps of the brother he adored. They had all gotten off. And as the days went by, his memory of that night began to change. He began to believe that Ariel had played a role in what had happened. Her very silence made her less a victim, or at least a *willing* victim. At last he felt he could return to normal life. He called Leah and arranged to meet her the following Saturday. He ached to be with her. It had been too long. He wanted to sleep with her so much, it hurt to think of it. He returned to the natatorium, pouring such energy into the practices and meets that his coach began considering him for an All-American candidate. In such a way did he hold the terrible knowledge of that night at bay. But he could not keep it there forever.

Too soon, Brian Tyler had to confront the knowledge that he was a coward. The hatred he'd felt toward Jordan turned inward. His future, his dreams, even his love for Leah was tainted. He had ruined someone's life. And he had kept quiet about it. But more than that, he began to understand the reason Ariel had lied. In spite of what they had done to her, she had lived by the unspoken code: the Service protects its own. The knowledge was like acid on his soul: Ariel had more honor than he did.

CHAPTER THIRTY

She had told her story in a deadened whisper, horrid in its lack of emotion. When she was done, the whisper simply ceased. The silence was eerie. Kate wanted desperately to say something, but it was far, far too late for words. Only one question seemed proper, but that, too, was futile. She doubted if Ariel even knew why she hadn't reported those who had taken her to the tower that night.

"You should have told."

The woman's eyes were flat with contempt.

If only you had, Kate wanted to scream. If you had, my son would be alive now. She heard a noise from the hall and wondered if the mother had been listening. She looked over at the fragile, stooped girl in the wheelchair. She was as crippled by her fears and doubts as surely as if the nerves in her spinal cord had been severed by a knife.

More than one life had been lost that night in the natatorium.

"Perhaps if you saw another doctor . . ." she began.

The eyes were expressionless now, as if the person behind them had withdrawn.

There was nothing she could do here, Kate thought. She had to leave. She rose, reacting in shock, not yet ready to deal with the burden of her ghastly knowledge.

At the door she turned. Her voice trembled. "Thank you for telling me this, Ariel."

The reply was in a monotone. "My name isn't Ariel. I'm Shirley."

Somehow Kate managed to stay in control until she was out of view of the house. She didn't look in the rearview mirror. She knew that if she had, she would see the figure of a rigid,

261

bony woman standing on the sagging porch, hopelessly watching her drive away.

She stifled all thought, concentrating on straddling the ruts with the car tires, but the spirit of the house—a miasma of damp dog and wood rot, of illness and despair—clung to her, and she rolled the window down, gulping the frigid air that poured in on her face, filling the car with its freshness until she was shivering. Still she did not close the window.

She longed to pull over, to bend over the steering wheel and sob, but she knew if she lost control now she wouldn't regain it. So she kept driving, gasping in the piercing Vermont air like a drowning person. She clung to the steering wheel so tightly that when she reached the airport it hurt to unclench her fingers. On the flight back to Baltimore a sadness more profound than any she had ever experienced, more penetrating by far than that which had followed Brian's death, took hold of her. She remembered Max's words. *What if the truth is that he killed himself?*

And she remembered her ignorant reply. *I have to know the truth*. Her innocence had been remarkable.

The pain was not in knowing that he had killed himself. It was much worse; it was knowing the agony he must have been in before he died.

Oh, my son, she wanted to cry. *My son. Why didn't you call me? Why didn't you turn to me? We could have seen it through.*

By the time she returned to Baltimore it was late afternoon and the setting sun stained the sky. She slumped with exhaustion as she crossed the airport parking lot to where her car waited. As she slid behind the wheel, she shuddered, remembering the body of the cat on the seat. Poor Max. In spite of his denial, the cat had belonged to him. You cannot negate need simply by denying its existence.

She realized then that her life had been going on, even while she'd been trying to freeze it in grief and in her search to understand Brian's death. The thought brought both pain and release. Whether she wanted to be or not, she was a survivor. She possessed the strength of endurance. She was too whipped at the moment to draw on it; it was enough to know it was there. Later she would need it. During the long nights when she woke in mourning and could not sleep, she would need it to see her through until sunrise. And she would need it for Leah. Leah possessed her own strength, but they would need each other's courage in the days ahead. Certainly when the baby came. That helped. The knowledge that there would be a baby. Brian's child. Thoughts of Leah pressed on her. She dreaded telling her about the part Brian played in Ariel's story, dreaded having to bring her acknowledgment of Brian's suicide.

Michael had been right. Brian did kill himself. Seconds later anger reasserted itself. But he had lied to her, too, and she knew she would confront Michael with his lies about their son. Why had he come to her with the story about Brian cheating? Was he so afraid of what she would discover? Or—the thought suddenly occurred, bringing fresh anger—could he, and the Administration, have known about Ariel all along?

She started the engine and pulled out of the lot. She would call Leah and Michael from the motel. And Max. She owed him that. He would be hurt, she knew, by the story she had to tell him. He believed so in the midshipmen and in their Concept of Honor.

She drove directly to her motel, and exhausted, stretched out on the bed, but sleep eluded her. There were the calls to be made. Max. Leah. Michael. She lay in the dark and stared into the darkness. Her nerves were so raw, so close to the surface, that she jumped when the phone rang.

"Hello, Kate? Kate, is that you?"

A flood of relief washed over her. It was so good to hear Nina. She had missed her terribly. And then she remembered the angry accusations of their last conversation, and she retreated into caution. "Yes. This is Kate."

"Oh, Kate, did I wake you? I've been so worried. I've missed you. We all have. Are you all right?" There was no reserve in Nina's voice, only warmth and concern. Kate's constraint melted.

"I'm fine, Nina. I've missed you too. I—I'm sorry I was so angry before I left—"

"Don't even speak of it. It was my fault. Michael brainwashed me," she admitted softly. "It sounds like you've been giving him a hard time. He phones every day trying to get me to call you. Last week he called Hal and kept insisting you're doing this to get even with him for Wendi and the divorce."

"It has nothing to do with that."

"I know. I should have understood before." She paused, as if taking a deep breath. "Katie..."

Kate detected the change in her voice immediately. "What's wrong?"

"Kate, do you remember the letter you got from Bri? The one in the mail that day? When we were going out to lunch?"

Did she remember? The breath went out of her lungs. She could not answer.

"Kate? Are you there? Do you remember?"

"Yes." She was surprised at the strength of her reply. She knew the truth now. Brian's letter couldn't hurt her.

"I don't know how to tell you. It... well, Hal was cleaning the car and he found it. It had slipped between the seat cushions. God, Kate. I feel so awful. It's been there all the time."

The line was hollow between them. Brian's letter. Nina had Bri's letter.

Nina continued uncertainly. "I have it here, Kate. What do you want me to do? I mean, I could mail it to you or ... or I could read it to you...."

"Keep it for me, will you, Nina? Keep it for me until I get home."

"Is there anything I can do?"

"Nothing." There was so much to tell her, but this was not the time to begin.

"I love you, Kate."

"I love you, too, Nina." She thought of all the times she had wanted to say that before. Odd, how easily it came now. She repeated it again before they hung up.

She was so tired, but now she knew that she would be able to sleep. She undressed in the dark. Before she crawled into the bed, she made her calls. Leah's voice sounded raw and weary. Hearing it, Kate could not tell her Ariel's story over the phone. The need to protect her was strong. Leah would have to be told, but the least she could do was tell her in person. As if sensing what was to come, Leah suggested she drive to Annapolis to meet her the next night.

"I have a late class. How does nine sound? Too late?"

"That's fine. Are you sure you don't want me to come in to D.C.?"

"No. I would... I would like the drive." The silence of

what they were leaving unsaid hung heavily in the air. "You found out why, didn't you?"

Kate felt as if her heart would break. "Yes."

"Is it bad?"

What word could she put to it? Bad? Yes, it was bad. It was painful, horrible. A nightmare. Unbelievable. That was it. Most of all, it was unbelievable. The feelings she'd been fighting since she left Vermont threatened to overwhelm her. She wanted to scream. She had finally learned what had happened to her son. A senseless, stupid, tragic flow of events had become too much for him to bear. It was unbelievable, and she ached with the torment he must have felt. "Yes," she finally said to Leah. She wanted to say more, to find comfort or strength to give her until they met, but futility swept her. "We'll get through it together," was all she could think to say.

She phoned Max next. The concern in his voice warmed her. He didn't press her for information, and she was grateful. They agreed to meet the next afternoon, after he returned home from classes. "I'll be waiting for you," he promised.

Finally she dialed Michael. While she waited for him to answer, her hands shook. Her rage, submerged since his visit, surfaced. Wendi answered the phone.

"He's not here." Her voice was cool.

"When will he be in? I need to talk to him."

"Can't you just leave him alone? Haven't you done enough damage?" The accusation in his wife's question, the trace of smug protectiveness, triggered Kate.

"If anyone has done damage, it's not me. You can tell him for me that I found out the truth. Oh, his performance last night almost convinced me. He'll be happy to know he nearly had me believing Brian was a cheat, and for that I'll never forgive him. I hope to hell he can live with himself. There's a liar and cheat and coward in the Tyler family, but his name is Michael, not Brian."

Her attack shook Wendi. "He didn't want to hurt anyone," she protested. "He was only trying to protect us. Brian's dead. He can't be hurt. Nothing anyone does or says can touch him, but we're alive. You kept pushing and he just wanted you to stop. Can't you understand that? Haven't you any loyalty? To Michael? Or the Navy?"

She heard the voice of Michael's arguments in Wendi's words.

"I wonder if you would feel that way if he lied about your child."

She hung up before the woman could respond. She felt completely free, released from any tie to Michael.

She slept deeply until afternoon. As she showered and dressed, she felt drained, but also strangely peaceful. On a whim she flipped through the Annapolis directory and dialed a salon. She was smiling, a tentative, fragile smile, when she left the motel.

Ninety minutes later she left the beauty shop. Her hair was inches shorter, softly curled around her face. She felt younger, freed. She bought a bottle of wine to take to Max. Not to celebrate, certainly not that. To share.

Suddenly aware that it was nearly five, she headed toward Max's home. She was almost outside of town when she saw the sign propped against the tree in the yard of a small house. The lettering was that of a child. She swung the car around and pulled into the driveway before she even had time to think about it. Moments later, a smile playing on her lips, she was on her way to Max.

He opened the door before she even had time to turn off the ignition. The knowledge that he had been standing at the window watching for her, waiting for her, made her heart leap. She picked up the bundle at her side, wrapping it snugly in her wool coat, and walked toward him. He watched, puzzled.

When she reached him he leaned forward and kissed her cheek, a movement so natural it surprised them both. When they were inside the hall she handed him the coat. "Careful," she warned, softly. And when he had taken the small bundle of fur from its shelter of wool, she said, "Say hello to Athos." Tears sparkled in her eyes.

She sat at the kitchen table and drank tea while he fussed with the kitten, warming milk for it, making a bed of soft clothes, stroking it, and marveling at its tininess. Watching him, she knew she had done the correct thing in bringing him the cat. When she drove into his driveway she'd had a moment of doubt, fearing the gesture would be misunderstood, or worse, that she had misunderstood his feeling for the dead cat and would regard the new pet as an unwanted nuisance. Now, watching him, she knew everything would be all right.

At last, fully satisfied that the makeshift cat bed was going to be acceptable, he came and sat opposite her, meeting the sorrow in her eyes.

Reaching across the narrow table, he cupped his hands around her cold fingers; his touch was gentle. He studied her face. "It was tough for you, wasn't it? You learned something about Brian?"

His empathy and perception weakened her, and unable to speak, she nodded. He's so different from Michael, she thought, and then—immediately—I will not compare them. It's not fair to either of them.

"Tell me," he said. And she did.

While she spoke he held on to her hands. When she was finished, he got up and came around the table. He pulled her up and held her. She rested her head on his shoulder. They were nearly the same height, but he was broad across the chest, and she leaned gratefully into his strength. He held her that way for a long time, comforting her without words. She had no idea how long they remained in that embrace, only that she welcomed his gentleness. Finally she stepped away and looked into his eyes. "Thank you."

He stared at her, and then she saw his expression change. She knew the hesitation he had felt two nights ago was gone. He would not pull back. Deliberately he leaned forward and kissed her. It was a tentative kiss and very sweet. He stepped back, still holding her hands, looking again into her face. He did not speak. Nor did he smile. Slowly he pulled her close, embracing her. This time the kiss was longer, searching, and it grew into hunger. She was shaken by it, and by her response.

He led her wordlessly from the kitchen. Behind them Athos was curled into a tight fur ball, slumbering contentedly in his new bed.

They were in the hall, at the foot of the stairs, before she froze. I'm afraid. I'm afraid of where this will lead, of what will happen after.

But it was more than a fear of the future that caused her to stumble. She was terrified of disappointing him. Would he find her old, ugly? Panic closed her throat. She knew so little about him. Maybe he was involved with someone else. She remembered the scar from her caesarean, the puckered flesh around the incision. It had been a very long time since she had made love with Michael. And he had been the only man she had ever gone to bed with. I can't do this, she thought.

Max felt her hesitation. He paused.

If he says one wrong thing, Kate thought, I'm leaving. If he says that everything is going to be all right or, oh God, especially if he says he loves me. Please, she silently prayed. Please help me.

His voice was so low, she could barely hear him. "I'm afraid too," he said. "But I don't want to turn back." He put his hands on her shoulders, turning her until they faced each other. "But I understand if you do."

And Kate knew then that she wanted to make love to this man. She wanted everything that it would mean: simple animal comfort and warmth, a satiation of the desire that now squeezed her throat shut, spreading through her with an aching softness, and finally, a reaffirmation of life.

She shook her head, and side by side they climbed the stairs to his room.

After, they lay in bed, the huge down comforter pulled up to their necks to ward off the chill of the big room, and they laughed. Much later Kate was to think that the laughter had been as healing, as much a part of the newly forged bond between them, as their lovemaking had been.

He had not turned on the overhead fixture. The only light was the glow from the adjoining bathroom. Shyly, Kate thanked him for his sensitivity, confiding her earlier fears. She was amazed at how quickly she trusted him with this knowledge. Then he confessed he had been terrified of the same thing. That was when the laughing had begun.

They cuddled, spoon fashion, and talked, asking hundreds of questions about each other's childhood. She told him about her father, his career, the illness, her feeling that he had betrayed her, left her behind, the pain of isolation. He listened silently, understanding.

With one hand he played with the short curls at the nape of her neck. She drew his other hand from beneath the blankets and ran her fingers over his palm, then kissed the tips of his fingers. She was overcome with tenderness for him. He looked down on her with such intensity that she blushed. "You're beautiful," he told her.

"I'm not," she denied. As if driven to display her flaws, she pushed the covers back and in the indirect light showed him the scar. He bent and kissed it, the gentlest of kisses. Then he stretched out beside her. His voice was infused with sadness. "I always wished I'd had a child."

She talked to him then of Brian. He listened, without interrupting. For more than an hour she talked, recalling Bri's birth, childhood, everything she could remember. It was so absurdly easy to talk to him.

When she was finished, he got out of bed. He crouched against the cold air on naked flesh and walked toward the closet. She looked at his pale buttocks as he walked away from her, touched by his vulnerability. His legs and back were sturdy and muscular. There was a slight thickening at his waist.

"You're beautiful," she said. His chuckle made the laughter begin again.

"Be right back," he promised. He shrugged on a blue calf-length bathrobe and disappeared. She snuggled down in the bed and waited, content.

He returned bearing a bottle of Dubonnet, two stemmed glasses, and Athos. While they sipped the wine, the kitten padded inquisitively around the bed, stepping with weightless paws on his chest, the pillows, her breasts. They laughed at his antics, and she spilled a droplet of wine on her arm. Athos licked it away, his rough little tongue tickling her. "Lucky cat," Max said.

Finally the kitten settled down in a curve of space between them, warming them both with his delicate body and the sound of muted purring. They talked softly, so as not to waken him.

The conversation returned to Ariel. "It haunts me," Kate confessed. "Why didn't she fight them? I can't escape the feeling that she was almost a willing victim. Why didn't she report them afterward?"

"I don't know, Kate. I'm not a psychiatrist, but it probably has something to do with the psychology of a victim. The feeling of being in some way responsible for the action, a sense of guilt. Does that make any sense to you?"

"If you mean the guilt of a rape victim, something like that, yes. It is so difficult to think of Bri being a part of that. It's almost impossible for me to believe."

"What are you going to do about it? Are you going to see the admiral tomorrow?"

"I haven't even thought about it." She was silent for a while, stroking his arm absently. "I do want to do something for Ariel. I *must*. I have a feeling she will reject any offer of help I make, but I have to at least try. Other than that, I guess I'm not going to do anything. The others who were involved—Jordan, Webb—it's their lives. I don't want to hurt them, or punish them for Bri's death. I came here to find out why and how he died, nothing else."

"You're a very understanding woman."

"Don't misconstrue how I feel, Max. My motives aren't that pure. The truth is, I almost hate them, I have absolutely no respect for them, and they have diminished what respect I had left for your Academy. They're hypocrites at best. I'm sick to my soul of their hypocrisy. I feel soiled by it. I am sickened to my marrow by the knowledge that Michael would lie about Brian, would destroy his memory, just to protect himself. I don't know if that was his idea or the Navy brass's. And to tell you the truth, it doesn't matter. The corruption of spirit is there, and I want to run as far from it as I can. 'Cover your ass.' Isn't that the expression? Well, they covered their asses on this one, and it didn't matter who got hurt. I don't know if any of them sitting in that Administration Building really knew what happened or why Brian died, or if they just were afraid of what I might find out, but I hope they burn in hell. I hope their souls are damned eternally." She swung her head on the pillow to look at him. "So, do you still think I am so terrific?"

"In a word, yes." He leaned over and kissed her. He pulled her to him, gently moving the kitten aside. His eyes were fierce with unshed tears. They stayed that way for a long time, each lost in thought.

"Hungry?" he asked after a while.

"Starved," she confessed.

"Come on." He jumped out of bed and pulled on the robe. Kate began to dress, not turning from him, comfortable with her nakedness now.

She set the table, pleased to feel how at home she already felt in his kitchen, while he made French toast using thick slices of oatmeal raisin bread dusted with cinnamon. They wolfed down the first batch, proud of and embarrassed by their appetite. He made a second platterful, which they ate more slowly, breaking off tiny pieces for Athos.

It was nearly nine, and she was afraid of being late for Leah.

"Are you sure you don't want me to be with you when you tell her?" he asked.

"I need to be alone with her," she replied. They left the dishes in the sink. He walked her to the front door. "I'll call you in the morning," he said.

They kissed again. As she walked out the door, feeling safe and secure, wrapped in his care, he said, "Thank you. For Athos. And for you."

When she slowed to make the turn at the end of the street, she looked back and saw him standing in a pool of light by the front door, waving. Even at that distance she could still see his bare feet and ankles revealed below the hem of the robe. "He should be wearing slippers," she said softly.

She drove slowly, unaware that she was smiling. She was sleepy, satisfied, hugging this wonderful sense of well-being to her, hardly daring to question it. Then she thought of Brian and the past pushed in again.

It was a deep pain, a soul-deep sadness, one she knew would be a part of her as long as she lived. Minutes before, she had been laughing and loving—living—while her son was dead. Guilt flickered and then died. Brian would understand. Her only regret was that he would never know that she had found Max. She was glad that Max had known Brian, had taught him. It was another bond they shared.

She pulled into the motel parking lot and switched off the ignition and lights. She was humming lightly as she turned the key in the lock. She opened the door, and when she saw the three people waiting in her room, gasped in surprise.

CHAPTER THIRTY-ONE

Spider stood at his locker and stared at the poster that hung inside. He had bought it at the Naval Institute Bookstore on the third floor of Preble Hall when he was a plebe. It was a color print of the Blue Angels, their jets in tight formation as they flew over the Navy-Marine Corps Stadium during the Commissioning ceremony. This poster represented everything he worked for and dreamed about. A combination of emotions warred in his chest: fear, shame, anger, and a regret stronger than anything he had ever felt in his life. For four years that poster had traveled with him. Now he took it down, prying it carefully from the locker door. He could not bear to rip it. He folded it neatly and dropped it in the metal wastebasket by his desk.

He looked down at Jordan's note. He didn't need to read it again. The words were burned into his brain: *Tyler knows about Greene. She's been to Vermont*.

Capturing the past four years in simple words was a task to which he knew he was not equal. How could one person sum up the Academy experience? The plebe panic that evolved into a midshipman's pride? The periods of boredom (no outsider ever understood about the boredom, the hours on Worden Field while the entire Brigade was at P-rade) that fluctuated with periods of back-breaking work. Maybe no one who had not lived it could ever fully comprehend what it meant to be a mid. What had he read in an issue of *Shipmate*? A letter from a graduate. "I regret everything I missed by going to Annapolis, instead of a regular college," the man had written. "I regret the women I couldn't sleep with, the hours I had to spend slaving over engineering. I regret it all, but I wouldn't change a minute of it."

In that moment Webb perceived that he could be redeemed, but that the cost of his redemption would not come cheap.

But he knew, too, that the crippling sense of shame he bore could be erased. If he had the courage. He was so afraid, he was sick with it. Did he have the courage?

But courage was what his four years had been about. Honor. Doing the right thing in the face of fear. He suddenly understood that if he did the right thing now, his four years at Navy would not have been in vain. It would not matter whether or not he was commissioned. If he acted now, he would be an Annapolis man in the truest sense of the words.

To act would be to earn his freedom after weeks of imprisonment. He wondered what would have happened to him, what would have become of him if Kate Tyler had not come to the Academy to learn why Brian had died.

He owed her something, if only the knowledge that her son had tried to stop the events of that night in the natatorium, and later, that he had been tormented by what they had done, had intended to do something about it. Webb wanted her to know that Brian had been a man of honor. He wanted to tell her that. And as much as he wanted to tell her about Bri, he was also seeking her absolution.

He wondered how to reach her, then remembered Dr. McNulty's visit. As he moved to telephone McNulty, Jordan's note slipped to the floor. He picked it up and saw that his roommate had continued the message on the back side of the paper.

A dread worse than anything he had ever known settled in his bowels. "Don't worry," he read. "Buck and I are going to take care of her."

At first, Kate could not take the scene in, but her instinctive reaction was that something was wrong. Leah was there, sitting on the swivel chair by the bed. Jordan Scott stood behind her. He looked jittery, nervous, but not threatening. His aquiline face turned for direction to the third person—a stranger to her—and Kate knew at once he was dangerous. She felt his menace, his deadliness. Purposely she ignored the stranger and spoke to Leah. The girl was pale, the strain drawing lines near her mouth, but she was controlled and her gaze met Kate's resolutely. "Are you all right?"

Her daughter-in-law nodded. Her arms were crossed in

front of her stomach, the protective stance Kate recognized.
Good girl, she said with her eyes.

The man leaning against the dresser splashed bourbon into
a plastic cup and swallowed it. Kate noticed that the bottle
was half empty. She deliberately faced him.

"I don't know what you are doing here or why you are
frightening my daughter-in-law, but I want you to leave now.
I would like you both to leave."

Jordan's eyes were confused, and he looked pleadingly
toward the other man. "It's too late for that," the man said.
His voice was arrogant. "We've got a lot to talk about, you
and me."

Kate steeled herself and reached for the phone. "If you
don't leave, I will call the police."

The man stood away from the desk. "Don't even think of
moving." He looked her up and down insolently, and Kate
fought to keep from giving him the satisfaction of recoiling
from his frankly sexual appraisal. "It's too bad old Bri didn't
have his mother's guts," he said to Jordan.

"Who are you?" she demanded.

"This is my brother, Mrs. Tyler," Jordan said. "Buck."

Kate continued to direct her attention toward Buck, remembering fragments of Brian's comments about Jordan's
brother. She knew the battle for control was between them.
"I presume my trip to Vermont has something to do with
your decidedly unwelcome visit." She might have been speaking to an unruly student.

"You shouldn't have gone up there, messing around in
things that are not your business."

"My son's death is very much my business."

"It's too bad you had to go and take that trip. Too bad a
nice lady like you had to make trouble." Again he gave her
that crude appraisal. It bothered Kate less this time. She was
beginning to understand that he wasn't a sexual threat, he
was simply trying to find an area of vulnerability to use
against her. Or so she hoped.

"You think I am going to report you, that's it, isn't it?" she
said to Jordan. "Because of what happened in the natatorium."

"I don't want to leave Navy," he said. "Only a few more
weeks and I'm out. I can't let you ruin it for me. We weren't
trying to hurt her. We just wanted to make her jump. It
wasn't fair. Why the hell should they change the rules for

them, for the women, you know? *We* had to make the jump. They keep telling us everyone operates by the same rules, it doesn't matter if you are male or female, but it isn't true. She brought it on herself. It was her own fault."

"Shut up." Buck's contempt was a mask on his face.

"I'm not going to tell on you, Jordan. I'm really not." Kate's voice was gentle. "You have to live in your own hell. I'm not going to tell anyone about Ariel."

"Don't give me that bullshit." Buck rapped the plastic cup against the bureau top. "A man's got to take care of his brother. You know what I mean. And I can't take the chance that you won't go making trouble."

"I told you, I'm not going to tell anyone about Ariel. Now I want you both out of here." She waited a moment and then crossed the room and picked up the phone. Behind her she heard Leah gasp.

"Buck." The name was drawn in horror from Jordan.

"Put the phone down, Mrs. Tyler."

That's what death must sound like, Kate thought. Turning, she saw the gun. He motioned for her to go and sit near Leah.

It was the first time in her life Kate had ever stared at the barrel of a revolver. The snout looked evil and deadly. Even sitting, her knees were weak.

"What are you going to do?" She forced her voice to be normal, willing it not to show her fear. Ignore the gun, she told herself. Focus on it, and he'll know how frightened you are. She saw that Leah was trembling, and she reached out to clasp her hand. The girl's fingers were cold.

"Jordo, check and see if anyone's out there." Buck nodded toward the door.

"Jesus, Buck, what the hell are you doing?"

"Cleaning up after you, little brother. Just what I've spent my entire life doing. Wiping up the shit after you."

His eyes were clear, watching every motion vigilantly. He seemed to like holding the gun. His grasp was relaxed, as if he were at ease, more whole, with the weapon at his side.

This familiarity made Kate more afraid.

Jordan's dark eyes darted nervously around the room. "Listen, Buck, let's get out of here. She said she wouldn't tell. That's all we wanted. Just her to promise she won't tell."

"She might. We want to make sure that won't happen, don't we, little brother?"

Kate wondered if he meant to kill them. She shifted her gaze to Leah and saw the girl didn't yet understand.

The phone on the bedside table rang shrilly, shattering the silence. Kate noticed that Buck's reaction was the most violent. She was grateful, for it revealed he was not as calm as he acted. The ringing seemed to go on for an eternity. After the seventh or eighth ring Jordan made a motion as if to pull the cord out.

"Don't." Buck's voice cut like a knife. "You pull that out, someone might come to find out what's wrong. Use your head, little brother."

"Jesus, Buck, you aren't going to kill them, are you? That's murder."

"Murder is just a word. Shit, Jordo, I shot dozens in 'Nam. Dozens. Murder? Hell, no. I got a medal for it." His eyes rested on Kate. "We're just going to have a reasonable talk. You look like a reasonable lady. I'm sure you won't be as stubborn as your son was."

CHAPTER THIRTY-TWO

Brian stared at two of the four bronze dolphins supporting the marble sarcophagus that contained the remains of John Paul Jones. Like so much at Navy, the crypt was a reminder of the infinite possibilities of man. Jones had been born a peasant in Arbigland, Scotland. Now he was honored as the "Father of the American Navy." Unbidden, the hero's immortal words echoed in Brian's mind. "I have not yet begun to fight."

I wonder, he mused. I wonder what Jones would have done in my place? Stupid question. Jones would never have been involved in the first place. He shifted position impatiently. What the hell was keeping Buck? Why does he want to meet me anyway? Jordo probably went crying to him. Well, if he thinks he can make me change my mind, he's wasting his time.

He glanced at his watch, regretting that he had agreed to the meeting. "Probably a waste of time anyway," he muttered. In ten minutes the crypt would be locked up for the day. Buck had better step on it. Behind him the Marine honor guard paced in precise steps around the tomb. The echo of his measured footsteps was the solitary sound in the dimly lit shrine.

Brian felt weighed down by the grandeur of the crypt. He knew the details of this place by heart, had since his days as a plebe. He knew that the massive columns were of the same marble as that of the sarcophagus: dramatic black-and-white stone that was Grand antique Pyrenees marble. In the deck encircling the tomb were inscribed the names of Jones's seven commands. Brian could recite them by rote: *Bonhomme Richard, Alliance, Serapis, Alfred, Providence, Ranger.* And the seventh one, of course. He dropped his gaze to look at the letters chiseled into the deck in front of him. The coincidence stung ironically. *Ariel*.

He shifted his weight. Christ, what was keeping Buck? The hell with it. He wouldn't wait any longer. As he turned to leave, he saw Jordan's brother watching him from the shadows near one of the exits. A chill of foreboding suddenly swept Brian. He pushed it away, substituting anger. How long had Buck been there? Jesus, he was always playing games.

As if sensing his mood, the older man stepped forward. He was grinning. "How's it going, Bri?"

"Let's cut the crap, Buck. What did you have to see me about? What was so damn important? 'Urgent,' I believe you said."

The Marine guard drew near. He did not look at the two men but stared dead ahead, a toy soldier, mindlessly marching. Buck stayed in the shadows, waiting until the guard passed by.

"Jordo told me you were going to sell out." The grin was gone from his face.

Brian studied Buck's face, wondering how much Jordan had confided. After a minute he said, "I'm quitting. That's true."

"That's shit-eating dumb. Four years and you're just walking away."

"Did Jordo tell you why?"

"He told me about the cunt." Buck spat the word. "You'd let a stupid cunt ruin your life?"

"We ruined hers."

"Jesus, Tyler. So what? She didn't say anything. Why should you bring it all down?"

"I can't explain. It's what I've got to do."

"What about Jordo and Spider? You going to ruin them too?"

"I have to do it. I can't live with myself. Can't you understand? Jesus, we almost killed her. And then we walked away and just left her there. I mean, it's a matter of honor." Then he saw the iciness in the narrow eyes and admitted defeat. He turned to leave.

"Wait a minute. For Christ's sake, just wait a minute," Buck reached out and grasped Brian's arm. His voice relaxed, friendly again. "Okay, man. You do what you have to do. It's cool." The change was so abrupt, Brian was thrown off guard.

He looked warily at Buck. In the distance the bells chimed. On the other side of the crypt, the honor guard started to lock one of the exit doors. Buck draped his arm over Brian's shoulder and led him up the steps and through the heavy door to the walk outside.

"You're stupid, Tyler. You're a stupid, pissless wonder. And it isn't over yet. I have a feeling the shit is about to hit the fan." Buck leaned in, so close Brian felt his breath on his cheek. "And the person who usually ends up covered with shit is the one who threw it at the fan. What you're going to do will fucking finish my brother, you understand that?" His eyes were black with menace. "I hope the hell you do, Tyler, 'cause people have been killed for doing less. You hear what I'm saying?"

Brian ignored the threat and strode off. His shoulders were braced with pride and dignity.

Kate looked across the room at Jordan. His patrician face was slick with sweat. "You won't tell, will you?" he pleaded. "Just tell him you won't tell."

"Shut up," Buck repeated. "Just shut the fuck up. You friggin' pussy. I've always taken care of you."

The initial shock had worn off, and Kate's concern about Leah grew. The girl was deathly pale and her eyes were dazed. Kate returned her attention to the gun and the man holding it. He couldn't just shoot us both, she silently reasoned. He's just trying to frighten us. Willing herself to be calm, she felt less paralyzed by fear.

"You don't have to get involved, Jordan. Don't let him drag you down."

"You shut up." Enraged, Buck reached out and slapped Kate, a blow that snapped her neck back. She heard Leah gasp. "I am going to tell you something, lady. You don't want to mess with me." He set the revolver down on the bed and reached into his shirt pocket for a cigarette. He seemed to ignore the gun. Kate gauged the distance. At least five feet separated them. And Leah was between them, sitting in the chair. Buck's knees almost brushed the girl's thighs. As if reading her mind, Jordan sat down on the bed next to his brother, shielding the gun from her view.

Casually, Buck struck a match and inhaled. He began to

speak, softly, precisely. Kate recognized the tone. It was that of a playground bully. While he talked he held the match in front of his face, his eyes on the blue flame. Leah and Jordan, too, were transfixed by the flame. Buck held the match upright and the fire burned down slowly, eating the flat matchstick, easing down Buck's fingers. No one spoke. The flame mesmerized them. After what seemed hours it reached his flesh. Kate could almost feel the burning, smell the singed flesh. Slowly, casually, Buck blew out the flame.

"No one has to get hurt," he said, lighting another match. "No sense in anyone else getting hurt. You understand. I mean, what good is it going to do now if you go and tell the brass about Greene? 'Course, if you did feel you just *had* to tell, then, well, then there's no telling who might get hurt. Accidents, you know. Shame if you had an accident. Or Brian's pretty wife." The flame burned low, and he watched it as if from a distance. The way he was lighting the match, holding it, reminded her of something but she couldn't pin it down. "Or his kid. Accidents like those that happen to cats. Soft black cats." He blew out the match and lit another. She could see the burnt flesh of his fingertips.

"You killed the cat." Her voice was without emotion. She saw the horror on Leah's face.

"What cat?" He blew out the match and lit another. The game was beginning to fray her nerves. Then it hit her. She realized what it reminded her of. A game of chicken. He was like a playground bully playing a game of chicken, pushing another child to the limit. And when she realized this, his power to frighten her disintegrated. With swift insight she knew that it was a role he had probably played for most of his life, knowing the other guy always backed down.

She looked from the flame to his face. "This has gone on long enough," she said calmly. "You have disturbed me and frightened my daughter-in-law, and I would like you to leave now. I'm sorry for you and I'm sorry for your brother, but it's time you both grew up and faced reality. I want you both to leave and then I am going to call Admiral Thatcher. I owe my son that much." Deliberately, she turned her back on him and his gun and stepped toward the door.

"Sit down!"

She ignored the barked command, reached for the handle and turned it. Cold, clean air rushed in, hurting her lungs. She heard the shot behind her. She braced her shoulders, stiffening the muscles to accept the pain, waiting for it. When she didn't feel the bullet, she cried out, knowing with horrible insight that the gun must have been aimed at Leah.

Max was on the edge of sleep, the kitten a warm ball against his side, when the door bell rang. He awoke to full consciousness immediately, certain that Kate had returned. Pleasure flooded through him. So much for holding back, he thought wryly.

Anticipating her face, it took him a minute to recognize the mid standing on the porch. One look at Webb Garrick told Max the boy was in trouble.

"Dr. McNulty? I'm sorry to bother you. It's Mrs. Tyler, sir. I think she might be in danger, sir." His voice cracked. "I don't know what to do. You were the only one I could think of for help."

Cold with dread, Max stepped aside to let the midshipman enter.

He was not ten feet into the tunnel before Brian regretted it. Nothing could change his mind about leaving the Academy. Nothing Buck could say. Nothing Jordan could say. And nothing Ariel could say. *Ariel.* Just her name made him feel ill.

He quickened his pace, almost running through the deserted tunnels to the agreed upon grate outside of Michelson. Five minutes, he told himself. I'll give her five minutes. He felt sick at the thought of facing her. The last time he had seen her, she'd been lying unconscious on the natatorium tiles. They said she had been able to walk all along. He was glad now. At first he'd been afraid of facing her, but now he welcomed it, wanted the opportunity to ask her forgiveness face to face. And why had she come? What could she want from him? Or had Jordan talked her into the meeting as he had Brian? He thought about the lies she had told to cover up for them. Surely she wasn't going to try and convince him not to tell what had happened in the natatorium.

"Tyler?" The query came from above, outside the grate, but peering up into the darkness, Brian couldn't see who waited there. The figure was nearly invisible, melting into the night. The whisper was distorted, familiar but elusive. One thing he did know was that it wasn't a woman's. Ariel wasn't here yet.

"A man of honor, aren't you?" The disembodied words were raw with sarcasm. "Step over here. On the rung of the ladder." There was a snap to the tone now—an officer's command—and without thinking, Brian responded. The sound of breathing floated down from above him.

"Your mind's made up, isn't it?" the voice prodded relentlessly. "No matter what I say, or how I beg you, you're fucking determined to go through with it, aren't you?"

"You're getting my message," Brian answered curtly, at last identifying the voice, furious that he'd allowed himself into being tricked into the meeting, realizing that Ariel wasn't coming. This was just one more attempt to get him to change his mind. If you only knew, you stupid bastard, he thought. All your asinine game does is make it easier. He concentrated on keeping his balance on the ladder below the opening. The rungs were damp. Then three things happened at once. A blow landed on his shoulder which knocked him from the ladder, a cord encircled his neck, and the grate slammed shut above his head.

Immediately, before he could even speak, he felt the cord—noose? Oh Christ, was it a noose?—tighten, chewing into his flesh. Disbelief, then fear, flooded his mind, his veins, his body. This could not be happening.

"Okay, hero. Game time is over. Say the word. Just promise you won't bring it down. Promise and I'll let go." The voice jeered at his helplessness. Frantically, Brian tried to ease his fingers between the rope and his neck. His foot kicked out in a vain attempt to find the rungs of the ladder, to relieve the pressure on his throat. "No." The word was no more than a gasp. He couldn't be sure his captor had heard it.

The rope jumped and strained in the grasp of the man above him, tugging his arms from their sockets. Perspiration covered the man's face as he wrapped the rope around the bars of the grate.

"Back down, damn you." He breathed the words. Sweat poured from his face, trickled down his back. "I'm not fuckin' kidding. Just back down." He knelt, hoarsely whispering the challenge between the icy bars. "For Christ's sake, just promise you won't tell. I just can't let you ruin everything. That's all." The veins in his neck stood out sharply. "Damn you, Tyler. Say it." Silence. "Is it worth it? Is your fucking honor worth your life? Is it?"

It was some minutes before the man realized that it had been a while since there had been sound or movement beneath the grate. "Tyler? Tyler, can you hear me?"

The faint, foul odor of defecation wafted out of the tunnel. "Oh Christ," the man whimpered. "Oh, Jesus-fucking Christ." The acrid odor of his own sweat mingled with the stench of death. He rose from his knees, and in a half crouch, ran brokenly through the darkness, across the Yard.

Below, in the tunnel, Roy Banks stared in disbelief at the midshipman hanging from the noose. "Jesus, Mary and Joseph," he breathed. His first impulse was to believe it was a joke, a gag the stupid middies were playing on him. They liked to do that, call him out in the tunnels with their noise and then roll a smoke bomb at him, escaping in jeering laughter. Fuckin', stupid middies, always fucking with his mind. Resentment flared into rage. Fool around with him would they? Then, almost immediately, he saw this wasn't a joke, some stuffed effigy they swung from a rope to scare him. Even in the darkness he knew the body hanging from the grate was a living mid.

But not for long. The rope swayed and the body twisted toward him. For one long, agonizing moment, the eyes of the dying man stared straight at Roy Banks. Later Roy was to think he heard the man speak. One word. *Please*.

He stared at the midshipman in his pressed blue military uniform, the dress of his despised enemy, and felt a rush of power. "Please." A ragged, haunted plea. Later he would try to convince himself that the mid hadn't said a thing. It was the eyes that had spoken, begged, pleaded for life. And in one mean moment of burning hate that added up to every insult he had ever swallowed, every taunt he'd ever heard flung at his half-wit brother, every injury, imagined or real, in one mean moment of burning hate, Roy turned from Brian Tyler and walked away.

"Which room is hers?" Webb had his door open before McNulty had even brought the car to a full stop. Before Max could answer him, they heard the retort, the unmistakable bark of gunfire.

Along the front of the motel other doors opened and faces peered out, saw two men running toward the motel, and quickly disappeared behind slammed doors. Max did not notice them. His eyes were riveted on one door. And on the figure framed in light silhouetted there. Man? Woman? From across the parking lot he could not tell. In that split second, he prayed. Let it be her. Please, God, let it be her. He froze, afraid to move, terrified to learn what waited in the motel room. Spider's command broke his paralysis.

"Come on. Move." The first-classman was younger, fitter, but Max reached the room first, holding out his arms, taking all the weight as the slender figure slumped forward, collapsing in his arms. He tightened his embrace around the already familiar body, greedily inhaling the scent of her. But he did not really dare to believe until he took hold of her chin and tenderly tilted her face toward his. "Kate. Oh God, Kate. Are you all right?"

She nodded, dazed, and gently Max carried her back into the room. Webb Garrick followed wordlessly. He saw what Max and Kate did not. "Dear God," he whispered.

Leah lay on the bed, weeping. On the floor Buck cradled his brother in his arms. Blood covered them both.

"You stupid shit. Oh Jesus, Jordo, you poor, stupid shit. Why?" There was more pain than seemed possible in Buck's voice.

Blood bubbled from the wound in the side of Jordan's chest, streaking his face. The wounded man strained to get the words out. "I was just . . . trying to scare him, Buck. I was just trying to be like you. I didn't mean to kill him."

The sound of a siren echoed in the distance. Dimly, Kate heard Max ask Webb to go to the office for help. Leah's sobs had turned to whimpers. Buck bent on the floor by his brother, his arms around the young man's body. Blood had sprayed the bed, the floor, and the wall. "Christ," Max mirrored her thought. "It looks like a battlefield."

"It is," she said.

Webb returned, bringing another man with him. When the night manager saw the room, his face went ashen. "Druggies," he spat. "God damn druggies." Hysterical giggles welled up in Kate's throat. Max went to her and held her.

"You're going to be all right, Kate. It's going to be all right."

She pushed him away and went to Leah. "This woman's pregnant," she told the motel man. "Has someone called a doctor?" She sat on the bed beside her daughter-in-law and held her hand, stroking her shorn hair. "You okay?" she asked softly. The color was beginning to creep back into Leah's cheeks. The girl nodded.

"What happened?" Webb asked. In his shock he looked both ancient and terribly young, defenseless.

"Jordan killed Bri," Leah answered. "He killed Bri and he was going to shoot us." Her voice began to tremble, but she continued to speak to Webb. "When Mrs. Tyler—Kate—started to leave, Buck didn't shoot her. I thought he was going to, but then I knew he couldn't. Jordan knew it, too, and that's when he tried to get the gun himself, to shoot her. Then it went off and he fell down. His face...he looked so...so surprised." Then her composure crumpled and she began to sob, making no move to cover her face.

Max moved closer. "Kate? Are you all right?"

She pulled back from him. When she spoke, accusation and sorrow rang in her voice.

"For God's sake, what are you creating down here?"

Max flinched but did not look away. His eyes met hers. "The best we can," he said softly. "Men of courage. A few of cowardice."

"Not good enough," Kate replied in a voice that shook with tears and horror. "And what of your precious honor? Are these the men of honor you told me about? The polite young men, the motivated wonderful men?" She pointed to Jordan. "He killed my son, you know."

She knew the mid was dying and tried to care, to feel compassion, but she was glad he was dying, and because of this she was afraid. Max reached for her hands. She tried to pull them away but he wouldn't let her, and after a minute she let them stay in his grasp, willing his warmth to spread through her.

The sirens were closer now. Their sounds cut through the March night, swirling like bagpipe music, dirgelike, filling the air of the motel parking lot, then expanding like waves until the sound reached past the street, dispersing across the town.

* * *

At Mother B. the last bell of the night rang. Inside the
sprawling multiwinged home forty-six hundred midshipmen
began to bunk down. Some were laughing, others cursed
injustices suffered at the hands of upperclassmen or professors or the system. As they lay back in their bunks, some
counted the days until Commissioning Week. Plebes thought
with relief about the day when come-arounds would be over
forever. They turned on their mattresses, knowing to the
minute how long their cherished sleep would last before
reveille, for the moment soaking up the hours of reprieve
from constant Navy life.

Outside, the grounds were deserted, the buildings and
landscaped lawns and monuments and cannons looming dark
and silent. And if by chance a lone midshipman had been out
there, walking across the Yard, he would have heard in its
silence—from the distance, from beyond the wall—the faint
sound of sirens.

He would have turned away. The sound would not have
registered. It came from beyond the Yard, and life outside
the wall had no relevance.

EPILOGUE

Spring bulbs bloomed on the grave. Jonquils, pale yellow and white, trembled in the slight breeze.

A woman stood at the base of the stone; her face was reflective, her sorrow no longer evident. There was a child by her side, dancing with the joy of life and the freedom of the season. Unable to remain still another moment, he darted forward and tugged the flag out of the ground. His face was as cheerful and sunny as the April day.

He peeked up at her to see if he would be ordered to put his prize back. Then he trotted off. He waved the flag jauntily and marched up and down the rich green grass of the grave. His toddler legs were stiff. "I'm in a 'rade, 'nana. I'm 'arching in a 'rade."

Kate had to laugh. She bent over and hugged the child. Her grandson held still for a moment and then squirmed and was off to continue his marching.

The man watched from a distance of several yards. He heard the sound of her laughter, and a spasm of pain crossed his face.

He wondered whether to approach her, acknowledging that all along he had known he would find her here. On this day of all days, she would come here. He walked toward her at last. "Hello, Kate."

If she was surprised, she did not show it. "Hello, Michael." The child ducked behind her legs and peeked out shyly. "Say hello to your Grandfather Tyler," she said softly.

The tot shook his head and watched the man suspiciously, as if he were afraid the stranger would make him put the flag back. "Mine," he said, holding the flag up. His face was fiercely stubborn. Looking down, Kate felt a pang. He was so very much like Brian.

287

"You got your judgeship," Kate said. "Congratulations, I know it meant a lot to you."

He nodded. "And I understand you're getting married."

"Yes." He waited for her to continue, but she added nothing. She did not want to talk to him about Max.

He looked at the gravestone, the flowers. "Did you plant them?"

"Last fall." She stared at the stone. "It's his birthday today. Is that why you came?"

"Yes. I suppose I should come more often, but I can't. Can you understand?"

"Yes."

"Sometimes, I wonder."

"What?"

"Oh, if we had tried harder, if we had both worked more at it, I wonder if we could have made it."

Kate did not answer. She wasn't sure if he was serious or if the words were spoken out of misplaced sentiment. Didn't he remember the bad years? Didn't he remember he left her for Wendi? She looked at him as if she could read his thoughts on his face. There were brown spots on his temples. Age spots, she saw with amazement. She never thought of Michael growing old.

"I still care about you, Kate."

She could think of nothing to say.

"Kate, I always wanted to talk to you. About your going down to the Academy. The whole thing about finding why Brian died. I wasn't mad at you when you went there. You do know that, don't you?"

"It doesn't matter."

"You haven't really forgiven me, have you? That's it. You're still angry because I believed he committed suicide. You still haven't forgiven me."

Kate scooped up her grandchild. "It's over now, Michael. There's no point in talking about it."

"That's it, though. I can tell you haven't forgiven me."

Kate's voice was gentle. "I'm not the one who has to forgive you, Michael. The forgiveness you need is not mine to give." She picked the child up and settled him on her hip, then walked back toward the car. The boy clung to her neck with one arm, waving the tiny flag with the other. Behind her, Michael stood near the grave and watched them walk away.

ABOUT THE AUTHOR

ANNE D. LECLAIRE lives on Cape Cod with her husband, son, and daughter. She is now at work on her third novel.

DISCOVER THE WORLD OF PAT CONROY

FIVE UNFORGETTABLE NOVELS
by
CELESTE DE BLASIS

☐ **THE NIGHT CHILD** (25458, $3.50)
The story of a proud, passionate woman and two very special kinds of love.

☐ **THE PROUD BREED** (25379, $4.50)
THE PROUD BREED vividly recreates California's exciting past, from the wild country to the pirated coast, from gambling dens to lavish ballrooms. Here is Celeste De Blasis' beloved bestselling novel: a world you will not want to leave, and will never forget.

☐ **WILD SWAN** (26884, $4.50)
Sweeping from England's West Country in the years of the Napoleonic wars, to the beauty of Maryland horse country, here is a novel richly spun of authentically detailed history and sumptuous romance.

☐ **SWAN'S CHANCE** (25692, $4.50)
SWAN'S CHANCE continues the magnificent saga begun in WILD SWAN: an unforgettable chronicle of a great dynasty.

☐ **SUFFER A SEA CHANGE** (26023-5, $3.50)
Her love, world and very future change under the light of an island sun as Jessica Banbridge comes to grips with the past and opens herself up to life.

Available wherever Bantam Books are sold or use this handy coupon for ordering.

Special Offer
Buy a Bantam Book
for only 50¢.

Now you can have Bantam's catalog filled with hundreds of titles plus take advantage of our unique and exciting bonus book offer. A special offer which gives you the opportunity to purchase a Bantam book for only 50¢. Here's how!

By ordering any five books at the regular price per order, you can also choose any other single book listed (up to a $5.95 value) for just 50¢. Some restrictions do apply, but for further details why not send for Bantam's catalog of titles today!

Just send us your name and address and we will send you a catalog!

THE LATEST BOOKS
IN THE BANTAM
BESTSELLING TRADITION

☐	25891	**THE TWO MRS. GRENVILLES**	$4.50
		Dominick Dunne	
☐	25540	**MOONDUST AND MADNESS**	$3.95
		Janelle Taylor	
☐	25547	**SWEET REASON** Robert Littell	$3.50
☐	25800	**THE CIDER HOUSE RULES** John Irving	$4.95
☐	25675	**BEACHES** Iris Rainer Dart	$3.95
☐	27196	**THE PROUD BREED** Celeste DeBlasis	$4.95
☐	24937	**WILD SWAN** Celeste DeBlasis	$3.95
☐	25692	**SWAN'S CHANCE** Celeste DeBlasis	$4.50
☐	26543	**ACT OF WILL** Barbara Taylor Bradford	$4.95
☐	26534	**A WOMAN OF SUBSTANCE**	$4.50
		Barbara Taylor Bradford	
☐	25418	**FACES** Johanna Kingsley	$4.50
☐	26583	**SCENTS** Johanna Kingsley	$4.50
☐	25709	**ARDENT SPRING** Anthony DiFranco	$3.95
☐	26354	**NEVER LEAVE ME** Margaret Pemberton	$3.95

<u>**Prices and availability subject to change without notice.**</u>